WISTERIA WINTER

ANN SWANN

Published by:

5 Prince Publishing and Books, LLC

DBA 5 Prince Publishing

PO Box 865

Arvada, Colorado 80001

Digital ISBN: 978-1-63112-444-0

Print ISBN: 978-1-63112-445-7

Cover design by Marianne Nowicki

Interior design by 5 Prince Publishing

First Edition F06022026

For more information about this title, visit: www.5princebooks.com

ALSO BY ANN SWANN

All for Love

Stutter Creek

Lilac Lane

Copper Lake

The Remains in the Pond

Telephone Road

Stevie-girl and the Phantom Pilot

Stevie-girl and the Phantom Student

Stevie-girl and the Phantom of Crybaby Bridge

Stevie-girl and the Phantom of Forever

A Crossbow Christmas

A Copper Penny Christmas

Wistera Winter

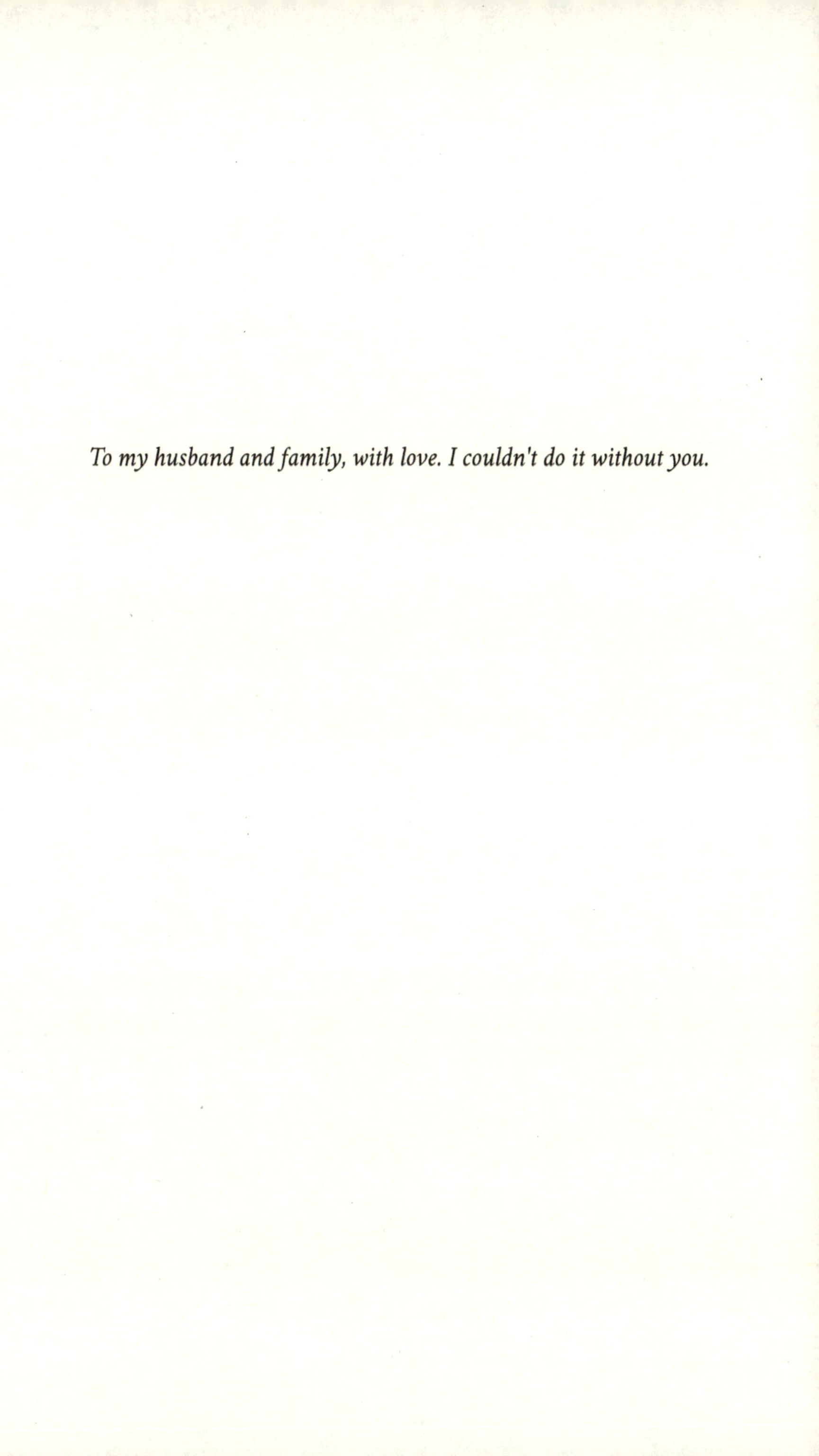

To my husband and family, with love. I couldn't do it without you.

ACKNOWLEDGMENTS

Many thanks to the entire 5 Prince team, especially publisher, Bernadette Soehner, for allowing me such creative freedom over the years, and editor, Cate Byers, for her endless patience and keen eye for detail.

I certainly can't forget our talented cover artist, Marianne Nowicki, whose beautiful work has added so much life to my books, and our lovely publicist, Lauren Lipp, who works hard to make us all look good.

But mostly, I would like to thank my dear friends and readers for standing by me through thick and thin.

I deeply appreciate your steadfast support throughout the years.

NOTE TO READER

Like so many of my stories, this one has a tiny kernel of truth tucked away inside the words and images. Human trafficking is, unfortunately, very real. I live near a large city which has been deemed one of the worst places in the country for this sort of tragedy.

This particular tale is fiction, but as you know some folks will do anything for money, including murder and the selling of other human beings. Evil is real. Of that, I have no doubt.

As for Sasha's hallucinations and memories, all of those are mine. When I was hospitalized for three months with Covid-19, I was put on a ventilator which requires the use of paralyzing drugs. The hallucinations were vivid, but they did not come to light until I was taken off the drugs, then it was like another world.

I don't understand where all of the fantastical visions originated, but I know some were from my own background of experience, while others came straight out of books and movies and even snippets of songs. Still others had to be courtesy of things happening around me in the ICU unit itself. Who knows?

A couple of my memories have no basis in reality at all. Thank God!

If it hadn't been for the constant prayers of my daughter and grandchildren—she had everyone we knew on a prayer chain—I don't believe I would have made it out alive. So, in case I've never said it … thank you, Sara Swann-Barnard. You helped to pull me back from the brink of the abyss.

Now, if you're still with me, kind readers, I say … on with the story. And as always, happy reading.

WISTERIA WINTER

1

THE END OF HALCYON DAYS

Linzy Everly lay curled up in her cozy bed, staring at the moonlight outside her window. The lacy curtains were open just enough for her to see the old pecan trees draped with colorful Christmas lights. The teardrop-shaped bulbs glowed softly against her windows. They also dripped from the eaves of the rambling ranch house. She and her sister, Sasha, had used those same lights to decorate the bare wisteria vines curling over the entrance gate. In the summer, those vines would be laden with showy clusters of purple flowers instead of colorful lights. Linzy loved their small pecan farm. She loved everything about it.

Eyelids growing heavier and heavier, Linzy dozed as she watched the swaying lights. Because her room was at the front of the house, she could see all the way to the gateway wisteria. The actual pecan grove was behind the house. It consisted of only a few acres now, but Linzy had seen photos from years past when it encompassed much, much more. Although she was fifteen and certainly didn't believe in Santa Claus, Linzy still adored their traditional holidays. Everyone seemed kinder and more patient, even the teachers at the high school where she was a sophomore and Sasha a freshman. Dozing comfortably, Linzy barely heard the furnace kick on with a soft growl. She liked the reassuring sound of it, knowing it was on the job, keeping them warm.

"Linzy! Linzy! Get up, something's *wrong*."

Linzy struggled to open her eyes, certain one of the pecan tree branches had reached through the window and grabbed her shoulder. Then she realized it was her sister's fingers digging into her flesh, shaking her, trying to wake her. She managed to sit up, rubbing at her eyes. "Sissy? What is it?"

Sasha's pale blonde hair obscured her face as she attempted to pull Linzy from the bed. "It's—I don't *know*," Sasha said. "It's a black cloud." She tugged at her sister's arm.

"A cloud? In the house?" Linzy formed the question in her mind, but she wasn't sure she said it aloud. Her head ached something fierce. All she could bring to mind were tree branches and Christmas lights, not a cloud … what was she talking about?

"It's *like* a cloud," Sasha said, exasperated. "Like something dark and smothery and it's going to kill us if we don't get out of here *right now*." She yanked with all her might and Linzy tumbled out of the covers, scrambling to get her balance.

The tips of her flip flops poked out from under the bed, so she shoved her feet at them. Their rural farm community lay half an hour north of Galveston near the tiny town of Brookville. The winters were sometimes cold, but not frigid. Linzy wore flip flops nearly year-round.

Sasha pulled at her again.

"Hang on, Sissy!" Linzy had one sandal on and was trying for the other.

But her younger sister yanked her again. She would *not* hang on. Not even long enough for the flip flops. Sasha continued to force Linzy across the room and into the hall, dragging her toward their parents' bedroom.

Near the doorway, Sasha tripped over something. "Mom!" she shouted.

Their mother lay crumpled on the floor.

Both girls fell down beside her. "Call 9-1-1," Linzy said, taking charge. "Hurry!" She gave Sasha a shove toward the kitchen.

Sasha stumbled through the living room. "Oh, my God," she cried, "Dad's in his chair. He's not *breathing*."

"Go!" Linzy screamed. "Call 9-1-1. I'm starting CPR." She rolled her mother onto her back reciting the ABCs of resuscitation from her days as a lifeguard. *Airway, breathing, circulation.*

The hallway was so dim.

She jumped up to flip on the light and swooned so severely she had to grab the wall for support. Looking down at her mom on the floor, she noted the bright red spots on her cheeks. Carbon monoxide. "Sasha! Tell them to hurry."

Making her way through the door into her parents' bedroom—holding on to the walls because of the dizziness—Linzy threw open both windows. Then she turned back to her mom, checked her Airway, listened for Breath sounds, then started Chest compressions.

From the kitchen, she could hear Sasha on the phone, telling a dispatcher how to find their farm.

"Call Blue," she shouted. "Tell him it's carbon monoxide. And open the *doors*. We've got to get them outside."

Her sister did as she was told.

Linzy heard the clunky wall receiver hit the floor. "Sash!" She was about to say *are you okay?* But then she heard the windows going up all over the house and figured the dispatcher had also given her instructions.

Sasha reappeared. "I can't wake Dad." Her voice cracked. "I can't wake him at *all*."

"Come on," Linzy yanked her sister by the hand. "Grab a

blanket off the bed. We'll roll Mom onto it and slide her down the hall and out the door. We've got to get them to fresh air."

Sasha grabbed the blanket from her bed and together they got their mom outside onto the lawn. Although their small acreage was only a few miles from Brookville, the volunteer ambulance would still take a few minutes to arrive.

Linzy fell to her knees beside their mom, listened again for breath sounds, rechecked her airway, then instructed Sasha to restart the chest compressions. "I'm going to get Dad," she said. "You keep up those compressions. Don't stop!"

Sobbing, Sasha nodded, dragging in air, hair stuck to her wet, blotchy face, hands pushing into her mother's chest—hard—just the way they'd both been taught.

Linzy inhaled the fresh air once, twice, three times as she glanced up at the cold December moon. The multicolored Christmas lights were like artwork in the dark sky. She blinked, swiped at her face, coughed twice, then ran back into the house to get her father. She could see the muted light of an old movie on her dad's late-night TV.

Adrenaline coursed through her veins as she grabbed the heavy woven blanket off the back of the couch and threw it on the floor beside her father's recliner. "Dad," she croaked. "Dad … wake *up*."

But he wouldn't wake up.

It took every ounce of adrenalin-fueled strength she could muster to push his motionless body over the arm of the chair and onto the blanket. His head hit the carpeted floor with a hard thud, but all Linzy could think about was how cool his skin felt. How dusky it appeared in the scant lighting.

She grabbed the blanket near his head and began to pull. The front door was only a few feet away, but even pulling with all her might, Linzy realized she wasn't going to make it. The carpet held onto the blanket like Velcro.

Her heart pounded from the headache and all the bending over, struggling, and she had to stop to get her breath.

Dropping the edge of the blanket, Linzy fell backward through the propped open storm door and landed hard on her bottom. She dragged in fresh air, gagging, coughing up phlegm, spitting it into the grass.

She glanced through the door into the living room where her father lay, unmoving, neck bent unnaturally, one arm pinned beneath his body, cheeks as red as apples in the light she didn't remember turning on. In the silence, the dispatcher's voice could be heard from the dropped phone in the kitchen. "Help is on the way, stay with me, girls, stay with me." The dispatcher probably didn't know if they were dead or alive.

Linzy gulped in the clean cold air and forced herself to stand, staggering back through the door, yanking up on the end of the blanket, tugging her father's body inch by inch across the carpet, bumping his head over the threshold unmercifully.

The Christmas tree stood like a sentinel in front of the big window. Linzy stared at it as she struggled, praying for the strength to save this man who had always delighted in stringing those colorful lights.

Finally, she had his head out the door. Falling to her knees, Linzy checked his airway and started chest compressions. "Breathe, Dad," she begged, trying to ignore how cold he was, how incredibly still. *Just breathe.*

She thought about rescue breathing, but they hadn't been trained on that, due to their ages, so she continued to pump her hands into his chest as hard as she could, counting compressions, aiming for at least one hundred per minute.

Then Mr. Ash was there, Blue's father, from down the road. Maybe Sash had called Blue like she'd told her to do, or maybe he and his folks had got the call from Brookville, the county seat. Their whole family were Wister County volunteers.

"I've got it, Linz," Mr. Ash said, gently pushing her aside as he took over compressions. "Go ahead and help your sister."

Linzy sat back on her heels. "Is the ambulance coming? Mom and Dad need oxygen. I'm sure it's carbon monoxide poisoning."

He nodded, obviously counting compressions just the way she'd been doing. "They're on the way." He looked up and over her head, shouted, "Blue! I need you."

The rangy, black-haired teen ran over. He had on flip flops just like Linzy would have done. Linzy glanced up. Their families had been friends and neighbors all their lives.

"Take over here, son," his dad indicated the compressions. "I'll do rescue breaths."

They worked together like a well-oiled team. Blue had been going on emergency runs with his dad since he was old enough to stay out of the way.

Linzy stumbled to where Mrs. Ash knelt over her mother, performing the rescue breaths while Sasha continued compressions, counting out loud between sobs.

The nightmarish scene temporarily overwhelmed Linzy, the dew on the grass glimmering in the moonlight, the lighted branches grasping at the sky, and the house, open and breathing as if it, too, teetered on the verge of collapse.

From behind her, she heard Mr. Ash say, "He's still not breathing. I don't think he's been breathing for a while."

She glanced back, surprised to see a paramedic fitting an oxygen mask on her dad's face. *When did they get here?*

Sinking to her knees beside her sister, she said, "Let me take over, Sis." But it wasn't Sasha doing the compressions anymore, it was another paramedic, and now she was fitting a breathing mask over her mom's face, too. *Did I pass out?* She recalled hearing the siren in the distance, but when did it come through the gate?

She pushed her disheveled hair off her face and looked around, surprised by the way the ambulance lights washed over the scene, bathing everything in red and blue, competing with the Christmas lights swaying in the breeze.

Near the door, someone yelled, "Clear!"

She turned her head just in time to see her dad's body jump and fall back as the portable defibrillator shocked him.

Sasha cried out as they upped the voltage and tried again. And again. Linzy stood and pulled her younger sister to her chest to shield her from the horrific sight.

Finally, the paramedic shook his head and removed the leads from her dad's chest. "It was worth a try," they heard him say.

Linzy looked at Blue. Her friend was on his knees, breathing hard, a wing of black hair plastered to his tanned forehead.

Meanwhile, another EMT cut open her mom's nightgown with a pair of bent scissors, readying her for the defibrillator that hadn't helped her dad. When they began attaching the sticky pads and leads all over her mother's bare chest, Linzy turned herself and her sister away.

Their dad's inert body lay near the front door where Linzy had dragged him from the house. His t-shirt had also been split, and his chest lay exposed to the cold night air. Linzy could see the disposable defibrillator pads stuck in his dark chest hair. Spots of wet conductivity gel glistened on his skin.

All those videos we watched while preparing to pass our CPR tests are really paying off tonight, she thought darkly. And then her stomach clenched, and she had to squeeze her eyes shut and dig her nails into her palms to gain control of herself.

She pulled Sasha to their mom's silver Buick and opened the rear car door, thankful they never felt the need to lock up at night. Tucking Sasha into the back seat, Linzy crawled in after her.

Sasha pulled the car blanket across their laps, still sobbing. "It's so stupid that mom always kept this blanket in the car along with that stupid first aid kit. Always be prepared. She told us that again and again—"

"Shhh," Linzy said. "Shhh, it's all right. It's gonna be okay ..." She held her sister and stroked her hair, thinking, You're right. It is stupid. And ironic. Be prepared. She knew her mom had meant to be prepared if you break down beside the highway. She'd told them the story of how she'd once spent a cold and harrowing night alone beside the road when she couldn't get the machine-tightened lug nuts off her wheel to change a flat tire. But seriously, how does one prepare for *this*?

Linzy pushed those thoughts from her mind and pulled the door closed so the interior light would go off. They couldn't go back inside the house; their dad's body blocked the doorway. It probably isn't safe yet, anyway. Something is leaking. Maybe the old furnace. Talk about ironic, it was my safe-night-sounds-furnace, my white-noise-going-to-sleep-furnace. Now this. *Traitor.*

She closed her eyes so her peripheral vision couldn't acknowledge the flickering light from her dad's late-night TV in the living room. Or the Christmas lights swaying from the eaves and the branches of the pecan trees. Or the unnerving swirl of the red and blue lights of the ambulance parked on the driveway behind them. Or worst of all, the way the lights met and meshed across the glowing white fabric of her dad's ruined t-shirt and bare chest.

Sometime later, the car door opened, and a kind voice said, "Let me check your oxygen level," before clipping a pulse oximeter onto her forefinger.

The same was done to Sasha and they both passed muster.

"I just had to check," the voice said. Then he backed away, saying, "Leave this door open for a bit, for the fresh air." The kindly face attached to the voice was somewhat familiar, a different neighbor, perhaps. Another rural volunteer like Blue and his folks.

Linzy nodded.

Later, someone else said, "C'mon, girls. The ambulance has

gone. I'm going to take you both to the hospital to be checked out. That's where they've taken your folks. Is there someone I can call … a grandparent or an aunt or uncle?"

Linzy opened her eyes and looked around, surprised to find that the bodies of her parents were gone, and she hadn't even seen them being loaded onto stretchers. "Oh, my God." She pushed her auburn hair away from her eyes. It seemed to be stuck to her cheeks, her entire face wet with tears. "Are they? I mean did they ever …"

Mrs. Ash shook her head. A portable respirator hung to one side of her face, away from her mouth and nose. "They were not able to revive them," she said. "That's why we need to call someone to be with you." Leaning into the car, she reached out to both girls at the same time, just the way the man with the pulse oximeter had done earlier. "I am so sorry," the kind woman said. "I'll take care of you. We need to get you both checked out more thoroughly, right away. I don't know a lot about carbon monoxide, but I know you need to be looked at."

Linzy glanced at her sister. *Is that why we're both so rum-dumb? Didn't even know the ambulance had left?* "Okay," she said. "Umm, we don't have shoes on or … clothes." She clutched at her baggy sleep shirt and looked up into her neighbor's caring eyes.

"I'll get them," Mrs. Ash said. "Mr. Ash went in earlier and turned off the furnace, opened all the other windows." She pulled her respirator back into place, then lifted it to say, "You two leave this door open. Okay?"

She waited until Linzy nodded.

"Alright, then. I'll be right back. Is there a cell phone in the house with all the contact numbers we may need?" She slid the mask into place and paused.

Linzy nodded. "On the kitchen counter, my mom's phone is charging. Dad's is probably beside his chair. Mine is in my room. Sasha's will be in her room."

The sweet woman squeezed Linzy's hand again. Then she turned and walked into the wide-open house.

Sasha looked at her sister, confusion evident on her face.

"We'll be okay, Sissy," Linzy said. "We'll be okay." But deep within her body, something began to vibrate. There were no grandparents. The last one had passed away a few months ago in California. Now there were none.

Somewhere, Los Angeles maybe, there was an uncle. Her dad's estranged half-brother. Someone she and Sasha had never met. According to her mom, he hadn't even bothered to tell them when their grandfather passed. Not until recently.

Beside her, Sasha began to sob.

Linzy wanted to repeat the 'it'll be okay' mantra, but even then, she knew it would be a very long time before either of them would feel okay again.

2

NEW LIVES

After the shock of their parents' deaths, the sisters found themselves mired inside a nightmare from which neither of them could shake the other one awake. They went from having no worries—aside from making all As and Bs the way their parents required—to worrying about every little thing like where they would live, when they would return to school, how they would pay the bills … the list was endless. Every day Linzy thought of something to add to that list. It was absolutely unreal. Truly a dark cloud.

Having no parents infiltrated every aspect of their lives. Linzy was afraid the worst of it hadn't even hit them yet. The dark cloud lingered, fat and grotesque, full of grief and confusion, ready to rain down on them at any moment.

And then there was the guilt.

Sasha blamed herself. As if the blaming could make things better, put things back in order. "Why didn't I wake Mom first?" she asked her sister. "Or even Dad? If only I'd gone to them first, maybe …"

Linzy would hug her and tell her it wasn't her fault. "No

matter who you went to first, our parents were already gone, Sissy."

After the funerals, when things had quieted down somewhat, the two of them had researched and read everything they could about carbon monoxide poisoning. And none of it mattered. Their folks were still gone. Still buried in side-by-side plots out in Brookville Cemetery.

"Faulty furnace," the fire inspector had said. "Surprised Mr. Everly didn't have it serviced each fall."

The girls didn't know if their dad had it serviced or not. That tidbit of information wasn't even a blip on their radar screens. They were teenagers. Home maintenance, to them, meant changing a light bulb or hanging Christmas lights, helping with yard work now and then.

Now we know, Linzy thought bleakly. Always have your furnace checked—every year—before time to turn it on. But as someone once said, the knowing doesn't change the doing. Especially if the doing was already done.

It was a terrible lesson. And it made for a horrible Christmas.

Blue and his family took them in, tried to make things easier, but seeing their home sitting there, empty, windows peering at them like eyes every time they passed by—pleading with them to come back home—was more than surreal. Wisteria Way had lost its yellow-brick-road feel. In fact, it was dreadful. A never-ending reminder of despair. The funerals had been the worst. Straight out of that same nightmare playbook.

Sasha had been given a mild sedative, and after a while, Linzy wished she'd taken the doctor up on that offer, too. As it was, she'd clung to Blue and Sasha and never heard a word the pastor said. When the service ended—it had been huge, the whole of the community turning out—both girls had tossed lilies into the twin graves and stared at each other in abject horror.

Back at the Ash residence after the double service, Blue tried to be there for both her and Sasha. His mom and dad saw what he was doing and made certain the majority of well-meaning town folk gave them room. The Ash family had stayed with the girls in the sympathy pew at the church, they didn't need to do it all again at the reception.

Afterward, both girls slept, wrapped in each other's arms on the guest bed in the Ash home. When one got up, the other did, too. They couldn't stand to be apart.

Finally, in the new year, Linzy threw herself back into school and tried to make certain Sasha did the same.

But that's when she realized her sister was still being eaten alive with grief and guilt.

"We were young and healthy," Linzy told her, each time she started the *what if–,* or *why didn't I–?* conversation. "If only I'd gotten to them first," Sash would say, "we probably would have all survived."

"It wouldn't have mattered if you had done every single thing differently," Linzy said, for the umpteenth time. "The living room and their bedroom were both closer to the furnace. The poison got into their systems quicker than it did ours. That's just what happened..."

But Sasha would shake her head and stare into space, berating herself for not understanding the dark cloud she had sensed. She would often say how she wished *she* had stayed asleep that night.

Even at fifteen, Linzy knew that was a cry for help.

She confided in Blue's mom that Sasha seemed to be sinking further and further into gloom. Mrs. Ash was the one trying so hard to keep them stable while their dad's attorney worked out how to keep them out of the foster system,

"Let me see what I can do," the dear woman said. "I think Sash needs outside help. Let's start with our pastor. If she can't help, I'm sure the family doctor can refer us to someone who can."

Linzy agreed. She had almost gone to the school counselor more than once, but now, a few weeks later, she was glad she'd confided in Mrs. Ash instead.

They began with the minister at the Ash's church. The same one who had conducted the funeral service. Linzy and Sasha's family had been sporadic churchgoers, so they were all familiar with each other, but not close. In fact, the Ash family's worship habits had been almost as sporadic as the Everly's. But Pastor Sue didn't hold that against any of them. She had been checking on the girls every couple of weeks since the deaths.

It made Linzy smile every time the pastor drove up to the Ash's farm in her tiny smart car. It looked like a toy sitting near Mr. Ash's giant farm truck parked under the carport.

The first time she had come to visit, Pastor Sue had simply opened the front door and stuck her head inside. "Hello," she'd called. "Anyone home?"

"We're in the kitchen," Linzy called back, recognizing the pastor's voice.

The cheerful woman leaned her curly-topped head around the corner of the door. "Everybody decent? Or should I come back?"

"We're all decent," Linzy said. "It's just the two of us right now. Blue is out helping his dad on the back forty,"—one of their inside jokes about the farm—"and Mrs. Ash is at the grocery store." She smiled at the pastor to let her know she was aware that Mrs. Ash had called her.

"Oh, well, then," the pastor said, "I'll just sit here and take a load off my feet, if you girls don't mind." She perched on one of the barstools at the kitchen island and placed her bag on the other one.

"It's good to see you," Linzy began. "Let me just get this laundry finished before Mrs. A gets home." She glanced at her sister. "Sash, would you get Pastor Sue a glass of iced tea?"

Sasha looked up from the notebook in which she'd been writing. "Tea?" She looked at the pastor as if she'd already forgotten her. "Oh, sure," she smiled. No matter how sad or miserable she felt, Sasha would never be rude. It was not in her nature.

"Thank you, hon. That would be great." The pastor returned her smile. "How's school going? It looks like you're doing some homework. I wouldn't want to interrupt."

Sash looked back down at her notebook in which she'd been writing. "Nah. I'm done with my homework. That's just a letter I'm writing."

That piqued Linzy's interest, but she didn't stick around. She knew her sister would be more likely to talk to the pastor—honestly—without her standing there.

In the laundry room, she opened and closed the dryer even though it was empty. She wanted sound effects to make them think she was truly folding clothes. More than anything, she wanted her sister to talk to this kind woman so she could start coming to terms with everything.

"Writing a letter to a friend?" she heard Pastor Sue ask.

"Yes ... well, sort of." Sasha's voice trailed away with the sound of the fridge opening and closing.

Linzy could hear both speakers clearly, could easily tell what her sister was doing as she spoke. Open fridge, take out tea pitcher, close fridge, fill glass with ice, pour tea over ice ...

She sat on the floor and crossed her ankles, prepared to sit and listen for as long as it took. Privacy never entered her mind. This was her Sash, her little sister, practically the only family she had left. Whatever she was going through, Linzy needed to know about it so she could help fix it.

"When I was a child," the pastor began. "Back in the Stone Ages ..." she grinned. "We were assigned pen pals in our English class. Mine was a gal from Maine. Randomly drew her name out of a hat. To this day we still write each other regularly. We've even met in person a few times."

Linzy heard the sound of a glass being placed on the kitchen island, as if the pastor had taken a sip and set it back down.

After a few seconds, the voice said, "Oh, that tastes good, Sasha, thank you." The sound of another sip. "Not too sweet. I'm not a fan of syrupy tea, are you?"

Linzy imagined her sister shaking her head in response. She was surprised by what her sis said next. "I kind of wish this *was* a pen pal," Sasha said. "I—umm. I never—I'm not really writing a letter. I don't have anyone to write a letter to." She stopped talking and Linzy imagined her taking a drink of her own iced tea. "I was trying to write a poem, actually."

"A school assignment?" the pastor asked. "Creative writing, perhaps?"

Even though she was in a different room, Linzy held her breath.

She wished she could see her sister's face as she spoke. Linzy scooted a little closer to the laundry room door. There. Now she could see them both, just barely. The concrete floor of the laundry room was cold. Christmas and New Year's had come and gone, but it wasn't February yet, and spring was just a promise. They were so busy taking things 'one day at a time' that it was easy to lose track of how quickly time was passing. *Until you find yourself sitting on a cold cement floor.*

"No," Sasha said. "Not an assignment. Just me, talking to myself." She lifted one shoulder in a half shrug. "It is *kinda* school related." She tilted her blonde head in that self-deprecating way Linzy knew so well. "And a little different."

"How so?" Pastor Sue prodded, sipping her tea as if asking a nonchalant question.

"I'm not using my tablet." She picked up the ballpoint pen again. "Our creative writing teacher said there's something about writing on paper that makes the words come out differently. She said it slows you down, makes your mind focus on the thought process."

Linzy was all ears. She hadn't heard any of this.

Pastor Sue seemed to mull it over. "I think that's true," she replied. "I write my sermons in long hand each week, then rewrite them on my computer to edit. But if I try to write directly on the computer, the words don't sound the same."

That appeared to get Sash's attention. "For real?"

The pastor nodded. "Oh, yes. And by the way, you said you don't have anyone to write letters to?"

Sasha looked at her face without answering.

The pastor slid a business card across the island. "Write to me. Anytime, all the time, anything you want. I'm here. I promise. And nothing you say will ever be repeated or belittled. You can tell me or ask me anything ... about God, about heaven, about grief."

She smiled a rueful smile when she said that last part, and Linzy suddenly remembered that the pastor's husband had been killed in terrible car accident a few years earlier. "We can discuss anything. That's my job. To listen and to help." She patted Sasha's hand. "And you know who else you can write to anytime, all the time?"

Linzy knew she would say God, or Jesus, maybe even Mary, instead, she said, "Your mom and dad."

Linzy saw her sister grip the ballpoint tighter. "How? How can I do that? Oh, I want to do that. I have so much to tell them. I want them to know how sorry I am I couldn't save them—" The flood gates opened.

Pastor Sue stood, taking hold of Sasha's fingers, and walked around the end of the island. She took the sobbing girl in her arms, pressed her head into the hollow between her shoulder and her chin, and held her. "There, now," she said, patting Sasha's back. "Of course, you need to tell them all that, and much, much, more. Just because they're in heaven doesn't mean you need them any less. They know that. God knows that. You talk to them just the way you always have. Talk to them and write to them." She inhaled slowly. "And you may even get some answers, if you listen closely."

Linzy watched from the doorway. She could feel the tears coursing down her own face, but she was careful not to make a sound. It wasn't easy. The sleeve of her sweatshirt was soaked.

She sent up a silent thank you to God for giving them such caring people. *I don't know why you took our parents away, or let it happen that way, but I thank you for sending us Pastor Sue.* And then she immediately amended her thoughts to include Blue and his parents. Without them, Linzy didn't know where they would be.

3

CURRY & PEACH

Insurance inspector, Jed Curry, exited his rental car in the parking lot of the historic Wister County courthouse in Brookville. He passed through a well-pruned tangle of bare wisteria vines which met over the entrance doors. Jed thought he'd like to see those climbers when they were covered with clusters of purple blossoms this summer. On the other hand, he hoped this case wouldn't take that long. He had some reservations, though.

Putting those thoughts aside, he entered the cool dimness of the old building and located the Sheriff's Office by following the signs that led down a short flight of stairs to the basement level. He was impressed with the magnificent marble floors. He might've taken the elevator, just to the right of the stairwell, but after his flight, he felt the need for a bit of exercise.

The sheriff's department appeared to encompass the entire basement. Curry continued to follow the small, no-nonsense signs, making his way to the main office.

Handing the secretary his business card, he said, "Need to speak with the sheriff, please. I'm here to investigate those two accidental deaths out on Wisteria Way." He placed his briefcase on the counter and smiled. "Rural Wister County, I believe."

The secretary nodded, picked up her telephone receiver, pressed the number one key on the phone's base, then relayed to the person on the other end exactly what Jed Curry had said. Without another word, she replaced the receiver, rose from her desk, adjusted her uniform belt, and nodded at the newcomer. "Follow me, please."

Jed followed her down the short hallway to the last door on the left.

The door opened just as they reached it.

A burly, mahogany-skinned man in white shirt and brown slacks stepped forward. "Sheriff Peach," the man said, offering a mitt-like hand in greeting. "Welcome to Wister County." His voice had a big Texas drawl to match his size, and his dark eyes seemed to take in every detail of the visitor's appearance.

The secretary smiled and headed back toward her office.

Jed Curry held out his hand to the sheriff. "American Home Life Inspector. We hold the policy on a generous double payout on Wisteria Way." He hesitated. "Pecan farm, if I'm not mistaken."

"Yessir," Sheriff Peach replied, motioning to an empty chair in front of his massive oak desk. He strolled back around, picked up his BIG BOSS coffee cup from the old-fashioned blotter covering the glass top, tilted the cup toward Jed Curry. "Coffee?"

Curry nodded. "Yes, please. I noticed your coffee bar in the hall. Looks well-appointed." He leaned back, loosened his tie. "Nothing better than a good cup of joe."

The sheriff left the door open and stepped across the hall where he poured black coffee into his own mug, then chose a clean cup from the ones resting upside-down on a paper towel. "Cream or sugar?" he called across the hall, picking up a spoon.

"Just black, thanks," Jed Curry called back.

Sheriff Peach returned and placed a mug in front of him. It was heavy white ceramic, unadorned, no-nonsense like the signage. A visitor's mug. He waited until the sheriff had gone back around to his own chair, then he picked up the coffee, took a sip. "Ahh, that's the good stuff. You're a lifesaver." He sipped again, then chuckled. "I arrived in Houston three hours ago. Traffic was rough. I thought DC was bad."

Sheriff Peach laughed, too, a big, rumbling laugh that should have shook his good-sized middle like the proverbial bowl full of jelly but did not. "I hate that place." He leaned forward and took a careful sip from his own mug. "Take a minute," he said. "Make y'self comfortable." He indicated a door to the left. "My private restroom if you need to slap some water on your face."

Curry nodded. "Appreciate that. I'm good for now." He sipped again, letting his eyes take in the bank of gunmetal-gray file cabinets lining the far wall.

As if on cue, the sheriff closed a folder already open on his desk. He handed it across to Jed Curry. It had some heft to it. "Brookville's a small community here in Wister County," the sheriff said. "Real tragedy out there on Wisteria Way. The Everly family. Little pecan orchard at the intersection of Wisteria Way and Pecan Road. Ward Everly inherited the place when his mother passed. He already owned it when he married Betty as a young man. Good people, Ward and Betty, carbon monoxide took 'em both. Left behind two teenage daughters. Whole community, devastated at the loss."

Inspector Curry put his coffee aside and opened the file reverently. He wasn't surprised to find the sheriff personally involved in this case. He'd done his research. Wister County hadn't seen a double-death accident since 2017 when an 18-wheeler wiped out a sports car on the loop that skirted the town. Driver had claimed brake failure. Of course that was a different insurance company, but word got around.

Besides, small town sheriffs know their residents, especially the ones with roots.

Sheriff Peach pointed at the folder with his mug. "Basics are there. Death certificates. Family names and numbers. Financial paperwork. Cell phone records. Photos from the scene. Witness statements." He sipped his own coffee as Curry paged through the documents.

"There's one thing in there I think you will find especially interesting."

Curry glanced up, waiting.

"Furnace was inspected shortly before the deaths."

Inspector Curry's hand stopped turning pages. "Are you kidding me?" His bushy Sam Elliott eyebrows went up. "I'm not in the habit of assuming anything in this line of work, but I would've bet my last dollar on this furnace *not* having a current inspection report." His eye continued down the page.

"So said we all," the sheriff replied. "Hard to understand how a reliable inspection could miss a leak big enough to kill."

The inspector finished reading, then sat back. "That's a short report considering two folks are dead. Says everything was in fine working order." He looked up at the sheriff again. "You've interviewed this guy from ..." His eye roved back to the top of the page. "Texas Pride HVAC?"

The sheriff leaned back in his oversized chair the same way the inspector had leaned back. The sheriff's chair let out a squeal. "Gotta lay off the biscuits," he joked. "My Sara makes the best biscuits in three counties. I don't mind sayin'." He linked his fingers behind his head. "As for this HVAC company, we did interview the owner and the service tech. They've been doing business in Wister County for decades. Been Ward Everly's furnace company for a number of years."

The inspector downed the rest of his coffee. "Completely fine, huh?" He looked up, one finger marking his place in the file. "Mind if I get another?" His glance traveled toward the hallway coffee station.

Peach smiled, "Help yourself."

When the inspector returned a moment later, fresh cup in hand, he said, "Any conflict in the family, Sheriff?"

"Looking into that," Peach said. "Here in Wister County, Brookville High School, those two surviving girls are top notch students in both academics and in sports. The younger one's on the swim team with my own daughter."

Inspector Curry glanced back over the basic report. "Linzy's the elder daughter?"

"Yes. Sasha's her little sister."

"What about other relatives? How was the marriage, the wife? Could there be a love triangle or a mistress, someone who stands to profit from the deaths of this fine couple? Besides the daughters, I mean."

Sheriff Peach let his chair down and leaned forward over the desk. "Betty, the wife, was a pillar. Volunteered for Meals on Wheels, kept the books for Everly Acres, the family pecan business. She was a saint, no doubt about it. Ward, too. Nothing but good ol' country folk. I've known 'em for years. No hanky-panky on either side. Marriage solid." He leaned back, just a little. "Who else might profit from these two deaths? That's my question, exactly."

Looking down at his desk blotter, the sheriff cleared his throat. "The only living relative we can find is a cat named Turvy Bedane Everly out in California. He's the half-brother of Ward Everly, the deceased. But he won't inherit anything, Ward and his wife left everything to their daughters."

The sheriff leaned back a bit before he continued. "This poor Everly family was devastated by Covid a few years back. Took out both of the girls' grandparents on their mom's side, left only the dad's dad on his side. He passed a few months ago. Heart disease is what I heard. Don't believe they were close though. After he died, that left only Turvy. Oh," Sheriff Peach laughed. "And before I forget to tell you, Turvy goes by Ancho, now. Even had it made legal. Signs all his paperwork that way."

"With a name like Turvy," Jed Curry said, "who can blame him. Jeez. Some parents, right?"

"Exactly," the sheriff agreed. "Jim Everly was also Ward Everly's dad, but Turvy's mom was the one some folks called the homewrecker."

"Homewrecker?" Curry asked.

Peach nodded. "Yeah. You know, had an affair with Ward's dad while he was still married to Ward's mom. Seems he split from her only *after* he got the homewrecker pregnant. Then he gathered up his new woman and lit out for California leaving the pecan farm and all the bills to teenaged Ward and his mom. It hit Ward's mom—her name was Raella—so hard she had a stroke. Practically an invalid afterward. Church ladies looked after her while Ward and a couple of close neighbors worked the farm to keep them from losing it completely."

The inspector rubbed one finger lightly across his upper lip as if checking for stubble. "Ward Everly seems like a fine figure of a man. Surprised he was able to take over at such a young age. Sounds like he had good help though—"

"After his mom had the stroke, Ward called his old man out in California and told him what his selfish actions had caused. Guess that made his dad feel guilty. He signed over every bit of land, plus the house, to his wife and son right then and there. Had an attorney out in California make it legal and send it to a newly minted lawyer here in Brookville by the name of Carla Brushow. She had just graduated law school and returned home to join her father's firm. He knew all about what had happened."

"A real mess, right?" Jed Curry said.

Sheriff Peach nodded. "Carla vowed to help Ward figure things out. She wasn't too much older than he was, back then. Made them have quite a bond, I think. Poor Raella Everly hung on for some years, but she was never the same. The boy did his best with the farm. However, over the years he was forced to sell off more and more of the acres. By the time his mom passed, the farm was down to the ten-acre orchard that's out there now. It sits directly behind the house."

"That's heartbreaking," Curry said.

"At least she had a decent life insurance policy," Peach said. "It allowed her boy to keep the house and those ten acres free and clear. Made an insurance believer out of him, too. As soon as he married, he took out those policies with your company on himself and Betty. God rest their souls." He sat back, crossed his hands over his midsection. "I still can't believe they're both gone, one fell swoop."

Inspector Curry ran a finger over his upper lip again. "They do sound like good people."

Peach nodded. "Ward finished high school, then he went to work for one of the oil refineries down on the coast. He never let go of that last pecan grove though, even if it wasn't enough to support the family anymore. Fortunately, it was just an hour's drive from Wisteria Way to the refinery."

His cell phone buzzed, and he pulled it out, glanced at the screen, stuck it back in his shirt pocket. "All those good folk are gone now, excepting Carla Brushow. She's still the best attorney in town. And still looking out for the Everly family. What's left of it."

Jed Curry said, "I see the girls stand to inherit everything when the older one turns eighteen. They're supposed to split it evenly, right down the middle." He glanced at the sheriff without expression. "Not a bad inheritance."

Sheriff Peach shrugged. "They won't have to worry about college or selling the farm, that's for sure. Especially not with your company's double indemnity payout. And not only will they inherit the ten-acre property here, but they will also take possession of their mom's family vacation cabin at Stutter Creek, New Mexico. Little resort town in the mountains."

Inspector Curry closed the file, leaving the Texas Pride furnace inspection receipt on top. "Thank you for copying all this," he said. "Most would've sent me the files on Google docs or some shit." He finished his second cup of coffee.

Peach leaned back. "Some things are better old school. Damn computer hurts my eyes." He smiled ruefully. The light through the window blinds seemed to warm his bare scalp. He rubbed a hand over it before he spoke. "It was a miracle those two girls got out of that house alive."

Inspector Curry sat up straighter, never taking his fingers off the receipt, as if he might learn more through osmosis. "It certainly appears that way. It also seems like this family has had its share of hardship."

Peach agreed. "And still managed to rise above, until now."

Inspector Curry pressed his lips together. "I've got a suspicious nature, Sheriff. Our line of work, I suppose." He paused. "Last year I investigated the case of a son who took his mom out on a midnight cruise the night before his college graduation. She didn't come back to see him walk the stage, so he didn't bother to show up. Come to find out, he'd flunked out months earlier. Kid inherited a small fortune and never had to tell his mom about his failure."

Peach shook his head a bit, as if he knew what Curry would say next.

"Woman's body washed up eventually. Weighted down by the boat's anchor. Fool kid couldn't explain how it got wrapped around her ankles. Nor how she got that paddle shaped dent in the back of her skull."

"That's cold," Peach said. "His own mother?"

Curry nodded. "Yep. Small anchor was no match for decomposition gases. The kid did the murder like he did everything in his life—"

"Half-assed it," Peach said.

Curry set his empty cup on the desk blotter. "You took the words right out of my mouth. Kind of a Menendez approach to gaining the family's fortune. No chance of that with these daughters?"

Peach shook his head, scattering the light from his shiny scalp. "Not no, but hell no. One of the best families in the whole county. Like I said, I know those girls personally."

Jed Curry sat up straighter. "Good deal. That's what I like to hear. So, I guess all that's left to do now is go out and see the furnace for ourselves."

"Now you took the words right out of *my* mouth," Sheriff Peach said. He stood, eased into his jacket, and plucked a gray Stetson from an antler peg above the file cabinets. Placing it on his head, he said, "Propane is turned off now. We'll turn it back on when we get there. I've got a reliable man ready to come out and repair the thing as soon as we give him the go-ahead."

Inspector Curry also stood. "I can't wait to have a look."

The sheriff unlocked the side drawer of his desk, took out a hand-tooled gun belt, fastened it around his hips below his belly, checked the load and the safety on his revolver before shoving the weapon into what appeared to be a custom-made holster. He tied the old school leather thong around his thigh so it wouldn't bounce if he had to chase down a suspect, then he opened the office door and waited for the inspector to precede him into the hall.

The secretary glanced up, gave the sheriff a short dip of her chin, acknowledging his departure, smiled at Inspector Curry, then returned to her computer.

"A well-run office says a lot about the man who runs it," Curry said.

Sheriff Peach grunted and followed him up the stairs and out a back door to the parking garage where his Ford Police Interceptor Utility vehicle sat, front and center.

Inspector Curry said, "If you'll allow me, I'll go around to the visitor's lot in front, grab my tool bag out of the rental."

Peach nodded, opened the driver's door of his Ford, smashed

his large frame behind the steering wheel, and fired up the engine.

Curry retrieved his bag in record time, then slid into the Sheriff's passenger seat and resumed talking. "After I look things over, we can compare it point by point with the previous report."

The sheriff grunted in acknowledgement, shifted into reverse and backed out of the space marked with a Skull & Crossbones sign. His actions were smooth, no motion wasted, likely a result of years spent driving miles and miles every day.

Curry buckled his seatbelt. "Thanks for taking me along. I've had enough of driving today. To be honest, I can't wait to get a look at this furnace, especially now that I've learned it was recently inspected."

The sheriff chuckled, but it wasn't a jolly sound. "I appreciate the speed with which your company is moving on this. We don't get many of these cases. Not where the whole family is sickened, and two killed. Seems suspicious to me, too. Even though it appears to be an accidental carbon monoxide poisoning, I had my deputies work it like a crime scene, fingerprints, photos, everything I could think of, just in case."

Curry watched as the big man felt above the rearview mirror where several toothpicks—likely from local restaurants—were stuck beneath the trim.

Plucking one from its home, Peach placed it unceremoniously into the corner of his mouth. "Gave up snuff a while back," he explained. "Had to replace it with toothpicks or Tootsie Pops. Wife threatened to skin me if I went with the candy." He patted his hard midsection.

His voice took on a new tone, maybe due to his need to keep the toothpick in place. "Even if there hadn't been such a big life insurance policy, I would want to pursue this case." He drove straight arm, big right hand clutching the wheel at twelve o'clock. His gaze never left the horizon, simply scanned from windshield to rearview, to side mirror, and back again. "I want to believe it was accidental, because I can't imagine the Everly's having a single enemy in this whole county."

He scanned the windows and mirrors again. "Except for that large payout and the recent service receipt, I might have automatically chalked it up to a tragic accident."

"I hope that's all it was. I sincerely hope we don't find anything untoward out there. An accident would be the best outcome for everyone concerned." He gazed out the passenger window at the blur of grass and trees along the highway. "But in our business, both mine and yours, we can't leave anything to chance. Money and power, lust and greed. If not for those things, I might be out of a job—"

"You and me, both, buddy. You and me, both." Peach inclined his head toward the upcoming intersection. "On the right, the turn into the driveway. Purty place, ain't it? Especially in the summer, when the purple flowers bloom. Back when they named the streets, Wister County gave everyone facing newly named Wisteria Way free bushes."

"Nice," Curry agreed. "I see the vines on the archway. They certainly frame the entrance gate." He craned his head around. "Very well-kept. Good place to raise a family I'll bet. Just the name makes me want to live here, and that long, curve-around drive. Very nice. Such a tragedy." He made a sound deep in his throat. "Just out of curiosity, did the county hand out free pecan seedlings at some point, too?"

"They may have," the sheriff said. "Way back in the day." He chuckled. "But this particular pecan farm's been here even longer than the Pecan Road sign."

The Ford Interceptor bumped across the iron-pipe cattle guard, and the sheriff drove right up the drive and underneath the attached carport beside an older model Ford farm truck. "When we get this mess straightened out," Peach said, "those girls can come back to their home. They're staying down the road with the Ash family since it happened."

Without further ado, he slid a ring of keys off his turn signal lever, sorted through them—each one labeled with letters in some sort of code—until his fingers happened upon the ones with WF on one label, and WB on the other. "The garage is automatic, disabled until further notice." He nodded toward the rollup door. "The mom's car is inside. But it's only a one car garage so Dad's old pickup truck lived out here under this carport."

He turned off the Interceptor's engine and nodded toward a second, oversized carport beside the house. "I asked Ward once why he had that giant thing built even though he didn't have a Recreational Vehicle." He opened the door to get out, but said, "He told me it was for those times when he wanted to drive his pecan shaker up to the house for a glass of iced tea." He jerked his head sideways, as if clearing the emotion from his eye. "Good people, those two. Damn good people." He pulled latex gloves out of a box in his console, offered a pair to Curry as well. "We've done all the dusting for prints, and what-have-you, this is just a little insurance on my part." He grinned at his own pun and went to unlock the front door.

Inspector Curry stuffed the gloves in his pocket, then climbed out and straightened his jacket before he began snapping photos with his digital camera. He liked to have a general picture of a home to jog his memory after he got back to the office.

Once inside, he photographed the smoke detector/carbon monoxide alarms in the hallway and kitchen area.

"Had no batteries," Sheriff Peach said. "Fairly new detectors but had no batteries. We dusted 'em for prints before the fire inspector opened them up. I can't imagine Ward putting them up and then forgetting to put in the power source." He clenched his jaw. "But I also can't imagine how anyone could take out the batteries without old Ward knowing about it. I have a couple theories about that, but nothing concrete. Don't want to sway your thinking before you even begin your investigation." He shifted the toothpick around with his tongue. "Bad thing about good folks. Sometimes they're too trusting." He stood back a moment, perhaps to allow his eyes to adjust to the dim indoors, then he flipped on the hall light and made his way to the furnace closet. "Here ya go," he pulled open the vented door and stepped aside.

The inspector placed his clipboard on the floor, tugged on the latex gloves, slipped a head lamp over his head and leaned in, tracing lines and examining things up close and personal.

"Ready for me to turn the gas back on?" the sheriff asked.

Curry stuck his head back out. "We will in a bit, to get a CO level, but I can already tell you the problem."

Peach shifted to one foot, held on to his gun belt with his right hand, his Stetson at his thigh in his left. He appeared to be bracing for unexpected news. Come to find out, it wasn't unexpected at all. "Whaddya see there, Inspector?"

Leaning back into the narrow closet, Curry shined his light up the side of the unit to the vent on the roof. "See this vent pipe?"

Peach leaned in beside him, a tight fit. "Yep ..."

"It's crimped right there where it goes out of the closet ceiling into the attic."

"Sure is," Peach said. "I see it. What's it doing, forcing the fumes back into the house?"

"Exactly," the inspector said. "And I don't believe that happened by accident. I see tool marks on that pipe." He shined the spotlight again. "See 'em?"

"I sure do," Sheriff Peach said. "Looks like somebody crimped it on purpose. Now we've got to find the son of a bitch who did it."

Curry glanced at the big man. "You already knew, didn't you?"

Sheriff Peach stepped back. "Let's just say I dusted the entire surface of this furnace for prints, just in case."

The inspector leaned down, opened the tool bag, and pulled

out two respirators. One reusable, and one disposable. "Let me take a few more photos of the vent pipe, then we'll put these on and fire this baby up, get an actual reading on the CO levels for the judge." He pulled out a combustion analyzer—it would test the level of carbon monoxide generated by the furnace—and waited for Peach to go outside to open the unit's propane fuel line so they could turn the system back on.

"Let's do it," Peach said, when he came back in the house. He put his toothpick in his shirt pocket and pulled his respirator on before setting the wall thermostat to ON.

Once they got a reading over 400ppm, Inspector Curry shook his head. "I'm surprised anyone survived."

Peach turned his head to hide the emotion that seemed to keep sneaking up on him. "Would it have killed them immediately?" he asked.

"Nah," Curry replied. "It would have taken a number of hours to build up in such a rambling structure. Maybe a few days. It's a high reading in the closet, but they weren't in the closet. It had to spread out, build up in the entire house. Does that make sense?"

The sheriff nodded. "Perfect sense. Plus, we don't get many really cold days down here, as a result, we don't know for sure when they turned the furnace on, or how long it ran. We will check the weather history. See how cold it was between the time the service company came out and the night the Everly's passed." He hesitated, then said, "I'm sure they ran that heater off and on since having it serviced in the fall."

He didn't elaborate anymore, simply shut the unit off, then the two of them sat out on the patio, leaving the doors and windows open so the house would air out completely. "I'll get my repair crew here as soon as our investigation is over," Sheriff Peach said. "We will all pitch in for the girls, if they decide to move back in." He seemed to think about that for a moment. "Need to share these findings with the feds before I do anything else. Now that you agree this 'accident' appears suspicious, there will be a detective going through everything." He glanced up at the roofline above the door. "I'd like to put up some cameras."

Curry looked up. "Yeah. Too bad they didn't have any already, otherwise, we might have visual proof of who came and went before Christmas." He paused. "I thought I saw a camera inside the furnace closet."

Sheriff Peach pulled out his smart phone and touched an app. "Put that baby in myself. After the fact, of course. Was afraid the bad guy would come back and try to undo his dirty work before we could make a case." He showed Curry the video of the two of them opening the closet door.

"Darn good video," Curry said. "Even in the dark of that closet."

Peach nodded. "Has audio, too. Since County can't afford to keep a man posted out here day and night, this is the next best thing. It will send an alert to my phone if anyone opens that closet door."

"That's good thinking, Sheriff," Curry said. "And would have been good for the trial if you had caught the one who crimped that pipe. Juries love video."

"I aim to nail this bastard one way or the other," the sheriff said.

"How long before you get results on all the fingerprints your man took?"

Peach shook his head. "Weeks and weeks, probably. There's a lot to sort through. And of course, most of the prints from inside that house will not be on file. Innocent folks' prints are not usually in the system unless their jobs require it."

Inspector Curry nodded. "I'd hazard a guess that whoever crimped that pipe is not one of the innocents."

4

PRAYERS

On Saturday afternoon, about a week after Pastor Sue visited Sasha at the Ash's home, Sash asked Linzy to walk down the road to their old house with her. It was a cool, clear day. High white see-through clouds streaked the sky like swaths of gauze. The girls knew nothing about Inspector Curry's visit. He wasn't finished investigating. Neither was Sheriff Peach. The propane gas was still turned off, the valve locked. All the girls knew for certain was that it wasn't time to move home yet.

"Those are cirrus clouds," Sasha said, gazing upward. "They're icy. They usually mean a change is coming."

Linzy looked at her. Just like Sash to say some random weather thing as they walked along. Linzy suspected it was because they were both so nervous. They hadn't been to their house since the sheriff had given the okay for them to go in and get the rest of their clothes and things.

"What's in the bag?" Linzy indicated the small mesh bag hanging from Sasha's shoulder.

Her sister inhaled slightly. "My prayers," she said. "Some letters to Mom and Dad." She looked at the hard-packed road, kicked up a little dust with the toe of her sneaker.

Linzy was confused. "Wanna talk about them?"

Sasha gave her the side eye. "No. Why would I?" She huffed a little, then softened. "I want to burn them. In our firepit out back. Or in the old chiminea." She pulled her hand out of her pocket and showed Linzy a book of matches.

"Sissy," Linzy began, "I wish you would talk to me about all this. It happened to both of us, remember?" She had to lengthen her stride to keep up with Sasha who suddenly seemed to be speed-walking.

Sash uttered a strange, half-strangled laugh. "That's exactly why I *can't* tell you." She sped up a little more, the gate now in spitting distance.

Linzy threw her thick auburn braid over her shoulder and hurried to catch her sister at the cattle guard. "What does that mean?"

Sasha's blonde ponytail bounced as she turned with a huff. "It means, you and I both lost our parents and everything. Our whole entire *lives* were lost." Tears spilled over her bottom lids. "But look at you ..." She eyed her older sister up and down with an expression of disdain.

Linzy couldn't help it. She glanced down at herself. "What about me?"

Sasha turned and toe-walked across the cattle guard pipes like a tightrope.

Linzy followed, careful not to touch her sister until they were both safely across—good way to break an ankle, her dad had said, the first time she tried to jump across the guard. She certainly didn't want to see either of them with their lower leg jammed between the spaced-out pipes now.

But Sasha didn't slow. Not even once they were across.

Linzy trailed her up the long, winding drive. When they neared the house, she could see the reflections of the thin clouds smeared across her bedroom window. The tall pecan tree still reached for the sky the way it always did. Her entire childhood was contained in that one reflection. All of a sudden, she was back in bed and Sash was trying to pull her awake. "Stop," she called, a flash of nightmare rooting her to the ground. She bent over, palms grasping her thighs. "Wait," she said. "Wait on me, Sash."

At last, Sasha turned, her face shiny with tears. She didn't seem to notice Linzy's physical distress. "I can't wait, and I can't talk to you. Not really. Not about this, or about anything 'cause you're always *okay*. I mean, you just, you take everything in stride and just handle it. Handle it and keep going."

Linzy straightened up, one hand going to her abdomen. "You really think so, Sis?" She bent over again, slightly, palm pressing her middle harder. "I hope you do. It means I've hidden it well. That maybe we will both be okay, eventually." She clenched her teeth. "I've always tried to look out for you, Sash. Ever since you were born. But man … going back to the house? I think it might be a mistake. I don't think I can." Linzy glanced toward the windows again. "I've been having these stomach pains." A grimace crossed her face. "They just hit from out of nowhere—"

Sasha hurried back to her sister, took her by the arm. "Oh, Linz, I didn't know. You always seem so strong."

"That's for you," Linzy said. "When you started kindergarten, you and Mom were both crying so hard it made me want to cry, too. I told Mom everything would be okay, that I would look after you." She tried to smile. "So, I always have."

Sash frowned. "You were only six years old then." She straightened her backbone. "What a burden you've been carrying." Gripping her big sister's arm a little more firmly she said, "C'mon. Help me burn these letters. We won't look inside. Just out back." She tilted her chin up. "It will be okay. I'm a big girl now, but I need to do this for me. Maybe for both of us."

Linzy felt something inside her relax, felt her vision begin to clear, she began to feel lighter somehow, even though Sasha tugging at her elbow still reminded her of the way she'd tugged her out of bed that horrible night. "Okay." She pushed the hateful memory aside and exhaled the breath that had been trapped in her lungs. "Okay," she inhaled fresh air. "Yes. We can do it. Together."

Arm in arm, they walked the rest of the way up the winding drive, bypassing the front door—an image of her dad's body staining her mind like a grief shadow—through the carport, and around to the back yard. Can't believe it's still winter, Linzy thought, seems like it's been winter forever.

They stood together on the wide back patio, looking across the acres at her dad's new shop building. "He hardly got to use it," Linzy murmured.

Sasha let go of her arm and went to the big-bellied clay firepot with the tall chimney. She opened her small mesh bag and pulled out a fat packet of folded papers. "I've been looking forward to doing this ever since Pastor Sue mentioned it."

Linzy dragged a heavy patio chair closer to the chiminea which sat a little distance away from the patio on a small slab of cement. Further out in the yard, their dad had dug a firepit and lined it with river rock, but Linzy was glad Sash hadn't wanted to use it. An open fire felt dangerous now. Even if it was built for that purpose. Some days, everything felt dangerous. As if death lay everywhere, just waiting to be discovered.

She watched her sister place the paper packet in the bottom of the thick clay belly and pull out the matchbook. "You said they're prayers and letters?"

"Yes." Sasha lit one corner, but the match went out, and the packet didn't catch.

"Try pulling one page out a little, like a fuse."

Sasha loosened the pages from the rubber band holding them together, and did as Linzy suggested, pulling one letter halfway out, like a tongue. She struck another match and held it to the tongue-fuse. It caught immediately. "I write down my prayers to God. And I write down all the bad things, and then I write to

Mom and Dad about my day, and how much I miss them, and how I would've done it all differently if I had only known."

Linzy looped an arm around Sasha's shoulders and pulled her closer. "I feel like we've each been battling this horrible grief alone instead of together." She pointed at the tall chimney. "Look at that smoke going up."

Sasha's eye followed the growing white wisp curling into the blue. "Right up to heaven, just like Pastor Sue said it would." With a teary-eyed half-smile, she bent into her big sister for comfort. "Thanks for coming with me." She swiped at her nose with the back of her sleeve. "I'm sorry I never thought about how you feel." Tucking a strand of hair behind her ear, she continued, "You think we should go out to the cemetery soon?"

Linzy nodded. "Maybe so. Take some fresh flowers." They hadn't wanted to go since the funeral. Mrs. Ash told them there was no hurry. But maybe it was time. Baby steps, Linzy thought. Baby steps. "You know we have to lean on each other from now on, don't you?"

Sash murmured something that sounded like "sure." Then she said, "Look up there." She pointed toward the wispy clouds. "That smoke looks like wings, doesn't it?"

Before Linzy could agree or disagree, Sash pointed toward a cloud formation. "And look, that one is a complete angel." She hesitated. "Angels and angel wings. Right up there in the blue." She held her hands out toward the heat coming from the opening. "The sky is always so blue in the winter. Pastor Sue was right. This is good."

"You had quite a packet of letters. Does it feel better, to imagine your words rising on the smoke that way?"

Sash nodded. "And it feels so warm, kind of cozy, even out here in the yard." Her voice had taken on a softer tone. "Glad there's no breeze to blow the smoke away. Maybe we can do it again, soon." She looked at Linzy. "Do you ever talk to Mom and Dad, or write to them that way?"

"I do," Linzy said. "I write in my journal now and then, but I talk to them in my head all the time. You know, just kind of pretending they're still here so I can run things past them, see what they would think. I know it's silly, they aren't going to reply, but somehow, just thinking about it that way makes me feel more in control or something."

Sasha let her hands fall back into her lap. "It's just all pretend, really. I mean, I feel better for a minute or two, then it all goes away, and I feel sad and hopeless all over again. Just like that very first night. Like nothing will ever be okay again."

A shadow fell across the yard.

Sasha turned with a jerk.

"Hey, y'all," Blue's long silhouette stretched his already tall frame to cartoonish proportions. "Everything all right?" He shoved his hands into his back pockets and rocked on the balls of his feet. His deep brown eyes scanned the scene, his usual smile, somewhat concerned at the moment, still firmly in place.

Linzy returned his smile and loosened her grip on her sister. "We're good." She sent him a look that said not to ask questions. "Just had some things to take care of."

He nodded, pushed his too long dark hair off his brow. "I'll head on back, then. I was following Dad in from the winter field. Thought I saw a bit of smoke as we turned off Pecan." He glanced in the direction of his house. "Dad went on, but I wanted to make sure everything was okay."

"Thanks, Blue," Sasha said. "I'm burning the evidence from my latest crime spree." She smiled and Linzy's heart fairly leapt in her chest. It was the first time her sister had made a joke since before. Minor breakthroughs, baby steps. We *can* do this, she thought. Maybe talking about it, and writing about it, burning it ... maybe it does help, just like the pastor said.

Blue laughed a bit uncertainly, then gave a little half-salute and said, "If y'all need me, just holler. Or, you know, send up another smoke signal." He glanced at Sasha, stretching the usual smile a little wider.

Two years older than Linzy, Blue didn't let any grass grow under his feet. Between school and working for his parents on their organic fruit and vegetable farm, he also helped his dad—and a seasonal crew—take care of the pecan trees on the Everly's place. When the pecans were picked and sent off to be shelled each year, the bags were labeled *Fresh from Everly Acres.* The Everly family's business was a small operation compared to the Ash Family Farm. Blue's dad sold their fruits and vegetables all year, rotating crops depending on the season, utilizing greenhouses as well. Their products were sold to restaurants and specialty grocers all over the Houston area.

"We don't see much of you these days," Linzy said, thinking how Blue hadn't even had time to get a haircut lately. "Sometimes it's hard to believe we all live in the same house." She smiled to let him know she was only half-joking. If she hadn't, the next thing she knew he'd be making it a point to look in on her every day.

He shrugged. "Sometimes, I think Dad is keeping me extra busy."

That made the girls laugh.

Blue jerked his thumb over his shoulder. "Anyhow, I better get going. Just wanted to check on y'all." He was careful not to ask exactly what they were doing. He didn't mention their folks or that night or even what might happen next.

For such big feet he seemed to know how to tread lightly. But was that a good thing, always avoiding the obvious? Linzy wondered but didn't press it. "We're okay. Don't worry, Little Boy Blue. We'll douse the embers with the water hose before we leave. Thanks for checking on us." She smiled again, softer this time. Linzy always teased him by calling him childish nicknames. But this time her smile said even though she sounded like she was teasing, what they were doing wasn't a joke.

Blue gave a tiny nod, and a sideways smile aimed at her—they'd been best buddies and down-the-road confidants since grade school, they were used to deciphering each other's unspoken messages—and then he loped away, hoofing it around the corner of the house to the winding drive where his red pickup waited.

Linzy wouldn't have minded him staying, but she felt as if she'd broken through some transparent wall with her sister in the last half hour, not to mention the easing of her own stomachache.

And they hadn't done it by walking on eggshells but by starting a fire.

Seems like some sort of lesson there, she thought. Maybe one I should write a letter about. In her head, she imagined herself writing to her mom in Heaven. Why not? What could it hurt? Maybe Sasha and Pastor Sue were onto something. She reached over and squeezed her sister's shoulder. "Smells good, like our old campfires at Stutter Creek."

"You think we'll ever get back there, to Stutter Creek?" Sasha's voice sounded forlorn. It made Linzy sorry she'd brought it up.

"Sure, we will," Linz said. "I guess we own the cabin, now." Her mind started down a new, more adult, pathway of thinking. Do we own everything? How do we pay for utilities on both places? What about property taxes, insurance? *Oh my God, so many things I don't know.*

They sat awhile longer, watching the last of the paper curl and blacken as the end of the thin smoke wafted into the air. It didn't take much longer before the letters and prayers were nothing but ash.

Sasha got up and stirred the burned leavings with a stick they'd kept there for that very purpose. The end of the branch, for that is what it was, an old pecan branch from the orchard, was black and hard. Sash stirred the mess, watching tiny sparks jump every now and then. "How about some dirt?" she asked.

Linzy grabbed the pail from beneath the patio cover and shoveled a few small spades of dirt onto the hot ashes.

Sash had gone for the water hose, for insurance, perhaps, but Linzy shook her head. "I know what I told Blue, but now I'm thinking cold water might crack the hot clay chiminea."

Sasha nodded, and they rewound the water hose and hung it back on the sturdy hose-hanger mounted on the rear wall of the house. "Everything in its place," Sash murmured, quoting their dad. She looked about the yard and patio. "I guess we'd better go." It seemed obvious she would rather stay.

"Yeah," Linzy agreed. "We don't want to worry Blue or his folks. They've been so good to us." She started toward the corner of the house, but Sasha kept looking at the back door.

"I wonder if the Christmas tree is still up in the living room?" she said.

Linzy felt the words like a punch to the gut. She thought they'd already decided they would not look inside, because of course the tree would still be up. Mr. and Mrs. Ash had gone in with the sheriff earlier, and they had brought the Christmas gifts to their house—all the ones that had been gaily wrapped and already under the tree—and even that had been awful. Then she and Sash had scurried through their bedrooms and bathrooms gathering things they needed to return to school. Mrs. Ash had been a tremendous help with that, saying, "Just show me what you want, and I can come back for it tomorrow."

The atmosphere had been bleak. Cold without the furnace. Empty.

It had been as bad, or worse, than when they'd tried to exchange gifts on that too-soon Christmas morning. Each time Linzy had opened a gift from their mom or dad, the knife in her heart seemed to sink in a little deeper. She knew her sister felt the same way, maybe even worse. If Blue hadn't been sitting beside her on the couch, his arm touching hers from time to time, she might not have been able to get through it.

Sitting between Blue and Sasha, Linzy had looked at the small pile of gifts growing on the coffee table in front of her as the Ash's own pretty tree cast its old-fashioned twinkle across them all. She had thought about giving their intended parents' gifts to Mr. and Mrs. Ash instead of simply leaving them unopened, but Sasha had blanched at that idea. "Just leave them be for now," she'd muttered. "I don't want to see Mom's little glass bluebird on someone else's kitchen windowsill. Too much of a reminder."

Linzy understood. And then she had realized there were several under the tree labeled from her mom to her dad, and vice versa. She didn't know what to do about them.

"Just give it some time," Blue had said when she sought his opinion. "There's no rush about any of it."

And of course that was true. Blue spoke the obvious. No rush. Nothing said they couldn't deal with the gifts next year. Put them in a closet for now.

"Should we just bite the bullet and go inside?" Sasha asked. "I mean, here we are ..."

Linzy stared at the back door, her gut churning. "Yeah. Okay. If it means that much to you, let's do it. No time like the present." Let's rip off the band-aid, let the healing begin. Her folks always said face your fears, don't hide from them. It's only a few gifts left under a decorated tree. We can handle that. We'll just leave them there a while longer. No rush.

Together, they stepped inside the house using the back door key Sash kept clipped to her bag. Just over the threshold, Sasha stopped. "Oh," she said. "This is awful."

Afternoon sunlight limned the edges of the closed drapes. A stillness hung over the dining table like a shroud. Shadows crowded the silent living room, jumping away only when Linzy flipped on the light.

"I was wrong," Linzy said, finger still on the light switch. "I don't think I can handle this, after all. We need Blue or Mr. and Mrs. Ash, maybe Pastor Sue." She gazed at the place where the tree had stood. Someone, probably Mrs. Ash, had gone in and taken the Christmas tree down and stored everything away. The little pile of presents had disappeared, too. I'll ask about those later, she thought. Right now, we need to go. "C'mon, Sash." She reached toward her sister and Sash nodded.

They backed out and locked the door. "I'll bet it was Mrs. Ash who cleaned up the decorations," she said.

Linzy's heart pounded in her chest. "I'm glad she did. But sad, too. Someday, I'll ask her about it. But not today." Without another word, she linked arms with her sister and together, they walked back to the Ash's home on the opposite end of Wisteria Way.

Mrs. Ash met them at the door. "Come in, girls. We've had some news."

5

CUSTODY

"What do you mean we can't stay here anymore?" Sasha's face drained of color.

Mrs. Ash clasped her hand tightly. "I'm so sorry. I can't believe it, either. Someone from your dad's side of the family has filed a petition saying he should be your legal guardian." Her eyes were cast toward the floor as she spoke, as if she didn't trust herself to look at them and say the words, too.

Mr. Ash reached for Linzy's hand. "We *want* you both to live with us. We'd like to petition the court to make us your legal guardians. If that's alright with you girls."

Both girls nodded vigorously.

Mr. Ash glanced at his wife. "We hope that will make a difference with the judge."

His wife said, "I will call Carla Brushow and tell her to go ahead with the paperwork."

"But who is left on our dad's side?" Sasha blurted. "Who filed for guardianship? All our grandparents are dead." Her eyes darted to her sister. "Mom was an only child, and Dad too. Except for ... was there someone else, Sis?"

A dense feeling of dread expanded inside Linzy's gut. Her

dad's half-brother. That had to be who filed. Just a couple of days before the accident, she'd been getting ready for bed when she overheard her parents talking about her dad's half-brother, something about a recent visit. Linzy had been intrigued. She knew nothing about a visit. But as she listened, she realized they were also discussing her Grampa Jim's death. Another big surprise.

Linzy had overheard her mom say, "Ancho. That stupid nickname. He never even told us when Jim passed. Just showed up here unannounced and blurted it out. Probably wanted to make sure we knew he got all the money from the life insurance, that's what I think." Linzy had never heard such vehemence in her mom's voice.

"I'll bet he had that payout spent before the water got hot," her dad had murmured. "Some nerve coming here crowing about dad's passing six months ago. Maybe since he got all the insurance money, we will never hear from him again. Thank God he can't touch the farm. It was my mother's … we don't owe him a thing."

Linzy heard her father pause, imagined him shaking his head the way he did when something perplexed him. "Truthfully," he'd continued, voice even lower. "I never expected him to show up like that. Ancho. Said he felt the need to break the news in person. Six months after the fact." Her dad's tone had grown even wearier. "Let's just let it go. I'm sorry I didn't get to say goodbye to my father, but I'm *sure* we'll never see his other son again."

Linzy heard her mom reply, "At least he left before the girls got home. The less they know about him, the better I like it."

The next day, Linzy hadn't been able to contain her curiosity. She had gently questioned her mom about what she'd heard.

Her mother's expression said she hated having to tell Linzy about Ancho. "He is a vile creature," she huffed. "Trust me on this. I'm just sad we are connected to him at all." She went on to give

Linzy a nutshell version of the events that caused Grampa Jim's divorce and move to California where Ancho was born.

Linzy remembered being horrified that a once-loving spouse would leave his wife and child that way. And yet, she didn't see how anyone could blame the child, and she said so, still gently, of course.

"Oh, no one blamed him for that. He was a victim of circumstance, like your own dad, back in the day. But over the years it became apparent that Ancho fostered great resentment toward your father because he'd inherited the pecan farm. Your dad told me all about it before we married."

Her mom hesitated then seemed to decide she was old enough to hear the rest. "After Jim took his mistress and fled to California, the woman gave birth to Ancho. Within a few years, the mistress turned out to be every bit as selfish as Jim had been. Big surprise there, right? Later, she did to him exactly what he'd done to your dad and his mom. She up and left Jim and took Ancho with her. Apparently, they lived a very hardscrabble life moving from one man to another and another and so on. I assume that's when Jim took out the life insurance policy on himself so that the boy would at least have something in case he died."

Voice growing sterner and sterner toward the end of her speech, Linzy's mom had concluded her tale with a whispered secret. "A couple of years ago, Ancho called your dad and asked for money to start his own vape store. Your dad said he sounded drunk. Come to find out, Jim had already turned him down."

Her mom seemed like she was talked out as she concluded, "Anyhow, your father turned him down, too—you know how he feels about those vape things that target teens—that's when Ancho gave him an F-bomb-filled cussing and called him names I'd never even heard before. Your poor father. I don't think he told another soul about that call. We both lost all respect for

Ancho that day, and that was a year or two before he showed up here yesterday, unannounced."

Linzy recalled how her mom had smoothed her hair down and physically calmed herself before saying, "And now, that's the last we'll ever speak of him." Then she'd retreated to the pecan grove, the place she called her "thinking spot."

Quite taken aback at the news of her grandfather's past indiscretions, and the visit from his other son—not to mention the fact that her Grampa Jim had been dead for months and she'd never even had a chance to meet him—Linzy realized there was a lot she didn't know. But all of that was forgotten when her parents perished in their own unbelievable nightmare just two days later.

Dragging her thoughts back to the present, Linzy said, "Did this petition come from California?"

Mrs. Ash nodded. "I gather it was filed by your Uncle Ancho. Apparently, he's your dad's half-brother." She shook her head slightly, as if in disbelief. "It says he will come here when it's signed."

"You mean he intends to be our guardian, someone we've never even met?" Linzy stood, ready to run.

The couple glanced at her, sadness in their eyes. "I'm afraid so. Unfortunately, your folks did not leave specific instructions for your care in case of—"

Blue erupted from the hallway where he'd been listening. "Of course they didn't leave instructions. No one expects to die like that. Not both of them at once. Why would they leave instructions? The girls are nearly grown, anyway. Like me." His eyes flashed and his whipcord body appeared as tense as chained lightning.

Mr. Ash stood. "Calm down, son." He started toward Blue, but the young man—already much taller than his dad—danced away, putting himself behind the couch as if behind a barricade.

"He can't take the girls to California, Dad. That wouldn't be right. They belong here." Tears of anger, or maybe frustration, appeared in his lashes. He swiped a thumb beneath his eyes, defiant.

Linzy wanted to go to him. Stand with him, but he had that couch between them.

"He doesn't want to take the girls away," Mrs. Ash murmured. "He wants to move here. Live in their house. Let the girls stay in Brookville, finish school. With himself as guardian."

Linzy dashed toward the bathroom, one hand covering her mouth, barely getting to the toilet before everything in her system came up. When she was down to thin strings of yellow bile, she managed to stand from her half-crouch surprised to see Sash and Blue standing there, equally horrified expressions on their faces.

Sasha reached around and flushed the toilet, sat her sister on the edge of the tub, smoothed her hair from her face.

Blue wet a washcloth, and Sasha used it to dab Linzy's lips. Her voice was low, worried, sick. "It'll be better than us having to move, right?"

Linzy tried to be positive for Sash. "Yeah, and maybe the judge will say no, and we won't have to worry about it at all."

"Did you know dad had a half-brother?" Sasha asked.

"Yeah. He showed up here unexpectedly just a couple of days before Mom and Dad died. Mom said he wanted to crow over the fact that our grampa Jim had passed away six months earlier and named him as sole beneficiary of his life insurance policy." She took a shaky breath. "But we were in school when he came. I just overheard Mom and Dad talking about it that night. I've never even seen a picture or anything. He didn't get along with our dad at all. Or our mom."

Sasha sat on the edge of the tub beside her sister. Blue stood in the doorway. "Why would dad want us to stay with him?" Sasha asked.

"He didn't," Blue said. "I was listening to my folks just now." He leaned against the doorjamb, determined to answer Sasha's question. "Your folks made a general will years ago leaving everything they own to you and Linzy. And no one else."

"Well, that's good, right?" Sasha sounded hopeful.

Linzy's cynical side reared its ugly head. "So, what's the catch. Why is he coming?"

Blue stepped in, took her washcloth, ran water over it, handed it back. He seemed to be stalling, trying to figure out how to say the bad news Linzy knew was coming. Finally, he sat on the closed toilet seat and held out a hand to each girl.

What a funny place to talk, Linzy thought, right there in the tiny guest bathroom, giant Blue-boy sitting on the closed toilet while she and Sasha perched on the edge of the tub. "Go ahead, Little Boy Blue," she said. "Blow your horn." She grasped his big hand with her smaller one. It wasn't a new thing. She knew that hand. He was their buddy down the road. The one they could always depend upon. The one she and her sister had always called Little Boy Blue just to make him chase them.

Blue inhaled before he spoke. "The catch is this, y'all own everything, but not until you turn eighteen. Until then, you need a legal guardian. And apparently, a blood-relative, even half-blood, is the court's first choice."

"But we don't even know him," Sasha said.

Blue nodded. "I heard my dad say the guy probably just wants the property. I mean, he didn't even come for your folks' funeral, right?"

"Oh, my God," Linzy clutched her abdomen. She shoved Blue off the toilet and Sasha flung up the lid and held her hair while she retched again. Just the mention of her parents' funeral seemed enough to make her sick.

"I'm sorry, Linz," Blue said. "I didn't mean to make you—"

She sat back on the tub, flushed the toilet even though it had been mostly dry-heaves, and handed him her washcloth.

He took it and ran it back under the tap.

"It wasn't what you said," she told him. "It was the truth behind it."

Blue and Sasha looked at her, and she repeated what her mom had told her about their dad's half-brother, Ancho. The news stunned them both into silence.

6

ANCHO ARRIVES

Carla Brushow sat at her big desk tapping the plastic cap of a Bic ballpoint pen against her teeth. She had fancier pens, a drawer full of them, but in Carla's opinion, an old Bic still had the truest ink delivery. Besides, fancy didn't hold much sway with Attorney Brushow. She was all about heart. And soul. In other words, family.

She'd lost the love of her life when they were both students in law school. Drunk driver outside a bar in Austin. After she finished school and moved back home to Brookville, she married a man who had wooed her relentlessly. Then he'd broken her heart in so many ways she was downright thankful they didn't have children. The pain would have carried over to them too. Perhaps that was the reason she took such a special interest in looking after the Everly girls. They'd suffered even more heartache than she had.

Now, Carla sat, going over Ancho Everly's pending arrival, looking at documents and notes sent to her from a very knowledgeable private investigator she'd hired with Sheriff Peach's blessing. Her head felt stuffed with questions and ideas.

The first thing that jumped out at her was the fact that Ancho currently shared a low rent apartment with his wife and her two children from a previous relationship. And even though his father had made him the sole beneficiary of a tidy life insurance policy, his bank account teetered on the edge of nothing.

Reading on through the report, she learned that he'd spent all of that money on games and gambling. Apparently, he had quite a penchant for online video casinos. The Everly home on Wisteria Way, along with the utility-grocery allowance, were both much larger than the low rent digs and disability payments Ancho currently received in Los Angeles.

It was no wonder the man wanted his chance at a slice of the Everly Acres pie. Even though it was only ten acres and a sprawling ranch-style home, Mr. Everly had sunk his own refinery paycheck into it all these years as well. The bank account was considerable, that much was certain. And all the property was paid for, free and clear.

The question seemed to be, just who was Ancho Everly? Could he really be the compassionate person he portrayed himself to be—willing to leave his home in Los Angeles and relocate to rural nowhere Texas to help care for two teenage girls he had never met? Or could he have ulterior motives?

Carla tapped the pen against her teeth again, thinking of ways to ferret out the truth. Until now she had allowed things to move forward while her investigator finished up his reports and Sheriff Peach continued his investigations into the furnace problem. They both had suspicions about the nature of the Everly's deaths. Ward Everly had receipts for furnace inspections from the same company year after year for at least a decade. They'd kept the system in tip top shape. So why had it suddenly malfunctioned?

Everyone was on high alert.

She glanced at the Regulator clock on the wall. It had graced this office since the day her own father had first hung out his shingle. She laid the black Bic on her desk blotter. Time to get this show on the road. Ancho's bus was expected to arrive within the hour.

She was glad he didn't fly. The airport was in Houston, and the traffic was crazy. If he'd flown, she might've sent an Uber to collect him.

Instead, Carla would drive the few blocks from her office on the Brookville town square and pick him up in her Land Rover. It would give her a chance to see him as he got off the bus, take his measure so to speak. Then she could get a bit more acquainted with him while driving out to the farm where the Ash family waited with Linzy and Sasha.

The drive took five minutes. She parked the car so that she had a clear view of all the bus passengers as they disembarked. Her short, white-streaked, black hair formed a salt-n-pepper halo around her head. No nonsense black glasses framed her sharp gray eyes.

Stepping from the car, she held up a handwritten sign with his name on it. Ancho shouldered his backpack and gave her a short hello wave. He headed toward her, then remembered to go back and pick up the rest of his luggage.

Carla opened the vehicle's cargo area and Ancho stored multiple bags inside. He appeared to be the picture of health. Disability for back injuries? Hmmm, Carla thought.

After formal introductory handshakes, he thanked her for coming to pick him up. She told him it was no problem since she'd been the Everly's attorney for years.

On the way to the farm, she listened while he regaled her with details of his life in Los Angeles.

Carla was a little surprised by his chattiness. Then she realized he must know she was there to check him out before allowing him to meet the girls. She also got the impression he thought they were nothing but a bunch of rural rubes. Good, she thought. Let him go on thinking that while we figure out a way to send him packing.

As they traveled the few miles from town to the farm, Ancho described his wonderful life which had, according to him, been terribly interrupted by the on-the-job injury that had wrecked his back. "Couldn't work a day after that," he said. "At least not in the trucking industry, the career that I loved." He'd leaned back and adjusted his bucket seat as if to make himself more comfortable.

Carla didn't let on that she already knew about his monthly disability checks. But he must realize she'd watched him climb off the bus and swing what appeared to be a hefty backpack onto his shoulder. He hadn't had any trouble with the steep bus steps, or with the rest of his luggage, either.

Being an attorney, she'd seen tons of on-the-job injury claims that were designed to get the recipient out of work for the rest of his or her life. This appeared to be one of those. "Did I read in your file that you have been on complete disability for several years?" She tried to keep her suspicions out of her tone.

"Oh, yeah. I was thrown off a faulty liftgate while delivering freight, and that was the end of my working days. Tried a few other careers over the years, but those crushed discs just won't let me sit at a desk or stand behind a counter for any length of time." He shook his head sadly.

Carla thought she knew a rehearsed speech when she heard one. She changed the subject, asking him more about his name.

Ancho laughed what she assumed was supposed to be a self-deprecating laugh. If he was surprised that she knew so much from his file, he didn't let on.

"My given name, Turvy, caused me nothing but grief from the first day of kindergarten. You wouldn't believe the teasing and bullying I put up with."

Carla thought that was probably the truest statement he'd made thus far.

He went on, "Anyway. I was about ten when I saw the word *ancho* on a bin of hot peppers in the market near our apartment.

Thought it would be cool to use as a gamer handle. Kinda tough. Spicy." He smoothed a scraggly mustache. "Liked it so much I made it legal when I grew up."

Doesn't he know anchos are simply dried versions of mild poblanos? Not hot at all. Surely, he knows. Doesn't he?

Maybe not. She glanced at him from the corner of her eye. What she really found difficult to believe was his statement—via email—that he didn't know about Ward and Betty's deaths until the State of Texas contacted him about becoming the girls' guardian. She had absolutely no knowledge of that. But she let it pass, for the time being. She was the executor of the Everly's wills and there was nothing in there about him. So how did the State know to contact him? More investigation was necessary.

Even if they really did contact him, all he had to do was say no to the guardian question and sign a paper saying he wanted to decline. Then he would've been off the hook and still living his cozy Ancho life, collecting his disability and playing his video games.

Instead, he'd jumped at the chance to accept. Don't pee on my leg and tell me it's raining, she thought. I'm not sure how you found out they'd died, but I think you saw your opportunity and couldn't wait to jump on it. Run it up the flagpole, so to speak. See how it might play out. Probably he just wants to ingratiate himself to these girls, get on their good side, live in a nice home, maybe bring the rest of his family down eventually.

So many scenarios ran through her head. Possibilities yet to be entertained, but he was speaking just now so she paid close attention. In her experience, folks who are lying will often tell off on themselves if allowed to babble.

For the rest of the ride, they discussed Texas and the rural area between Brookville and the Gulf. Carla wanted him to be as comfortable and off-guard as possible.

Carla wished she had tried to get Linzy alone before now, find out exactly what she knew about this character, but the unexpected guardianship filing had surprised them all. In her mind, the idea of a stranger as a guardian was every bit as suspicious as Ancho claiming he'd received a call from a state's attorney telling him Ward and Betty had died and left the girls without a guardian.

He had something up his sleeve, no doubt about it. She needed to somehow find out if he had been watching the online newspapers for obituaries in the Brookville area. The town didn't have an actual print paper anymore, not even the weekly publication from years past, but they did have a by-subscription newsletter called the Wister County Gazette. It was available to anyone who cared to pay for a subscription online.

All Carla knew for certain was that an attorney from Los Angeles had faxed her office the paperwork showing that Ancho was a blood relative. Probably the only one in existence. It also told her what day he would be arriving, in other words, today.

Ancho interrupted her train of thought with a pleasant stream of comments about the humid climate and abundant foliage of southeast Texas.

"Perhaps you will get to make the short trip to the coast," she said. "Galveston Island is only a half hour away, and quite popular, you know. Beach town and all that."

Ancho laughed. "I think you forget I'm from Cali. Best beaches in the world."

"You got me there," Carla admitted. "You got me there." So why on earth would you want to leave all that behind?

Twenty minutes later she turned onto Pecan Road, which was simply an extension of Hwy 517 off Interstate 45. Pecan would intersect Wisteria Way in less than a mile and then they would be at the farm.

Even though she was an experienced attorney, Carla could feel the butterflies fluttering in her belly. By the time she bumped over the cattle guard beneath the still-bare wisteria vines, she had the butterflies under control. But her so-called Spidey senses were definitely on high alert. The questions in her head would not be ignored.

Following the circle drive to the front of the house, Carla could imagine the Everly girls sitting together on the sofa, waiting. She knew the Ash family would be there, too.

"Here we are," she said, putting the Land Rover in park and killing the engine. She stepped out of the driver's side, glanced at the big, picture window and waved.

She waited on Ancho to join her.

"I freakin' love this place," Ancho said.

Carla saw her opportunity. "Oh, it's a lovely property. Have you ever visited before?" She pretended only mild interest in his reply as she opened the back door of the Land Rover and grabbed her purse from the rear seat.

"Only once," Ancho replied. "Ward was my big brother, you know. We just didn't see each other much."

Quelling an explosive impulse to say, "Are you serious right now? When did you visit? I need details … " Instead, she slammed the rear door of the Rover and came around the front of the vehicle adjusting the strap of the purse to her shoulder. Inside the bag, she had her camera. Carla intended to photograph every room, every surface, and every closet as she gave him the grand tour. She wanted him to understand that she was documenting everything. Just in case anything should come up missing later. After she figured out how to get him out of there.

This was already a nightmare for the Everly sisters. If not for this, they probably wouldn't even be back in the family home. The girls had settled in quite nicely with the Ash family down the road. In fact, Sheriff Peach hadn't even allowed them to turn the propane back on until recently, after the repairs were made.

Nope, they really didn't need this so-called uncle to move into their home and take over their lives, but for the moment, they had no choice. If they didn't allow him to come here, then he would technically have the legal option to make them go with him to California. Carla Brushow, Sheriff Peach, and the Ash family were determined to do everything possible to prevent that. And to make Ancho's stay as short as possible.

~

"I'll just move in, too," Blue blurted when they heard the car doors thunk shut. "I don't care if he is a blood relative, he's a stranger and shouldn't be allowed to do this. He might be a pervert for all we know."

Linzy told him the sheriff had already done a background check, and he had no criminal history other than unpaid parking tickets. Even though she and her sister had been devastated by the sudden, unbelievable, turn of events, they seemed to have no choice but to give Ancho the benefit of the doubt. It helped that everyone from the sheriff to Mr. and Mrs. Ash told them they were working with Carla Brushow to find some legal loophole to send him packing. They just weren't there—yet.

They all watched through the window as their new-to-them-uncle stepped out of Carla's vehicle. To their immense relief, he appeared harmless. At least there were no devil horns visible. Only his frizzy, dirt-colored hair and somewhat odd mustache were as they expected. Different. Linzy opened the storm door to greet him and Carla, and that's when she noticed up close that his mustache appeared odd because it had been filled in with some sort of brushwork.

Linzy glanced at Sash and then at Blue, to see if they had also noticed. She couldn't tell if the brushwork was tattoo ink, or some sort of eyebrow pencil. Was that even a thing, to draw on a mustache? What normal guy would do that? Not one around here, she thought.

She couldn't take her eyes off those tiny fake hairs. They fascinated her. Later, she would discuss it with Blue. No doubt, he'd have plenty to say. He wasn't usually one to hold back. But maybe she shouldn't make a big deal of it. Benefit of the doubt, and all that.

The big guy lumbered toward her, arms outstretched, and she allowed a brief hug. "The place looks great," he said. "Just like always."

"Hello," she said, taken aback by his statement. All she could think was, I would've sworn Mom and Dad sent you packing the one time you were here. But she didn't say that. He had already moved on to Sash and the others.

Her manners told her she should say she was glad to meet him, or welcome to our home, but Linzy couldn't make herself say it. That would have made her feel like a hypocrite. She was neither glad nor was he welcome. This was being forced on them. Besides, now that she could see the fake, drawn-on mustache up close, manners were the last thing on her mind.

This is temporary. Only temporary. Those words reverberated in her head as the scene unfolded. But they didn't ease her mind, just bing-bonged around inside her skull like the ringing of a bell.

When Ancho leaned in toward Sasha for a hug, Linzy couldn't help herself, she turned sideways so that her body slid between them. "Come and meet our home-away-from-home family. This is Mr. and Mrs. Ash. They live just down the road—"

Mr. Ash held out his tanned and calloused farmer's hand. "We're always around."

Carla Brushow grinned.

Blue stepped forward, offering up his big-knuckled paw. "I'm always around as well." He glanced at Linzy and Sasha. "We grew up together." In his best chest voice he said, "They're like my own sisters. If I had any." His cheeks reddened and he ducked his head before pumping Ancho's hand forcefully.

Linzy studied the ground. She couldn't look at Blue's face. She knew he didn't really mean sisters. Maybe Sash, but not her. Not since the end of last year.

Blue's mother seemed to take pity on his discomfort. She leaned in toward Ancho, her southern manners on limited display. "Welcome to Texas," she said. "Let us know if you need anything." Her smile did not quite match her polite words. In fact, there was a steel ribbon running through her voice that matched the new steel-gray streak that had recently appeared in her light brown hair.

I'm glad Mrs. Ash made us spend the last few nights back here, Linzy thought. This is going to be so hard.

7

ACCEPTANCE

Together with Ancho and Carla Brushow, they trooped back into the house where Mrs. Ash took to the kitchen to pour everyone a glass of iced tea.

Ancho accepted his and sipped. Then he mentioned he would have to get used to the lay of the land so he could make a grocery run later.

No one commented on that, but he didn't seem to notice. Instead, he took his tea glass and made himself at home, following Carla Brushow as she documented each room with her camera.

At the end of the hall, Ancho stopped in front of the furnace. "Is this it? The monster that killed my brother and sister-in-law?"

Linzy felt her stomach do a slow roll, then her temper began to rise like the mercury in an old-fashioned thermometer. *How dare he mention that night so casually.*

Mr. Ash was beside him in an instant. He glanced back toward the living room where Blue had moved to sit on the couch between Linzy and Sasha.

"I'm sure you can understand the delicacy of that topic," Mr. Ash said, standing directly beside Ancho. "It was a horrific night.

I know you and your half-brother were not close, but those two girls were right here when it happened. It's a wonder they didn't lose their lives. Please, try to think about their feelings before you speak."

Mr. Ash turned and opened the furnace closet doors so Carla could take pictures. "As you can see, the entire ventilation system was replaced after the tragedy." He seemed to want to say more but he checked himself at the sounds of running water and the clink of glasses from the kitchen. He wondered if he should mention the new camera tucked into the closet, but decided no. It wasn't filming anything except the furnace. No need to disclose it. Not even the girls knew it was there.

Linzy watched the hallway exchange, she could hear parts of what they were saying, but not everything. *I sure hope Ms. Brushow was serious when she said if there was a way to get him out of here and back to California, she would find it.*

"Sorry about that," Ancho said to Mr. Ash before he closed the closet door. "I didn't mean to ruffle feathers, it's just so hard to imagine them dead on the floor because of this thing." He thumped the front of the furnace with the knuckle of his index finger. The metal gave out a hollow *throng*.

Mr. Ash clenched his jaw. "You seem to be missing an empathy gene," he said. "Why don't we drop this topic for now, and forever?" He reached past Ancho and closed the furnace door before turning and marching back to the living room. His face was nearly purple from checked emotions.

Ancho murmured, "I just wondered if they ever found out exactly what caused such a terrible leak, that's all."

Mr. Ash's face grew even more thunderous.

Carla Brushow reached over and took Ancho by the shoulder, ushered him through the rest of the house before Mr. Ash could explode.

Somehow, they made it through the visit with Carla showing Ancho exactly where his part of the house was located, and where the girls had their domain. Linzy felt like saying, 'and never the twain shall meet,' but of course that would have sounded snarky, so she didn't say a word.

When all was said and done, Blue stayed with them after his folks and Carla Brushow had gone. He fell asleep on the couch with a pillow and a blanket, and he wouldn't budge no matter how many times Linzy told him they would be just fine.

It was not the best of beginnings, but between Blue and his folks, and Attorney Brushow, they somehow made it through Ancho's first week.

Initially, the girls stuck together, avoiding their uncle like the plague, spending a lot of time at the Ash residence, showering at home only if the other sister was there to guard their jack-n-jill bathroom door.

The second week, even though Ancho had been told to use the guest bedroom, he had slowly migrated to the master bath and the master bedroom. The girls weren't sure what to do about that since they were at school all day, so they went on with guarding each other at home, and staying gone as much as possible. They thought about just telling Ancho they would be spending all their time at the Ash's home, but the court said he was now their guardian. He could either say go ahead, and then he would have the house to himself, or he could say nope, you don't have my permission to do that. The girls didn't like either of those options.

When he could, Blue made it a point to be at their home with them. At least when his work or school didn't pull him away. But since his family sold organic vegetables from their farm to local groceries and restaurants, and he was finishing up his senior year of high school, being pulled away happened often. Clearing the winter fields and planting spring crops was a big job. Being a senior not quite so tough. Especially since he already planned to take fire science courses at the junior college following high school.

. . .

Before they knew it, another week had passed. And then another. The first few were smoother than anyone had expected. Once Ancho had moved out of the guest room and into the master suite, he seemed to go out of his way to accommodate them.

At first, the girls were upset. He has no right to take over that way, Linzy told Blue one evening. Why can't he stay in the guest room like Ms. Brushow told him?

Blue said he would make him move back, no problem, but Linzy thought of how that would look, how it would damage their unspoken truce, and she backed down. "I guess we can give it some time," she said. "See what he does next. Maybe Ms. Brushow will have good news soon."

"I'm sure she will," Blue assured her. "This can't go on forever."

Linzy could always count on her best friend, Blue, to bring at least a little positivity to the situation. She hugged him and told him she was glad he was there.

Another week passed with Ancho staying in the den or in their parents' room, playing video games and watching movies. "See, I really don't want to disrupt your lives," he told them. "I just knew I was the only relative you girls had left so it was only logical that I step in to help."

"Maybe he doesn't realize how fake that sounds," Linzy said, when retelling it to Blue later. "I mean, we were all settled in at your house before he came. We probably would've stayed there until I turned eighteen, you know?"

Blue agreed. He said he couldn't figure out why the guy appeared out of the woodwork that way. "But my daddy said that happens sometimes, when people die unexpectedly." He'd shrugged, as if he didn't want to say too much.

"Oh, well," Linzy said. "At least he hasn't attempted to make any drastic changes at the house. That has been a huge relief.

Now that he has the master suite, I think he might actually be trying to get along. Like he said." She dragged her feet on the asphalt as they walked along with Sasha from Blue's house to theirs. "But he's still a stranger," she said. "And I *would* like to sleep in my own bed without having to lock the door."

"Yeah," her sister quickly agreed. "I'd like to shower without having to wait until you get home." She picked at a cuticle. "But to be honest, I don't think it will ever be our home again. When we aren't there, he has the house to himself. Does he go in our rooms? Does he go through our parents' things we stored in the attic?"

She closed her eyes and rubbed her forearms as if she felt shivery. "Just thinking about him at our house while I'm at school gives me the creeps. I find myself looking for small signs every time I come home."

"Signs?"

"You know ... things moved around in my room, or in my closet or dresser drawers." Her eyes were haunted when she looked up at them again. "He can do anything when we aren't home."

Linzy nodded. She didn't tell her sister how she hated seeing him use her mom's favorite iron skillet in the morning. Standing there at the stove, making pancakes, using their parents' bone china wedding dishes to eat them on. We only ever used those dishes for special occasions. Christmas, Thanksgiving, Easter. The sound of his knife and fork on the delicate china almost made her cry. She wouldn't tell that to Blue either. No telling what he might do.

In her opinion, Ancho didn't belong in her mother's kitchen at all. She just said all the nice things so Blue wouldn't worry. But every night before she went to sleep, Linzy prayed that Carla Brushow would figure out how to get Ancho to go back home. To his home. He had his own family, he shouldn't be allowed to come in out of nowhere to disrupt theirs, especially not in the place that used to make their mom so happy.

She began to wonder if they should somehow be watching what was happening when they were gone. Sasha's words had made an impression on her. Maybe there's some kind of hidden camera system we could install to show what happens when we're not here. She vowed to ask Carla Brushow about it. If she didn't know, maybe she could find out from the sheriff.

Linzy didn't want to tell her sister what she had in mind about the cameras. Not until she talked to Ms. Brushow. She didn't want Sash to worry any more than she did already. Especially since they had gone back to school and found everyone treated them as if they were made of glass.

No, she thought, I won't add to her worries. Sadness seemed to be her middle name now. Linzy felt sad, too, but she had Blue to talk to. Blue to hug her and make her feel better. She was pretty sure Sash didn't have anyone like that, other than her and her good friend Rose. But Rose had a boyfriend. She stuck by Sash as much as possible, but in the end, three's a crowd. Especially in high school.

Oddly enough, Carla Brushow called Linzy the very next day. "I'm just checking on you girls," she said. "Wanted to see how everything's going. Let you know I haven't forgotten about you."

Linzy launched right into her questions about cameras.

Turned out Carla knew a bit about cameras. In fact, she had gone ahead and purchased four nanny cams. Linzy asked her to bring them to the house as soon as possible. She took them out that very evening. Ancho didn't even come out of the master suite except to say hello, then back to his cave he went. Before long, Carla had hidden tiny cameras in all the shared living areas of the house. The only places they were not utilized—because it would be illegal—was in bedrooms and bathrooms.

That was okay with Linzy and Sasha. The extra eyes made them feel a little safer. Nevertheless, being back in their home, without their parents, and with a stranger, was a lot like a page out of an Edgar Allen Poe novel. Or one of those Poe short stories her Literature teacher loved so well. Linzy wanted Ancho out of their lives. They didn't need him, and she didn't trust him. She just wanted him to go back to his life and leave them alone.

A couple more weeks went by and nothing happened. There was nothing bad on the cameras, he just seemed to be stagnating, enjoying his new home as if it were the Waldorf Astoria.

Finally, Linzy couldn't stand it any longer. One morning she arose, feeling out of sorts, wishing she could go sit in the middle of her parents' room and just talk to them, miss them, acknowledge their absence, but she couldn't do that. The door was closed. Ancho lived there now.

She shored up her nerve, prepared to talk to him like an adult, rehearsing her speech in her mind. "What are you doing," she planned to say. "You can't be enjoying this charade any more than we are. You have your own life back in California. A wife, stepchildren. Ms. Brushow told us so. What do you hope to gain here?" Better yet, when are you leaving?

But no matter how many times she rehearsed it in her head, no matter how many times she started toward the kitchen with the intention of talking to Ancho like an adult, Linzy just couldn't do it. She'd never confronted an adult about anything. Ever. The law said he was now her guardian, hers and Sasha's. Life see-sawed from horror story to black comedy and back again. Nothing made sense anymore.

Above all this crazed reality, Linzy was becoming more and more worried about her sister. She knew that was part of the reason for her foul mood and need to take some sort of action. Vague dreams had plagued her more than once. Dreams about Sash walking down the road and not coming back. She seems so fragile, Linzy thought. Even though she was doing well in her school classes, Linzy could tell their new home life was weighing on her. She didn't talk about her feelings much, but she had recently confessed to Linzy that she could barely stand to look at Ancho anymore. "Sometimes I get this feeling ... kind of that dark cloud feeling ... ever since that first day when he said that about the furnace. I just don't trust him."

Linzy realized she was saying the exact same thing she herself had been thinking. She also recalled the 'black cloud' her sister had felt on the night their folks died. Could that be the same depressing darkness she felt now? "I'm glad you told me," Linzy said. "This must be torture—"

Sasha shrugged. "It doesn't matter. It's out of our hands. We installed the cameras, we look at the footage, and it shows that he seldom comes out of his man cave. When he does, it's just to go to the kitchen for food, or to the den to play those stupid video games on the big TV. I just need to get past it. Grow up, or something."

Linzy heard the jagged tone of her sister's voice, as if she'd used a jigsaw to shape her words. She mentioned their conversation to Blue, and he made it a point to come in and sleep on the couch a few nights even though it required him to rise before dawn the next morning to go back to his house to shower and change.

On those nights, Ancho simply stayed closed up in the master bedroom or the den, playing his games or watching his movies, sleeping perhaps—something that Linzy confessed irked her to no end. "He doesn't even have to work," Linzy confided to Blue. "I've never known a grown man or woman who didn't do some kind of work. Have you?"

Blue had no answers, but he did have hugs and commiserating sighs and nods. And he would often take both girls into town for burgers and fries and, if nothing else, just a quick trip to the Dairy Queen for a milk shake.

But as the days passed, and Ancho grew more and more comfortable in their home, the two girls grew ever more uncomfortable. It was like Sasha said, when they were not there, he could do whatever he wanted. And eventually, he did.

The days crept past, turning into weeks and then months. They watched the camera footage carefully. Ancho did nothing illegal, but he gradually took over their home just like a crop of weeds takes over a garden.

Blue seemed as dumbfounded as anyone about how things had turned out. He jokingly told Linzy he could take the guy out in the Gulf and let him fall off the boat if she would just give him the go ahead.

Patting him on the back, she said, "I know you're only kidding, but don't tempt me." She'd slapped a hand across her mouth after she said it, realizing what she'd just admitted.

Blue slung his arm around her. "It's okay. If we can't joke about it, we might go crazy."

Linzy nodded, relishing his strong arm around her. Thinking all the while of Sasha and the dark cloud. If not for the reassurance of Blue and the nanny cams, they might have gone seriously stark raving mad. "We don't need a guardian," Linzy repeated. "We grew up that night. And we have you and your family, Pastor Sue, and Ms. Brushow." She ground her teeth together. "We don't *need* him."

Things rocked on. If the girls were home, one of the Ash family members was likely to be there, or to be in and out. Of course, Linzy and Sasha still went to the Ash farm almost daily. They were seldom left totally alone with Ancho. Not for long anyway. Not even with the nanny cams. After all, they could only record things as they happened, they certainly couldn't prevent anything.

Just as they began to think this would be their forever routine, or at least until she turned eighteen, Linzy walked in just in time to hear Ancho on the phone begging Carla to raise the monthly household allowance.

She knew the attorney had set a strict limit for household bills like cable, electric, and groceries, but right from the beginning, Ancho seemed to have trouble staying within the budget. His extracurricular activities like drinking beer, streaming games and movies, and ordering in snacks and fast food continually ate up the funds.

"You'll need to use your own money for extras," the attorney had told him at the beginning. "The Everly's finances are used strictly for necessities like groceries and utilities. Not for your extra luxuries."

Linzy recounted the incident to Blue later, and he said he'd overheard Carla telling his dad that she had an investigator checking into Ancho's monthly disability payment out in California. "If it is still being used to pay for an apartment he no longer lives in, then that might be fraud. And fraud could get him out of our lives." He grinned slightly when he told her that.

So how long till we know? Linzy had asked. But Blue didn't know that part. "I assume it has to be long enough to show that the rent is still being paid, but he isn't living there." He'd shrugged. "And I have no idea how long that might be."

"It's way more complicated than I would have thought," Blue said.

Linzy agreed. "I guess Ms. Brushow will let us know if something works out." She hesitated a moment, then blurted. "Do you know if Sheriff Peach is still investigating the furnace failure. I mean, it appears that he's done since he allowed us to move back into the house when Ancho came, right?"

Blue did not know that, either. The investigation was one thing *none* of them had been privy to. "Actually, I haven't heard one way or another, but like you said, since y'all are back in the house, I assume it's all settled. I do know the furnace company said everything was fine when they checked it beforehand." He shrugged slightly. "I know the sheriff and my dad are the ones who arranged for a company to come in and make the repairs . . . that was before Ancho, of course."

"I can't believe he left his wife and kids to come here," Linzy said. "Her name is Patty. He told us that one day just out of nowhere. Sash said he was probably hoping we'd invite her and the rest of the family to live here, too."

"Weird," Blue agreed. "Y'all don't need a guardian. But he sure seems to be enjoying his time away from his family." Blue raised one eyebrow. "Maybe that's the whole reason he came, because he wanted to get away."

Linzy pursed her lips. "I overheard him telling Carla Brushow that he needed more money in our day-to-day household fund."

Blue shook his head. "I'll bet Ms. Brushow loved hearing that, didn't she?"

"I wish I knew what she told him," Linzy said. "I could only hear his side of the conversation. But it didn't sound like he got what he wanted." She turned half away. "I can't believe we're even talking about it," she said. "Like, how can Mom and Dad really be gone? How can we be left with just him?"

Blue turned her back around, pulled her in close. "He isn't all you've got. You've got me, and Sash. My mom and dad, Pastor Sue . . . and about a million other folks I could name if you want me to."

Linzy sniffled and rubbed her face on his shoulder. "Thanks, Blue-boy. I appreciate that. I know it's true, I just—"

"Had a moment of weakness, like we all do now and then. It's okay. Good Lord, with what you and Sash have been through, most people would be falling apart right now. You are doing great." He tipped her face up with one finger beneath her chin. "I swear you are."

Nodding, Linzy dried her eyes and snuggled deeper into his embrace. "I'm lucky to have you," she said. "I guess we'll just have to see how things play out."

Blue pressed her to his chest and rested his chin on top of her head. "It's gonna be alright," he said. "I promise."

The next day, Linzy arrived home to find a scroungy new guy sitting on the sofa, grinning like the infamous Cheshire cat.

"Who're you?" she blurted.

The guy stood, pushed a hank of sun-fried hair away from his bloodshot eyes. "Name's Domino." He touched his right hand to his right eyebrow in a limp salute. "But you can call me Dom." His gaze slid over her body. "You're right, bro," he muttered to Ancho. "Choice."

Linzy ignored the stupid salute and told herself she didn't really hear what she'd just heard. Nobody is that crude, she thought. She turned her head to cough into the crook of her elbow. The ghost of their pot smoke was still evident. Would that show up on the security cam video? If so, it might be the very thing to get him out of their lives. She assumed smoking dope in the presence of minors was illegal. Especially when it wasn't even his house.

"Domino is my wife's brother," Ancho said. "He's got a weird sense of humor." He glared at Dom. "He's just stopping over for a few days. On his way back home."

Linzy hurried to her room and shut the door. A creepy pot smoker? Staying for a few days? No way. This is not a hotel. And it's not Ancho's smoking lounge, either. Smoking anything is not allowed on Sasha's swim team. Especially not smoking dope. We'll both have contact highs if we have to live with this—even for a few days.

She took out her phone to view the nanny cam footage in private.

The girls talked it over as soon as Sasha got home from practice. She wasn't as upset as Linzy thought she would be, and that scared Linzy in a different way. Her sister seemed almost detached, as if she didn't really care one way or the other.

"Think we should tell Mr. and Mrs. Ash?" she asked.

Linzy nodded. "I think we should. I mean, we have to, right? Especially about the smoking. Drinking beer all the time is bad enough, but at least we don't have to breathe that." She felt stupid saying it, but it all went along with the idea that Ancho could do whatever he wanted in their home when they were not there. She hated it.

Sasha nodded. "Will they call the cops or ... what? Is that stuff illegal?"

Linzy thought about it, she didn't know how much weed one could keep for private use. She also thought about how Coach wouldn't care about that. He'd probably just cut Sasha from the swim team if she came in smelling like weed, but come to think of it, Sash didn't even mention that. Swim team used to be her favorite thing in the world. Didn't she care anymore? Linzy thought they'd had a breakthrough the day they'd burned the letters, but now she wondered if Sash was even still writing her letters.

Living with a stranger was taking a major toll on them both. They didn't need this new guy and his dope on top of everything else. Maybe I won't even tell Mr. and Mrs. Ash, she thought. This is my house. Mine and Sasha's. Ancho is just a temporary guardian. I'll tell him what's allowed and what isn't. I'll tell him myself.

As soon as her sister was in bed, Linzy gathered her courage and called Ancho into the kitchen.

He ambled in, a bleary smile on his face.

Disgust coloring her words, Linzy said, "I want that guy out of here. And I don't want you bringing anyone else to this house. There won't be any more smoking dope, either. Sash and I are minors, remember? You said you wanted to be here to look after us. Not to drink beer and smoke dope with your buddy." As she spoke, her anger grew. It was a new feeling for Linzy, this actual fury at another person.

Ancho's already pallid skin turned the color of old paste. He raised his bloodshot eyes to hers and the look there was frightening. "We don't have no dope," he said. "I've got a medical prescription for my disability, but we don't have no illegal dope. And you ain't seen us smoking nothing."

For a moment, Linzy wished she hadn't confronted him without Blue. He was right, she hadn't seen anything, just smelled it, and breathed it. She hadn't seen them actually smoking because they confined it to the master suite. Probably the little sitting area her mom had called her reading nook.

Heart pounding, she turned on her heel and stalked back to her room, praying he wouldn't follow. She closed and locked the bedroom door behind her and stood with her back pressed against it.

When her heart rate returned to normal, she pushed her small dresser up against the door and then went into Sash's room and quietly did the same there. Only their jack-n-jill bathroom remained open between their two rooms. I'll tell Blue and his folks about Domino and the pot smoking tomorrow, Linzy thought. She washed her face and brushed her teeth and hoped she could go to sleep as easily as Sasha had done. Then it occurred to her that Sash might be sleeping *too* much. If she was at home, she was in bed. Linzy didn't know what to do with that idea. Except the same thing she did with everything these days … tell Blue and Mrs. Ash. Maybe Pastor Sue.

After half an hour of tossing and turning and flipping her pillow over and over to find the 'good' side, Linzy finally dozed off. She jerked awake once, certain she'd heard something, but after lying perfectly still for several minutes, determined it was nothing but a dream. Once she went back to sleep, she slept soundly.

Morning came early, as her dad always said, and while she

didn't feel rested, once she got up and pulled aside the bedroom curtain, the daylight actually made her feel a little better.

She and Sash got ready for school as always. They didn't mention the night before. Linzy didn't want to start the day on a sour note, she just hoped Ancho and his buddy would be holed up in the master suite and stay there until she and her sister were gone.

To her surprise, Ancho came into the kitchen while they were eating their cereal and said she was right, he should not have had a guest over without their okay. Then he apologized and told her Dom already had his bus ticket on to California. He was scheduled to leave the very next day.

Linzy accepted the apology and felt something akin to pride that she'd handled the issue on her own. She didn't smell any smoke that day when they came home, and since Dom would be leaving soon, she didn't say any more.

That evening, the girls avoided being in the same room as Domino. Ancho seemed tame in comparison to his raggedy friend. Even though Linzy didn't smell any odor, the guy seemed to always *lean*. As if he walked a thin, unseen, tightrope.

"He seems high all the time," Sasha muttered. "I don't like the way his eyes look."

Linzy nodded. "It's not right, him being here." She'd hesitated before continuing, "But Ancho says he's leaving tomorrow so—"

"Hey, Sis—"

Linzy stopped to listen. Something in her sister's tone made her think a secret was forthcoming. "What is it?"

Sasha shook her head. "Oh, never mind. It's nothing." She glanced at the living room where her father's chair once sat. Blue and Mr. Ash had replaced the recliner before the girls moved back in.

"Is it too much, Sash? Being back here in the house, I mean?" It wasn't the first time she had broached the subject with her sister, but it may have been the first time she'd asked her that directly. She also had to admit that even after nearly three months here with Ancho, she still thought about her folks every time she came in the door. The same door she and her sister had dragged their parents out of when trying to save them.

"It's okay, Sissy," Sasha assured her, hollow eyed. "I wouldn't want to be anywhere else. All we have left of Mom and Dad is here, in this house. On this farm." She coughed and cleared her throat. "Like you said, Domino will leave soon. And before too much longer, you will come of age and then Ancho will have to leave, too. Then we'll have our lives back."

Linzy hugged her. "I don't think it will be that long, Sash. Something will change, and in the meantime, I'm here. Always. And we've got all our other peeps looking after us, too." She pulled back and looked at her sister's face. "If these guys bother you in any way, say anything that makes you uncomfortable, let me know. In fact, just don't even come home anytime I'm not here. Just go down to Blue's house. Okay?"

Sasha nodded. "You don't have to worry about that."

Linzy smiled, but in her heart, she thought, is this any way to live?

8

SWEET SIXTEEN

The very next day, Linzy turned sixteen with the saddest party known to mankind. It was organized by Ancho, with balloons and a store-bought cake on a day when she really wanted only one thing, her parents. Even getting her upgraded driver's license earlier in the day could not get rid of the creeping sadness. Before this, she'd been on a hardship license, only allowed to drive herself and Sasha back and forth to school. Now that she was sixteen, she should have felt happy and unfettered, allowed to go and do anything.

But she certainly didn't feel happy and unfettered.

In addition to missing her parents on her birthday, Linzy had just learned of a new development with Domino. He claimed he'd stepped in a gopher hole and sprained his ankle while roaming the acres with Ancho. "We were just taking a little stroll before heading into town to the bus station," he said. "Now, doc says I have to keep it elevated." He raised his pant leg to show her an ace bandage wound around his ankle. "Doc said absolutely no two-day bus trips until the swelling is gone."

Immediately suspicious, Linzy blurted, "What doctor did you

see? There are only a couple in Brookvi—" She glanced at Sash who had just walked in and sat down.

"Doc on Demand," Ancho said. "We just called 'em up on Facetime, showed 'em the bruising and swelling." And then he'd flourished a grocery store birthday cake on the palm of one hand like a concierge in a cartoon. It was complete with sixteen candles.

Linzy had been raised to be polite. But she had never mentioned that it was her birthday, so how did he know? I certainly don't want anything from him, she thought, except for his absence, *and* that of his bushy-haired friend, of course. Nevertheless, she swallowed her sharp unspoken remarks and tried to show her appreciation. At the same time, she had the distinct impression that the spur of the moment celebration was nothing more than a lame attempt to detract from the fact that Domino was still here when he was supposed to be gone.

Now she had to pretend to be thankful when all she really wanted to do was grab Sash and walk out the door. The two of them had already been invited to dinner with Blue and his parents. A nice dinner at the only steakhouse in Brookville. Linzy felt stressed and exhausted. She was beginning to think Ancho was counting on her "polite" upbringing to keep her from throwing a fit about Dom still being here. Maybe I need to be more forceful, like before, she thought.

Instead, she thanked him, mentioned their already planned dinner reservations with Blue's family, and smiled sweetly. I'll practice standing up for myself later, she thought. I don't really seem to have it in me again.

He set the cake in front of her, lit the candles, and waited.

Linzy leaned in, blew out the candles, and made a silent wish for strength. "Thank you so much," she said. "We will have some when we get back. The Ash family is waiting for us right now."

Ancho's cheeks went red, then purple. His eyes narrowed to

half-closed blinds. The look on his face bordered on rage. "Well, then, by all means, feel free to go. Sorry I kept you from your *real* party." He took the cake and still smoldering candles and made a show of sliding the whole thing into the garbage bin in the kitchen.

Linzy waited a moment, then took her glass of water and dumped it in the bin as well. You may not care if the house catches fire, she thought. But I sure do.

Dom sat in a dining room chair, droopy eyed and slump shouldered, as if trying to fathom what had just happened. "Hey, sweetheart," he said to Linzy, "don't get your panties in a twist. Ever'things aw'right." His slitted eyes traveled down her body like before. "Jus' like *you.*" He stuck his bandaged foot out in front of her. Not quite far enough to block her path, but enough to get her attention.

Linzy couldn't believe their childish behavior. She was angry and alarmed. Both of them were acting like complete morons. And Dom was beginning to frighten her. It's the beer and the weed, she thought. Makes them act even more like idiots.

"I didn't think you even knew it was my birthday," she said. "Mr. and Mrs. Ash planned this dinner weeks ago." She grabbed her purse, touched Sash on the shoulder to let her know she should grab hers, too, and then they hurried out the door to the carport.

Please, God, let my car keys be in my purse. She had stopped hanging them on the decorative KeysPlease hook beside the door even though it had been the place to put them ever since her folks had hung their keys there. Something about not having them with her when she and Sash went to bed at night just wouldn't let her rest.

Now, though, she had a horrible feeling her keys would be missing from her purse, that she would be forced to go back through the house to look for them. But no. They were in her bag —thank God—just where she'd put them.

Sasha opened the passenger door and slipped inside. "He was

mad," she said. "Do you think it's because we didn't invite him to go with us or because we wouldn't cut the cake?"

Linzy shrugged. "Maybe it was because I dumped the water in on top of the candles. I don't know, and I don't care. I think it would be rude of us to invite them to the steak house since Mrs. Ash is the one who made the reservations. He and his friend weren't even here then. Besides, it's not a party, just dinner. She said she knew I might not feel like a full-on birthday celebration."

She tossed her bag in the backseat. "He's high and unstable, if you ask me. But I'm not going to blow off the people who really love us just for his last-minute attempt to make brownie points. I'm sure the birthday cake came right out of our own grocery funds. Besides, Dom was supposed to be gone today." She rolled her eyes and slid behind the wheel. "I don't believe that sprained ankle bull for one minute."

Pressing the starter button, she put the gear shift in reverse and backed out just far enough to access the circle drive leading down to the gate. *Neither of those idiots should be here, making our lives miserable. He is just sponging off us.* Does he think he's going to stay forever? What about his own life, his wife and kids? And now here's Dom and his supposed injury? *What next?*

Unanswered questions floating around in her head, Linzy tried to put on an act for Sasha's sake. "Let's forget them for a while. What will you have at The Roadhouse?"

"Probably chicken," Sasha said. "With the salad bar." Sasha seldom ate red meat, and if it wasn't for her swim coach insisting that they load up on protein, she probably wouldn't eat meat of any kind.

"I may get the little sliders," Linzy said, just to keep up her front. "Blue will insist I get a steak though. He thinks I should have filet mignon on my birthday, crazy guy."

"He loves you," Sasha said. "It's obvious. Always wants the best for you." She swallowed and Linzy heard it in the quiet confines of the car. She reached out and turned the radio on low.

"Are you okay, Sis?" she asked.

Sasha nodded but swallowed again. "Someday I want someone to look at me the way Blue looks at you. Someone who always wants the best for me, too."

When she smiled at Linzy, it almost broke her heart. "I know what you mean, Sash. But just remember, we all love you and want the best for you. All of us." She grasped her sister's hand. "And you will fall in love one day. I promise. Blue and I have been best friends forever, and he's your friend, too. One day, there will be a special guy. You're not even quite fifteen yet, you know."

Her birthday was coming up soon, but she hadn't even mentioned taking Driver's Ed classes yet. Didn't seem to really care. That worried Linzy. She glanced at her sister in the waning light. Sasha gazed out the window at the sunset. Her face had gone pensive, impossible to read.

They drove into town and met the family at the steak house. Blue had been out late, making a grocery store vegetable delivery, or he would have come to the house to pick them up.

The Ash family made things bearable, as always, and for an hour or two, the girls forgot to be sad. Blue gave her a beautiful locket holding a picture of the two of them, and Mr. and Mrs. Ash gave her a lovely dress which Linzy had admired one day at The Galleria in Houston. It had been one of the weekends Mrs. Ash had insisted on taking her and Sash on a shopping spree to get their minds off the home situation.

That was before Domino had appeared out of the blue like a virus. She still hadn't told anyone else about him. Everyone always had so much on their plates, she hated to add to their worries.

Plus, she believed he would be gone today, but now that had changed. And she was still processing all that. At the restaurant, the steaks and baked potatoes were eaten and thoroughly enjoyed. Sasha had her chicken and salad, and slices of red velvet cake, with scoops of vanilla bean ice cream, were served alongside an energetic birthday song performed—seemingly out of the blue—by members of the waitstaff.

Linzy grinned in spite of herself. Even Sasha got into the spirit. Along with a new curling iron—their old one had died just a few days earlier—Sash had been thrilled to give her big sis a *Sweet 16 and Never Been Kissed* key chain as a joke. It turned into a surprisingly lighthearted celebration during which all their troubles seemed to fade away, at least for a while.

When the meal was done, and the girls started home, Blue followed in his truck. He wouldn't take no for an answer.

At the house, he walked them inside and they noticed the double pocket doors to the den completely closed.

Blue inclined his head toward the doors, a question on his face.

Linzy shook her head. "Just forget about it," she said. "We're getting ready for bed anyway." She paused, listened. "Sounds like video games. Ancho loves his games."

Blue didn't appear convinced. He could not understand a grown man—completely unemployed—who played video games all day and night. "If he can do that," he indicated the door. "Why can't he work from home? Most computer jobs are remote anyway."

Linzy shrugged. She'd asked herself that very same question.

Blue said, "I'd feel better if you just let me sleep on the sofa tonight."

Linzy wouldn't hear of it. "You've got school *and* work again tomorrow," she said. "I'm not going to be the reason you fall asleep in class or driving down the road to make a vegetable delivery." She laughed to show her bravado. "Everything is fine, Little Boy Blue. No worries."

She ushered him back to his truck before Domino could make an appearance. Linzy didn't want to have to explain him. She already felt like a fool for not telling him earlier.

Blue gave up.

Linzy gave him a chaste goodbye kiss and watched as he climbed into his driver's seat. But as she watched the old red pickup drive away, she immediately had qualms about her decision to keep quiet. Just as she'd been making herself do with so many things since her folks died, Linzy realized she was simply trying to put on a happy face because she didn't like pity. Or feeling helpless. *Dom will leave soon. He has to leave soon.*

Turning out the living room lights, she checked the kitchen. Linzy never left dirty dishes in the sink overnight, one of her mom's rules, so she washed a couple of glasses and placed them on the drainboard. No use putting them in the dishwasher, who knew when they would have enough random dishes to run a full load?

She found nothing else that needed her attention, so she turned out the light and went down the hall toward hers and Sasha's bathroom-connected bedrooms. I'll check the nanny cams on my phone in a minute. Make certain everything is 'normal' before I go to bed.

Since the den doors were still closed, sounds of some kind of cyber warfare emanating through, Linzy assumed everything was all right. At least they weren't too loud. The old house was well built, well-insulated. Her dad had taken good care of things. Which is why the leaky furnace still boggled her mind.

At the entrance to the hallway, she looked back into the dim living room. Moonlight draped soft rays across the old couch and new chairs.

It was the same but different. Mrs. Ash had changed out the throw pillows, keeping the same type, just changing to a different shade of mauve and jade. Linzy liked the changes. She also liked when Mrs. Ash had whispered, "Don't worry, I've got everything in storage if you want it. I just thought a few new colors might make things easier."

Linzy had given her a big, teary-eyed, hug.

Now, she took one more glance at the moonlit living room.

The dimness was comforting, but strange, like seeing things through a filter. This is our life now. This is us, moving on. Things change. Who said the only certainties in life are death and taxes? Linzy didn't know, and she didn't understand much about taxes, but life and death? She was learning all about that.

Stopping to say goodnight to her sister, Linzy wasn't surprised when Sasha ushered her into the bathroom where they could wash their faces and brush their teeth in tandem. The way they'd done when they were little kids.

The sinks weren't dual in this bath like they were in the master, the one Ancho had stealthily taken over—probably in preparation for Dom's visit, so he could have the guest room—but the two girls took turns at the single sink without even speaking. Linzy had a quick flashback to the day she'd sat on the closed toilet, sick as a dog, while Blue and Sasha mopped her face and held her hair.

Bad, bad, memory. She shoved it away, tried to bury it. Allowed herself to be comforted by this new-old routine, getting ready for bed at the same time, one after the other. The atmosphere in the rest of the house was surreal. But this, this togetherness, that would be their safe place, always.

Linzy convinced Sasha to sleep with her that night. "I just need you with me," she told her. "My first birthday without the folks. It's kind of brought me down." That wasn't exactly true, but close enough.

What she really needed was to know her sister was safe. If Sash had sensed a black cloud coming down the night the furnace malfunctioned, then Linzy felt she was experiencing something similar tonight. It was once again an overwhelming sort of feeling that something ugly was hanging over them, waiting to fall.

9

SIXTH SENSE

The next morning Linzy and Sasha got ready for school, ate their bowls of cereal on the patio, then left the house. All without seeing either Ancho or Dom. It was quite a relief. Both girls were in good spirits as they exited the house.

Sasha rounded the front of the car and pointed at a square of white sticking out from under the driver's side windshield wiper. "What's that?"

Linzy reached over and yanked it free. As soon as she opened the folded paper, she realized exactly what her sixth sense had been warning her about. In an incredulous voice, she read the lines scrawled across the page. *'Linzy, you're all I ever wanted. If your uncle says it's okay, we can get married. You can go back to LA with me. I've seen how you look at me. I know you feel it, too.'* A pair of entwined hearts were scribbled at the paper's bottom edge.

Opening the Buick's door, Linzy fell into the driver's seat and started the car without speaking. Sasha climbed in beside her. Linzy handed the note to her and backed out of the carport in a daze. "I don't even know what to think," she finally said.

Sasha read the note and began to giggle.

Linzy glanced at her in amazement. "Are you laughing?"

Sasha giggled again. "I can't help it," she said. "It looks like something a third grader would write. Or maybe a fifth grader." She shook her head and started to crumple the paper.

"Oh, no. Don't toss it." Linzy grabbed the note, refolded it. "That's going to Mr. and Mrs. Ash. I first thought I'd show it to Blue, but I don't know how he would react." She tucked the paper into the center console. "If Domino isn't gone when we get home, I'm taking this straight down to the Ash's house to show them. Tell them what's been going on. This is ridiculous."

They drove on to school in near silence. When they arrived, Sasha said, "You're right, Sis. I'm sorry I laughed. It isn't funny. It just looked so comical, somehow. Like a joke, you know? To think you would ever be with someone like that."

Linzy rolled her eyes. "All that weed they smoke. Makes 'em live in their own little world. At least, I think that's what it is." She pressed her lips together. "Seriously, I never looked at him, did I? I mean, like that?"

"Not no, but Hell No," Sasha said, invoking their mom's favorite, and only, curse word euphemism.

"Thank you," Linzy said. "This life we've got just keeps getting stranger and stranger. I'm ready to put the brakes on these two clowns."

"I'm with you," Sasha said. "We probably should have told Mr. and Mrs. Ash about Domino right away."

"Yeah," Linzy signaled for a lane change. "That's my bad, trying to handle stuff on my own. But I believed them when they said he was leaving and then—"

"It's okay, Sis," Sasha said. "Learning as we go, right?"

"Learning as we go," Linzy repeated. "That's right. That's exactly right."

They arrived at school before they knew they were even close, and thankfully, the rest of the day passed uneventfully.

Sasha texted Linzy at lunch to remind her she had swim practice after school. It bothered Linzy that Sash still didn't sound excited. "I forgot we have a make-up meet coming up next weekend."

"Oh, that must be for the team that was sidelined by the flu for a couple weeks?"

"Yes," Sasha said, "I couldn't believe it. Then a couple of our girls got it, too. Must be a bad strain this year."

Linzy said a silent prayer that they wouldn't come down with it on top of everything else. After all, doesn't the immune system take a hit when the body is constantly under stress? She rolled her eyes when that thought crossed her mind. Oh, brother, she thought. I'm beginning to sound like an old worry wart, even to myself.

Properly self-chastised, Linzy went straight out to the car after school. All the way home she worked on building up her nerve in case Dom was still around. Something will have to be done, she told herself. He has to leave. That's all there is to it.

At the intersection of Wisteria and Pecan, Linzy looked to her left. It would be so easy to simply go to the Ash's home, avoid a confrontation with Ancho. But she turned right instead. Apparently, she had boosted her nerve just enough. Through the gate she went without giving herself a chance to back out. Bumping over the cattle guard, she drove the silver Buick around the right side of the circle drive and parked under the carport as usual.

The farm truck was there, where it always sat when not in use. Linzy got out and went inside. Without hesitating, she headed straight for the kitchen anxious to learn if Dom had left. Before she'd even crossed the living room, she could hear the sound of Ancho's raised voice.

He seemed to be speaking into the phone again. "That's right, Ms. Brushow," Linzy heard him say, "there was a note, but it was from her boyfriend. I saw her pluck it off the windshield this morning. I also overheard her talking about running off to get married." He stopped talking abruptly, then said, "No. No, ma'am.

Not my brother-in-law. Not Dom. He wouldn't do anything like that. Of course not. He's only been here a couple days, would have gone on to Cali by now but—" He stopped talking again when Linzy dropped her backpack in the floor.

She was livid. "What are you talking about?" she yelled. "I just turned sixteen. If I have anything close to a boyfriend, it's Blue. And we sure as *hell* aren't talking about running off to get married. Dom left that stupid note on my car and you know it!" She couldn't believe Ancho would stand there lying like that. For a moment she was certain steam must be escaping from her ears like some mad cartoon character.

Without considering the consequences, Linzy yelled even louder, "Everything he just said is a lie, Ms. Brushow, I don't have a boyfriend. And I'm sure not getting married."

Ancho's face paled and he ended the conversation and shoved the phone in his pocket before glancing around at Domino who was leaned up against the counter, sipping a beer and smiling.

"Thought you had to keep that leg elevated," Linzy spat at him as she turned and marched out of the kitchen. She finally realized what a mistake she had made in trying to handle this situation by herself. I should have told everyone about Domino the moment he arrived. But how did Carla Brushow find out about the note?

Linzy yanked her own phone out of her back pocket, intending to call the attorney, but it rang in her hand. She smashed the green answer icon. "Ms. Brushow?"

The attorney's voice held a hint of alarm. "What's going on, Linz? I just got off the phone with Ancho, but before that, Sasha called me. She was so worried about some note left on your car this morning. Then she finally got around to telling me about this new character staying out there."

Linzy's breath whooshed out. "I just got home from school and walked in on Ancho talking to you. The character you mention is named Dom. He was supposed to go home today, but then he left that note this morning. I was going to go down to the

Ash's home if he wasn't gone, show them the note, but then I heard Ancho talking to you." She pushed her bangs upward with her palm. "I'm glad Sash called you. I didn't know she was going to do that." She pulled in a slow, deep breath, clearing her head before speaking again. "I think Ancho and this new guy, supposedly his wife's brother, may be cooking up some kind of a plot—"

"I want to hear more about that," the attorney said. "But plot or no plot, there should be no one staying there. Especially not some pot-smoking letch."

Linzy felt a weight lifted off her shoulders. Thank you, Sasha, she thought. You saved me again. "Ancho says Domino is from California, too." She felt her nerves begin to calm as the attorney peppered her with questions.

"Yes," she said, in answer to another question about Dom. "He's been here for a couple of days." She walked out the back door to the patio. "No," she said into the phone, "I did not invite him to stay. He was supposed to be gone yesterday but he said he sprained his ankle, and some tele-doc told him not to get on the bus until the swelling went down. But if he keeps hitting on me and leaving stupid notes it won't be the swelling he has to worry about—"

Carla Brushow interrupted with another question.

Linzy blew out an exasperated breath. "You know, hitting on me—looking at me like I'm a piece of candy, saying how *choice* I am." She stopped pacing and pulled the slightly crumpled paper from her other pocket. "And then there was the note stuck under my windshield wiper."

In a trembling voice she read the stilted lines. *'Linzy, you're all I ever wanted. If your uncle says it's okay, we can get married. You can go back to LA with me. I've seen how you look at me. I know you feel it, too.'* She cleared her throat. "And then he drew two big hearts at the bottom." Linzy paused. "It really made my skin crawl."

There was shocked silence from the other end of the phone, and then the attorney said, "No signature?'

"No," Linzy said, "but Dom's the only other person here from L.A. besides the one who calls himself our uncle."

Carla huffed, "Snap a pic of that note, send it to me. Then save the original. Don't let anything happen to it. Bring it to me tomorrow. I'll call you right back."

Linzy clicked off. Inside the house, she could hear Ancho's ringtone blare out a heavy metal song popular from before she was even born. She laid the note on the patio table, took a picture, and sent it to the attorney via text. Then she carefully folded the paper back up and slipped it back into the pocket of her jeans.

From inside the house, she heard Ancho answer his phone. "H'lo?" he said. "Oh, no. Of course not. Nope. Uh-uh. Ain't no one living here with us. Just me and the girls. My wife's brother stopped by on his way home to L.A. Had business out in New Orleans, but he's leaving soon."

Linzy heard him mumble an expletive. When she glanced through the kitchen window, she found herself staring straight into his furious face. Her own anger melted into fear.

"Nah," she heard him say, voice flat. "Ain't nothin' going down like that. If Dom was flirting, I wasn't aware of it." He halted, obviously listening. Then he continued in a snarky tone. "Aww, hell no. He never wrote no note. That was from her boyfriend. Like I told you."

He stopped, listened again. "The note said he wanted to take her back to L.A., huh? Yes, ma'am. I didn't know that." His tone had changed, humbled. "Yes. Yep. Dom will be leaving tomorrow. Today? Well, I guess he could. See, he's got this ankle injury. Nope. I understand ... not my home. No overnight guests. Not even my own brother-in-law." He paused again. "Of course. No visitors, none at all. Got it. No problem."

He ended the conversation but immediately called someone

else. Even from outside, Linzy could hear him speaking. She couldn't make out the words, but his voice sounded like the hiss of a rattlesnake.

Suddenly, her phone startled her like before. She yanked it out of her pocket, glanced at the screen to see who was calling. "Ms. Brushow?"

"I'm heading that way," the attorney said. "The creepy friend should be gone before I even get there. He can sit in the bus station and wait on his transportation back to California. Absolutely no more overnight guests at Ancho's invitation. You and Sash own that house, he's just a temporary guardian. You can have all the overnight guests you want, but I'd watch them around him. I no longer trust that character. At all. Cameras or no cameras." She inhaled, then continued. "I'm looking into ways to get you girls out from under his umbrella. What did he say when you showed him the note?"

Linzy barked a short laugh. "I haven't even had a chance. I don't think I will, though." She felt she could speak more freely now that she knew Dom would be leaving. She recalled Ancho's doughy face in the kitchen window. "I hope you can get rid of him. I can't believe how our lives have been turned upside down." I won't start bawling, she thought. *I will not.*

"We'll get it worked out, Linz. I promise. Don't give up."

"Thank you," Linzy said, imagining the no-nonsense woman brushing her salt-n-pepper hair off her forehead as she spoke. "I don't know what we'd do withou—"

"It's okay," the attorney interrupted. "Go ahead and go on down to the Ash residence until Ancho gets his visitor out of there. Keep my number on speed dial. As a matter of fact, just stay on the phone with me. I don't like this turn of events. Go ahead and go to your car. I'm on my way."

Linzy slid into a patio chair, both alarmed and relieved. "I will," she said. "And thank you, wait. Hold on." She held the phone away and listened. She could hear Ancho and Domino moving through the house, voices raised in heated conversation.

"Everything okay, Linz?" Ms. Brushow said, voice barely audible.

"I think so," Linzy whispered. "Sounds like they're mad at each other, Dom saying he can't get a ticket that leaves before tomorrow."

"Stay on the phone with me," the older woman said. "Go on out to your car. If they are angry, I don't want you there alone—"

"They're leaving," Linzy said, totally relieved. "I just saw Ancho walk past the window with a duffle bag. I think he's mad at Dom for messing up the plan somehow."

Carla Brushow chuckled. "I'm still coming," she said. "Let's just stay connected until you get out to your car."

"It's okay," Linzy said. "They're both getting in the truck. I heard Domino complaining about no place to stay tonight, and Ancho said there was a motel right by the bus depot."

Ms. Brushow chuckled again and Linzy said, can you hear this? She held her phone up to see if Ancho's voice would carry through to Ms. Brushow. "It sucks, man," he said. "It seemed like a good idea for a minute. You shouldn't have put in that part about L.A., but no worry. We'll come up with something else. Just gotta think it through."

Linzy's whole body turned cold when she heard him admitting it that way. Especially when Domino's thin, scratchy voice apologized and agreed with him.

"You should see them, Ms. Brushow," she said, putting her phone back to her ear. "Domino has this pot belly hanging over his jeans where his t-shirt doesn't meet his pants, and scraggly blond hair that sticks up all over like the raw ends of a torn blanket. Oh, hold on, I can't hear them anymore—"

She hurried to the front window, then said, "Whew, it's okay. The truck just started up. They're leaving already." She watched the truck trundle through the wisteria gate and onto the road.

"They're gone. I guess Ancho will be back after he drops Dom off somewhere."

"That's what I need to talk to you about, Linz," the attorney said. "I think it's time we file for emancipation. It's a little early according to your age, but there are definitely extenuating circumstances."

At lunch one day, Linzy's friend, Sara, had told her she might be able to become emancipated at age seventeen. "Oh, I hope you're right, Ms. Brushow," she said now. "That would mean Ancho would have to leave, too, right?"

"That's right," the attorney said. "I'm in the middle of drawing up the papers to petition the court. It would make me your conservator, and you would be Sasha's legal guardian until she's old enough to become emancipated, too."

"That would be an answered prayer," Linzy began, and then a thought occurred to her. "You know, I think I just figured out what 'the plan' actually meant. If I married Dom, the way the note mentioned, then everything I own would also belong to him, right? Oh, what a horrible plan. I must seem like a real hick to them."

"They think they're smarter than everyone," the attorney said. "I believe that was one of their harebrained ideas, but don't worry about it, anymore. I've told Ancho in no uncertain terms there is to be no one else in the house but him. From now on." She softened her tone a bit. "And I'll put the pedal to the metal on my own plan of emancipation."

Linzy sniffled, then laughed self-consciously. "Thank you for coming to my rescue, you and Sash. I hope we can we start the proceedings soon?"

"Yes, they're in the works now," Ms. Brushow said. "And those aren't the only irons I'm heating in this fire. In fact, I'm thinking we need to have a sit-down meeting sooner rather than later. Can you girls come to my office tomorrow after school?"

Linzy didn't hesitate. "Of course."

"Great. Don't mention it to Ancho. Just hang in there. If anything changes, call me immediately. And if Blue wants to stay over, that will make me feel better. In case Ancho is still steaming, I mean. In fact, if Blue can't make it, let me know. I haven't had a slumber party in years."

Linzy laughed out loud at the idea. "Okay, that's a deal." She thanked her again, looking forward to telling Sash all the news. She had messaged Linzy to say that a friend was going to bring her home from swim practice so Linzy wouldn't have to drive back into town. Since she didn't mention the note or the call to Ms. Brushow, Linzy assumed there were other swimmers standing around.

After clicking off the call with Carla Brushow, Linzy went to her room and attempted to concentrate on a paper she was doing for social studies class. She stayed in her room until Sasha got home. Mrs. Ash had called to invite them down for dinner, and the two girls enjoyed a quiet time with the family. Blue escorted them back to their home where they drank glasses of iced tea on the back patio, as always.

Linzy asked Blue and Sash to accompany her on a walk through the pecan grove. The trees were beginning to leaf out, and it was actually very pleasant. In the back of her mind, she had to make certain Dom was really gone and not hiding out. He'd said that "strolling the acres" was how he sprained his ankle, so she wanted to keep an eye out for gopher holes, too.

There were none. And no signs of any ratty tent camp or other hide-out either.

They all went back to the patio door and into the kitchen just as Ancho came in through the front door. He went into the master suite without a word.

After hearing about the entire Domino incident, while they were walking the "acres," Blue elected to sleep on the sofa just the way Carla had hoped he would. Linzy didn't try to dissuade him.

For the first time in months, she felt a glimmer of hope. Carla had called her again and told her the judge had signed off on the paperwork for the next phase of their legal battle. She explained that when Linzy signed it tomorrow, she would become emancipated and the legal guardian of Sasha all in one fell swoop.

The attorney also told Linzy that although she would be made conservator of their accounts, as she'd mentioned previously, she would also ask Mr. Ash to be her second voice. That way both adults, plus Linzy, would have to sign off on all major purchases or changes to finances or real estate ownership.

Now all they had to do was break the news to Ancho. Carla said, "I'll make certain Domino got on that bus to California, and then tomorrow, while you girls are in school, we will invite Ancho to a very important meeting in my office. What we won't tell him is that Sheriff Peach will be there, too."

10

THE MEETING

Linzy whispered to Blue and Sasha what was being planned, and he grabbed them both in a major bear hug before literally walking them to their bedrooms and making certain they were tucked into their rooms for the night. "Call me if you need anything," he said, holding his cell phone aloft.

Ancho was not seen again that night. Video game sounds emanated from the master suite sitting area as before. This time, without Domino.

Linzy felt fortunate that he hadn't tried to set any rules for them when he became their so-called guardian. All he'd had on his mind were things that benefitted Ancho.

"Thank you for staying," Linzy told Blue as he turned away after escorting her and Sash to their rooms. "I feel kind of shaky about all this."

Sash had gone straight into their connecting bathroom.

Blue pressed Linzy close and kissed the top of her fluffy caramel hair. "I'm here," he murmured. "Not leaving you."

They'd always been inseparable—best friends bound by something no one ever thought to question. "Joined at the hip," his mom used to say.

But ever since Linzy's parents died, something between her and Blue had shifted, grown heavier, tangled with grief and something harder to name. Sasha called it love, Linzy wouldn't argue with that. Not at all. Blue pressed one more tender kiss to the top of her head before allowing her to slip into her bedroom and turn the lock.

She heard Sasha open the other side of the bathroom that went into her own bedroom, and so she gave her a few minutes, then went through to check on her. Sasha had gone right to sleep.

In the guest bathroom, she could imagine Blue utilizing the toothbrush he'd brought down the first time he'd stayed with them. Linzy vowed she would repay his selflessness one day. He was their rock and their champion.

The next morning, they all got up early for work and school. Blue would be graduating high school this year, so he went to school earlier and got out earlier than they did. Senior privilege, it was called. He still worked for his dad while volunteering with the rural fire and EMT service in the evening. It was comforting, everyone getting up and getting ready together, even if Blue did have to leave first.

On the way out of the house, they saw that Ancho's bedroom door was open. That meant he was also up and about. He usually slept in until after they were gone. Linzy felt a bit of trepidation when she saw that open door, but she tucked it away and hurried past.

As the three friends gathered Blue's bedding and stacked it on the end of the sofa, Linzy caught a glimpse of Ancho pacing the back patio, talking on the phone. He hadn't said a word yet, but he seemed to go out of his way to avoid running into them.

Linzy peered out the window, watching him. Today, he had on a clean t-shirt and jeans and had combed his frizzled hair. She wasn't certain, but he may have even touched up his skimpy mustache.

She moved closer to the storm door, listening. Lately, she had zero qualms about eavesdropping. His voice was barely audible, but Linzy could make out what sounded like him telling someone that he thought the attorney might offer him a cash deal to leave and go back home.

"Dom may have had an unexpected result, after all," he was saying. "They *really* didn't like him being here. Now, they don't want me here, either." He was silent for a moment, listening. "Yeah," he laughed. "You know I'll tell her where she can put *that* kind of deal. I deserve this house, or at least half the value."

Linzy felt her throat constrict to the size of a pencil. She couldn't seem to get enough air. She already knew Ancho had received their estranged granddad's only life insurance benefits. She didn't understand why he felt entitled to anything from her mom and dad's estate.

Unnerved, she crept away from the back door motioning for Sasha and Blue to follow her. She didn't want to alert Ancho that she'd overheard, but she didn't want to hang out once Blue left, either.

They all hurried out the front door into the early morning.

Once out front, Linzy could breathe again. "Oh, my God," she said, ushering Sasha into the passenger seat of the car. "I'll tell you what I heard when we are on the way."

"Call me," Blue said. "I've got to head on to school now, but you two go on down to my house or stop for coffee or something, okay? I don't want to leave y'all alone with that guy anymore."

Linzy nodded and climbed into the driver's seat of the Buick. She touched Blue's picture on her phone and put him on speaker so she could relay the entire conversation to both of them as they drove.

Sasha said it made her think Ancho was not going to leave without a fight.

Linzy crossed her fingers and hoped Sheriff Peach and Attorney Brushow had some tricks they hadn't yet revealed.

Once they ended the conversation with Blue, Linzy told Sasha they had plenty of time for a side trip to The Coffee Spot Café in Brookville.

As they enjoyed their coffee and pastries, Linzy noticed Sasha had her fingers crossed, too. Neither of them mentioned the meeting they would have after school. Linzy knew why. It meant her sister wouldn't want to draw attention to it. Don't upset the juju gods, Sash always joked, meaning if you drew attention to a thing—good or bad—it often had a way of falling apart or getting worse.

At school, they exchanged one look in the parking lot, tipped their coffee cups at each other, then went their separate ways.

Sash's fingers had still been crossed.

The day wore on.

Linzy watched the clock in every class. Was the meeting with Ancho over yet? How did he react when he walked into the attorney's office and saw Sheriff Peach there ... and come to think of it, why *was* the sheriff there?

Linzy's mind raced.

Finally, around two o'clock, Carla Brushow sent her a text. "It's over. You've got your life back. Call me when you can."

Walking out the back door of the school an hour later, Linzy couldn't contain herself any longer. She let out a whoop and punched her fist in the air.

"Everything good, Linz?" her friend, Tonya, asked.

Linzy laughed and tapped the attorney's name to call her. "Everything is looking up, Tonya. Finally looking up." Not many of their friends knew exactly what had been going on the last few months, but a few did. Sasha's friend Rose was one, and her own friends, Tonya and Sara were the others. Those three girls had been their good friends since grade school.

Tonya ran to Linzy and gave her a high five just as Carla Brushow answered her phone. "Call me later," Tonya mouthed at Linzy before backing away to give her some privacy.

Nodding, Linzy spoke into the phone, "Hi, Ms. Brushow. Is it really over?"

"Yes," the attorney said without preamble. "In fact, it went so well, you girls don't even have to come in." She paused, then said, "You should have seen him, Linzy. He turned forty-three shades of red when he came in and saw Sheriff Peach standing there." She chuckled as if remembering. "He said we had no right to accuse him of anything. And that was before a single word had even been spoken."

"Oh, no," Linzy said.

"Oh, yes," the attorney retorted. "Then Sheriff Peach laid a copy of the note in front of Ancho, hitched up his gun belt, and told him that the legal papers were all in order, and the jig was up. He said we all knew he'd been simply trying to bilk you girls out of your inheritance."

"What did he say to that?" Linzy asked on a whoosh of breath.

"Oh, he started to yell that we had no right to do this because he was the only living relative, blah blah, blah—as if he was the victim here."

Linzy inhaled to speak, but Ms. Brushow continued, "Then the sheriff took off his hat, and placed it upside down on my spare chair."

"Uh oh," Linzy said. "I can imagine how that looked."

"Ancho pushed his hair out of his face, prepared to argue, but Sheriff Peach dropped the bombshell. He told Ancho about the hidden camera in the hall closet—the one with the vented door." She chuckled a bit. "We had both forgotten about it having audio on it. He made certain Ancho knew he had placed it there as part of the investigation into your parents' deaths."

Linzy felt her eyes grow wide.

"It took Ancho a minute to digest all that—"

Linzy thought carefully before she spoke. "What did become of that investigation?" she asked. "With everything else happening, I'd almost forgotten about it. Especially since nothing was ever said."

"Oh, the investigation is still ongoing," Carla assured her. "And once I told the sheriff about the note from Domino, Peach went through footage from every camera. But it wasn't until he accessed the audio portion of that furnace closet camera that he hit paydirt."

She snapped her fingers. Linzy heard it over the phone. "Can you believe that little camera actually picked up part of the conversation in which Dom agreed to place a note under your windshield wiper? Wasn't his idea at all, he was just doing what Ancho wanted."

"Wow," Linzy breathed. "You know, I once overheard Ancho and Dom whispering in the hall. I figured they had spied one of the nanny cams in the living room, so they went to the hall to tell their little secrets."

"I'll bet you're right. They thought it was a safe, unrecorded space. Seriously though, the camera Sheriff Peach placed was only intended to catch anyone who might open the furnace closet," she said. "He wanted to make certain no one messed with the pipes again."

"I'm sure glad he did that, I'm not sure I even knew there was one in there," Linzy said.

"You would have, soon. It was just an investigative tool. And while the note itself is not a crime, the fact that we now have a recording of Dom and Ancho talking about it—together—gives us leverage to get him out of your house for good."

"Thank God," Linzy said.

Carla agreed. "You should have heard Sheriff Peach when he cleared his throat and said, 'That could also be considered soliciting a minor. Especially since she's only sixteen and you yahoos recorded it *and* put it in writing.'"

"Gross," Linzy said. "That's so, so ... *gross.*"

The attorney chuckled. "That's why the sheriff got in Ancho's face and asked him if he would like to listen to the recording himself. I swear, I thought the guy was going to pop an eyeball. Peach said only a few sentences are audible, but it was enough to convince a local judge of their intent."

"And I'm sorry to tell you this, part, Linz," Attorney Brushow said, all the jolliness gone from her voice, "but he is now the number one suspect in the furnace leak that killed your parents and almost took you girls as well."

Linzy felt the blood drain from her head. She was glad she had reached her car. She had to sit down, quickly. For a moment, she wasn't certain she could form words. Finally, she said, "Number one suspect? Why? Do you really think Ancho did something to them on purpose?"

The attorney cleared her throat. "Our investigator found a subscription to the online newspaper, The Wister County Gazette. It's in Ancho's wife's name, but she has no connection to this area, so why would she want to read about it?" She took a breath, then continued. "We believe *someone* intentionally damaged the furnace vent pipe, causing the carbon monoxide to leak back into the house. Not sure how Ancho could have done it, but pretty sure he thought he would inherit all the Everly family property if the four of you succumbed to the poisonous gas."

"But when that didn't happen," Linzy mused, "he decided we were left all alone, so he would just swoop in and take over anyway."

"Yes," Carla said, voice taking on a soothing tone. "But when he got here, Ancho discovered you girls were not alone at all. You have an entire community wrapped around you. I guess he became desperate for a new plan. I believe he thought getting you into his family through marriage would solve everything."

"What was his response to all this?" Linzy asked.

Carla Brushow's voice was cool. "When the sheriff told Ancho we knew the pipe had been damaged intentionally, the guy almost leapt out of his chair. Probably would have if Peach hadn't been leaning over him. But once Peach told him that was the *reason* he had placed the camera in there, that's when Ancho's face really fell."

Linzy's stomach did a sickening roll. Her voice came out as a whisper. "What did he say then?"

"Oh, he denied it, but Sheriff Peach went on to tell him that he intended to prove it beyond a reasonable doubt. And that when he did, Ancho would be looking at premeditated murder." Carla lowered her tone. "That's a death penalty charge."

"Murder," Linzy said. "Premeditated murder. And he's been living with us, all this time."

"I'm afraid so," Carla said. "Of course, we never thought he could be involved and then be so bold as to actually move in, but here we are. Still, even knowing all that, we must find something concrete to tie it all together."

Linzy said, "He probably killed Mom and Dad. I just can't wrap my head around it. He's been in our house, in *their* house, in *their* bed, just feet away from us, for months."

"I'm sorry, Linzy. We never would have allowed him to stay, had we known. I mean, we knew he was lazy and greedy, but we thought he was just an opportunist. Hoping to inherit something, anything ... then we found the subscription, and it raised a big red flag."

The attorney cleared her throat then continued, "It's horrible to think he may have orchestrated the entire plan from the beginning, but Peach made certain the creep understood *all* our suspicions. You should have seen the sheriff flex those massive shoulders as he laid down the law."

"I sort of wish I had," Linzy murmured, realizing the attorney was deflecting the conversation away from the topic of her folks' murder, and how she and Sash may have been living with the murderer all this time.

"Oh, yes," Carla said, gaining her attention again. "Peach

commanded the room. He told Ancho to stand up, and then two deputies appeared in the doorway as if on cue."

"They arrested him right then?" Linzy asked.

"Most certainly," Carla said. "It isn't proof, yet, but the note, the recording about the plan, and the newspaper subscription that was taken out *before* your folks died, all of that together, is enough to hold him on." She cleared her throat. "When Sheriff Peach told him he would be in jail until the investigation was complete, he lost all the color in his face. Peach says he already has enough evidence to go to trial, but he would like to have what he calls 'a smoking gun'."

Linzy was momentarily speechless, mulling over the meaning of the phrase. Then it hit her. "I may have the smoking gun," she said. She took a deep breath and launched into the story about Ancho's surprise visit to Wisteria Way shortly before the tragedy.

"That's unbelievable," Carla Brushow said, shocked. "I can't believe I didn't know about it. You're right, this could be our smoking gun." She began to speak, then stopped, then started again. "Tell me everything," she said.

"I'm sorry," Linzy said. "I never realized it might mean something." She lowered her car window, wondering what was taking Sasha so long. Then she continued, "I guess it didn't stand out with me because I didn't actually see him. I just overheard Mom and Dad talking about it one evening, talking about how he'd appeared at the house that day, without warning."

The conversation with her mom popped back into her head. "I'll try to tell you everything … it was the day after he visited that I begged Mom to tell me who she and Dad had been talking about. And she did … boy, did she ever. She did not like him at all. In fact, she told me to never mention his name again."

"Oh, my," the attorney replied. "He might've damaged the furnace vent that very day, then took out a subscription to the local newspaper in his wife's name in order to keep up with the outcome of his plan. Just the fact that he used his wife's name is suspicious. Why would he feel the need to hide it? That's cold. Really, really cold." She exhaled. "Definitely premeditated."

Linzy felt awful that she hadn't mentioned it before, but he was a distant relative, not someone she would ever call upon. Truthfully, though, now that she knew him, she wasn't surprised. She hadn't trusted Ancho from the first, and Sasha had experienced such a bleak feeling about him it had nearly dragged her back into depression.

After hearing everything Attorney Brushow had to say, Linzy felt both relief and a new sense of fear. What if the evidence was *not* enough to hold him … what if he got out? What if he wanted revenge?

11

AFTER THE MEETING

The day after Ancho was arrested, the Ash family helped Linzy and Sasha install outdoor cameras and a brand-new indoor-outdoor security system. They left the nanny cams in place as well. "That simple camera in the furnace closet really made a difference in getting Ancho out of here," Mrs. Ash said.

Linzy closed her eyes. "I just wish it had been there *before*." She felt tears threatening her speech. "I mean, how could Ancho crimp the pipe? And when? My dad would've have known if he did something like that, right?"

She swallowed to clear her throat. It floored her to think the death of her parents was now considered a murder. And the fact that the number one suspect had been sleeping in her mom and dad's bed made her feel like Little Red Riding Hood being hoodwinked by the Big Bad Wolf.

Mr. Ash said, "I should have known something suspicious happened. I *never* knew your dad to let any of his equipment fall into disrepair."

"But *how* could he have done it?" Sasha asked.

"Your parents were in the house with him, right?" Blue said as he plopped down beside Linzy on the sofa.

Linzy nodded, recalling the way her mom's voice had sounded when she said Ancho's name. "I assumed they were, but I didn't come right out and ask. I mean, he may have gone to the bathroom, or Mom could have stepped out on the patio to call Dad. Doubtful he was already home, in the middle of the day like that."

Sasha began to pick up the trash from the new camera packaging. "I can see how that could happen. He could have done something to the vent pipe while Mom was outside or even in another room." She wadded plastic and flattened boxes for recycling. "I knew there was something evil about him, showing up that way. Saying he wanted to be our guardian. I think he really did want to kill us all, don't you?"

"Maybe," Linzy said. "And you know what?" She let the memory of her parents' voices run through her mind again. "If I had told someone sooner, these last few months might have been avoided."

Sasha fell onto the sofa beside Blue. "Oh, Sissy, don't you start the 'what if' game. We already know how that plays out."

Linzy looked at her sister. She was right. They'd already been down that road. "It's beginning to make sense, isn't it? After all, someone damaged that pipe. Who else would've had the motive and the opportunity?" She sat in one of the new recliners. "Who else would profit from our deaths?"

Blue spoke up. "Even if it was Ancho," he glanced up at his dad before continuing, uncertainty palpable in the tone of his deep voice. "Even if it was him … how can it be proved?"

Linzy bit her bottom lip and stared at the space between Sasha and Blue. "I've been trying to figure that out.

"It wouldn't take but a minute to crimp that pipe," Mr. Ash said. "If he had the right tool that is."

"Could he have brought a tool with him?" Mrs. Ash asked.

"Not on a plane," Linzy said. "But there is a hardware store in town. He could have stopped by Ace Hardware and bought the—"

"Channel locks," Blue said. "You know, large adjustable pliers. That's all it would take to crimp it that way." His eyes were dark, much darker than his usual cheerful brown. "We can talk to Mr. Montoya at the hardware store. Ask him to go back through his receipts for December, see if he sold some channel locks to a creep meeting that description." He thought for a moment. "We can show him a picture. Did anyone take a picture of Ancho?"

They all looked at each other. Linzy shrugged. "Maybe social media?"

"If we're lucky," Mr. Ash said, "Or perhaps Sheriff Peach already thought of all this. He probably ran a check on his driver's license. We could use that photo. If we're even luckier, Ancho may have used a credit card to purchase such a tool. Wouldn't that be something?"

"Ha!" Linzy barked. "I don't believe he *has* a credit card. Who would give him credit?" She lowered her eyes, shocked at the ugly passion in her own voice. "Maybe the sheriff will let us use his mugshot."

"He's bound to have a debit card," Mrs. Ash added. "He has to have some way to access the funds from his California bank account."

Linzy jumped up, ready to head to the car. "You're right. He must have a debit card to access those disability payments. Let's go—"

Mr. Ash was way ahead of her. He held up his phone. "Calling Sheriff Peach now. He will have no problem getting a look at those records. To be honest, I'll be very surprised if he isn't way ahead of us on this."

Linzy sat back down. "You're right. Besides, we can't go barging into the hardware store, demanding answers. Mr. Montoya sold my dad his tools for years. He would probably tell us, but we can't just go around playing detective, can we?" She closed her eyes, pressed her hand up across her forehead into her hair. It was such a desperate gesture, so like someone at the end of her rope, that Blue stood and pulled her up, crushing her to his chest, right there in front of his parents.

"Dad and Sheriff Peach will check it out, Linz. Don't worry." He looked across the top of her head at his father. "We won't let him get away with it. I promise."

Sasha burst into tears when Blue spoke those words, giving voice to what they'd all been thinking. She covered her face with her hands and Linzy broke free of Blue's embrace and dropped back to the sofa beside her. "Don't worry, Sissy," she slid an arm around her sister's shoulders. "We'll make sure he's convicted. He won't bother us, ever again."

"If he is the one who killed Mom and Dad, though," Sasha mumbled, under her breath. "Nothing will ever make that right."

Linzy couldn't argue with that.

After Mr. and Mrs. Ash left, Blue stayed on. "I'm not going to leave y'all again," he said. "Not until we get this all straightened out and get him behind bars on more than just a lot of suspicion."

"What if it isn't him?" Linzy murmured. "Could we be jumping to conclusions?"

"I know it's him," Sasha said. "I knew there was something wrong with that guy from the very first day."

Linzy nodded. "I remember what you said." She went to lock the back door. In her mind, one thought began to circle, if we don't find anything connecting him to the furnace, and he gets out on bail, he will want revenge.

For a moment, the room was quiet. The last rays of the sun striped the west-facing picture window in yellow, pink, and orange. It was beautiful but wasted. Too much stress and worry to appreciate a simple sunset. Too much heartache.

12

MOVING ON

When Linzy called Attorney Brushow to ask about all the questions they had raised with Mr. and Mrs. Ash, she assured her that Sheriff Peach was connecting all the dots to bring Ancho to trial and put him away forever. "We are finding more and more bits and pieces tying him to Wysteria Way," she said. But she did not elaborate.

At the arraignment, however, the District Attorney presented the charges to the judge and Ancho pleaded not guilty. But seeing as how he was charged with a double murder along with two attempted murders and considering that he was likely to be a flight risk, the judge set the bail so high that Ancho couldn't meet it even if he hadn't blown all of Grampa Jim's life insurance payout.

When the judge announced the amount of bail, Ancho's court-appointed attorney simply shook his head, fastened his briefcase, and headed back to Houston. "I'll be in touch," he told Ancho. "Call me if you need anything."

The girls agreed with each other that they should have felt comforted that Ancho was going to remain in jail until the trial, but after several months passed, and they learned how slowly the wheels of justice could turn, it became more and more difficult to stay hopeful. Especially when Ancho fired one attorney after another because he claimed they were incompetent. Each time he did so, it set his trial date back a few more months. To Linzy, it seemed the nightmare would never end.

But at least he was out of their house.

School progressed and Blue graduated. The entire family, plus Sash and Linzy, sat in the audience to cheer when he walked the stage. He planned to begin his fire training classes at the junior college as soon as possible. His plan was to become a city firefighter while continuing to work at the family farm on his days off.

After graduation, the Ash family held a huge backyard barbecue to celebrate Blue's achievement, and then they gave him an open-end airline ticket to travel anywhere he wanted. "We understand if you don't want to do it at this time, but it will be right here when you are ready."

Linzy knew they were saving him from having to say he wouldn't fly off on a vacation and leave the girls in limbo, and she appreciated that. But it also made her sad. He shouldn't have to postpone his celebratory trip on account of their troubles. Of course, they would have done the same for him. In a heartbeat.

At least the barbecue was nice. Lots of his class members stopped by on their way to the senior dance, but Blue wouldn't go with them. Not even after Linzy tried to guilt him into it. Once again, Linzy ended up wishing she could do something to make him change his mind, but he simply said he didn't feel like dancing just then.

The rest of the summer slid past in the wink of an eye.

Linzy became a junior and then began to eye her senior classes. She also began to tutor students online after school and on Saturdays. It was through a nationwide company called Quest Online Schools. Linzy had found it by accident when she was doing research for a Social Studies project. They were asking for high achieving high school students to apply as tutors. She applied thinking she might use it as part of her project about how education is constantly changing, but the supervisor who contacted her was so kind and encouraging, Linzy accepted the actual position of part time tutor. Then she fell in love with it. Helping younger students work out their stumbling blocks gave her great satisfaction.

She began to look forward to completing her own high school career. The regimen of it grated on her now. The way other students, and sometimes even the teachers, treated her with kid gloves … it just drove her crazy. Made her feel less than real. No one at Quest knew her backstory. It felt good to have a clean, blank, slate.

Sash said she felt some of those same challenges. She drifted through the end of her sophomore year and straight into her junior year. Swimming seemed to hold less and less appeal as one year morphed into the next. Finally, she stopped swimming altogether.

To fill the void, Sasha signed up for art class. Linzy wasn't surprised. She and Sash had once loved taking sketchbooks out to the orchard, trying to sketch the birds that flitted from branch to branch.

Sasha confided to Linzy that she hoped letting go of competition would be a good thing because ever since *that night*, she'd felt as if she were moving through deep water even when she wasn't swimming. Linzy worried that meant her battle with depression wasn't behind them.

She wasn't surprised at the water analogy, though. Swimming had always been Sasha's superpower. And yet, this tragedy had ruined it. The thought of a trial loomed over both of them just like the previous dark cloud feelings. But as Carla Brushow said, the wheels of justice were turning, they just had to have patience and let them.

Eventually, the wheels did turn. Just like the wheels of time.

. . .

Not long after Linzy's senior year began—and Sasha's junior year—the prosecuting attorney called and said they were finally at the point that they needed to start preparing their testimonies. He wanted both of them to come to the courthouse and give depositions in preparation for being put on the witness stand.

The girls practiced what they were going to say. They were both incredibly nervous, afraid they would somehow screw it up and let the murderer walk free.

Carla Brushow helped. She told them to answer the questions simply and truthfully. It's all on record already, she said. The jury just needs to hear it.

Things were finally moving forward.

One Monday instead of going to school, the girls found themselves sitting outside a conference room on the third floor of the courthouse. The District Attorney said it could still be weeks before the trial actually got underway. In fact, the defense attorney was making noise about a change of venue.

The District Attorney's name was Jared Dunhill. He was nice, but the girls didn't really understand the process. "Why can't you be the prosecuting attorney?" Linzy asked Carla Brushow.

Ms. Brushow smiled patiently. "I'm not really a criminal attorney, sweetie. I wouldn't be much use in a murder trial. But I'll be there with you. Trust me. Jared Dunhill is the man for this. We wouldn't want anyone else."

That had been good enough for Linzy, especially when Carla told her she would be in the conference room for the deposition as well. "I'll be right here every step of the way. Don't you worry. Everything is working exactly the way it should."

So, on that Monday, Linzy and Sasha went into the conference room, one at a time, accompanied by Carla Brushow, to be questioned by Jared Dunhill and cross examined by Lex Carruthers, Ancho's court appointed defense attorney. During questioning, the girls were both encouraged to tell their stories straight through from just before their parents died until the day Ancho had Dom leave the note on Linzy's windshield. Of course, they added all of the odd happenings in between. Especially the part where Linzy overheard her parents talking about the unexpected visit from Ancho. They told things simply and without embellishment.

After that, both attorneys, Dunhill first, questioned them on the finer points. Just as if they were actually testifying in the trial. There was no judge nor jury. Each girl went in by herself, sitting at the long conference table with Carla Brushow on one side and a court appointed representative on the other. Their attorney paced back and forth as he asked questions, glanced at papers, and made notes on a legal pad. Although both girls were technically still minors, Linzy had been emancipated, so only Sasha had a children's rights representative in the room. The only other people there were the defense attorney and a court reporter with her stenotype machine hooked up to an open laptop.

It was during this questioning that Linzy learned about all the pieces of evidence Sheriff Peach and Carla Brushow had accumulated on Ancho. Jed Curry had signed his own report describing how the furnace pipe appeared to have been crimped, and the sheriff's investigator told about tracking down a flight Ancho had taken from L.A. to Houston just two days before the tragedy.

The investigator had also tracked down the digital receipts showing that Ancho had rented a car at the airport before driving to Brookville where he was seen on camera purchasing a set of channel lock pliers at Ace Hardware. Linzy learned everything about how they intended to prove Ancho then made that terrible visit to their house on Wisteria Way.

Blue and his folks waited for them in the courthouse hallway while each girl completed her deposition. They kept Sasha company while Linzy was being deposed, and then did the same for Linzy when it was Sasha's turn.

When Linzy sat on the hall bench with Blue and his parents, she felt as if she had aged ten years. Her meeting had been eye-opening. Nerve-wracking. Heart-wrenching.

Sasha stood when the representative came out to get her for her turn. She grabbed her sister in a panic. "I don't know if I can do this, Sissy."

Linzy held her for just a moment, then took her by the shoulders, looked into her eyes, and said, "You can do it. And you will do it. You're my sister and you saved my life. You're strong. So strong. Always remember that." She squeezed her shoulders, then gave her a slight push toward the waiting woman. "Carla Brushow is in there, she will be right beside you the entire time."

Sasha took a few steps forward, then glanced back at Linzy over one shoulder. Her eyes were wide, cheeks pale. She hesitated, then straightened her spine and marched the rest of the way toward the woman waiting beside the open door. "I can do this," Linzy heard her murmur. "I can."

Trembling, Linzy sat back down beside Blue just as Sheriff Peach walked past the end of the hallway, probably on his way to his office in the basement. There wasn't much traffic on the third floor since both courtrooms were located on the second floor.

The sheriff was speaking to someone on the phone as he walked, but he obviously had the speaker on. Linzy and the others could hear him relaying information about the charges and the digital proof to someone he called Inspector Curry.

They were all surprised when they could hear the inspector's reply. "What an idiot he must be. Is he the kind of guy who smokes a lot of dope?"

"Oh, yeah," Sheriff Peach said. "Just wish it would have kept him on the couch, stuffin' his face with munchies instead of coming up with the plan that killed two good people and nearly killed the girls, too."

Blue pulled Linzy closer to his side when they heard that.

Mr. Ash got up and followed the sheriff. They could no longer see him, but his voice was still quite audible. He seemed to have stepped into a doorway or an alcove. A stairwell, perhaps. No doubt, he thought he was speaking in private.

Before Mr. Ash could alert him to how clearly his voice was carrying, they all overheard Inspector Curry say, "That's pure evil. Just let me know if you need me to testify."

The sheriff chuckled. "I've got your name at the top of the list. May not be necessary, though. The idiot left such a great digital trail his lawyer knows a jury will likely be quick to convict. In fact, his attorney is already talking about a plea deal. Life in prison without parole."

"Ahh," Curry replied. "Taking the death penalty off the table, huh?"

"Exactly," Peach said. "We would have got to this point a lot sooner if the dope smoker hadn't kept firing his attorney. Went through two others before this one. 'Course each one had to have a couple months to review the facts of the case." He laughed. "The idiot didn't realize he was keeping himself locked up by doing so. These depositions are just in case something goes awry. But I'm pretty certain it's a done deal. Of course, it will be up to the girls and the District Attorney, but in my opinion, it would be the best way to move forward, avoid a lengthy trial, and prevent him from ever hurting anyone else."

Linzy barely heard Jed Curry reply, "Can't say as I blame you, keep those girls from reliving everything in the courtroom. Between you and me, I wouldn't mind seeing that vermin strapped to the table."

In an even lower tone, Sheriff Peach said, "I knew Ward Everly my whole life. Betty, too. Seein' their bodies layin' out on the grass that night, the two girls huddled up together, shaking … I could easily push the plunger on that killer's death needle myself." All of a sudden, he made a throat-clearing sound that caused Linzy to think Mr. Ash had finally found him to let him know how loudly his voice echoed through the near-empty halls.

Mr. Ash returned to Linzy and Blue, and a short time later, Sasha came back through the double doors, a wad of tissue clutched in one hand. She was smiling though, either because she was glad it was done, or because it hadn't been as horrible as she'd feared.

Linzy stood and brought her back to the bench. She couldn't wait to tell her what they'd just overheard. "It's going to be okay now, Sash," Linzy told her. "You'll see. Sheriff Peach said we probably won't even have to go to trial."

Carla came out then. When she heard Linzy's statement, she put a finger to her lips in the classic *shh* motion. "Let's not get our cart before our horse. However, if you both agree with a plea deal, in the event one should be offered, I will be glad to relay your decision to Jared Dunhill." She smiled. "Just make sure you know that even though the killer would be spending the rest of his life in prison, he would still have a life." She didn't say, unlike your parents, although Linzy knew that's what she was implying.

Sasha took her sister's arm. "I don't care what kind of life he has as long as he is locked away from now on." She cast her gaze at the floor. "I don't know if I can ever retell all of that stuff again. It's bad enough that I replay it in my head nearly every night." She shuddered and closed her eyes.

Linzy pulled her sister to her side and said, "That's that, then. We both agree a plea deal would be better than having to testify."

After that, things began to move quickly. It felt as if everyone in the county was ready to put Ancho and his horrific crime behind them. Based on the evidence gathered, plus the depositions, Ancho's attorney somehow managed to convince him of the wisdom in accepting a deal. Come to find out, the other two attorneys had told him the same thing. Which is why he fired them.

This time, he pled guilty to murder and attempted murder and went straight to prison. There would be no possibility of parole.

The evening after the District Attorney, Jared Dunhill, gave them the news that Ancho would never again see the light of day outside a maximum-security prison, the Ash family, the two Everly sisters, and Sheriff Peach, all gathered in Carla Brushow's office.

"You don't think he could break out, do you?" Sasha said.

Sheriff Peach assured them Ancho was gone from their lives, forever.

Linzy hadn't been surprised to hear her sister echo one of her own fears. In a horribly twisted way, it seemed logical to worry, they'd been doing it for so long now, but she didn't want to admit that to Sasha. She would never share how she'd already had nightmares about Domino—and even Ancho's wife, Patty—attempting to break into their home to exact revenge in Ancho's place. No. She would never admit that. Instead, she put on her brave face. "We'll be fine now, Sissy. I promise. We'll be just fine."

Sheriff Peach surprised them by hugging Sash and telling her to call on him, day or night, any time she felt the need. He probably would have hugged Linzy, too, if Blue had ever turned her loose. He couldn't seem to keep his arm from sneaking around her shoulders at every turn.

At last, Blue and his folks took the girls to their home where Mrs. Ash served a lowkey celebratory dinner of chicken and rice, garden salad, and iced tea. "We're simply celebrating the fact that the Ancho chapter of your lives is now closed. You girls can finally begin to move forward."

Linzy smiled. She felt her spine soften, as if it no longer needed to be ramrod straight in case of attack. "I wish we could take that trip to Stutter Creek that we talked about," she said.

"We can," Blue replied. "Why not? At least for a long weekend."

They all raised their tea glasses and clinked them together. "Go and have fun," Mr. Ash said, "We will take care of the farm. You know we love you girls just like family, and we'll always be here for you."

Across the table, Blue's head bobbed. "Yes," he echoed. "That goes double for me." A bit later, he drove them home and escorted them inside. "Are y'all sure you don't want me to stay again tonight?" His voice held such a caring note, it was difficult for Linzy to say no.

She glanced at Sasha for her approval. They had spoken to each other about their need for independence more than once. "We may be still in our teens," she told him. "But we aren't helpless. Life dealt us this hand, now we have to learn how to play it. We can't depend on others forever."

Blue looked like he might argue, but then he hugged them both and left, telling Linzy to call him for any reason. After he was gone, Linzy said, "I am so ready for everyone to stop walking on eggshells around us."

"And I'm ready to stop looking over my shoulder all the time," Sasha said.

"Same, Sissy," Linzy replied. "Exactly the same." She glanced around the room, poised to say something else, when a quick knock surprised them.

Linzy's heart lurched. Her gaze arrowed toward the door. The evening sun had slipped away, and darkness had dropped like a theater curtain. She glanced at her sister.

Sasha's arms were crossed over her chest protectively, hands gripping her elbows.

Nanoseconds of indecision ticked past.

Then Blue said, "Hey, y'all. It's me. I left my phone."

All the pent-up breath whooshed out of Linzy's chest.

Sasha relaxed her grip on herself.

Linzy rushed to the door, unlocked the deadbolt, and pulled it open. The heavy oak door moved slowly, impeded by the thick carpet.

Blue stood, one hand in his pocket, a look of embarrassment on his face. "I know. I'm a dolt. Sorry." He pulled his empty hand out of his pocket. "I must've laid it down somewhere."

Linzy rolled her eyes, tugged the door a little wider. "You gave us a start."

Her best friend nodded and ducked his chin. "It didn't feel right, leaving the two of you alone. I mean, I've been staying ..."

Smiling, Linzy took pity on him. "Okay, Little Boy Blue. If it bothers you that much, you can sleep on the couch one more night. Just like you've been doing, or you could sleep in Mom and Dad's room. We really *do* appreciate it." She stopped speed-talking, inhaled, and fessed up. "I might be a little nervous. I mean, it feels like we should stay alone, start being adults right now, but I keep imagining how angry he must be, knowing he will spend the rest of his life in a cell." She looked up at Blue's face, thankful he was so stubborn. Sometimes she put on the brave big sister facade for Sasha's sake. But sometimes it felt good when she didn't have to.

"I'll take the couch again," Blue said. "I still don't want to sleep in your folks' room," he indicated the master bedroom with a tilt of his head. "I seriously think it's time to fumigate it." He grinned a little, but Linzy suspected he was serious. Memories of Ancho and Domino permeated that room even after all this time.

"I was afraid to put everything back to normal—"

Sasha spoke up. "You didn't want to jinx us."

"Yeah, but now that it's behind us, we *should* make some changes." Linzy looked at Blue. "You know, like your mom and dad did for us?" A grimace crossed her face. "I've been itching to get in there, to be honest. Especially the bathroom. It seems like such a waste, not to use it at all."

"You sound like Mom," Sasha said.

"I guess I do." Linzy looked at Blue to gauge his reaction. "I guess this whole thing changed me."

"Yep," Blue said. "Life changes us all. But you are doing fine. Great, as a matter of fact." He glanced toward Sash. "You *both* are." Looking down the hall toward the master suite, he said, "Maybe I can help renovate. New paint, carpet, new drapes."

Linzy appreciated the positivity, and she liked the idea. The time since their parents had been gone felt like a lifetime. Or some old home movie she'd been watching.

"I like that idea, too," Sasha said. "Let's plan on starting it soon. After we get back from Stutter Creek, maybe. I mean, I wouldn't want to live anywhere else, but Mom and Dad's room is tainted now. We just have to figure out how to fix it." She glanced toward the suite, then looked away.

"We'll do it," Linzy and Blue said at the same time.

Sasha smiled. It looked a little sad. "Goodnight you two. Don't stay up too late." Her voice ended on a joking lilt as she made her way to the farthest end of the hall where hers and Linzy's bedrooms were located.

Blue crashed on the sofa that night, but the following morning, Linzy insisted he head back to his own home immediately. "I'm practicing being the new boss," she joked. "You and your folks have looked after us long enough, and you've spent way more than enough nights down here, babysitting. Now, for both my and Sasha's benefit, it's time we take charge of our own lives. I mean we've got all this surveillance stuff; the murderer is in prison for good … nothing else is going to happen." She pressed her lips together in an expression that showed she meant what she was saying.

Blue agreed that he wouldn't be the babysitter anymore. But Linzy noticed he had his fingers crossed when he said it. She led him toward the door before he could say more. Her senior year was rolling past like a high-speed train, and while she was ready to be finished, it was high time to reclaim some small bit of normalcy. She had worked hard and had all the necessary requirements to graduate. Many of her classes had also been dual credit. That meant she already had a number of college credits under her belt.

She hadn't mentioned it to anyone yet, but Linzy was thinking of applying for early graduation. Not only did she have all the required credits, but she had also passed the final state test last year as a junior. That meant she didn't have to take it this year. She enjoyed her tutoring job so much that she had decided to get her teaching degree online.

Linzy had been serious when she said she felt it was time to start acting like an adult. She also intended to continue working part time while taking her college classes. And she really couldn't see any reason to put it off. However, as Sasha said, Linzy was a little bit superstitious, she hadn't wanted to start a big project until the threat of a trial was nothing but a bad memory.

She pulled herself out of her reverie as Blue backtracked and picked up his phone from the coffee table, tucked it down in his pocket, and strolled out to his old pickup truck. At the last second, one foot on the truck's running board, one hand wrapped around the steering wheel to hoist himself inside, Blue pointed his chin at the silver Buick, then turned and said, "You ever going to start parking in the garage?"

Linzy shrugged. "Maybe. But Mom often left the car out here. Besides, enclosed spaces and running cars ... know what I mean?"

He nodded. "I sure do, boss lady." He started to swing inside the cab, then hesitated. "Fix me supper tonight?"

Chuckling good-naturedly, Linzy replied, "Of course, but I know what you're doing. You just want to spend the night again, don't you?"

"We-l-l," he said, dragging the word out in a suggestive tone, "when you put it that way ..." He left the sentence hanging and climbed inside the cab to start the engine. It seemed loud in the still of the morning but there were no nearby neighbors to disturb, just a mockingbird that flew from one pecan tree to the other, scolding as she went.

Blue drove down the wide circle drive, gave Linzy a little wave, then bumped over the cattle guard, and through the wisteria-framed gate. "See ya tonight," he called out. "We can plan our long weekend."

Linzy waved as he went. After going through the gate and turning left, it was only a short drive across the intersection with Pecan Road, and then straight on to his home at the western end of Wisteria Way.

To herself, Linzy murmured, "I can't wait to see the Stutter Creek cabin again. And all our friends." She grinned when she thought of Turk the wonder dog. "I wonder if we should honeymoon there someday?" They hadn't actually discussed it, but she had seen a black velvet ring box on Blue's dresser months ago.

Throwing one last wave at the receding red truck, Linzy fought back the familiar feeling of being exposed. Being outside, alone, made her feel nervous and vulnerable even though she knew Ancho was in prison and Domino was back in California. She shivered in the warm morning air. The mockingbird scolded again. *Must have a nest nearby.*

Stepping back inside, Linzy pulled the door closed and locked it. She clicked on the TV weather to check out the conditions at Stutter Creek. Snow had been falling steadily for a couple of days. A late snow, slushy and dangerous. Due to a severe forest fire the previous year, much of the usual foliage had been burned away. A heavy snow melt was expected to cause flash flooding. Geez, she said aloud. That report was more than I bargained for. Even though Stutter Creek was ten hours away by car, she'd forgotten how the mountainous, New Mexico weather could be the polar opposite of the weather here, near the Texas coast.

Linzy hoped their cabin wasn't going to get flooded. Should they go up to check? That didn't sound like much of a celebratory trip. Maybe it would be best to call Beth or John before making any sort of plans. Looking at the clock, she recalled that it was an hour earlier in New Mexico. Too early to call anyone. She made herself a mental note to try Beth later.

Still gazing out the dining room window, Linzy could see the first rows of the pecan grove behind the house. It was small now, just a few dozen trees, but it had always been her favorite place. Hers and Sasha's. They'd had picnics in the shade as kids. Climbed every tree just because they could. Played hide and seek for hours and hours.

All their childhood friends had loved slumber parties at their house because it was so much fun just to be out there in their own private forest-like setting.

But now the little grove was not quite so inviting. In the early morning light, it seemed full of shadows. Could someone hide there? Linzy peered into the slight distance. Could they? Ancho is in prison she kept repeating to herself. No more worries. He isn't getting out. Ever.

It was all she could do to keep her fingers from pressing the buttons to call Sheriff Peach. To make sure the killer hadn't escaped on his journey to his new prison home. Get busy, she told herself. When you're busy, you don't worry.

"Sissy?" Sasha called. "Is that you?" She stepped out of the bathroom with a towel wrapped turban-style around her hair.

"Yep. Just me," Linzy replied. "Blue's gone."

Sasha nodded. "Sweet of him to stay over and look after us."

"Yes, it was," Linzy agreed. "I think it's unnecessary," she said, pulling up her armor, "but what can I do?"

Sasha bent, unwrapped her hair, began to fluff. "No matter

what I've said before, I like it when he stays. I've had enough sleepless nights to last me a lifetime."

"Me, too, Sis." Linzy started back toward the kitchen. "But we have to stand on our own feet someday." She hoped that didn't sound too harsh. It was only the truth. She inhaled slowly, tamping down the lingering anxiety with each breath. "Hey, I'm making a banana-blueberry smoothie, want one?"

"Yes, please."

Linzy started to the kitchen, then stopped. "Let's make a pact," she said. "From this day forward let's vow to enjoy every moment that we can. Let's never rush things and never avoid celebrations. Since we know that murderer will not get out of prison, we will start living our lives again, start using the good china—*appropriately*—whenever we can, and we will go back to Stutter Creek as soon as possible. Sound good to you?"

Sash nodded. "Sounds perfect. Especially the part about going to the cabin and not putting things off anymore." Her eyes flicked to her sister. "Maybe it is time we start living again, instead of just hiding out."

"Way past time. Now, I'd better go and fix our smoothies."

"Thanks," Sash said. "I'll be ready in a few."

As she added ice and milk to the blueberries and bananas in the blender, Sash yelled from the bathroom, "Don't forget the honey!"

Mrs. Ash was always talking to them about caring for their immune systems. "I won't forget," Linzy yelled back, reaching for the honey as her finger hovered over the ON button. Actually, she would've forgotten. Her mind was still on the idea that she might be able to graduate early. A visit to the counselor's office was in order. She could do that this morning during first period study hall. Her supervisor at Quest Online Schools had already told her she could have all the hours she wanted. "We're very satisfied with your work and your performance evaluations," the supervisor had said. "Once you obtain your degree and teaching certificate, we would be honored to offer you full time employment. You would have your own virtual classroom."

The more Linzy thought about it, the more she liked it. My own classroom, she thought. Lesson plans, incentives, choosing novels to read together as a class. All the lovely maps and geography. She was getting excited just thinking about it.

Sasha sailed into the room, grabbed her smoothie, then dashed out the door to throw her things in their mom's old Buick. She started it up and backed out, waiting for her sister to join her.

Linzy was glad she'd talked Sash into getting her license as soon as she'd turned sixteen. Even if it did mean she was sometimes stuck with their dad's old farm truck. Driving the big truck wasn't so bad. It always smelled like pecan wood and sunshine. Just like her dad. Even Ancho hadn't been able to dispel that sweet fragrance. Thankfully, he hadn't smoked in it like he had the master suite.

Linzy's phone jangled in her pocket before she finished gathering her things.

"This weather is so beautiful," Sasha said. "Seems like we've come out the other side of that bad dream we've been living." She laughed a little. "Everything feels great for a change."

"Exactly what I was feeling," Linzy said, watching from the door as Sash rolled down her window and stuck her hand out to test the breeze.

Linzy leaned out the house door and called Sasha's name, laughing because they were on the phone, waving and talking much as she had done with Blue earlier. "Don't leave me," she told her sister. "I'm hurrying." She ducked back inside, sipping the end of her smoothie while grabbing her backpack, and rushing out the door. She turned back once; to make certain the door was firmly locked behind her.

"We finally have our home back," Sash murmured when Linzy got in the passenger seat and fastened her belt.

"Yes, we do. I don't know about you, but I feel a little bit like Dorothy over the rainbow."

"Yeah," Sasha said, hesitating only a second before replying. "You know, I really do like it when Blue stays with us. I wouldn't care if he always did. I mean, I know Ancho is in prison for real but are we sure Domino won't show up again? Or even Ancho's wife? She's bound to harbor a lot of resentment toward us."

Linzy looked down at her phone, finger poised to key in Beth and John's New Mexico number. "It's like you read my mind, Sis. I'm sure the wife blames us for Ancho going to prison and leaving her alone. When he came out here, they probably all thought they had it made. I wonder if she knew he killed our mom and dad?"

"Yeah, I wonder that, too. I mean, did the sheriff investigate her and Domino?"

"I think so," Linzy said. "I know they looked into Domino's whereabouts, but as for the wife, I'm really not positive." Something to ask, she thought.

"I'm sorry I got off on that topic again," Sasha interrupted her thoughts. "I try not to give those evil people any more of my peace of mind, but it's hard."

She paused and Linzy said, "Let's make another pact … let's say we can always talk to each other about our thoughts and fears, even if they are negative. It would be abnormal to pretend to be cheerful all the time. Right?"

"Right," Sash said. "Thank you for saying that 'cause I do worry about sounding negative all the time. I can't seem to help expecting the worst now."

"Gee," Linzy quipped. "I wonder why?" She chuckled. "I tend to see the worst-case scenario first now, too. Maybe we'll get over that someday."

"I hope so," Sasha said.

"We will, Sissy," Linzy assured her. "We just have to stick together and talk things out along the way. Which brings me to an idea I'm entertaining for the future... remember how I learned that it's possible to graduate early if you have enough credits?"

Sasha nodded.

"Well, I found out that I have enough."

"Seriously? I'm not surprised, but still, the semester has already begun. They don't let you graduate just anytime during the year, do they?"

Linzy shrugged. "I'm not sure. Hopefully, it's just the actual credits that matter, not the length of time you've attended."

"I see what you're saying. Like the really smart kids who skip entire grades, right? But what about walking the stage? Have you talked to anyone about all of it?"

"Not yet," Linzy said. "But I think I will today. I love my tutoring job. The students are so sweet, and they need so much help." She glanced down at her phone. "To tell you the truth, right now, I feel like I'm kind of wasting time, taking classes to fill the day when I don't actually need the credits."

Sasha chuckled. "You could be helping a lot more kids, right? If you worked full time?"

Linzy looked up at her. "Well, yeah ..."

"And you are certainly used to helping," Sasha continued, as if Linzy hadn't spoken. "Good at it, too. I never would have made it through Algebra without you. Sounds like you know what you want. Just let me know if you need me to do anything."

"Thanks, Sis. I appreciate it." She glanced down at her phone again. "I'd better call Beth right quick, before we get there. I think it's late enough now." She hit the entry for Beth & John in her contact list and wasn't surprised when the sweet woman picked up immediately.

"Linzy," their old friend said in a warm voice, "it's so good to speak with you. We heard about the outcome of the trial ... we were so glad to hear that they sentenced that evil man to life in prison."

"We were glad, too," Linzy said, tapping the speaker icon so Sasha could hear the conversation, too. "In fact, we were thinking of making a trip to Stutter Creek to celebrate. But I saw on the news that y'all are having major snow right now."

"We sure are," Beth replied. "The ski resort is delighted. But down here at the base of the mountain, every bit of melt tends to create a new river. Heaven help us if we get too many warm days in a row. Those fires did a real number on our vegetation ... not much left to hold back the flood."

"Should we worry about the cabin?"

"Not at all," Beth replied. "John is keeping an eye on it. Truthfully, it's the village that's taking the biggest hit. You never know which streets will be impassable next."

Linzy pictured the one-way-in and one-way-out highway leading into the small mountain town. "Gosh," she said into the phone. "Maybe this isn't the best time to visit." In the driver's seat, Sasha was wide eyed, shaking her head.

Beth said, "Considering it could easily become more stressful than restful, you're probably right. Don't worry. We're taking care of the place. I promise."

"Oh, thank you. I don't know where we'd be without you and John."

"And Danny," Beth said. "You won't believe how that boy has grown. Can't wait for you girls to come up when the weather is better. We've missed you *both*."

Sasha and Linzy looked at each other. "We can't wait!" they chorused.

Beth laughed and promised to keep them informed about the weather and they all said goodbye and clicked off.

In a couple of minutes, they arrived and turned into the

school parking lot. They had talked the whole way to town without even realizing it.

Linzy got out and strolled toward the double doors feeling a little lighter, determined to find time to visit with the counselor, or at least to make an appointment. But before they got to the doors, Sasha was waylaid by her good friend, Rose. Linzy waved at the two of them and continued on inside the building.

13

NEW LIVES–NEW JOBS

"Look," Rose squealed, holding out her ring finger. "Matt and I are engaged."

Sasha lofted her hand up to the light to examine the sparkly diamond. "When is the date?" she asked, surprised.

"Right after Christmas break," Rose said. "We're going to elope."

"Rosie! Are you—"

"Pregnant? No, girl, not even. We just want to start our lives together now, not after some giant frou-frou wedding like my folks will want." The slight young woman shook her brown curls, a dreamy look in her eyes. "Besides, we both have enough credits to graduate early, and Matt already has a part-time job waiting."

Sasha tried to gather her wits. "Wow … I can't, I mean … wait, if you elope, I won't get to be your maid of honor." She examined the dainty ring again, tried to make sense of what her friend was telling her.

Rose threw her head back, laughing, seeming to have fun with her unexpected news. "No worries, bestie. Maybe I'll just wedding-nap you and take you with us, what do you think about that?" She winked to show she was teasing.

Sasha hugged her, but Rose hesitated, stopping them from entering the building. "I do want to ask you something else, though." The girl gazed into Sasha's face as if to make certain she had her attention.

She didn't though. Sash was still trying to get over the fact that both her sister and her best friend had accumulated enough credits to graduate even though their senior year had barely begun. I must be a slow poke, she thought. Here I am a junior and I'll be lucky if I have enough credits by the *end* of senior year, much less at the beginning. I must be doing something wrong. Was it all the hours I spent at swim practice and all those meets?

After a moment, she realized Rose was waiting for her to say something. "Sorry," she said. "What's your question?"

Rose leaned closer. "Would you be interested in working the half-day program the way I've been doing?"

That idea took Sasha completely by surprise. She'd thought of many secret things Rose might've asked her, but this was definitely not one of them. "Well, hmm. I've never thought about it," she said. "Until recently, I had swimming after school."

"I know … but now you say how glad you are when each school day ends, so I just thought, you know, maybe you would like to get out at noon the way I do." The girl twirled a curl around her finger and waited.

"Yeah, that sounds good," Sash laughed. "But it's kind of out of the question, isn't it? I mean, the half-day is for seniors, not lowly juniors."

"It's for seniors and some juniors on a case-by-case basis. Which is what I did all of last year, remember?"

"Oh, that's right," Sasha said. "I thought it was just because of your uncle. I guess I was so wrapped up with swimming and … everything that happened, that I didn't really question it."

Rose nodded and squeezed her best friend's hand. "I know, bestie. Totally understandable."

Sasha thought of all the changes they'd been through. "I guess

I was sort of in a cocoon. Plus, I kind of assumed you and Matt were together all the time."

"Aww, that's okay," Rose said. "We were most of the time." She went on to describe how much she enjoyed taking part in the work-study program and how she still loved working as a part-time receptionist in her uncle Cam's real estate office. "But now, I want you to take over the job."

"Why? You aren't leaving yet," Sasha said. "Why would I need to start now?"

"I'll need to train you before I leave."

"But—"

"I think you would love it," Rose interrupted. "And I'll bet the school counselor would help. I mean, after everything you and Linzy have been through. I'm pretty sure they will bend over backwards to accommodate your wants and needs."

Sash felt herself stiffen when Rose said that. Best friend or not, it was hurtful and crude and exactly the sort of thing she heard over and over when others didn't know she was listening. Especially in swimming. Which is partly why she didn't continue with it this year.

"Oh, Sash," Rose grabbed her and hugged her. "I'm so sorry. I can't believe I said that. I'm just full of myself today. Please don't—"

Sasha pulled away simply to get Rose to stop squeezing her. "It's okay, Rosie, I know you didn't mean anything."

"I'm such a selfish idiot," Rose said. "The truth is … I want my best friend to take over my spot with my favorite uncle, so I won't be leaving him in the lurch when we elope. Maybe it will soften the blow when everyone learns that we're not just getting married, but we're also moving to Colorado. Matt and I both worked so hard to have enough credits to graduate midyear, and I feel like you are the perfect replacement at CG Realty. You already met Uncle Cam at our backyard barbecue, remember?"

"I remember," Sasha smiled. "He is super nice, but didn't you say he's not really your uncle?"

"Oh, he's my Uncle Brandon's brother so not technically my uncle. Just by marriage."

Sasha nodded and started walking again. "I'll think about it. Really. I will. That's sort of a lot to take in." She adjusted her backpack. "I still don't think I'm ready to lose my best friend, though. Not to Matt or any*one*."

Rose squeezed her hand. "It's only while Matt gets his degree, then we might be back. Depending on how much we like Colorado."

Heaving a dramatic sigh, Sasha pretended to be crushed. But she couldn't pull it off. She leaned over and linked her arm with Rose's arm. "I can't be sad," she said. "I think the world of Matt. I know you two will be very, very happy."

"Thanks, bestie. And you think about my idea, 'kay? Just imagine getting out of school at noon every day and driving down to Galveston to work for three hours. Beautiful setting and you get paid. Plus, if you enjoy it, you can earn your real estate license someday. That's what I might do." Rose shrugged. "I've enjoyed it so much I can't stand the thought of just anyone taking over. I really want you to do it."

"Seriously, I'll think about it," Sasha said as they finally made it inside.

Rose blew her a kiss and skipped on down the hall toward her first class.

By the time she walked out to meet Linzy after school that day, Sash had decided she liked Rose's idea. But she wanted to talk it over with Linzy first. Although it was a huge step, she thought it might be a good one.

Thinking she might see Linzy in the parking lot after last period, she rushed out, but when she turned on her phone, she saw that Linzy had sent her a text saying she might be a few minutes late because she was visiting with the principal and the counselor about early graduation.

Sasha tossed her backpack in the back seat and slid behind the steering wheel. She opened all the car windows and made herself comfortable. It was easy to kill time scrolling social media while waiting for her sister. She pulled up the website for CG Realty, the one owned by Rose's uncle Cam.

An unfamiliar feeling of excitement drifted over her at the idea that she might be able to cut her school days in half while learning about a new career possibility. Before this, she had looked no further than a possible swimming scholarship to the University of Houston. But the last few meets she just hadn't been able to care … looking into the stands after each meet, not seeing her folks there the way they always were … that had been like ripping the scab off a wound every single time.

Her phone chimed with a message from Linzy. "On my way out," it read.

Sasha replied, "I can't wait to hear what you found out."

Her sister emerged from the building with a smile on her face. Once they were on the road, Linzy told her that the counselor thought it was a wonderful idea. She said the rest of the hour had been spent going over the requirements for her diploma. "Can you believe I'm going to finish up by Christmas break?" Her eyes were wide. "They pulled up my credits right there on the computer and gave me the go ahead. And I'll still be allowed to walk the stage with the rest of the class." She sounded a little stunned. "I'll soon be working from home, full time."

"Of course I believe it, Sis," Sasha said. "You've always been the best student."

Linzy seemed so happy that Sasha went ahead and relayed her own news about Rose's engagement followed by the possibility of entering the work study program.

"Wow," Linzy said, not even trying to hide her surprise. "I

don't know which to address first, Rose's engagement, her and Matt's early graduation, or the idea of you possibly going to school half a day."

"Well, if it helps any," Sasha said, "I'm completely shocked that all *three* of you have that many credits, I wanna know how I can do that. As for Rosie … I think she and Matt will be extremely happy when they're married, but we can't say anything to anyone yet. We're the first ones to know. Aside from all that, Rose's uncle is Cameron Gaines, the owner of CG Realty in Galveston. We see those billboards all over the highway, guy in a gray cowboy hat?"

Linzy nodded, a look of confusion on her face.

Sasha continued, "Rose went to work there last year through the work study program. She's still the afternoon receptionist."

Linzy's said, "Okay. That's the other reason I don't see her much, even though we're both seniors."

Sasha nodded. "Probably. Anyway, when she and Matt get married, Mr. Gaines will need a new afternoon receptionist."

"And you want to do it?"

"Yes."

Linzy sat quietly for a moment, thinking. "But you're a junior. Are you even eligible?"

Sasha smiled. "It's not a done deal yet. I told Rose I had to talk to you, first. But she said if school agrees—the way they did for her last year—then I can go in and start learning the ropes next week." Her voice softened. "She told her uncle about me. And I already met him once, at a barbecue at her house."

"So, we're talking about this program for next year, right?"

"Well, yeah, unless the counselor can convince the principal to let me start now. The semester just started so, hopefully there's a chance."

Sasha felt like she could tell what Linzy was thinking. She had just made her own plans for cutting her school career short. So how could she possibly disagree with Rose and Sasha's idea?

"You know," Sasha said. "Rose wants me to start training soon so that as soon as she leaves, I can move into the afternoon receptionist job right away. If I do well, I should be able to work full time the entire summer before senior year. Maybe even save up for my own car. And if I *really* like it, I might begin taking real estate courses online and on weekends. Become an agent in my own right someday."

"Wow," Linzy said. "I see you've given it plenty of thought. Maybe you really would love it. Guess there's only one way to find out." She had one more thing to say, possibly as a last attempt at dampening Sasha's enthusiasm. "You know, it is a bit of a drive to Galveston. Mr. Gaines wouldn't happen to have an office in Brookville, would he?"

Sasha laughed and made the turn onto the highway toward home. "No, sorry. It's definitely Galveston."

By the time they were near Wisteria Way, Linzy had agreed to give her blessing as long as the school okayed it.

Sash thought they would. But her sister had made some valid points, especially the gentle reminder that CG Realty was thirty minutes away. Not only would that be a lot of gas driving back and forth twice a day, but Sash would also be driving the same route, alone, every day, down some fairly deserted stretches of highway.

Picturing it in her mind, Sasha knew she'd be surrounded by little more than blue sky, yellow field grass, and not much else until the causeway bridge across the bay to the island. In light of all that had happened in their short lives, driving alone for miles and miles did sound somewhat daunting. Although, when she allowed herself to think about it, the driving wasn't the scary part, it was the possibility of breaking down in their mom's ten-year-old car that was the scary part. But of course they would get it checked out beforehand, make certain everything was in good working order.

She approached the intersection of Wisteria and Pecan and put on her blinker.

"Well," Linzy said, "It seems likely we will both be starting new adventures soon. Are you as ready as I am?"

"Yes," Sasha replied. "I am ready for an adventure." She spoke simply and honestly. "If the school allows it, I will work three hours each weekday afternoon, until the summer. I may even work some Saturdays. I'm not sure yet." After pausing, she added, "You know, I can't wait to get away from everyone walking on tiptoe around me."

Linzy nodded. "Same here, Sis. It got old in a hurry, didn't it?"

Sasha drove through the gate and across the cattle guard. "I didn't realize it bothered you," she said. "Until you mentioned getting your diploma early." Her voice grew quiet as she drove into the carport. "But now I know, and that gives me the courage to admit that I've been feeling the same things."

Linzy mentioned how they'd had a similar conversation the day Sash had burned her letters in the chiminea.

"That's true," Sasha said. "That was quite a while ago. And still the sadness overwhelms me sometimes. Does it you?"

Linzy tilted her hand back and forth in the air. "It comes and goes. But I've started praying for comfort *and* direction. Hopefully, this is it. For myself, with the online school, and for you with this new opportunity."

"Yes," Sasha agreed, shutting off the engine. "Maybe these are answered prayers. Rose said there are lots of things I have to learn before she turns me loose to fill her spot." She opened her car door but turned back to her sister. "I'm so glad she asked me to do this. I'll enjoy the time with her, and you *know* how I love those real estate shows on TV."

Linzy brayed laughter. "I know, Sis. Especially the beachy house hunters. I can already hear the excitement in your voice. Galveston Island. Honestly, you have my full support."

"Thanks." Sasha grinned. "I think it will be good. Rose's uncle couldn't be nicer. Plus, Rose said working in public helps to put high school in perspective."

Linzy's eyes widened.

"What's wrong, Sis?" Sasha asked. "Something in your face—"

"I just had a red flag moment." She unlocked the front door and went inside. "When did you say you met Rose's uncle?"

"It was at a barbecue at Rose's house a while back. Her mom's birthday party. Why?"

"Oh, you know me and my suspicious mind … an older man hiring a beautiful young high school girl …"

Sasha glanced at her sister as they dropped their backpacks on the couch. "But he's Rose's uncle. I mean he's her Uncle Brandon's brother, so that makes him family, right?"

Linzy started to speak, but Sasha plopped down on the couch and held up her hand. "I know you think I'm naïve, but don't worry. It's nothing like that. He's just like the rest of Rose's family, super nice, and caring." She pressed her lips together to suppress a giggle. "It's okay, Sis. I know you have to worry since you're my official guardian now." A giggle escaped her lips, "But you don't have to worry about this."

Linzy plopped down beside her. "Okay. I'm done worrying … at least for the moment." She reached over and tickled her little sister's ribs.

For a second or two, Sasha felt they were almost transported back to their childhoods. It was a wonderful feeling.

14

SASHA'S NEW JOB AND LINZY WALKS THE STAGE

Just as her friend, Rose, had predicted, Sasha was allowed to enter the work-study program the very next week.

Not long after it began, Sash found herself experiencing moments of actual happiness. She fell in love with the drive to Galveston every day. It felt like a safe space away from the prying eyes and pity she often felt in the classes and hallways. Living with Ancho for all those months—and then living under the blanket of waiting-for-the-trial-to-begin—had also taken a toll on her.

Working with the public, although daunting at first, turned out to be fantastic. Especially since she had her best friend, Rose, to show her the ropes. It helped that their boss, Cameron Gaines, was seldom even in the office unless he had an appointment to close a deal or meet a new client. He had other agents working for the company as well, so there was never a dull moment. Sasha loved it. When Rose and Matt eloped after the semester break, things were quite different at the office, but Sasha soon grew into the role. Rose had trained her well.

At home, Linzy seemed more relaxed, too. It became evident in the way her relationship with Blue continued to blossom. To

Sasha, it was easy to see the two of them were no longer just best friends, now they were spending every possible moment together. It didn't surprise her at all. She'd always known Blue was her sister's soulmate. Over the years, they had both come to rely on the dark-haired, soon-to-be-fulltime, firefighter. Sasha assumed he would be her brother-in-law one day.

True to her new plan, Linzy accepted her mid-year diploma and began her third-year college classes, online, in earnest. Her advisor was amazed at how many hours she had accumulated during high school. At the same time, she took on a few more students in need of tutoring. "It might take a couple more years to get my degree in education," she told Sash, "but that's okay, the company has assured me I will have my own classroom as soon as I do. In the meantime, I will have all the tutoring hours I can handle." She'd grinned when she said it, and Sasha felt thrilled things seemed to be working out just right.

At the end of the year, Linzy walked the stage in her cap and gown. It wasn't necessary since she'd already received her official diploma, but it was considered a near-sacred rite of passage. Afterward, she attended the big dance along with Sasha and Blue. It was sponsored each year by the school board and Mothers Against Drunk Driving. The end of year celebration was made even more special when Rose and Matt appeared as a surprise for their friends and family. A tremendous cheer went up, and the band broke into "Here Comes the Bride."

To Sasha's delight, Linzy hugged her and whispered that when it came time for her marriage to Blue, Sash would definitely be the maid of honor. Before Sasha could respond, Linzy hugged her a second time and danced away.

Everyone agreed that dancing in the school gym and on the school's large patio under the stars had turned out to be the perfect way to end her and Rose's high school careers. No matter what Sasha said, though, Linzy would not take part in the all-night movie lock-in that followed.

"I can't wait to do this again next year," Sasha declared when Blue drove them home that night.

"It was wonderful," Linzy agreed. "I'm just sorry we didn't do it when you graduated, Blue-boy."

Blue laughed and said, "I'm just glad Brookville is so small that the entire town is invited." Then he added, "But I agree with Sash. You should've done the lock-in, too. It's really the only thing that's strictly for seniors."

Linzy made a face at him. "And how did you enjoy the lock-in last year?"

Blue shook his head, one hand on the steering wheel, the other entwined with Linzy's. "Okay, okay, I get the point." He glanced at Sash who sat in the backseat, windows down to celebrate the sweet verge-of-summer air. "We all kind of got out of the school routine early, didn't we?"

Sasha laughed. "Yes, we did. Like Linzy says, we turned into a bunch of old fogies. But I'll tell you this, I can't wait to do the big dance again when I graduate. It's so good to feel young for a change." She saw Linzy and Blue glance at each other knowingly when she said that, but silly or not, she didn't care. Not tonight.

She began to hum the George Strait song they'd played at the end of the dance, and soon they were all singing along.

After graduation, the verge-of-summer melted right into full-on summer, and the days were full indeed. Rose and Matt returned to Colorado while Sash settled into her new role as full-time summer receptionist for CG Realty . The other full-time office clerk, a young man named Marc, busied himself with learning the business while taking his own real estate courses online. He hoped to move from office staff to agent soon.

Sasha listened to him carefully when he was in the office.

They had switched roles so he could work part-time while he concentrated on getting ready to take the license exam. Sash liked everything about the business. She was determined to learn all she could about her own possible path to a lucrative career in real estate.

The summer disappeared in a haze of activity and work, and her senior year began just before she turned eighteen. That's when time really sprouted wings. She went back to her afternoon-only shift in the Galveston office while obtaining the rest of her high school credits in the morning hours. Going to work for CG Realty had been just what she'd needed to give her life its new direction. She even enjoyed working half-days on Saturday, too.

Both Sasha and Linzy began to look forward to everything with joy, especially the holidays. Halloween once again meant hayrides with kids in the rural neighborhood, hosted by Blue and his folks along with the other volunteers at the rural fire department, and Thanksgiving and Christmas meant family and faith and giving thanks for the things they had overcome, not to mention all the wonderful things yet to come. She and Linzy spoke about it privately, more than once, and they agreed to begin decorating again, sparingly, instead of simply celebrating at the Ash family home the way they'd done for the past few years. They vowed to latch on to every simple pleasure that came their way. They knew their parents would want that.

As a result of all these events and revelations, Sash and Linzy began to live more in the moment. Linzy totally devoted herself to her college classes and her tutoring students, and most especially to Blue, the one who had been there for them through it all.

Sasha, on the other hand, finally began to explore her newfound adulthood. She felt as if she had the best of both worlds. Her trio of high school classes in the morning, and then back to her grownup job in the afternoon. They were in the last semester of her final year of high school, and she couldn't wait to finish up.

Mr. Gaines told her what a wonderful job she was doing and how he had grown to depend on her. He was always professional, always kind, and he answered all her questions about being an owner/agent while allowing her and Marc to tour new properties together. Sometimes, he even stayed behind and answered the phone. He told Marc he would help him begin to build his own client list since he had recently passed his licensure exam, and as a result, he often made it back to the office to sit in when Marc met with clients or wrote up contracts.

Every now and then, Mr. Gaines would tour a property with them. A couple of times, Marc stayed behind to work on contracts, so Sash went with Mr. Gaines by herself. She later told Linzy it made her a little nervous to ride with the boss, but she only said it once. The next time Linzy asked how it was going, Sasha said it was the best thing ever.

As the seasons moved forward and the pecan trees regained their spring leaves, Sasha began to look ahead to the finalities of her senior year. While the sprinkler company inspected the soaker system in the pecan grove on Wisteria Way, she and her friends began to look ahead to the after-graduation lock-in that Linzy had skipped. In her new, embrace everything state-of-mind, Sash couldn't wait to attend the all-night lock-in and movie-night—after the town-wide dance, of course. It seems absence really did make the heart grow fonder and Sash really missed—and appreciated—all the sweet friends she'd had in some of the classes she no longer attended. Of course, no one could take the place of Rosie.

"I wonder what it will be like during the senior lock-in?" Sasha asked

Rose on one of their frequent phone conversations. "Neither you nor Linzy took part since you both got your credits early …"

"Oh, I know. I can't believe we voluntarily missed out on so much fun," Rose said. "I heard that right before they lock the doors, all the girls go on a crazy school-wide search with flashlights to flush out any male stragglers who try to hide. Matt's friend said they pelted them with popcorn. By the way, you can use my cot and sleeping bag, if you don't have one. Mine are still at my mom's house, probably stored in the attic. Unused." She laughed. "I heard you will likely be so exhausted after all the food, drink—and chasing the guys—that you'll fall asleep as soon as the first movie is projected onto the big screen." She giggled again and Sasha put her on speaker so Linzy could join in the conversation, too.

"Linzy said Tonya told her that last year they chose to watch *Grease* and *The Princess Bride* and *Wicked*. Movies everyone could dance to and sing along with. In between, they showed SpongeBob cartoons."

Rose sighed. "Now, I'm really sorry we missed it."

"Yeah," Linzy called out. "Blue said his buddies had a ball. He said they stayed in the field house and had their own snacks and movies like Rocky, Reacher, and Die Hard."

"A testosterone trio," Rose said.

"Exactly what I thought," Linzy replied, a touch of sarcasm in her voice. "But they did have limited lists to choose from. Parent and school board approved, of course."

They spoke a while longer and after they all hung up, Linzy told her sister, "I'm glad you decided to take part in the lock-in so you can end the year with a bang. Just don't do like Roseie and run off to get married."

"Oh, Sis," Sasha teased. "You're so silly. You know that you and I are going to have a giant double wedding someday—if you and Blue will wait that long—I don't even have a steady boyfriend yet."

~

Linzy relished watching her sister blossom back into a fun-loving teenage girl who could laugh and act silly and enjoy pop music blaring out the windows of the old silver Buick as she headed off to school and work each day.

She wasn't surprised that Sasha had turned out to be a valued employee at CG Realty, always on time and doing a top-notch job. That was her sister's true nature. To do things to the very best of her ability—the way she'd always done in school and in swimming—before the nightmare.

Not the same girl, Linzy thought, waving as Sash bumped over the old cattle guard on her way out the gate each morning. Not the same girl at all.

Knowing her sister was happy allowed Linzy to begin enjoying life again as well. Little things at first. Coffee on the patio in the early morning. Iced tea in the evening when Blue's schedule allowed. They both appreciated relaxing and just being together.

Her teaching career blossomed, too.

The Quest Online school administration seemed quite thrilled with the progress Linzy's students made. "You've definitely found your calling, Linzy," the school administrator said.

Blue was also in the happy place with them. He'd been helping his dad on their organic vegetable farm since he was old enough to carry water. And while he wanted to inherit the farm someday, in the meantime he thoroughly loved his career as a brand-new Brookville firefighter. Growing up, he had always been an unpaid Wister County volunteer, like his dad. Now that he could make a living with it told him he had his career right on track.

"Thinking of getting my paramedic training, too," he told Linzy one evening. "They're just like medics in the field. You know, it's really hard to be on the scene of an accident and not be certified to do what you know needs doing."

Linzy had a sudden recollection of Blue bent over her father, performing CPR.

"Once I'm certified," he told her, "I'll have even better pay and benefits, and I will still have days off to help Dad—and you—on the farms."

He was referring to the fact that firefighters and paramedics worked 24-hour shifts on duty and 48 hours off. They ate and slept at the firehouse when they were on duty, and when they were off duty, they had other jobs. Like helping out on the farm or landscaping or a million other careers. One of Blue's closest buddies worked at the tractor supply store on his days off. Another had a safety consulting business.

In addition to Blue and his dad working their own farm, they also helped Linzy and Sasha oversee the Everly Acres pecan grove. They kept the trees pruned, and by hiring the same folks Linzy's dad had always hired, they were able to keep up with fertilizing, weeding, and harvesting. A local company shelled the pecans and sold them on-site by the pound.

Linzy was keen to learn everything about the business. She knew a lot of it by simply being there from day to day, but as a kid, she hadn't known all the whys of what was being done. Now, she was eager to learn. With her teaching career being online, it left plenty of time to keep up with the family business.

The Monday following Sasha's high school graduation, she returned to her now full-time job at CG Realty to find a new company car sitting in her office parking spot. She was by turns thrilled, shocked, and over-the-moon. Not only was it a beautiful, gold colored Cadillac, with all the bells and whistles, better yet, it was a testament to how well she was doing at the job she so dearly loved.

Linzy almost fell over when her sister drove it home that day.

Cameron Gaines followed her in their mom's old Buick. Linzy had met the man a few times over the past year, when she dropped by the office to take Sash to lunch or pick her up for some reason or other, and he often made certain to tell Linzy what an invaluable part of the business Sash had become. It always made her little sister blush when he said things like that.

The day Cam Gaines followed Sash home in the gold Cadillac, with Marc following in a gold-colored Lincoln in order to drive Mr. Gaines back to the office, Linzy felt a slight trepidation in her gut. She'd heard of agents earning fancy cars for selling a lot of listings, but not just for being a great receptionist. And the fact that the Cadillac and the Lincoln were the same exact shade of gold? That made her red flag senses flutter even more. Then again, perhaps the Lincoln belonged to Marc. It could happen, right?

Linzy tried not to jump to conclusions. There had been absolutely no hint of impropriety about the job. If anything, Mr. Cameron Gaines continued to act like a kindly uncle toward Sasha just as he always had toward Rose. Of course, in Rose's case, he really was part of the family. Even if it was by marriage and not by blood.

One thing the new car did was cement Sash's desire to become an agent in her own right. "According to the realtor school website, I can be ready to take the licensing exam in six months to a year through their online classes. And guess what? Mr. Gaines said he would pay for my classes the same way he is paying for Marc's."

That made Linzy feel a lot better. "He certainly is a kind man, isn't he?" she replied. In her head she wondered if there was such a thing as too kind. But then she told herself she was being paranoid. After all, he was paying for Marc's classes, why not Sasha's too? It sounded like everything was above board.

Soon Sasha began the real estate classes. She loved every moment of it. "Cam said he'd sponsor me to take my exam and then hire me as an agent as soon as I get my license." She smiled sweetly. "That's exactly how Marc became an agent. And I'm so glad. I really like Marc. He introduced me to his friend, Leandra, who is an art major at the University of Houston. One weekend we are all planning to get together and take one of those fun paint-with-me workshops on The Strand. I can't wait. Cam said he might go, too."

Linzy didn't know exactly when Sasha began referring to her employer as Cam instead of Mr. Gaines, but she knew it was after the gift of the car.

Before long, the four of them were going out regularly after work. First, they did the painting class with Marc and Leandra, next it was karaoke, and here and there they all made a couple of trips to the beach. Sasha fell in love with Pleasure Pier and everything else connected to the laid-back town of Galveston.

When she realized all the things that were going on, Linzy was furious. Not just because of the ten-year age gap between Sasha and Mr. Gaines, but because he was her boss. Linzy had always been taught to be skeptical of employer-employee relationships. This was exactly the sort of thing she had been worried about from the very first.

But what could she do? Linzy had pushed the suspicious feelings aside, just the way she always said she would not do, and now, look what had happened. They were spending loads of time together outside work. It wasn't just Sasha with Marc and Leandra, it was Sasha with Cam. Her little sister's first serious relationship appeared to be with her much older boss.

15

SHOUTS OF JOY ALL AROUND

Linzy told Blue about Sasha's worrisome relationship while they were drinking iced tea on the back patio. "I have such reservations," Linzy said. "So many concerns."

"But look how happy she seems. She's living her dream. That's what we all want, right?" Blue nudged Linzy's knee with his. "I mean, that's what good parents do, right? Give their kids wings to fly." He mock-cringed, as if he knew she might slug him.

"I'm *not* the parent," Linzy muttered, unwilling to be drawn into the old standing joke. "Besides, how do I know her wings will still work if her heart gets broken?" She swiped icy droplets of condensation from the base of her iced tea glass. "I just keep thinking about the age difference and the fact that he is her boss, he could hold that over her, you know."

"Understandable," Blue said. "It is kind of a shocker, but you can't keep her from making mistakes. Her happiness is pretty much all you've ever wanted—"

Linzy glanced at his tanned face. She was determined to force herself into a better mood. For herself, and for Blue. "Well, maybe it's not *all* I've ever wanted."

Blue smiled and bumped her knee again. Their connection

had continued to grow deeper and deeper. Soul deep, it seemed, just the way Sasha had always known it would. He'd been there—right by her side—through thick and thin. Before the tragedy, they'd been best friends and sort of sweethearts. Now, it was a whole other level. Triumphs in her life were triumphs in his life, too. And vice versa.

Linzy sighed. "So, you think I should keep quiet about her going out with him and accepting ridiculously expensive gifts? You don't think I should even try to talk some sense into her?"

Blue took a long swallow of tea. "I think you can point out all the flies in the soup, but then you just gotta step back and see if she sends it back to the kitchen, or whether she fishes out the tiny carcasses and digs right in."

Linzy rolled her eyes and *shoved* his knee with the heel of her hand. "You have such an elegant way of putting things, Blue-boy." She snuggled into his side and watched the sunset begin its nightly show.

The west-facing patio was still their favorite place. Mealtimes often found them carrying sandwich plates out to the small table, and they'd even started dancing now and then, if the playlist agreed with the moonlight.

"We're like an old married couple," Blue said. "Talking over our worries about the kiddos."

Linzy laughed. "Just the one kid. And the one huge worry." She glanced at his face to make sure they were still on the same page.

But Blue wasn't looking at her. His eyes were on the vibrant display of yellow-orange fire softening the horizon.

"I guess we are like an old married couple," she said. "Do you mind?" Her voice squeaked on the up part of the question, so she covered it with a gulp of iced tea.

"Mind? *Hell* no. It's my dream come true, sittin' here with you. I'm just waiting on the day we make it legal."

That got Linzy's attention. She planted her feet on the concrete. "What did you say?"

He took a quick gulp of tea, inhaled too soon, and began to sputter.

Linzy laughed and clapped him on the back.

After a few seconds of him spraying tea and laughter, Blue grabbed her by the hand and pulled her onto his lap. "I'm good now." He grinned. "You can stop whaling on me."

Good humor bubbled beneath his words as his hand snuck down to his jeans pocket. He stood, tumbling her off his lap without a thought. "Sorry," he said. "Sorry." He ignored the stunned look on her face as she righted herself on the arm of the glider.

She was about to give him a good scolding, but then she saw the tiny velvet jewel box he'd scissored out of his front pocket with his two fingers.

"Sash's shenanigans kind of blew mine out of the water," he said. "So, I've been holding onto this little trinket, just waiting for the right moment."

He went down on one knee and balanced the box in the palm of his outstretched hand. "Linzy Everly, will you marry me, make me the happiest old fogie on the block?"

Linzy grinned. "We don't have a block, you goof. We have acres."

Blue matched her wide smile. "Is that a yes?"

"Well, of course it's a yes." She leaned over and kissed his forehead. "But I don't know if there's actually anything in that box."

He raised one eyebrow. "What if it's empty?"

"Hmmm," Linzy murmured. "Maybe we should just leave it clos—"

He flipped up the lid. A dainty three stone engagement ring peered up from its satin lining. "It was my gramma's on my mom's side. Mom said to tell you it's vintage." His earnest gaze sought hers. "I hope you like it. I thought it was a good idea seeing as how you and I are kind of vintage anyway."

Tears flooded Linzy's vision. "It's perfect," she said. "Just like you."

He tugged the ring out and slipped it on her finger. "Mom said it would fit. She said you were slender and petite just like her momma was."

"Oh, Blue," she held the ring up to the waning light. "It really is perfect. I can't wait to be Mrs. Blue Ash." She laughed. "Linzy Ash. It has a nice sound—"

Blue stood and pulled her to him. "You can keep Everly in there, too, if you like. We aren't *that* old-fashioned." He laced his fingers through hers and together they admired his grandmother's ring. "I know your family name is important to you."

Linzy smiled. "You know me so well. I can't imagine ever being without you."

Blue took her chin, gently pressed his lips to hers. "That's what it's all about. Commitment. I've given it a lot of thought, 'cause I know we're young. But after all we've seen, and been through, I don't want to wait any longer. Don't see any reason to wait, do you?"

Linzy shook her head. "I want to marry you, but not unless you agree Sasha stays with us as long as she wants. I'll never leave her alone. Not ever."

"I wouldn't have it any other way," he said. "And we don't have to run down to the courthouse or rush into planning anything right now. I just wanted to make sure you would say yes. Make certain we would be our own little family someday."

Linzy nodded, whispered. "Yes."

He sat on the glider and pulled her onto his lap. "What was that now?"

She took his face between her hands and kissed his cheek, "I said yes." She kissed the tip of his nose, "Yes." Then she kissed his forehead, "Yes." Then his lips, over and over and over. "Yes," she said with each little kiss. "Yes, and yes, and yes!" She placed one more smooch right between his eyes. "It won't hurt to simply *visualize* what our wedding will look like, will it? You know, just for the sake of it."

He pretended to collapse even deeper into the glider. "Oh, no, here it comes."

She giggled and held her ring up to the sunset light. "It's so beautiful," she said. And then she kissed him some more.

After a while, they called Sasha and his parents to share the good news. There were shouts of joy all around.

16

LONG ENGAGEMENT

Linzy stood at the sink, rinsing the dishes that had accumulated over the course of the day. She could put them in the dishwasher, but there weren't that many since Sash had spent the weekend with Leandra and Blue was at work. Blue, her fiancé. Linzy loved saying it.

They had been engaged for a few months now and were talking about setting a date, but neither felt rushed to do so. It was enough just to be spending time together in their new couple status rather than simply as best friends from down-the-road. They'd both always known there was more depth to their feelings than simple friendship, and from time to time it had spilled over in private, but now it was public knowledge and that made it oh, so much better, like coming home. Like coming home after Ancho had finally been convicted. Like coming home to their *real* home, not just a place inhabited by a "pretend" uncle.

Linzy hated that her thoughts often turned to before and after Ancho, but she supposed that was just the way her mind worked. She pulled the drain plug and let the water run out of the sink, determined to direct her thoughts back to the after rather than the before.

Lately, life had taken on a seriously happy hue. Not only for her and Blue, but also for Sasha. After the initial shock had worn off, Linzy softened to the idea of Sash and Cam spending time together. Blue was right. She could not protect her sister forever. The girl was going to make mistakes, everyone does. Maybe this wasn't as awful as she'd first thought.

At least Sash seemed to be taking an interest in new people other than just her boss. Leandra worked in an art supply store on The Strand while also attending the University of Houston. Sasha had talked about visiting Leandra there on several occasions. Together, they explored many of the artsy shops and galleries in Galveston and Houston. Sasha had always been a sketcher, but because swimming had taken so much of her time in high school, she hadn't done much until now.

With Leandra, it seemed Sasha had rediscovered her love for color and sketching. Especially sketching beachy landscapes.

Not long after Marc got them together, Sash brought Leandra home to Wisteria Way where they spent the whole day, along with Linzy and Blue, when he got off work, grilling burgers, watching movies, and generally acting like young people without a care in the world. It made Linzy hope that Sasha was branching out, loosening up, seeing what else was out there in the world.

With Leandra's help, they started decorative painting in Sash's bedroom, something she'd always wanted to do. The first thing they did was to sketch an outline of wisteria vines in full bloom climbing around and dripping down above the doorways and windows. Sash finished adding the color to them little by little over the following week. "Even though it's winter, I can have my favorite purple flowers all year long."

The girls had talked about painting clouds on the ceiling and a beach sunrise on the wall opposite the bed, but so far, those were just pipedreams. In fact, now that she thought about it, Linzy realized she hadn't heard much about Leandra lately. She supposed they were both busy with work and studying so she was glad when Sash told her she was going to stay over with Leandra at the dorm this weekend.

Leandra seemed to be quickly taking the besties-place vacated by Rose. Linzy hoped that meant Sash was spending less time with Cameron Gaines. Her sister was private about her private life, and Linzy hadn't seen anymore red flags. Don't look for trouble, Blue often said. So, she tried to be chill and let her sister live her own life.

Leaving the dishes stacked in the drainboard on the counter, Linzy dried her hands on a dishtowel. Works in progress, she thought. That's what we are. Learning as we go. She hoped Sash and Leandra had the best weekend ever. She herself looked forward to a lazy Sunday afternoon with a new book she'd downloaded just yesterday.

She started toward the bedroom for her Kindle just as the front door opened and Sash appeared as if summoned. "Hey—" Linzy began.

Her greeting was cut short when Sasha said, "Please don't hate me, Sissy." Her voice held a pleading tone. "Just remember, I'm not a kid anymore, and I have something serious to tell you. It's about Cam." She crossed the room slowly.

Linzy motioned her to the living room couch and sat down beside her. She took hold of her sister's hands. It felt as if something life-changing was coming.

"You have Blue," Sasha said, squeezing Linzy's fingers. "And I've always *loved* what you two have together. Blue is like a big brother to me, you know that. But now," she smiled a wry little smile. "I understand how you feel about him because I feel the same way about Cam."

"Sis," Linzy began. "I know y'all have been seeing each oth—" But she didn't get to finish that sentence, either.

"He is *everything* to me," Sash continued, as if Linzy hadn't spoken. "He makes me calm. Just the thought of him takes away all my fear and anxiety." She dipped her chin, closed her eyes, and took a quiet breath.

Here it comes, Linzy thought. Here it comes.

Sasha tightened her grip on her sister's hands. "Two days ago, we flew to Vegas and got married in a chapel with Elvis as our witness."

Whoa! I thought she would say engaged or in love, not married. Is that even possible at her age? Don't you have to be twenty-one or something? Linzy opened her mouth to reply, but Sasha squeezed her hands so firmly she immediately closed her lips again.

After a second, Sash whispered, "There's one more thing, Sis."

And suddenly, Linzy knew. She gave her sister's hand a little shake. "You're going to have a baby, aren't you?" She couldn't keep the astonishment from her voice.

Sasha nodded. "We were going to be married anyway—"

Linzy turned loose of Sash's hands and jumped up to pace. She felt as if her head might explode. Hadn't they already had this conversation about Rose and about the two of them one day having a double wedding? And still she came up pregnant? *Pregnant!*

Before speaking, Linzy paced back and forth a few more times. She wanted to make certain she could tamp down the negative words that flooded her thoughts. A few leapt out anyway. "Oh, Sash. Pregnant? I can't *help* worrying. Having a baby and being a brand-new wife at the same time will be so challenging. I mean, usually you get used to being a couple before you bring a baby into the mix."

Sasha's face crumpled. "I hoped you would be happy for us." She dabbed at her eyes and nose with a ragged tissue from her pocket. "We're over the moon about it." She glanced toward the picture window. "Cam is in the driveway, waiting on me to tell him to come in. I wanted to tell you first."

Linzy stopped pacing. "It seems like you just recently told me that the two of you are dating. Excuse me if I need a moment to adjust." She looked around at the home they'd shared and almost lost. Is life always going to be such a roller coaster? Up and down from one thing to the next? She knew the answer to that. So far it was a big YES.

She imagined herself asking Blue that very question when she relayed the news to him later. His reply would doubtless be a jolly laugh. "Someone must've prayed to live in interesting times," he might say. "Was that you, Linz?"

She would poke him in the shoulder. "Seriously," she'd say. "What do you think?"

Once again, he'd laugh, then he might say, "What I think is that we've got each other, and we already know how to roll with the punches." His sweet smile would melt her like it always did. And then he'd go on to add, "I'd say we've got it made. Whatever life throws at us, we will handle it. Together."

Thinking it through, predicting how Blue would react, made Linzy feel better. Calmer. At least calm enough to break her silence. Sasha said Cam made her feel calm. Linzy supposed Blue did the same for her. So, she said, "Are you happy, Sash. For real? No doubts?"

Sasha smiled. "No doubts at all, Linz. I promise." She dabbed at her eyes and laid her hand on Linzy's forearm tentatively. "Please, be happy for me."

Linzy sat back down and pulled her into a sisterly hug. "I will, Sissy. If you're happy, I'll be happy, too. I promise." Besides, there's nothing to be done about it now. She squeezed her sister again. "And you know what? We will love the *stuffins'* out of that baby, as Mom would've have said. Oh, wouldn't Mom and Dad be thrilled at the news of a grandbaby? The first grandbaby?" She tried not to think about how they would question the age difference, the so-called shotgun wedding. What good would questioning do now?

Sasha pulled away and sat up straighter, as if she'd read her sister's thoughts. Or felt the tension. "They would be thrilled, after they got used to it. Aren't you going to ask me when the baby is due?" She patted beneath her eyes with the tissue again.

"Sure, I was," Linzy said. "Just as soon as I was able to think." She ventured a smile, praying it was not a rictus. Truthfully, she still felt stunned. Would this have happened if her parents were alive? No. Sash would be attending college on a swimming scholarship, not eloping and preparing for motherhood with a man who just happened to be her much older boss.

"August fifteenth," Sasha blurted. "A fall baby. Won't that be great? My favorite time of year." Tears sprang to her eyes again. "Anything besides Christmas, right?"

Linzy tilted her forehead against her sister's. "August sounds perfect. You'll be a great mom. And I'll be the super cool aunt." She pushed her bangs off her forehead and sat back. "When do we have a gender reveal party?"

Sasha laughed. "I don't know. I'm still a little overwhelmed."

Yeah, Linzy thought. I'm pretty dumbfounded myself. But I'm trying to be supportive. In truth, all I can see in my head right now is a fourteen-year-old girl waking me in a panic in the middle of the night and our parents lying dead on the lawn. Didn't we just get through all of that and the stuff with Ancho? And now you're jumping into marriage and motherhood. Wow, she wanted to say, what about your real estate career? Seems you barely started driving, then working, and then this man came into your life and here we are.

But Linzy didn't say any of that. Once again, what would be the point? It was too late, what's done is done. Bun in the oven her gran would've said. "Bring Cam in," she said.

Sasha dried her eyes, went to the front door and motioned for her new husband to come inside.

Linzy glanced over her head just in time to see the lanky man straighten up from where he'd been leaning against the gold Lincoln Navigator, smoking a cigarette.

Sash had once told her, jokingly, that he only drove a Lincoln because well-known Texan, Matthew McConaughey, was the spokesperson.

It was the first time Linzy had seen Cam smoking. She watched in amazement as he dropped the cigarette on the driveway, ground it out with the heel of his ostrich boot, then picked up the butt and put it in his jacket pocket. Maybe I should have seen this coming, she thought, taking a deep, spine-steeling breath to ready herself for whatever was coming next. Bad boys. Some girls like them. Sash must be one of those girls.

But then, to Linzy's surprise, she found something endearingly awkward about the way the tall man stepped through the door, one big-knuckled hand removing his Stetson while the other smoothed his hair self-consciously.

He nodded at Linzy. "Sash broke the news?"

"She did. I guess congratulations are in order—"

Cam ducked his chin, one long arm snaking around Sasha's waist. "This isn't the way we intended things to progress." His speech was hesitant, the cadence uncertain. "We were being careful," he said, and he might've added more, but Sasha squeezed him around the middle to shut him up.

"I don't think Linz needs details," she said, sounding embarrassed. "I'm sure she understands."

Well, not really, Linzy thought. He's supposedly a grown-ass man and you, my younger sister, little more than a kid, but—

"Anyhow," Sasha continued. "I haven't shown her the pictures from our Elvis wedding yet. I thought I'd let you do that." She guided him to the sofa where they all sat, side by side.

An Elvis wedding. And I missed it. Linzy fought back tears. And one little snort of laughter.

Sasha patted the sofa for Linzy to scoot closer while Cam pulled out his phone and opened the photos. There were dozens. Sasha wore a short, pearl-colored dress with a tiny little veil embroidered with sky blue flowers.

"The flowers were the 'something blue' part of the ceremony,"

Sasha said. "And the tiny Bible tucked into that baby's breath bouquet was the something borrowed." She grinned. "It belonged to the Elvis impersonator."

Linzy enlarged the photo with her fingertips and looked closer. The tiny Bible looked old, well-worn. "Did the Bible also stand for the something old part of the wedding?"

Sasha nodded. "Well, that and this." She turned her palm up to reveal a large, cushion cut diamond on a thin, gold band. It was accompanied by a narrow gold wedding band. "Cam picked out the diamond ring, but he already had this gold band." She twisted it around so Linzy could see it better.

"The gold band was my grandmother's wedding ring," Cam said. "My brother got mom's ring for his bride, so I got Gram's." He smiled and it seemed somewhat rueful. "I bought the engagement ring for Sash because I thought she needed a diamond."

Oh, Linzy thought, touching the ring on her own finger, that's so sweet. So similar to the ring Blue gave her.

Cam scrolled to another photo. This one showed him placing the wedding ring on her finger. He stood tall and proud beside her in a slim gray suit with a white shirt and black string tie. He looked like an old country-western singer just stepped off the stage. Or off the Galveston billboard, perhaps.

In the next photo, Elvis loomed large, one arm around each of them.

Sasha sighed. "My 'something new' was my beautiful dress." She gazed at her husband in adoration. "We bought it right there in the hotel. Cam simply called the concierge, and they had a selection of wedding attire sent up from the bridal shop downstairs." Eyes bright, Sash continued, "I felt just like a queen."

Linzy admired the pictures, remarking on how happy they looked while in the back of her mind remembering how Sash had told her she was having a girls' weekend with Leandra.

"So ..." Linzy began. "I suppose this means I'll be losing my roommate?" She thought of how empty the house would be without Sash in it.

"I bought my girl a house on the island," Cam said. "Nabbed it before it went on the market. Sunset Drift, a gated community with a private beach." He glanced down at Sasha's face. "I can hardly wait to start our lives together. It may seem a little rushed, but she's made me the happiest man alive."

His gaze strayed back to Linzy's face. "This may not be how we intended to start our lives together, but I assure you I will do everything in my power to make certain Sasha—and our baby—have nothing but the best, from now on."

Linzy swallowed the tears threatening to overwhelm her. She pulled her sister in for another hug and told her what a beautiful bride she'd been. Somehow, she refrained from mentioning any of her reservations. She wanted to, oh boy, did she ever, but she held her tongue. And praised herself for doing so.

"I know what you're thinking, Linz," Sasha said, seeming to read her thoughts as always. "And I missed having you there. But I was afraid you would try to talk me out of it." She hesitated. "I had to make this decision on my own."

Linzy nodded. She wanted to say of course I would've tried to talk you into waiting, but maybe that would've been wrong. I've got to let go. Even if it breaks my heart.

Sasha hurried on, "This just means we will have to make *your* wedding an even bigger event to make up for it."

"Yes, we will. But maybe not until after August. When do you find out the gender? They can do that so early now, right?"

Sasha laughed. "I'm not certain I want to know—"

Cam shook his head. "We kind of like the idea of not knowing." He closed his phone album. "Birth is such a mysterious, extraordinary thing, we want to enjoy every miraculous moment, wondering."

Those few words made Linzy feel somewhat better about her new brother-in-law. Did he often talk like some renaissance poet, or was that a little over-the-top for her benefit? She hadn't been around him very much. He was always busy with work. Was this the real Cam? Or an imposter? *Will I always be so suspicious of everyone and everything?* She came back to the present. "I suppose it's time to pack?"

Sasha nodded shyly. "Cam took the day off to help. All my clothes will fit into the Navigator. And I'd like to take some of my favorite things—"

Linzy softened. "Of course, Sissy. Take anything you want. Everything belongs to both of us." She looked around to see if she could discern what her sister might need. Nothing jumped out at her, so she said, "Soon, we will go shopping. For maternity clothes." She began to get excited in spite of her doubts. "We'll have to outfit the nursery, too." She clamped her lips together, embarrassed at her own enthusiasm. "I can't wait to see your beach house." If Sash is in this, she thought. Then I'm in it with her.

Sasha squeezed her sister's hand. "I'm so relieved to hear you say that. I hope you will come with us now, as soon as we load up my clothes and stuff."

"Only if your new husband is okay with it."

"Our home is your home," he said, sincerely.

Linzy mimed wiping sweat off her brow. "That's a load off my mind. Although you may regret saying it." She smiled to let him know she was joking. "I can't wait to tell Blue and his folks. They are not going to believe it."

Sasha grimaced. "I hope they don't think less of me for … you know." Her hand strayed to her midsection.

Linzy said, "Well, seriously, no one else needs to know, unless you tell them. I mean, you're a married woman and August is a long time from now."

Sasha's eyes lit up. "You're right. I'm only a few weeks along. No one does need to know, do they?"

"But it doesn't matter," Cam said. "Even if everyone knows.

We don't need to feel ashamed. We were already planning on marrying."

"That's right," Linzy agreed. "It's no one's business." She turned to Cam. "Having said that, I'm going to tell you now that the one thing people may question, including me, is the difference in your ages."

Cam's expression belied his shock at the blunt statement.

"Sorry, if that isn't what you wanted to hear," Linzy said. "But Sash and I have been through a lot." She caught her sister's eye to let her know she wasn't trying to cause an argument, just trying to clear away all doubts to start out on the right foot. No secrets. No surprises. To Cam, she continued, "I just want you to know I am extremely protective of my little sister. She saved my life."

Sasha closed her eyes, listening.

Linzy went on. "I won't ever let anyone mistreat her." She gazed at Cam's face, awaiting his reply.

To his credit, Cam nodded. "I wouldn't have it any other way. In that respect, you and I will always be on the same page." He smiled. "I feel the same way about my younger brother, Brandon." He slipped an arm around his wife's shoulders. "But that is nothing compared to how I feel about my new bride."

17

SUNSET DRIFT

The three of them were finishing up the packing when Blue arrived still wearing his paramedic uniform. The crisp new shirt made the freshly sewn-on firefighter-paramedic patches stand out.

The previous week, he had passed his exam to become a certified paramedic. After more classes, he would get his license. But that would be awhile yet. Before beginning, he hadn't realized there was a difference in being certified and being licensed. Of course he planned to go the full route, even if it did require a bachelor's degree.

Today had been his first shift under his new combined title at the Brookville Fire and Rescue Service. He would still volunteer for the Wister County fire company on his days off—the way he and his parents had always done—but this was for the city. Paid. With benefits. His new, life-long, career.

Linzy dropped what she was doing and hurried to the front of the house when she heard him drive up. She snapped picture after picture as he climbed out of his truck and strolled to the front door in his new uniform. "Whoohoo! You look so *handsome.*" She stopped snapping pics and held the door wide open. "How was your first day?"

Blue ducked his head, face red even under his farmer's tan. He pulled her to his chest for a kiss. "It was a great day. Who's here?" He nodded toward the Lincoln in the driveway.

"It's Cam and Linzy," she said. "I would've called you, but I didn't think you were getting off until seven o'clock in the morning."

Cam laughed. "My twenty-four-hour shifts begin next week. This week is more like orientation. Getting to know my way around doing two jobs instead of one." He glanced back at the Lincoln again. "Nice ride."

She took him by the hand and led him to the back patio. "Brace yourself," she said. And then she told him the news.

Blue's mouth dropped open, and then he began to laugh. "Good one, Linz. And it's not even April Fool's Day—"

She shook her head and sat on the glider. "Not even kidding." She pulled him down beside her. "They went to Vegas."

He let his head fall back against the top of the glider. "When's the baby due?"

"August," Linzy said. "But I don't know if I was supposed to tell you."

Blue raised his head, zipped his lips with his fingers, thew away the key. "I promise not to tell a soul. But thanks for trusting me. I hope we never have any secrets between us."

"We won't," Linzy said. "Never."

He picked up her hand and touched her ring. "I can't believe she beat us to the altar. Where will they live?"

Linzy told him about the private beach community called Sunset Drift. "It's on Galveston Island. I can't wait to see it," she said. "But it will sure be different around here."

Blue stood, stared out at the pecan grove. "I can't let you stay here alone, Linz. I would never be able to rest."

"I'm sorry, and I appreciate what you're saying, but think

about it. Soon, you'll be working twenty-four-hour shifts every third day."

"Damn," Blue said. "You're right. But I can be here the other forty-eight hours. At night, I mean." His face was earnest. His worry almost palpable.

"That's sweet of you," Linzy said. "But I need to be in charge of my own life. Don't worry. I'll be fine. We've still got the security system. As Bob Marley said, 'Every little thing's gonna be all right,' I promise."

He paced to the opposite side of the patio. Once again, the sunset painted the sky with pastel fire. Sash and Cam were inside the house, packing.

"We could go ahead and get married now," Blue said. "We were only waiting because of Sasha, anyway, right? Because we didn't want to rush her out of the nest." He smiled when he used Linzy's word.

Linzy walked up behind him and encircled his waist with her arms. She laid her cheek against his broad back. "Nah, I want that sweet 'friends and family' wedding we talked about. Then we can honeymoon at Stutter Creek. I'm looking forward to that. But we can't do it when you're just getting your career off the ground. Besides, I've got my online students to think about, too."

Blue pulled her arms more tightly around him. "Are you always going to be this damn practical?"

Linzy laughed. "I plan to be just that. Someone has to keep you and your future-heathen-children in line." She pulled her hands free and goosed him in the ribs, but he was fast. He turned and caught her in a clinch, capturing her lips with his.

When they parted after several breathless moments, Linzy saw Sasha watching from the picture window, a huge smile on her face and one hand flat against her midsection. "You told him, didn't you?" she asked, poking her head out the back door.

Linzy shrugged. "He tortured it out of me."

"C'mon," Sasha said, grinning. "Let's take my old stuff to my new home."

Linzy asked Blue if he wanted to go to Galveston.

"Hell to the yeah," he said. "Let me run to my house and change clothes."

"I'll go with you," Linzy said. "We can tell your folks."

"Yep," he gently pulled on the aluminum storm door to go back inside. "That, we will do."

Sash glanced toward the driveway where Cam was loading her final suitcase. "I think Cam and I should go to your house too. If that's okay with you, of course." Her eyebrows rose questioningly.

"I think they would appreciate it," Blue said, giving her a brotherly hug. "I just hope they don't have a heart attack."

Mr. and Mrs. Ash came out to meet them when the Navigator followed Blue's truck through the gate. They had been introduced to Cam on earlier dates, the most recent being Sasha's eighteenth birthday dinner. Now, Mr. Ash shook Cam's hand and Mrs. Ash made a fuss over the gorgeous ring. To everyone's surprise, they took the news graciously, hardly batting an eyelash between them.

Sash made Cam show the sweet couple the Elvis wedding photos, and then she invited them to come to the beach house for an impromptu tour. They agreed to go only if everyone would sit down and share a quick meal first. "It's only meatloaf and mashed potatoes," Mrs. Ash said, "but there's plenty."

Cam surprised them by rubbing his belly and telling her it sounded delicious. *Maybe he's all right, Linzy thought. Maybe he will fit in with the whole bunch of us after all.*

Over the dinner table, Cam let them know how much he appreciated being accepted into the family. "And this meatloaf is every bit as good as my Gram used to make." He grinned. "Well, almost."

Mrs. Ash laughed and used that opening as an excuse to learn more about him. She mentioned how she admired his billboards everywhere and remarked that his Gram must certainly be proud of him and his business sense.

Cam shook his head, patted his lips with a napkin. "Lost her several years ago. Mom, too. It's been just me and my brother, Brandon, for quite some time. He's got his own family now. Made me an uncle twice over." That brought another smile to his lips and to the faces of everyone around the table.

Cam went on. "I think that's one thing Sash and I bonded over." He looked across the table at Linzy. "The fact that our siblings are our core family members."

Sasha looked at Cam. "You have Brandon and Maura's family and Linz and I have Blue and his family."

"Yes," he agreed. "That's exactly what I was thinking."

Linzy nodded. It appeared they had more in common with Cam than she knew.

Mrs. Ash said, "Well, in case we haven't said it, let me just assure you that you will always be welcome at our house." She smiled and began to clear the table. Mr. Ash offered to help, but the younger guests quickly pitched in. Soon, they had the dishwasher loaded and the kitchen and dining room cleaned and shining.

Then they all climbed into their vehicles and followed Cam and Sasha to their new home on Galveston Island.

"I think he might be all right," Blue said. He and Linzy had elected to ride in the back seat of his parents' double cab pickup. It had way more room than his old truck, and Linzy and Cam had the Lincoln loaded down, no extra space at all.

Linzy sighed. "We can hope—"

"And pray," Janine Ash said. "We can always pray." She turned her head slightly toward them over the back of the seat. "And don't forget, an age difference can actually be a good thing if he's as stable and settled as he appears." She cleared her throat. "I take it Cameron has no children of his own?"

Blue laughed. "Way to sneak that in there, Mom."

She echoed his laughter. "You don't know how badly I wanted to ask him about that right there at the dinner table."

"Oh, don't worry. I got that scoop right away," Linzy said. "Sash said he was in a long-term relationship a few years ago, before he got his business up and running, but there were no children."

Mrs. Ash seemed to breathe a sigh of relief. "Maybe it was an amicable breakup. Sash deserves to start off with a blank slate. Especially at her young age."

Linzy agreed. "Maybe that's what's been bothering me. Not the age difference, but the difference in experience." As Mrs. Ash said, though, that could be a good thing. Maybe my little sis needed someone more mature.

They drove the short drive to Galveston, the night now black velvet with stars poking through like pinpricks from God's favorite seamstress.

The interior of the big double cab felt cozy. Holding hands with Blue in the back seat, humming along to Mr. Ash's favorite country radio station on the FM dial, Linzy began to feel relaxed for the first time all evening. "I hope it will always be this pleasant, driving to visit Sash and her new husband."

"Glad it isn't far away," Mrs. Ash said. "Maybe she won't get too homesick. I remember how it was when I was a young bride." She gazed out the window at the lighted causeway. "It's so pretty at night. It's been a while since I've been to the island after dark." She fell silent as they continued driving across the long bridge. "We do get in our routines, don't we?"

Mr. Ash chuckled. "You mean our early-to-bed early-to-rise routine?"

His wife giggled girlishly. "Eight p.m. comes earlier and earlier, doesn't it?"

"See what we've got to look forward to, Linz?" Blue joked.

Linzy grinned. "With any luck, we'll turn out just like them."

Blue pulled her hand over to his knee and laced their fingers together. "We will," he said. "And we'll have our own babies riding in the backseat. Two or three, maybe four, however many we can fit—"

"Whoa, now," Linzy said. "Let's not get carried away."

He leaned over and whispered in her ear, "Let's do get carried away." His tone turned lascivious. "I can't *wait*."

Linzy rolled her eyes and poked him with her elbow. He loved to tease her. She hoped Sash and Cam had that sort of relationship.

Ten minutes later, they were driving along the seawall, gazing out at the happy, carnival-colored lights of Pleasure Pier amusement park and a well-lit, offshore drilling platform in the distance. On the other side of Seawall Boulevard, hotels and condos loomed.

After a few miles, Cam pulled up to a private community gate. A tastefully lighted beach sign proclaimed the development to be Sunset Drift. Cam punched a short series of numbers into the entry box and drove through as the gate swung open.

They followed him in. Linzy wondered what kept the gate from closing on them and how it could possibly be considered secure if more than one vehicle could enter each time.

The first house was a small mansion. One of those multi-storied windows-lit-up-like-a-cruise-ship homes. Linzy forgot to wonder about anything after that. She was too busy watching for Cam to turn in somewhere.

There were six houses in the development. All were mini

mansions that shared a single stretch of pale beach shining in the moonlight.

Cam and Sash's house was the last one on the sandy street. It stood on tall stilts, pastel and beautiful beneath the rising moon. Cam swung the Lincoln around and underneath the ample carport area as the automatic garage door rose to reveal Sash's Cadillac snugged in tight. He pulled in beside it.

"There's Sash's Caddy," Blue said, a note of awe in his tone.

Mr. Ash pulled up behind the Navigator under the extended carport. Cam had not closed the overhead door.

"Very impressive," Mr. Ash said, stepping out at the same time Sash stepped out of the Lincoln. "I really like the carport attached this way. Reminds me of your Wisteria home."

Linzy laughed, thinking of the carports her dad had built for his pickup truck and pecan shaker at home.

Mr. Ash glanced at the front of the beach house. "I suspect the ocean side is even more magnificent."

"It is," Sasha said. "I'm still in shock myself. Cam just bought it." She glanced toward her new husband shyly. "It's my—our—wedding present."

Linzy wondered if Mr. Ash noticed how Sasha's hand snuck down to her tummy as she said "our." Probably not. After all, he's a man. Mrs. Ash would've noticed, though. No doubt about that.

Cam grabbed a couple of suitcases from the trunk of the Navigator and Blue and his parents did the same. They all trooped through the garage and up a few short steps to the interior connecting door.

Linzy came along with an armload of dresses from the backseat, and Sasha brought up the rear shouldering two different overnight bags which, Linzy was certain, held her makeup and toiletries.

Before the two of them reached the interior door, Cam came rushing out, grabbed the overnight bags, and set them down. "Nope," he said. "Gotta follow tradition." He turned his wife around, one hand on each shoulder, and guided her back out of the garage and around to the wide steps leading up to the wrap around deck.

Everyone followed to see what he had in mind.

There were seventeen steps in all with one small landing after the first ten.

Linzy mounted the last step. "This view is *magnificent*." Breath whooshed out of her chest on the word magnificent.

Sasha stood, facing the water, her back to the barely lit windows. She gazed out at the surf. "It certainly is." She turned to face her sister. "This is only the second time I've been out here at night." The breeze swished her thick blonde hair across her face, and she laughed and smoothed it away. "I can't believe we're going to live here."

Everyone lined up at the rail beside her, looking out to sea. In the distance, the other houses were visible. But they were way down the beach. It felt secluded, even though it wasn't far from downtown.

Behind them, Cam touched an icon on his phone and unlocked the broad double doors. "Now," he said, scooping Sasha up from behind. "*Now,* I will carry my new bride over our new threshold, and we will start our new lives together just right."

Sasha squealed and flung her arms around his neck as he grinned, walked them through the doorway, and kissed her soundly before setting her down in the large, open, living area.

Peeking through the window, the only lights Linzy could see came from underneath the kitchen cabinets across the way. Those lights were pale turquoise blue. They gave the entire living area an underwater feel. How fancy, she thought. How *chic*. Linzy couldn't help herself; she was totally impressed.

After a quick tour of the rest of the house with its vaulted ceilings and mile-high windows, they spent a few more minutes simply standing in the near-empty living room, drinking in the beach view. "We've got living room furniture ordered," Sasha said. "It's coming this weekend."

"Some of my bachelor furniture was okay," Cam said. "But my old beat-up couch just looked sad when we tried it in here." He flung his arms open to indicate the large space. Then he grinned and started back toward the kitchen and the door leading to the garage.

They all helped Cam bring the suitcases and other bags from the utility landing—the stairs leading from garage to kitchen—then the six of them trooped back through the living room and down the deck stairs to the sand. For a few moments they simply stood outside in the moonlight, breeze ruffling their hair, breathing in the salty gulf air.

"I'll be coming down to walk with you," Linzy said, hugging her sister as they made their way around the base of the home back to the carport.

"That will be wonderful," Sasha replied. "I plan to walk every morning and maybe in the evenings, too." She glanced around at Cam who remained slightly behind the rest of them. "I'm going to be calling you, a lot." She dropped her voice to a whisper. "Especially about cooking."

Linzy laughed. "I've got all of Mom's cookbooks. I'll bring them out next time. Oh!" She stopped talking. "We need to give you a wedding shower … is it okay to give a shower after the wedding?"

Mrs. Ash caught up to them. "I overheard the word shower." She took each girl by the arm, inserting herself in between them. "We *definitely* need to organize one."

And so, it was decided. A wedding shower would be held at the Ash family home. A few months later, it would be a baby shower. But that wasn't mentioned, yet. Linzy wondered if it would be prudent to have them both at once. Not my call, she thought. Not my call.

18

NEW TRADITIONS

As they were leaving the Sunset Drift development, Linzy, Blue and his folks exclaimed over the magnificent beach home one last time. No one mentioned the elopement or how suddenly the couple had gone from 'employee-employer' to 'dating' to husband and wife.

After a moment, Mrs. Ash said, "I wonder if Sash will continue working in the front office now?"

"Hmm," Linzy said. "I've been so stunned by everything; I haven't even asked."

"Why wouldn't she?" Blue said. "Now they can carpool—"

Linzy laughed.

"Let's drive by the office while we're here," Mr. Ash said. "I've never seen the place, have y'all?"

"I've come into town several times to pick Sasha up, or have lunch with her in Galveston," Linzy said. "It's a beautiful office."

"I wonder where they honeymooned," Blue mumbled, almost to himself.

Linzy rolled her eyes. "They stayed at The Bellagio in Vegas. I guess that was honeymoon enough."

Blue cleared his throat, waggled his thick eyebrows suggestively.

Even in the dark back seat of the pickup, Linzy felt her face grow warm. He loved to tease her with little comments when his folks were around, and she couldn't call him on it.

She decided to play his own game against him. "So where should we have our honeymoon, honey?" She said it loud enough for his parents to hear while making her voice completely innocent.

Mrs. Ash laughed and covered her mouth while Mr. Ash cleared his throat and turned up the volume on the radio.

Blue laid his head back on the seat and closed his eyes. He knew better than to continue down that road. He'd tangled with the best before. She'd say anything to get his goat. Besides, everyone knew Stutter Creek was their plan.

Linzy snuggled into Blue's side, and he wrapped his arm around her and pulled her even closer. They drove past CG Realty so Mrs. Ash could see the business, then the rest of the trip home went by in a flash.

Linzy wouldn't allow Blue to stay the night. She was afraid she would get used to it before she had the chance to see if she could make it on her own. She hoped her sister never felt too vulnerable to be alone, since she'd already jumped into the marriage pool and bypassed the chance to be independent.

The next morning, Sasha called Linzy around nine. "Cam's gone to the store for eggs. He's going to make breakfast for us," she said. "But I was worried about you, Linz. Are you okay?"

That made Linzy's eyes well up with tears, just a bit, and she had to admit she'd gone to sleep with the TV on an old movie just for the company. "Don't worry. I'll get used to it," she said. "I'll probably even learn to *enjoy* the solitude, you know me."

"I don't know why you and Blue don't go ahead and get married or at least move in together."

Linzy rose from her desk chair and stretched. She had three

students online, working on math problems which she would review shortly. "I think I have some strange need to find out if I can make it on my own," she said. And then it occurred to her that all of a sudden, the tables had turned, and little sis was now comforting big sis.

After that first morning, one of them called or texted the other one at some point every day, discussing meal plans, sending phone pics of the sunrises and sunsets over the Gulf and over the orchard, asking after each and every detail of their day-to-day doings. "When are you coming to walk the beach?" Sash asked on the second day.

"Tomorrow," Linzy said. "It's Saturday. What time should I be there?"

"If you come early, we can have coffee on the deck," Sasha said, "watch the sunrise the way we used to do on the back patio."

"That sounds like a plan. Cam won't mind?"

"Not at all. In fact, I don't have to go to the office this Saturday, since we're expecting our new furniture to be delivered, but Cam has a showing, maybe two." She'd smiled when she said that, proud of her new husband.

And so, the two sisters started their new tradition, coffee on the deck at sunrise every chance they got. The first time was glorious. They drank one cup on the deck with Cam, then he went inside to shower and dress for his showings. The sisters took the opportunity to walk the length of the beach where Sash stopped to pick up shells and bits of sea glass and pebbles.

Her eye was drawn to anything pretty or unusual. "There's the neatest little shop on The Strand," she said, "sort of a gift shop and art gallery combined. They sell the most wonderful handmade things."

Linzy heard real excitement in her voice. Everything about Sasha's new life seemed to suit her. "Let's visit the shop later, before I go home," she said. "Is it the one where Leandra works?"

Sasha shook her head and might have said more, but then a look came over her face that Linzy had never seen before. "Oh, no," she said, one hand over her mouth. "Don't look, Sis." She ran to a clump of sea oats growing near the house. Her coffee and croissant came back up with a vengeance.

"Uh, oh," Linzy said, standing back to give her sister a bit of privacy. "Morning sickness has come to call." She couldn't help the smile in her tone. "First time?"

Sasha straightened; her face bathed in sweat. "Yes," she swiped at her forehead and upper lip. "That was awful."

Her sister went to her side, took her arm. "Do you feel better?"

"Not much. I feel like I need to lie down." She looked toward the steps leading from the beach to the deck.

"Come on," Linzy said. "Lean on me if you feel dizzy. We'll get you to the house, make some tea and toast. That's what they always say on those British shows on PBS." She laughed. "Just part of being pregnant, I guess. When is your next checkup?"

Sasha told her it was scheduled for the following week. "I'm going to continue working in the office," she said. "As long as I can deal with this morning sickness."

They made it up the steps and into the cool dimness of the living room. The tall windows were tinted and shaded by the deep eaves.

"You rest and let me take care of you," Linzy said, fetching a cool wet cloth for her sister's forehead. "I'll brew the tea and make some toast—"

"Make it iced tea," Sasha said on her way to the bedroom. "There's a pitcher already made up in the fridge. And spread some grape jelly on that toast, would you?"

Linzy laughed. "Yep, I believe your pregnancy has kicked in. Wonder what it'll be next? Lobster and peanut butter? Mom wrote in your baby book that she couldn't get enough of those when she was pregnant with you."

"Oh, Sis," Sasha mopped her own forehead with the cool cloth. "Don't say lobster. I think it might make me hurl again."

"Surprised you didn't grow up loving it," Linzy said. "Also surprised mom craved them because nuts and shellfish are two of the worst allergy triggers in kids." She brought the snack to her sister on a bamboo tray. "This tray reminds me ... your wedding shower is set for two weeks from today."

"Argh," Sasha made a noise in her throat. "I can't go if I can't get out of this comfy bed."

"You'll get it figured out," she said. "Maybe the doc will have something to help."

Sure enough, the OB/GYN doctor knew just what Sasha needed to keep the pukies—her term for the relentless nausea—at bay. She was able to attend her impromptu wedding shower as well as continue working in the office right into her ninth month.

Everyone in the office, plus Leandra and her school friends, along with all the kind people she'd met through her teen years—Pastor Sue, Carla the attorney, several of the volunteers at the Brookville Fire Department, and even Sheriff Peach—attended the shower arranged by Linzy and Janine Ash. In the end, it turned out to be more of a delayed wedding reception rather than a shower.

When Sash announced the news of her pregnancy, Mrs. Ash immediately asked to help plan the baby shower as well.

"We are so blessed," Sasha told Linzy later. "Such caring families. Plus, I've got the love of my life, and you've got Blue." She giggled when she realized how that had sounded. "The love of your life, of course."

"We *are* blessed," Linzy said. "Like maybe God and the universe are trying to make up for everything that happened."

Sasha's eyes widened. "I wish we hadn't thought that. Don't want to bring down the juju—"

"No. No." Linzy said. "That's just superstition. It's fine to mention good things that happen. It doesn't invite bad. I don't believe that at all." She crossed her fingers down beside her thigh, out of sight.

Then, they stopped talking. Their mom had always said it was right to thank God for your blessings, but not to crow over them. They'd both taken that to heart. But Cam *has* been a blessing, Linzy thought. She'd been delighted to watch her sister's happiness and self-confidence grow almost as fast as her tummy and her newfound love of creating shell art. It seemed to go along with her new need for color in her home and in her wardrobe.

Linzy thought it might be a nod to the past few years, the dark cloud that had hung over them, but that was just her theory. In truth, Sash had always loved unique clothing, the more colorful, the better.

When it came to her maternity clothing, Sash had gone all out. Each piece she'd bought was soft and bright, pants, capris, even the boat neck sweaters and tops.

The only articles of clothing she still wore from her teenage closet seemed to be her old blue swim team windbreaker, and a voluminous tie-dyed t-shirt she and Linzy, along with Rose, Tonya, and Sara, had made during one of their infamous slumber parties back before they lost their folks.

Now, each time Linzy made the short trip from Brookville to the island—to walk the beach—she was amazed at her sister's growth. If the time they'd spent waiting on a trial had slowed to a crawl, this period of time seemed to have sped up, as if someone had pushed the fast-forward button.

When the urge to nest came upon her, as her doctor had said it would, Sasha filled her new home with the same colorful textures that made up her wardrobe. Soon, their home décor sported works of art that echoed those sea-bright colors. It delighted her to find shells and sea glass in the same hues she was using to decorate their new home. Thanks to YouTube DIY videos, she even began to create and sell some of her pieces in The Shell Shop on The Strand.

At first, Sash made small pieces, curio boxes encrusted with shells, tiny sea-creature earrings and necklaces, and later she even created one large piece, a lovely mirror bordered with shells and sea glass.

Cam was so enthralled with his wife's new art he promised to have a kiln installed in the store house beside the carport. She wanted to create pottery and decorate it with shells and ceramic sea creatures. Cam had already bought her a pottery wheel so she could take a ceramics class.

The next time Linzy went to the beach house, Sasha handed her an apron and a paint brush. She'd already outlined a scene from *The Little Mermaid* on the nursery wall. "We're having a girl," she said. "But I don't care about a gender reveal, or about having the doctor confirm it. In my heart, I know it's true."

They'd painted the nursery mural and walked the beach and a few weeks later they had a beautiful baby shower. And then the baby came.

Linzy Skye Gaines. Eight pounds and one ounce. Nineteen inches long. A clutch of baby fine hair the color of wet sand and eyes as dark as the sea.

"She's perfect," Cam told them when he emerged from the delivery room at two thirty-five a.m. with a look of stunned joy. "Absolutely perfect. She even appears to be wearing lipstick. That's what the delivery nurse said. 'I've never seen such perfect little rosebud lips.'" Cam grinned and dug in his pocket for a nonexistent pack of cigarettes. He'd given them up as soon as Sash had moved in. "Can't believe she's here. That she's mine." He grinned sheepishly. "I mean ours."

Blue laughed. "So, mom and baby are doing well?" He already knew the answer. Linzy had been in the delivery room, too.

"Perfect," Cam said again. "Just perfect."

In the waiting room, Blue whispered to his mom, "Wonder if he'll ever come back down to earth?"

Mrs. Ash just laughed. "What a blessing. I'll be glad when they get her tucked into the nursery so we can all see her."

Linzy walked out with her iPhone full of pictures. "Let the oohs and ahhs begin," she said, opening her screen. They all crowded around, remarking on hair color, complexion, and the fine shape of her head. "She might be tall, too," Linzy said.

Cam laughed and grinned, then went back inside. His feet never touched the floor.

That was mid-August. Mom and baby went home with new-daddy Cam to the beach house on the island. Everything was wonderful, perfect, just as Cam had said.

Linzy brought her laptop and her lesson programs and made her tutoring lesson plans at the beach house so she could be there to help out the new mom.

But Sasha took to motherhood like a pelican to the waves. After a couple of days, it was clear Linzy wasn't really needed. "I'm only a phone call away," she said when she loaded up her things to drive back to Wisteria Way. "Never hesitate to call me."

Sasha leaned in the car window for a kiss. "You know I won't," she agreed. "But don't wait for an invitation. As soon as Skye's doc okays it, she and I will hit the beach with her new balloon tire stroller." Her eyes gleamed. "I can't wait to try it out."

Linzy still couldn't believe how easily Sash had claimed her spot in the motherhood hall of fame. The new parents doted on the baby and were blessed by an unbelievably easy "fourth trimester."

"Is it really called that?" Linzy asked when she and Sash discussed it one day.

"That's straight from the doctor's mouth," her sister said. "The three months after the baby is born used to be called the postpartum period, but it's had such negative connotations, that it's now referred to as the fourth trimester."

"I'm learning," Linzy said. "Learning with you and the little button here." She touched the baby's nose gently. "She is such an incredible blessing. I'd give anything if Mom and Dad—"

"I know, Sis," Sasha murmured. "I've thought about it a thousand times, and it would probably get me down if not for you and Cam, and Blue." She smiled and Linzy tried to match it.

Linzy wondered if even their greatest moments of joy would always be tinged with sadness, or if it would get easier over time. But then she thought that it could always get worse. Best to go back to counting our blessings, and stop being so morose. Postpartum depression is supposed to be for the mother, not the aunt.

She drove on home, determined to put those thoughts away and not let the gloomies get a solid grip on her. Better to think of Halloween. It would be their first one apart, but she was determined to make it a fun one.

Blue always helped out at the volunteer fire department, and until the last couple of years, she and Sash had helped with the hayrides and sometimes the haunted fire station, too.

Even before she got home, Linzy was on the phone to her sister, reminiscing about their childhood costumes and Halloween parties, and wondering if it was too soon to make a costume for little Skye.

While they were chatting, Sash found an online pattern to make the baby a tiny pumpkin outfit with a green felt hat. Linzy began to feel better. They made plans to go to the fabric store soon. "Remember when we dressed up as detectives that year?" she asked.

"I remember," Sash said. "Mom helped us become Sherlock Holmes and Dr. Watson—"

"You really wanted to be Sherlock," Linzy said. "And I would've let you, if you hadn't been so allergic to that hat."

"The deerstalker hat," Sash murmured. "I so wanted to wear that silly thing. I think I fell in love with the name of it." She laughed self-consciously.

"You scratched your scalp so hard I told Mom you had cooties."

"Turns out, it was just made of wool."

They both had a good laugh, remembering how Linzy had become Sherlock instead. "Those were good times," she said. "What were we, barely in our teens?"

"Well, you were," Sasha said. "I think I was a tween. Hey, what are you going to wear this year?" She paused. "I think I'll go to the office as a milk cow. I just found the funniest black and white cow costume on Amazon. Here, I'm sharing the link so you can see it."

"You are one crazy new momma," she told her sister. "A milk cow!"

"Maybe a little crazy," Sash agreed, "but that's how I feel, especially at two o'clock in the morning when Skye thinks she is starving."

Linzy laughed to herself, thinking of her sister nursing her baby at the office wearing a Holstein cow costume. And just like that, the gloomies were gone, and everything was right in the world again.

Right up until it all fell apart.

19

THE JOKER'S WILD CLUB

Cam parked beneath the yellow and red neon sign depicting a winning poker hand—including a grinning joker—climbed out of the Lincoln and walked into the club. He allowed the door to close silently behind himself. "Hey man. How's it going?"

Gershwin smiled his golden smile, never making eye contact, looking directly over Cameron's head at the door. "Not too bad," the bouncer said, his deep baritone smooth as room-soft butter. "You good?"

"Can't complain," Cameron said.

Gershwin let one side of his wide mouth turn up. "Wouldn't help anyway."

"Never does," Cam murmured, sauntering on into the dark interior.

Cora was not at the bar, shaking her drinks, entertaining the regulars. Instead, there was a new bartender. A hairy-faced guy Cam had never seen before. His handlebar mustache resembled that of some old movie star from the 1970s.

Cam almost said, "Is that your Halloween costume?" but he checked his tongue at the last second. He didn't intend to be here long, just one or two hands of Texas Hold'em, win a few bucks, add it back to his bank account.

Maybe I should just cut my losses, he thought. Tell Sash that I lost so much money at the poker table that every gift I've given her—the beach house, the Cadillac, the three-carat diamond ring—are all in danger of being repossessed. He thought about it for a split second. *Nah. Not yet. I'll make some of it back tonight.* He didn't think he could stand seeing the disappointment in her big blue eyes if he had to tell her what an imposter he was.

He went on through to the men's room, washed his hands, checked his pulse—so far, so good—then walked out and took a hard right down the long hallway to the card room. It was nearly pitch black in that hall. Not a place anyone wandered into by mistake.

When he opened the hidden door, he was greeted by nods and smiles. Glad to see me, he thought. Ready to take some more of my hard-earned cash.

Pug indicated an empty chair at his table. "My friend," he smiled. "It's been a while." His thick bulldog lips smiled around the stub of a black cigar. He shifted his mountainous body in his specially made chair. The chair squealed in response.

Cam nodded hello, then sat in the proffered place. Let the chips fall, he thought. Win or lose. This would be the end of his gambling days. It didn't feel right anymore. If he could get back at least part of what he'd lost, he would tell Sash everything. Then he'd swear off the cards completely.

He leaned back in his chair, wanting to appear nonchalant. The game would be a long shot. He knew it. He'd lost a lot over the past year, before he married Sash. Hundreds of thousands, maybe even a little more. But it is what it is, he thought. Here we go.

He accepted a stack of chips from Sven, the dealer, and tried to focus. Time to get down to business, he thought. Take control of this thing.

He saw Cap'n, the charter boat captain with the wooden leg, waiting. They'd sat near one another a previous time. About the leg, he'd told Cam, "S'good for tourism. Folks come down to the hah-buh expectin' to see Cap'n Bligh or Ahab. I play it up, take 'em out to hunt fie'ce mah'lin."

He'd rolled up his pant leg. "Like the one got me this here," he said, tapping the leg. "Solid oak. Antique." He'd laughed like a drunk. "We hunt up some big'uns. Fightin'est bastuds you evah hooked." Then he had leaned back in his chair, laughing. "That's the reason my *Sheba's* never idle. Tourists love it." Then he had turned his attention back to the game, never having lost track of who played what, or how much was bet.

Later, Cam asked one of the other players, "He really lose that leg bringing in a fierce marlin?"

The player, a slim Latino dude called J-Man, rolled his eyes, fingered his poker chips, and muttered, "I heard it was a fishhook on that rust bucket he runs. Got infected. Cap was too drunk to get it seen by a doctor. Gangrene set in ..."

Cam recalled thinking how that story was almost as bad as the marlin tale. The thought of anyone having to have a leg amputated due to his own drunken stupidity made him cringe.

It felt as if someone, his little brother—or maybe the universe—had just sent him a message about sitting in a bar, drinking and gambling while his new wife and baby were home, alone. This will be the last time, he thought. Absolutely the last time.

He put everything out of his mind as the game began.

Cards were dealt, bets were made, bluffs were called.

Before long, Cam found himself nursing a beer at the bar. He wanted a shot of whiskey to go with it, but he vowed to swear off gambling and the hard stuff, starting now.

Tonight's game had been short and intense. He'd bailed out early when the cards didn't fall his way. Paranoia had set in. After one brutal bluff-gone-bad, Pug had joked about soon owning his own real estate office. Cam folded and bowed out. "Guess it's still not my night," he said.

Pug's comment about his real estate company had been like a splash of cold water. Pug might've been joking, but Cam knew if he didn't get control of himself, he really would be in danger of losing his business. And possibly his new little family.

He glanced at his reflection in the long mirror behind the bar. The planes of his face were blurred, distorted by all the bottles of liquor and stacks of highball glasses, but there was no denying the shock in that man's eyes.

What a royal screw up. He laughed at his own Freudian slip. As a kid, he'd been known as Royal, and his brother had been called Legend. But he had changed his name when his father went to prison. Later, Brandon had changed his, too. Since then, his life had been his own. New persona, new goals, new everything. He'd moved to Texas, built up his business with nothing but grit, and then he'd met Sasha. She and little Skye were the best things that had ever happened to him. He needed to focus on them and not on his losses. Trouble was, he'd worked his tail off for his business and the money he'd lost. It was hard to see it disappear simply because he'd made stupid gambling mistakes.

He tipped his glass toward his reflection and downed the remains of his beer. When he set the glass down, it thumped the bar a little harder than he intended.

Rodrigo, the new hairy-faced bartender, looked up and immediately drew another to replace it. "Take it easy, my man," the good-natured barkeep advised. "We like to keep our customers well and happy." He grinned beneath the bushy mustache.

Cam tipped his new beer toward the man and took a sip. "No problem, buddy, no problem." The guy didn't know Cam. And

Cam didn't know him. The only reason he even knew the man's name was because the cougar at the end of the bar kept calling him to come over.

Suddenly, a scratchy, feminine, voice floated toward him. "Hey, Cammie ..."

Cam glanced at the mirror again. It wasn't the cougar, instead, Teena could be seen coming up on his left.

He raised one hand in a kind of wave. "Hey, there, young lady. Where've you been keeping yourself?"

Teena held up her near-empty glass and Rodrigo nodded. Apparently, he already knew what she was drinking.

"Well, let's see," she drawled, moving closer. "Since you took yourself off the market, I've been out of town a lot." She drew a fingertip along the back of his neck while sipping her new drink.

An icy drop of water rolled inside his shirt collar from her fingertip. Cam shrugged slightly and twisted his head around to see her more clearly. "Well, I knew I hadn't seen you around, but then again, I don't come in here much anymore."

Teena laughed then lowered her voice to a soft growl, "Yeah. I heard you got married and had a kid." She slid onto the stool beside his. "Can't believe it's been that long since the night you took me home."

Cam looked at her face. She was right. It had been a long time. Another lifetime, in fact. Way back before he had Sash and Skye. "Yeah." He nodded. "It's been a while. I've got a wife and beautiful baby girl now."

The woman smiled. "So what'cha doing drinkin' in here if you got all that at home?"

Another slap in the face from the universe. Cam set the second glass on the bar. Time to go, he thought. Everything is telling me. Time to go. "Just a momentary lack of reason," he told Teena. "You're right. I shouldn't even be here—"

She smiled again and Cam was surprised to see her move his

beer glass closer to him. Did she take a drink of my beer? Why would she? Her own drink was fresh.

"I'm glad you're doing well," she said.

"Hell, yeah," a rough voice said. "I'm glad, too. 'Cause this 'ho is off the market. Off *your* market anyway. She's mine now. No more free rides." A tree trunk arm came down on Teena's shoulders. The branch-thick wrist lay inches from Cameron's chin.

"Shut 'cher ugly mouth," Teena muttered. "I ain't a 'ho to Cam."

Cameron let his gaze run toward Teena's glassy, half-mast stare. He knew when someone was tweaking. He wished he didn't.

"I don't believe I know your friend," he said, tearing his gaze away from her once-pretty face.

She attempted to shrug off the guy's heavy arm. "Chalk, this is Cam Gaines, my old real estate tycoon."

The beast clamped his hand around Teena's upper arm. His fingertips disappeared into her flesh as he leaned around to get directly in Cam's line of sight. "I'll tell you what, motherfucker," he leaned even closer. "You stay away from this ol' *gal* unless you got cash. She's mine, now. *Capiche?*"

Cam almost spit laughter in the brute's ugly face when he said the word *capiche* like some old mafia don. "Uh, yeah, ca-*peesh,*" Cam repeated, face as straight as possible.

Chalk looked at Cam's beer. "You finished with that?"

Cam picked it up, downed the dregs, threw some bills on the bar and set the empty glass on top of them. He made certain Rodrigo saw it, then headed for the door. He could feel Chalk's stare boring into his back all the way across the room to where Gershwin stood, arms folded across his massive chest.

Good, Cam thought. At least G won't let the mountain sneak up on me from behind. On the other hand, the bouncer sure didn't seem to have a problem with the way the creep manhandled Teena. Why was that? Was he getting a cut of her earnings from the guy? He certainly seemed chill about it.

Cam strode out to his Lincoln determined to drive straight home but knowing his car might pull into any of a half-dozen other drinking establishments on the way back if he wasn't extra careful.

Suck it up, dumbass, he thought, his finger on the start button. Suck it up, face the music, tell your sweet wife why you felt the need to gamble instead of simply working more hours to sell more property. Tell her what a dumbass you've been.

He slid into the driver's seat of the Lincoln, started it up and moved his hand to the shifter to reverse out of the parking lot. His mind was on autopilot, not thinking about the task of driving, simply listening to his ego tell him to stop looking for the easy way out, go home, confess to his wife, and then get busy selling houses and property to get them back in the black.

Confession is supposed to be good for the soul. Tell her the worst and be done with it. Everybody screws up sometimes. Besides, we weren't even married when I lost the bulk of that money. I can make it all back with two or three good listings on the beach. It's not the end of the wor—

A heavy fist thumped down on his hood. Not hard enough to dent, just hard enough to get his attention. Cam's hand fell away from the shifter, and he found himself staring into the eyes of the tree-trunk beast.

He blinked and powered down the window. "The fuck's your problem, asshole?"

The tattooed behemoth strode around to the passenger door, popped it open, and stuffed Teena inside. In the yellow and red glow of the neon, old bruises appeared on the woman's face like optical illusions under blacklight.

The monster crawled into the Lincoln's back seat. "Teena wasn't ready for you to go," he snarled. "She seems to have this thing for you."

Cam heard something rusty in the creep's voice. He soft fingered the safety on the 9mm pistol he kept in the driver's door pocket. Glancing at Teena but keeping the beast in his peripheral, he said, "You okay, Tee?"

She nodded, but it was clearly a lie.

Cam knew this had to be about money. A slow-motion robbery of sorts. He wanted to hurry it along before his temper got the best of him and escalated the situation. He could feel anger boiling beneath his skin, but it was like molasses. Thick, and slow, sort of sticky. His head felt strange. "So, what can I do for you folks?"

Chalk spoke in a raspy whisper. "Teena says you got cash. A lot of it." He shoved the tip of a large Bowie knife over the back of the seat just enough so Cameron could see it. "We want it."

Cam had to wonder where he'd had the large blade hidden. Maybe he'd stopped and retrieved it from his vehicle on the way across the parking lot. But it didn't matter now. He eased the 9mm up with his left hand and touched the tip of the knife with the barrel of the gun. "I don't think you came prepared, fuckhead."

The big man sat back and opened the car door. "Let's go," he ordered Teena. "Thought you said he didn't carry." He climbed out, the heavy vehicle rising on its springs, and slammed the door.

Teena placed her right hand on the inside door handle. With the left, she touched Cam's arm briefly, like an insect. "I didn't want no part of this." Her voice shook. "He made me—"

Her door flew open and the neanderthal yanked her out. "We'll be seeing you," he said, dragging poor Teena over the gravel like a rag doll. "And next time I *will* be prepared." He kicked her door closed with the heel of his boot.

Cameron ignored the kick. He could've smoked the guy, but why go to prison for that piece of walking-talking-crap? Besides all that, his vision was a little fuzzy. Guess I've already got out of the drinking habit, he thought. More so than I realized.

He waited until the couple re-entered the bar, then he laid the gun in the passenger seat, made certain his gray Stetson was secured in the ceiling holder, and then he hit the automatic lock button for the doors.

Finally, he drove out of the lot and headed home. He needed to get there right away. His vision was wavery, eyelids heavy. He hoped Sash wasn't waiting up, she didn't need to see him in this state. Would I have shot the creep? Cam knew he would have. No one took his belongings unless it was over his dead body.

His thoughts felt jumbled. Time to find another card game. Jokers has gone straight to Hell. I'm giving up gambling anyway. Forget about Pug's games and just be done. Be a family man like Brandon.

All the way home, Cam's mind spiraled around and around. He decided the attempted hold-up had been a good thing. Maybe even a God-thing. Maybe God's way of telling him it was time to get serious about changing his life. Just like his brother had been saying. Just like the universe kept saying.

But being behind on bill money was never a good thing.

The sooner he caught up, the better off he'd be. Wait, is my bank account really empty? His mind felt as fuzzy as an old peach.

He didn't go right home. Instead, he drove around Galveston hoping to sober up by looking at properties he'd listed, and others for which he hoped to get the listing. Three good sales and I'm back in the black, he thought.

At last, he headed home. His mind wasn't clearing, in fact, it felt fuzzier than ever. His eyes kept closing of their own accord. Twice, he jerked himself awake after drifting out of his lane. Thank God for the Lincoln's lane-alert system.

His mind replayed the events in the parking lot. Something about that encounter kept gnawing at him. Teena had seemed so strung out. Was she like that the one time I took her home? No. I never would've hooked up with a chick that wasted.

He wondered if he could help her, somehow? Hell, I'm nobody's hero, he thought. And then a new thought dawned on him. The one time he'd taken her to his condo, before he met Sash, she had jokingly asked for his security code to open his door.

They'd been acting silly that night, lovey-dovey. Had he given it to her? And more importantly, do I still use the same code at Sunset Drift? Sash and I moved into the place in such a hurry, with the wedding and the closing and the baby all coming so close together. Surely, I didn't use the same code ... *did I?*

He couldn't seem to focus his thoughts. I'll figure it out when I get there. S'not that important. Not right now.

Except what about the mountain Teena had called Chalk? Where'd he come from? Never saw him before tonight. There had been four other cars in the lot outside the bar. Cam wasn't certain which one belonged to the creep, but he suspected it was the ancient Chevy with the rusted rocker panels.

He had no clue what Teena might drive, if indeed she even had a vehicle. The poor girl seemed to have fallen quite low. Very sad, but not his fault. He hadn't looked at another woman since he'd found Sasha.

As thoughts of his perfect wife invaded his mind, he finally let in all his worries. Besides the money he'd lost and spent, now he was finding that a new baby has lots of needs, and his best agent, Shelley, was eyeing a move to Houston, a much larger market. Marc, his other office staffer, had earned his agent's license, but he wasn't nearly the salesperson Shelley was. Not yet anyway.

Feeling like the world's biggest loser—not just in cards—Cam finally made it back to Sunset Drift. His vision was so wonky he could barely focus on the road. Driving around hadn't sobered him at all. Instead, he felt even more toasted.

He kept his eye trained on his rearview mirrors to make

certain no one followed him. The fact that Gershwin allowed Chalk to walk around armed kept gnawing at him. Especially since the jerk seemed to be new in town.

Too bad Teena couldn't keep her mouth closed. Of course, it was his own fault. I'm the drunk who never should have hooked up with her in the first place.

Cam shook his head. Maybe I should just cut-out now. Send Sasha home to her sister. She'd be better off. Her and the baby. At least she'd be out of harm's way in case Chalk followed to get his money. No. It's not his money. He won't try me again. I'd know if I was being followed. He glanced into his rearview. His brain was so muddled he couldn't really remember why he thought they might follow him. Do I owe Pug for the poker game? No, Pug doesn't loan money. And he sure doesn't allow credit games.

What a sorry night.

He checked his rearview mirror once more as he approached the Sunset gate to punch in the security code. No one followed him and the house was dark except for the twinkle lights on the deck and in the nursery. The other houses had their twinkles on, too. He drove the quiet asphalt street through the small community until he got to the last house.

I need therapy, he thought. Twelve Steps might be a starting place. A place to help me figure out why I've stayed out late drinking and gambling when my girls are waiting for me here at home. I can always earn more money to pay my debts. I can never replace my girls.

He parked the Lincoln in the garage—somehow without hitting Sasha's Cadillac—and stumbled up the steps to enter the utility room door. The kitchen was just to the right of the utility room, through a separate, open, door. But he couldn't seem to key in the correct numbers on the security pad. After a couple of tries, he finally did, but once inside, he turned and smashed his thumb against the pad, turning off the security system completely.

The house was quiet. As he started through the utility room, his toe caught the bristles of the broom leaning against the wall. It fell over in slow motion and smacked the washing machine with a hollow *thwong*.

"Son-uva-bish!" His voice came out slurred and much louder than he intended. "Wha'sa broom doin' there?"

In a fit of drunken stupidity, he kicked the broom. This time, it hit the dryer.

From inside the house, he heard the baby cry, then Sash attempting to comfort her.

Cam tried to be more careful, but he stumbled over the corner of the kitchen mat. "Gaw-dammit!" He could not get his balance. He lurched across the wide space toward the living room, finally catching himself on the back of the couch. Standing there, in front of the moonlit windows, he found it impossible to keep from swaying. The immense ocean-facing windows made him feel poised on the brink of the universe, looking out at the entire salt-washed and star-swirled galaxy.

Letting go of the couch, Cam stumbled across the room to turn on the lamp over Sasha's rocking chair, the one where she sat and nursed the baby every night. The chair beckoned him, but it was closer than he thought. He fell against it and kept on falling.

By the time he righted himself, and the chair, Sash stood in the doorway, holding the baby in her arms. "Honey, is everything all right?"

He turned to face her. Why was everything so blurry?

"Cameron, are you *drunk*?"

Something in his mind shifted. A red film melted down over his good sense. He looked at the sweet baby that demanded all his new bride's attention. "Maybe I've had a few drinksh." His voice didn't seem to be his own. "It'sh my fuckin' *buinness*."

Sasha's mouth fell open, and her eyes appeared to gloss over. The baby cried louder. The look on Sasha's face showed utter disappointment. It almost brought Cam to his senses. His hand found her arm "Sash, I . . ."

She pulled away with a look of alarm.

"Whassa matter?" he muttered. "I ain't gonna—"

"You're drunk. Just leave me alone—"

The red anger spoke. "Leave you *alone?* 'Zat what'choo want? Okay, then. I'll leave you alone." He grasped her upper arm, pushed her toward the double doors.

"Cam, what are you—"

Twisting the dead bolt and yanking the door open, he shoved her out, then slammed the door and locked it behind her. "There," he yelled. "Now you're alone." He chuckled at his funny joke, pulled out his phone, and touched Linzy's picture.

By the time Linzy answered, he'd staggered to the bedroom.

He spoke a few words, then flopped across the bed and passed out.

20

PHONE CALL

Linzy crawled into bed while talking to Blue on the phone. He was on duty at the fire station helping to decorate for the next night's expected trick-or-treaters. "We're gonna do a big candy giveaway early in the evening," he said. "We'll close Station 2 and let Central handle our calls for a couple of hours. I can't *wait.*" He sounded as excited as a little boy.

Laughing, Linzy said, "I can only imagine what happens at Christmas time."

"Oh," Blue replied, "that'll be the toy drive. It's going to be *epic.*"

It made Linz feel proud to think he was something of a superman, out there helping people when the calls came in, but still just as sweet as the boy she'd always known.

She hung up, opened her most recent novel, and read until she began to drift away. The sound of her ringtone dragged her right back out of her slumber.

Fumbling around on the nightstand, knocking her paperback to the floor, Linzy finally got the phone close enough to her face to see who was calling.

She pressed the green answer icon. "Cam?"

Her brother-in-law's boozy voice cut through her confusion like a buzz saw. "Hey, Lizny. Come ge' yer sister. Shees ou'side on the deck, waiting."

Linzy tumbled out of bed, panic sending her scrambling for keys and shoes. "Cam? Is that you? What the hell?"

He chuckled and clicked off.

Still holding the phone, feeling like an idiot, Linzy immediately touched Sash's picture in her phone favorites.

The call rang and rang and then went to voice mail. Is this some kind of Halloween prank? She left a brief message. "Call me, Sissy. This is not funny." Then she clicked off and tapped Cam's picture.

His phone also rang and rang, then went to voice mail.

She pulled a jacket on over her fleece pajamas, grabbed a clip for her bedhead hair, and called him again. "C'mon, Cam, answer the phone." She snatched up her purse and made her way through the kitchen to the garage, dialing again as she went.

Still no answer. She continued straight out the connecting door and slid behind the wheel of the Buick. Hitting the automatic door opener, she buckled her seatbelt, then backed out and pressed the *close* button on the garage remote. It was dark as a cave outside. Clouds dimmed the stars and moon.

At least there won't be much traffic, she thought. Should I call the cops? Get them to go out and see what's going on? Find out why no one is answering their phone?

Everything had been going so well. What could have happened? She'd never known Cam to drink, but then what did she really know about him? He'd certainly sounded drunk.

She thought of calling Blue, but he was on shift, and he would probably turn around and call his folks right down the road. She didn't want him to do that until she knew what was happening. If it was some kind of stupid prank, she didn't want to disturb the Ash family. They had done so much for them over the years, she hated to add another worry to the list. I'll be there in less than thirty minutes, she told herself. Everything will be okay. I can always call them then, if needed.

As she drove around the circle to the big gate, Linzy couldn't help noticing the soft autumn ground mist swirling along the edges of the drive, wafting away into the orchard and beyond. Perfect pre-Halloween setting, she thought. Eerie and still.

She pressed the accelerator a little harder and bumped over the cattle guard, twisting the wheel roughly to make the sharp turn out of the driveway onto Wisteria Way. Linzy couldn't take her eye off the rearview mirror as the long L-shaped ranch house grew smaller and smaller behind her. She'd left the kitchen light on as she made her way through the house to the garage, but the glow was barely visible through the encroaching mist. It clutched at her heart.

Their childhood home, hers and Sasha's. They had been through so much, surely God wouldn't let anything else go wrong. That thought jarred her. Why wouldn't he? What made them so special? Bad stuff happens to good people all the time.

She grabbed her phone out of the cup holder and dialed 9-1-1 asking the operator to direct her call to the Galveston County Sheriff's Office for a welfare check on her sister and baby.

"I know it isn't frigid outside," she told the Galveston County dispatcher when the transfer went through, "but it is cold. And the wind always blows at the beach. I don't know why she would choose to wait for me outside. Unless she is afraid to be inside." She took a moment to control her emotions. "It makes no sense. And now, neither of them will answer their phones."

"That's fine, ma'am," the dispatcher said after getting the address. "Better safe than sorry. We're sending a unit out to check. Have they had marital problems before?"

Linzy steeled her voice, trying not to let it crack. "Not to my knowledge. And I've never heard of him drinking, either." She paused. "But he sounded as drunk as a skunk when he told me to come and get her."

"Yes, ma'am. I understand. We'll see what's going on and I'll call you back at this number."

"Thank you," Linzy replied, relief settling around her. "I'm on my way from Brookville," she said. "I'll be there soon."

"Don't speed," the dispatcher replied. "I have deputies on the way."

The trip went fast but slow. There were few cars on the road but trying to keep her anxiety in check made time seem to stand still. After a few minutes, Linzy covered the clock with one of the pink, sticky notes she kept in the center console.

Her mind drifted to the last time she'd visited her sister while Cam and Blue were at work. Sash had seemed so happy. On one hand, she had been thinking about going back to the real estate office after maternity leave was over, while on the other hand, she'd been having second thoughts about going back at all.

She'd confessed to Linzy that she simply adored being at home with her baby. "I feel like we live in paradise," she said. "And I only want to stay home, walk the beach, take care of Cam and the baby, and make art. Do you think that's ridiculous?" She'd turned her head in a newly acquired questioning manner. Linzy felt the mannerism might be a direct result of carrying little Skye around in one arm all the time.

"Of course not," Linzy said. "I can hardly believe it myself. I'm just thrilled you've found your soulmate." She recalled how they'd laughed at that. "As for paradise?" she said. "Yeah, I think it might be. Especially now that you've got that new stroller."

Sasha's smile had lit up the whole room when Linzy agreed she did indeed live in paradise.

And now this, Linzy thought. What could have gone wrong? Did I miss something, one of those red flags?

She could almost imagine some reporter sticking a microphone in her face, asking how she felt about what had happened, looking for a sound bite for the evening news. "They'd seemed so happy," Linzy imagined herself saying.

A lump formed in her throat, and she swallowed, hard, and turned up Tom Petty. *Freefallin'* came on. It had been one of their dad's—and consequently hers and Sash's—favorite songs.

It felt like a sign. Oh, no, Linzy thought, listening to the words about a bad boy who didn't even miss the girl he'd left behind. Is Sash sending me a message? Why do I always look for signs? And why are they so hard to accept when I find one? After the dark cloud that woke Sash just in time to save the two of us at the house that night, it seems I would be inclined to believe in signs. Maybe if it had awakened her in time to save all of us, it would be a lot easier to believe.

She reached down and touched the dash screen for a different Sirius station. E-Street Radio. The Boss and all his minions. There ya go. Safety. *Cadillac Ranch.* Rock out. Linzy opened the window. She was getting close. She could feel the Gulf air in her sinuses. Taste it on her tongue.

Where are you, Sash? Give me a sign like when we were little and tried to guess which card the other was holding up behind the Science Fair posterboard in our rooms.

Linzy didn't realize she was crying until she tasted salt in the corners of her lips and realized it wasn't from the Gulf air after all.

The Tom Petty song kept reverberating through her skull even though she'd changed the station. And on the tail of it, the thought that some regrets are easy, like not hanging on to her mom's old CD radio, the one that had played everything from Elton John to George Jones in the big laundry room. That was a small regret. It had seemed a thing she would never use, and so she'd let it go in the estate sale, but now Linzy found herself longing for it.

She still had the CDs, and others by Heart, Tom Petty, and even Willie Nelson and Charley Pride. More of her mom's and dad's old favorites. Why did I let it all go? It didn't take up much space; it could've continued to sit right there on the laundry room counter the way it had for years. Why on earth did I keep the CDs and not the player?

Grief, her sister had said, comforting her. We were sick with grief and didn't know what we were doing.

That was a simple explanation and now a simple regret.

Others were much worse. Like the one her sister carried with her about not being able to save them.

Linzy smashed the radio icon over to Sirius XM Hits and rolled down another window to blow away the blues, the regrets, the past, all of it. But it didn't work. Not completely. Post Malone came on singing about how he had some help making a mess of his life.

She sang along for a minute, but then her voice morphed into prayer the way it often did. God, please help me contact my sister. She's not answering, but her phone shows to be at home. I pray she's asleep in her bed, unaware of what her husband is up to. I wish I could track his phone, but we aren't that close. We don't keep up with each other's whereabouts the way Sash and I always do. Maybe he is out at a bar entertaining a client. Can I get there before he does? What did he mean, she's outside, waiting?

And why, oh *why*, doesn't she answer?

Her mind spiraled around and around these questions, so Linzy turned the radio down to background noise and began a litany of prayers for Sasha and little Skye, prayers for everything to be all right, prayers for this whole thing to be nothing more than a big misunderstanding. Prayers that it's simply some stupid, twisted joke. Anything except the horrific feelings creeping over her like cold mist.

. . .

At last, Linzy entered the causeway to the island. Her phone jangled and she touched the dash screen to answer. "Hello?"

"This is the Galveston County Sheriff's office. You asked for a welfare check on your sister?"

Linzy's heart raced. "Yes, that's me—"

"We have her," the dispatcher said. "The deputy is sitting with her now. She and the baby are both fine. Are you enroute?"

"Yes," Linzy breathed. "Thank you, I'm turning onto Seawall Boulevard right now." Within minutes, she came to the entry gate into Sunset Drift. It was already open.

She drove into the exclusive oceanfront community surprised to see that all six of the homes had twinkling, outdoor lights.

Linzy didn't know what she expected, police cars, flashing lights, news cameras. There was none of that. When she pulled into the driveway at Sash and Cam's home, she saw a Galveston County squad car parked beside the street. A female deputy sat in the driver's seat, and she could see the silhouette of someone in the backseat as well.

Linzy slammed the Buick into park, jumped out, and rushed over to the patrol car. Everything was quiet except for occasional bits of conversation from the officer's in-dash radio.

"I'm Linzy," she said as the deputy stepped out of the car. "Linzy Everly. I'm Sasha's sister. I'm the one who called for the welfare check."

The deputy nodded and opened the rear door. Sash looked up at her with a wounded expression.

Linzy crawled in beside her and enveloped her and the baby in a massive hug. Sasha's eyes were as large as the moon. It was obvious she'd been crying.

"We looked through the bedroom window from the side deck," the deputy said, "and we can see Mr. Gaines passed out on the bed." She glanced toward the house. "But we can't get inside without breaking the lock or window."

"So, Sasha and the baby are locked out," Linzy said. "I'm so thankful y'all got here quickly." She visually inspected the sleeping infant in her mother's arms. "Is Skye all right?" she asked.

Sasha nodded. "I was able to breastfeed her. Otherwise, I don't know what might've happened." Her voice grew faint. "Thank you for calling the Sheriff's Office. I didn't know what to do without my phone or my car keys." Her voice trembled. "I couldn't make the code work at all. The door panel was dark, as if he turned it off inside. Why would he do that? I banged and banged, but he wouldn't come."

She dropped her head, as if ashamed for causing trouble. "I tried the house next door, but no one answered. I was about to start walking on to the next one, further down, but the wind kicked up, and I was shivering in my night gown, and poor Skye, not even a baby blanket." She gazed down at the infant's face. "I finally remembered the beach towels in the big trunk under the deck. I knew we could wrap up in those. At least be out of the wind."

Linzy stroked her sister's blonde hair remembering their silly conversation about wearing a milk cow costume to the office for Halloween. "You did just right, Sissy. Just right. Did y'all have a fight, or something?"

Linzy noticed movement up on the deck and observed a second officer standing there, looking out to sea.

"He came home drunk," Sasha said. "I've never seen him that way. He was so loud. Yelling and cursing, falling over things." She shivered as she retold the events. "He kept shaking his head, like he was dizzy. Then he grabbed my arm, and I told him to leave me alone."

She began to sob.

"Shh, it's okay," Linzy said, stroking her arm this time. "I'm here, now, Sis. Everything's going to be fine."

Sasha gulped, wiped her nose with what appeared to be a fast-food napkin, and said, "He told me he'd leave me alone alright."

She began to cry again. "And then he pushed us right out the door onto the deck." Her voice disintegrated completely.

Linzy felt her blood pressure rise. "That low-life, piece-of—"

Sasha shook her head, laid a palm on her sister's hand. "He was just drunk, that's all. He wasn't my Cam at all. I don't think he even knew what he was doing."

Glancing at the deputy's face, Linzy whispered, "He called me on the phone, Sis. He told me you were outside waiting for me. He must've known what he was doing." She tried to relax her facial muscles. "This is not how it's supposed to be. He put both of you outside in the middle of the night. There's no excuse for that."

The female deputy, O. Pollard according to the nametag on her uniform, closed her clipboard. "We think it would be best if you took your sister and the baby home with you tonight, Ms. Everly. Give Mr. Gaines time to sober up and cool off. After that, we suggest family counseling or mediation. Maybe some AA meetings if need be."

Linzy nodded. "I'm onboard with all of that. C'mon, Sash, let's get while the gettin's good." Their dad's old saying fell flat. "You know what I mean." Linzy wished she hadn't said it at all.

Sash craned her neck to look up at her tall, stilted, two-story home. "But we have no diapers or anything."

"Walmart is open all night," Linzy said. "They'll have anything we need. Let's go."

Sasha reluctantly allowed her sister to take the baby. "What about a car seat?"

Deputy O. Pollard looked at her partner, Deputy F. Ramirez, who had quietly walked up to the car. "I think I can open that front door without damaging it too badly." She shrugged. "They gotta have the baby's car seat."

F. Ramirez said, "Get it. The creep has slept long enough."

Linzy thought that last part was supposed to be on the down-low, but she heard it. They probably knew Cam was big in the real estate business on the island, but it obviously garnered him little respect in this instance.

In two minutes, they were inside the house with minimal damage to the door frame. Deputy Pollard had used her tire iron to force the lock, and since Cam hadn't set the alarm, he never even woke.

"He looks dead," Linzy said as they followed the deputies inside.

Deputy Ramirez leaned over, felt the pulse in Cam's neck, and rolled her eyes. "Not dead. Just dead drunk." She looked at Sasha. "Do you want to file assault charges?"

Sprawled across their king size bed in his sport coat, Cam let out an ugly snore. His Stetson was on the bed, something no self-respecting cowboy ever did—just an invitation to bad luck—and he hadn't even removed his boots.

"Oh, no," she said. "He didn't hit me or assault me. I don't think he even meant to lock us out." She glanced through the doorway to where he slept on, oblivious to everything. "He was just so drunk he didn't realize what he was doing." She hurried through the kitchen to the garage so she could retrieve the baby's car seat from the Cadillac.

Officer F. Ramirez assisted her, then fastened it into the old Buick. "I've got a couple little ones, myself," he said. "Getting these out and put into another vehicle can be a real booger. If you want it done right, that is."

Sash thanked him profusely and went back inside to pack the baby's diaper bag with clean clothes and other necessities. In the bathroom, she grabbed a small hamper of dirty clothes. "I'm not going into the closet," she murmured, rushing. "That might wake him. I'll just grab my clothes out of here and put them on. Wash the rest at your house. "

Linzy tried to help, but thinking about how her sister had said, 'He was just so drunk?' upset her greatly. Do you hear how that sounds, Sissy, she thought. I mean, how much worse does it have to get before he's no longer 'just drunk'? If the baby gets sick because of this little incident, will that be bad enough? She shook her head. No use bringing it up right now …

The deputies left a note on the table detailing why the front door was damaged and where they'd sent his wife and child. Then they closed up the house and escorted Sash and Linzy out to the Buick.

"Drive safe, ladies," Deputy Ramirez said, helping Sash put the baby into the car seat.

"Thank you," she said. "Both of you." She allowed her gaze to take in both deputies.

Deputy Ramirez waited as she slipped into the shotgun seat, then he closed her door and patted the top of the car to let Linzy know they were ready to go.

Linzy had a sudden vision of Cam stumbling down the steps, bloodshot eyes wild, sport coat flapping in the breeze, yelling, "Where you going with my baby?"

But it didn't happen. As far as Linzy knew, he was still passed out on the bed, oblivious.

All the way back to Wisteria Way, Linzy thought about Sash and the baby huddled up beneath the deck in a chair. How could Cam be so cruel? And how had he kept that side of himself so well hidden? Talk about Jekyll and Hyde. She made a mental note to ask Sasha if there had been any other signs of alcohol abuse.

She glanced at the passenger seat.

Her sister appeared to be dozing, exhausted, head tilted over against the side window, eyes closed. Baby Skye slept peacefully in her familiar rear-facing seat behind them.

Linzy thanked God all the way home. For answered prayers and for the fact that she worked from home. I'll catch up on sleep later, find out what those power naps are all about. As she drove, she tried hard to make herself relax, but her thoughts kept replaying every detail. Her sister had apologized over and over about Linzy having to come to her aid in the middle of the night.

"Don't be ridiculous," Linzy assured her. "I'm always here for you—day or night—just the way you've always been there for me."

Now, her eyes scanned the blue-black roadside. Wild grasses glowed when her headlights picked them out of the darkness. Quite a bit of traffic going to and from the island now. Guess some folks go to work early. At least it isn't deserted. That would have made things worse, somehow.

It will be okay, she told herself. We will work it out.

We always do.

21

WHAT NOW?

Cam awoke after daylight, neck stiff, bladder full. But his head felt clear. Well, clearer, anyway. Clear enough to be disgusted at the fact he was still in his clothes and boots. And what was his hat doing on the bed? *I know I didn't drink that much last night.*

He recalled how muddled his thinking had been when he left The Joker's Wild. He didn't owe Pug a darn thing. He'd drained his savings account playing poker at Pug's tables over the past couple of years. Spent almost everything he had in checking on Sash the past few months. Then two of his big sales had fallen through, buyers backing out at the last second, so last night's card game was just an attempt to make some of his cash back before Sash found out how broke they really were.

Suddenly, he remembered having trouble with the keypad last night. Jiggling with that thing, he'd lost his temper. He vaguely recalled jamming his thumb against the keypad in anger once he'd gained entry. Then he'd turned and tripped over the broom.

Groaning, Cam made his way to the bathroom and then to the kitchen. He needed coffee, and lots of it. He remembered Sasha scolding him for being too loud, so he wasn't surprised there was no coffee made. Instead, what he found was a note on the table from the Galveston County Sheriff's Department.

Head pounding, eyes glued half shut, the stink of cigarette smoke in the clothes he still wore, Cam read the note, then read it again before stumbling through the house from room to room, searching everywhere for Sash and the baby.

Finding the house empty, he collapsed into a dining room chair and tried to recall exactly what had occurred after he arrived home. *I remember getting drowsier and drowsier as I drove home. Then I tripped over the broom, and Sash was there with a look of thunder in her face, but her voice was sweet and shocked and then we—and then I—yelled and pushed them out. Oh, my God. I pushed them out. Into the night. Into the cold.*

Forcing himself to his feet, Cam crossed the living room to the front doors and flung them open. The deck was empty. He shaded his eyes with one hand, gazing into the distance. The waves were the only movement on the beach. No Sasha, no stroller, no baby Skye.

He closed the doors, went to the garage. Sash's Caddy sat right there next to his Lincoln. Cam closed that door and went back to the dining table. He picked up the note and read it again.

"Your wife and child are with her sister. You were drunk and locked them out, but she didn't press charges." It was signed Deputy O. Pollard.

Cam dropped his head into his hands and wept.

When the pity-party was over, he went to the bathroom and turned on the shower. I know I only had one or two beers. Why does it feel like I've been on a three-day bender?

He stripped out of his wrinkled clothes and stepped into the warm flow of the water. As he soaped and rinsed, he did his best to remember everything.

. . .

After his shower, while the coffee brewed, Cam toweled his hair and took up his phone to formulate a text. "Dear, sweet Sash," it began. "Let me start by saying I'm *so* sorry for pushing you and the baby out into the cold. Please tell me what I can do to make this right. You know I love you and Skye. I was out of my mind to do what I did. Literally, I think I was out of my mind somehow. I had one or two beers. I *wasn't* drunk. I had only been to a card game." He hit enter on the lengthy message and then started another one.

"I can't understand what happened, but I will make it up to you and the baby. Just give me the chance." He sent that last part with a red heart emoji, then began a third message.

"I want you to know I'm going to talk to someone about the way I acted. I'll do anything to get my girls back home. It will never, ever, ever happen again. I promise."

Okay, he thought, pouring his first cup of dark roast. The ball is in her court. He laid his phone down, then thought of one more thing.

"I'm going to head your way in a few minutes unless you say otherwise. You don't have to come home today, but I need to see you. I can't stand being away from you and Skye."

He laid the phone down a second time and sipped the hot coffee. I hope that was right, giving her a heads-up that way. She hates to be caught unaware … but she also might bolt if she knows I'm coming. He sometimes forgot her and her sister's history. They were suspicious by nature, especially Linzy. Maybe I shouldn't have tipped my hand. Bluffing was never my strong suit. That thought reminded him of the disastrous games at The Joker's Wild.

Little by little, all the memories of the previous night filtered into his thinking. He couldn't believe he'd even tried to win back his losings that way. Desperation, he thought. Nothing but desperation. The idea of losing two fantastic sales in a row, coupled with his own crazy gambling losses over the previous two years, plus his recent spending … it just sent me over the edge, that's all.

Pouring another coffee into his insulated mug, Cam continued to second guess himself. Maybe I should stop and get some flowers or candy, those chocolate things she loves so much. Or is that over the top? I've already showed my hand through the texts. And our bank account is in the hole. No wonder I never win. *Dumbass.*

He finished dressing and was out the door before he could lose his nerve.

The predawn traffic was scant. It would pick up later in the day, when families made their way to the beach with toddlers and teens in tow. Even in winter, Galveston Island was a magnet for shore lovers.

When he was nearly out of town, Cam's belly began to growl with hunger. That's when he realized it was really too early to visit Wisteria Way. He sipped his coffee and wished he'd taken the time to grab a bite of something before he left the house.

He couldn't remember the last time he'd had an actual meal. He'd skipped lunch yesterday to show one of the properties that had fallen through. Not wise, skipping meals, he thought, his growling gut reminding him of the feel of the ulcer that had plagued him since his teen years. Skipping meals and drinking beer were not part of his doctor's orders.

"You've got to stop drinking and start eating right," the doc had said years ago. "Take these antibiotics to start the healing, then continue with the omeprazole acid blocker. And limit your intake of spicy food, alcohol, and caffeine, especially three hours before bedtime. Let your stomach heal, for crying out loud. This ulcer will land you in the hospital next time."

That had been back before his real estate business began to show a profit. Now, Cam shook an antacid into his mouth from the bottle he kept in the car's console. Seems I've come full circle, he thought.

He wasn't really that stupid. He knew why he always turned to the bars when things felt heavy. It was just like that old Springsteen song, one step up, and two steps back. Every time he tried to move forward, he forced himself back. Self-defeating, his brother, Brandon, always said. Just another thing they'd inherited from their old man.

Crunching the antacid on his tongue, Cam spied the Galveston Waffle House and whirled the Lincoln into the parking lot. He knew he would feel better after a bite to eat. He opened his wallet, peered inside. Two twenties and one last credit card not maxed out. I have to get it together. Work harder. Make a plan, stick to it. I've made more than one fortune; I can do it again.

He stepped out of the car into the fresh, salt air. The diner was already half full. Choosing a booth beside the east window, Cam ordered bacon, eggs over easy, and Texas toast. A side of home fries and another hot coffee completed his order.

He settled back into the padded vinyl seat and listened to the kitchen chatter while watching the sunrise through the plate glass. The humidity from the steamy kitchen made the windows run with condensation. It created an artsy watercolor effect on the coming sunrise. His heart ached to share it with Sasha. She would love that. She should be here.

Once again, he allowed himself to feel the self-hatred welling up from his gut. *How could I do that to the two people I love more than anything in the world? What is wrong with me? Am I a monster?*

The waitress set his plate down on the table and swished away.

Cam took up his fork and dug into the eggs, bit off a mouthful of crispy bacon and swallowed the bite with a gulp of just-right coffee.

The whole mess congealed in the back of his throat. Water sprang to his eyes, either from choking or from the taste of reality, and he stood, threw down a twenty, and rushed out the door to the parking lot. He was proud of himself for not gagging it up into his plate.

In the Lincoln, he spat the sorry wad into a clutch of fast-food napkins, then sat for a few minutes, gathering his composure. His phone dinged. It was a reply to his text asking Sasha if he could come and see her.

"Come on," the message read. But it didn't end with a heart or a happy face.

His anxiety ratcheted up a notch. His belly roiled.

Cautiously, he backed out of the parking spot and entered the roadway. The drive from Galveston to Brookville took less than thirty minutes. He kept the cruise control set and passed other motorists with ease. Wisteria Way was just the other side of the small community.

Before he knew it, Cam was slowing to make the turn onto Pecan Street. Soon, it would intersect with Wisteria Way.

In the near distance, the ranch house nestled into its neat little pocket of pecan trees and early morning mist. The Lincoln eased over the cattle guard and through the bare bones arch of wisteria. He hoped the curt message meant Sasha wanted to see him. He was pretty sure Linzy would not.

22

REUNITED

Linzy stepped out of her car under the carport and waited as Cam's Lincoln crossed the cattle guard. He must not have noticed her. She had just returned from the Ash's house down the road. She tried to keep her expression from betraying her shock at seeing him. Linzy secretly hoped they'd gotten rid of him for good. The fact that he'd shoved her little sister outside while she was holding the baby made him persona non grata in her book.

The Lincoln continued slowly up the circle drive to the house.

Linzy leaned into her car, pulling out a reusable bag full of vegetables from the Ash Family Farm.

Coasting to a stop, Cam appeared to notice her at last.

He exited the Lincoln hesitantly. "Linzy, how are you? I didn't see you there." He waited for a reply, when none came, he continued. "How are my two girls?"

He seemed to be trying to make his statements light, as if the incident had been blown out of proportion. But to Linzy, there was no lightness in what had happened.

"I can't believe you have the nerve to show up here," she said. "As far as I'm concerned, you aren't wel—"

"I've been texting with him, Sissy," Sasha said from the

doorway. "He's made his apologies, and I told him he could come."

Linzy was surprised at the way she stood up for him. She clenched her teeth and marched into the house to put her produce away. Sasha held the door open for her sister, but then she stepped out to speak with Cam in private.

In the kitchen, Linzy unpacked the veggies and stored them in their proper places. It was all she could do not to rush out and drag her sister back in the house. With every onion and every bunch of radishes, she muttered to herself, "Let Sash handle it. Let Sash make her own decisions."

She listened to herself right up until the moment the two of them came back inside. Then she could stand it no more.

Sasha had a forgiving heart. Linzy, not so much. Even though she heard her sister telling him that if he ever hoped to be a family again, he would never take another drink, she thought he was getting off too easy. It never should have happened in the first place.

"It's too soon," she said, striding into the living room. "You both need time to regroup, make certain your issues have been resolved." She looked straight at Cam. "Words are easy to say," she seemed to dare him to contradict her. "The truth is you both need distance and perspective." She set her jaw. "And maybe professional help."

Her eyes flicked toward her sister. "Sasha has a huge, forgiving, heart. But I judge people on actions, not words. Ancho taught me that. Besides, Sasha shouldn't have to save an adult … she needs an *adult* to help her raise this precious baby." She stood with both hands clenched. "If you're not up to that task, let me assure you, I am."

To Linzy's surprise, she saw no anger in Cam. "I deserve that," he said.

"Then you'll understand when I say that I think Sash and Skye should stay here." She looked straight at her sister. "He forced you and the baby out in the cold without a second thought."

"Sissy," Sasha said. "I think he—"

"Yeah, yeah," Linzy interrupted, waving one hand. "I know you think he's sorry and it will never happen again, but Sash, it should not have happened at all." She cut her eyes toward him. "Alcohol is no excuse for hurting the ones who love you. In fact, alcohol sometimes brings out a person's true nature."

Cam didn't look away. He held her gaze. Linzy was still amazed by his lack of animosity.

"I'm going home now," he said to Sasha. "*Our home*. I know I screwed up, and I'm sorry. I only had two beers. I really don't know what happened, but you have my solemn promise it will never happen again. Linz is right. I must need professional help. I'm going to go to AA and start from there." He waited for their response. None came. "It just doesn't make sense, the way I felt. And acted. Nothing like that has ever happened before."

The baby fussed from the porta-crib Linzy had bought and Sash went to the bedroom to retrieve her. She could hear Sasha soothing Skye before bringing her to the living room.

Cam reached into the swaddling blanket and touched his baby girl's face. Linzy saw Sasha hold her breath, but she pretended not to notice. He placed a tender kiss on Skye's forehead. "Hope you come home soon, little one," he whispered. Then he turned and strode outside without a backward glance.

Linzy thought she saw a glint of moisture in his eye as he turned. She and Sasha watched from the window as he slid behind the wheel of the Lincoln, folding his long, jeans-clad legs into the space with ease. "He's leaving it up to me," Sasha said.

"You need to stay here awhile," Linzy replied. "I wasn't kidding about that. Get some perspective on what really happened. How serious it could have been."

He might not be begging her to come home, but he was

reminding his wife of what she was missing, and Linzy knew it had worked. She could see the hope on her little sister's face.

They didn't speak as they watched the brake lights of the Lincoln blink and then disappear when Cam made the turn off of Wisteria back onto Pecan.

~

The next day, Cam went to work with a renewed sense of purpose. He didn't sell any mega-million-dollar properties that day to recoup his recent spending spree and previous losses, but he did manage to generate a showing for a mansion on a bluff.

And that was a start.

He stayed busy, only checking his phone about twenty million times to see if he'd missed a call or a text from Sasha. When quitting time came around and still no word, he began to get worried.

His phone dinged when he was nearly to the Sunset Drift turn. He reached over and touched the answer symbol on his dashboard screen. Sasha's picture appeared.

"Hey, there," he said, going for casual, working to slow the gallop of his heart.

"I miss you," she said, voice soft. "I miss our home. The life I thought we had."

Her words cut into him. "I'm coming to get you. Right now. I just left the office so it will be a few minutes."

She said something he didn't catch.

"What was that?" He waited. "I couldn't hear you, sweetie …"

"I said, I don't know how to tell my sister. She thinks we should be done. Over. That I should stay here." A beat of silence, then, "I don't want Linzy to think I'm a pushover. A *victim*."

That hurt. The word victim gutted him. Her the victim, him the abuser.

He knew he deserved it. She *was* the innocent party. Hadn't done a thing except ask him not to wake the baby, ask him if he was drunk. All the rest of it was on him. Every bit of it.

"It's going to be all right," he said. "We belong together. We're family."

She stunned him when she said, "Maybe we should wait one more day. Just until tomorrow. By then I'll have found a way to break it to Linz."

Cam felt his blood pressure rise. He twisted his head to the side, a sudden kink grabbing at the muscles in his neck. "Alrighty, then." He bit his tongue to keep from telling her that Linzy could go screw herself. That wouldn't do anyone any good. It would only make matters worse. That was something his father would have done. Not him. It wasn't in him. *Right?*

Somehow, he managed to keep his voice calm. "I'll be waiting," he said. "I've got a big house to show tomorrow—the one on the bluff at Narrow Point—but I'll be free after that." He paused. "Or I could head to Wisteria right now."

He imagined he could hear her thought-wheels turning even over the phone. Finally, she said, "You know I'd like it if you came to get us right now, but I owe Sissy. And she's going to take some persuading. She was really upset that you locked us out and turned off the alarm so I couldn't use the code to get back in."

Cam suspected she'd sneaked in that part about him locking the door because she still needed more reassurance. "Yeah," he said. "I need to tell you about that. First of all, I had two beers and that's all. I don't know how I could've been drunk, but I was so dizzy I could barely stand. It happened at the Joker's Wild Club where I used to play cards, before I met you." He swallowed, hard, then continued. "I know I shouldn't have done it, but I thought I could make some cash at the card table. Cash to pay off some debts I accumulated way before we got married. It's a long story, sweetie, and I promise I'll tell you all of it when you get home. Just not over the phone, it's too complicated." He took a quick breath so she couldn't cut him off.

"And here's the thing I really needed to tell you, I didn't turn off the alarm on purpose. I just smashed it with my thumb when I had trouble making the code work. I didn't mean to disable it. Not at all."

He sucked in his pride, suddenly aware of how lame it all sounded. "But I will tell you this. I will never forgive myself for doing that to you. I thank God I somehow had enough sense to call Linzy—"

"I'm not fishing for another apology," Sasha interrupted. "I'm just saying I owe my sister. She came to get me and Skye in the middle of the night. She'd never hurt me." The phone made a funny noise, and he thought she'd probably taken him off speaker before saying what she really wanted to say. "You know, locking us out wasn't just cruel—"

Here it comes.

"—it was dangerous. What if Linz hadn't been at home? What if she hadn't answered the phone for some reason—"

"Then I would have come out and got you," he said. "Brought you back inside." He reached down and turned up the volume. Her voice through the dashboard speakers had grown fainter and fainter as they spoke.

"See," she whispered. "That's the part you still don't seem to understand ... you were willing to leave your baby daughter out in the chill night air just hoping my sister would come and get us. You were passed out cold when the deputies broke into our house to get the car seat. You never even knew they were there. And why did you do it? To punish me for asking you to be quiet?"

He started to speak but hesitated. Aside from Linzy, no one had ever been so blunt with him. In his family, secrets had been the norm. He was rendered completely speechless. She had laid it all out for him to explain.

"Passive-aggressive," she said, filling the conversation gap.

"Pretty sure that's what my counselor would call it. You not only wanted to use the excuse of your drunkenness to punish me, but you wanted to punish the ones I love too. Baby Skye and Linzy. You got us all in one fell swoop."

Her voice had begun to tremble as she spoke. He knew she needed to get it out, but if he allowed her to keep talking, she might talk herself out of *ever* coming home.

He cleared his throat, swallowed his pride one more time, and let the emotion flow. "I'm so sorry, honey. You're right. Hell, I need a counselor, or better yet, a psychiatrist. To hear it said like that, the way you just did, makes me sound like an absolute monster. I don't blame you for not wanting to come home. I don't deserve you—or the baby."

Silence for what seemed like an eternity, then she said, "Are you really going to go to AA?"

"Yes. I may be a lot of things, but I'm not a liar." He cracked open the window to feel a burst of fresh air on his face. Stress had been his lifelong companion. Sometimes, it seemed near impossible to shake. Maybe AA would help with that, too.

"Cam?"

Something in her voice chilled him. "Yes?"

"You were completely unconscious when the sheriff's deputies came to the house." She paused. "I don't know how long you would have been asleep before you let us back inside … probably all night long."

He didn't think he could feel any smaller, but he was wrong. She had already mentioned that once, because it was such an awful thing. And he had no idea how to explain it or make it better. But he had to try. "I'm so sorr—"

"What will prevent that from happening again?" Her voice sped up. "Because I will never go through something like that again. Not ever."

Cam drew in a deep breath. "I promise, Sash, it won't ever happen again. I swear on my mother's grave. I will never take another drink of alcohol for as long as I live. Not even beer. You have my word." But in the back of his mind, he knew it wasn't the beer that had made him drunk. In fact, that was something he couldn't explain. Do I have a brain tumor? Would that explain it? I'll call a doctor, hell, I'll go to the Emergency Room if Sasha thinks I should.

Sasha sighed. "That's what I needed to hear. You don't know how close I came to taking that metal patio table and heaving it through the big window just to get back inside." She hesitated. "But to be honest, I was afraid it would anger you further. And I didn't know what you might do." She stopped talking, maybe to let the full weight of those words sink in.

And sink in, they did. Cam couldn't help himself. His voice caught in his throat, and he began to sob. Knowing his sweet Sash, the best thing that had ever happened to him, the mother of his precious child, was now afraid of him, it broke his heart.

Sasha's voice came through the speaker, soft, but resolute. "I'll text you later. After I've spoken to Linzy."

"I'll be waiting," he finally managed to say. He wanted to apologize again, but he remembered how he and his brother used to play a game where each would say a tongue twister so fast and so repetitively that it would cease to have meaning. Just a stupid game, he thought. But probably the same principle applies to apologies and I love yous. If you say them too much, too often, maybe the words begin to lose their shape.

23

GOING BACK

Sasha disconnected from her husband and raised her eyes to the view that had changed so little since her childhood days. Through the front door glass, she could see all the way to the end of the curved driveway where the slender, leafless branches framed the gate.

Since it was fall, and tomorrow was Halloween, the sun went to bed early, and the moon rose pale and white, brightening the cloudless night.

No clouds to cloud my view, she thought. Wish I could say the same for my thinking.

With a sigh, she turned away. Behind her, in the porta-crib, baby Skye fussed, wanting her dinner and her bath, not knowing ghouls and goblins would be ringing the doorbell about this time tomorrow, hoping for treats.

But that wasn't tonight. Tonight, she and the baby were both worn out and ready for a good night of calm before the cheerful storm.

Sasha was glad to be back home, but she longed for a reset button to turn back time. She couldn't understand how her amazing husband had flipped that way. Loving new father in the morning, mean cartoonish drunk that evening. Mean cartoonish drunk bordering on abuser, her subconscious whispered. Don't start whitewashing what happened, especially not to yourself. She dozed off with the memory of the cold night events in her head and an ache in her heart.

The next morning, she didn't wake until Skye began to stir. The baby had slept peacefully in the little porta-crib right next to her bed. Walmart, Sasha thought. Good old Wally World. And Linzy. She had brushed off Sasha's protests when she bought it that night by saying she'd planned to get one anyway. "I'll need it when I babysit, you know I'd been planning on getting one anyway." Then she had hugged Sasha and dried her tears, making the best of the tough situation.

Now, Sasha sat up and cooed at the sweet, innocent child. Her heart broke a little more, wondering if this would be the end of their brand-new little family. Is my husband a Jekyll and Hyde? Does he have some sort of split personality I knew nothing about?

Before she could follow those depressing thoughts down that depressing rabbit hole, Linzy surprised her by calling out, "Hey-y-y, do I hear my favorite girlies in here?" She opened the door a few inches and stuck one hand into the gap. A gift bag dangled from her fingers.

"What's this?" Sash asked. "It's not my birthday and we've never done gifts on Halloween, have we?"

Linzy shook her head, an odd look on her face. "Cam dropped this off a while ago. He said not to wake you, but when he got back home yesterday, he saw it on your sewing table. He said he knew you'd worked hard on making it, so you should have it for Skye's first Halloween."

Sasha put her hand in the gift bag and pulled out the tiny pumpkin outfit she'd made, along with the little felt hat. Tears welled up in her eyes. "He was here but didn't ask to see me or the baby?"

"No, he said he told you he would wait on you to call him, but he couldn't let all your work on Skye's little outfit go to waste." She reached out and stroked the soft orange felt. "He said to please send him a picture or video of her wearing it tonight when the trick-or-treaters come."

"Her first Halloween," Sasha murmured. "This isn't how I thought it would be." She thought of calling or texting him right then, to say thank you for bringing it, and to tell him to come back and celebrate the fun holiday with them tonight … but something stopped her. Some nagging little worry that he might be manipulating her. Knowing how she would respond to the kindness, how she would *likely* react.

Sasha rose from the bed and dismissed any more thought of calling her husband. She told Linzy she couldn't wait until the kiddos came around in the evening. "Will you be riding on the hayride with them?"

Linzy paused in the doorway. "Not this year," she said. "I thought I would just answer the door when Blue's mom and dad bring them around. Blue will be getting off work too late to drive this year. But the other volunteers have it covered." She ducked into the guest room and came back with a box full of small treat bags shaped like ghosts. "I bought these a few days ago. I hope you'll help me fill them with candy and some tiny treats."

Sash grinned. "Of course. The kids will love them. Just like they'll love the lighted jack-o'-lanterns we still need to carve." Linzy had bought pumpkins at the farmers market just for this purpose.

"Skye will love all this when she gets a little older," Linzy added.

"Yes, she will," Sasha agreed. "We'll make sure she enjoys everything, just like we did as kids." She hesitated, look of nostalgia crossing her face. "Do you remember the year Dad helped us make a spooky trail through the pecan grove and Blue dressed up like the headless horseman?"

"That was so much fun," Linzy said. "Especially when he rode his pony across the path holding that lighted jack-o'-lantern in the crook of his arm." She laughed, and Sasha laughed with her, but the sounds were a little bittersweet.

They both glanced at the baby as if to inject some good humor back into the day.

"Okay," Sasha said, "let's do this ..." She smiled at her sister. "First, breakfast and coffee, then carve the jacks, fill the treat bags, make it a *great* Halloween. She pushed the idea of calling Cam into the back of her mind and readied herself and Skye to start their day.

It *was* nice of Cam to drive all the way back out here to bring Skye's little outfit, she thought, but it certainly didn't mean all was forgiven. I'd like to go back to the way it was, she thought, pretend nothing happened, but that would be naïve. Things have changed, but maybe all is not lost.

She glanced at Skye's little face as she nursed. "It could have been so much worse," she murmured. Then she caressed the baby's soft cheek and forced herself to look forward, instead of backward. "It will be okay," she told Skye. "Mommy will never let anyone hurt you. And that's a promise."

After dressing the baby and then herself, she met Linzy in the kitchen where she was cleaning the pumpkins and gathering the carving utensils.

Together, they created the jack-o'-lanterns, roasted the seeds, made a pumpkin pie—something neither had ever done from scratch, they had to follow a video on YouTube—and then it was time to fill the treat bags, and get ready for the kids to arrive.

All in all, it was a very good day, and they enjoyed each other's company tremendously. If Sasha felt a slight pall hanging over the festivities, by the time the ghouls, ghosts, goblins, princesses, and superheroes had flung themselves off the hay wagon at dusk —pulled by Mr. Ash's old John Deere tractor—and rushed to the front door yelling "trick-or-treat, trick-or-treat," the two of them were more than ready.

With a spooky Halloween light glowing over the front porch, Linzy waited for the first knock. Sasha and Skye hung back, watching and videoing, ready to take it all in and maybe send it on to Cam.

When the first fist tapped the door, Linzy yanked it open and shouted "Boo!" In her old witch's hat and sparkly black eye mask, she was quite a sight.

The kids drew back when she cackled and raised her broom at them. But then she immediately smiled and hoisted the large bowl of treat bags with the other hand. Relieved laughs rang out as she offered the bowl to each child brave enough to step forward. When all dozen or so had taken a bag, they yelled "Happy Halloween," and scurried back toward the hay wagon.

Linzy let them get settled back onboard, and while they were busy digging into the little bags to see what goodies they'd scored, she crept out into the darkness and began to chant a spooky rhyme:

Witches high and witches low,
Watch your feet before you go,
She'll pull you down and whisper boo,
Then stir you in her witch's brew!

And then she ran the tip of her feathery broom across the kiddos' hanging legs and cackled again. Kids squealed and yanked their feet up beneath them. Someone yelled, "Go! Hurry! Before she gets us." But they all knew it was in good fun.

Linzy raised her broom at them again as the tractor chugged back toward the gate.

"Now back to the volunteer fire department spook house for some real scares," Sasha said, laughing, as Linzy came back to the door.

Eyes twinkling behind the sparkly mask, Linzy said, "Yes, I

got them primed for it." She pulled off her witch's hat. "What's Halloween without a little fright?"

"This has been the best one we've had in a while," Sash said. She wondered if Linzy had been trying extra hard to make it that way. They'd both been a little worried that the baby would be scared of all the front door activity, but it didn't seem to alarm her at all. Her eyes widened a bit when the kids yelled trick or treat and when her Aunt Linzy cackled, but that was it. She was in her mother's arms, warm in her tiny pumpkin outfit. Her world was safe. In fact, it was almost time for her nightly bath, and a bedtime story.

Such a good baby. Not yet sleeping through the night, but close. Sasha didn't mind. She relished the night feedings when it was just the two of them. As she bathed and changed her, she thought of how it would be if they were at home at the beach house. When she awoke in the night there, Sasha would carry her to the living room, the wall of windows bright with stars and moonlight and whispery with the sound of the waves *shush, shush, shushing* along the shoreline mere steps away.

Cam had gotten up with them once or twice in the beginning, but since she was nursing the baby, there had been nothing for him to do other than nod off again.

Now, the thought of the big middle-of-the-night window was a little painful. She missed it. Sasha remembered imagining the two of them like an old-world painting, child at her breast, moon lighting the tall glass, white foam lacing the waves to the shore ... a mother and child reunion as Paul Simon once sang.

A drowning bout of homesickness washed over her like one of those foamy waves. That's it, she thought. I need to go home. Linzy's feelings are important, but so are mine, and Cam's. He's not perfect, no one is. And he's given us such a beautiful home, everything I ever wanted. If he needs me to help straighten out the finances, I will do that. I can't give up on him. I won't give up on him. As long as he is serious about not drinking or gambling anymore … and about always being honest.

She carried the baby to the bedroom and got her phone from the nightstand. Without giving herself a moment to back out, she typed and sent a text to her husband. "What time can you be here tomorrow?" She added the video of Skye in her first Halloween costume.

The nerves started after she walked back to the living room and told Linzy. It was the look that did it. The look that said you're crazy, Sis. But she didn't argue. Linzy simply told her she could call if things didn't work out. "Call anytime," she said. "Day or night."

Then she said one more thing that made Sasha almost think twice. "Hide a car key somewhere outside, and always keep your phone charged and in your pocket." She swiped her bangs up with the back of her hand. "Maybe make a go bag. A little carry bag to hold your keys and some cash. Hide it in a safe place, outside."

Sasha opened her mouth to protest and Linzy held up her hand. "I know what you're going to say, but I'm telling you now, put one of those new prepaid phones in the bag. Just in case your clothes don't have a pocket. I'd also stuff the trunk of the car full of baby blankets and diapers. Just in case."

A deer in the headlights couldn't have appeared as stunned as Sasha felt after Linzy's little speech. It definitely made her think, just as Linzy had doubtless intended. She continued to think about it as Linzy went to clean up the kitchen. She hadn't lectured, not exactly, but when Sash had shared her intent to return home to Cam, Linzy's mind seemed to go into overdrive with ways to keep them safe in case it ever happened again.

Sasha didn't question her sister just then. She knew they were all tired. Instead, she simply followed Linzy to the kitchen and changed the subject to Skye and her new terrycloth onesie. "She's gone up to a three to six-month size already," she told her sister.

"And she's not even six weeks. It must be those long legs. Just like her momma."

"Haha," her sister said. "Very funny." Sash stood barely five foot two inches in her stocking feet. The top of her head aligned perfectly with Cam's shoulder. Any length or height the baby inherited came from him, not her.

Linzy laughed. "Good thing we went shopping last week." She glanced at Sasha. "If you have some already-too-small clothes gathered up, I can come and get them. Take them to the charity shop for you."

"Thanks, Sis." Sasha thought Linz might be formulating a plan to come and check on her in a day or two. "I did gather a few, along with a couple outfits of my own. Then I realized I wanted to save some of my maternity tops and newborn clothes in case *you* need them someday. Or in case I have another baby later." She smiled sweetly when she said it, to let Linzy know it was a possibility not an agenda.

"I get 'cha," Linzy said. "Come to think of it, someone once told me it's bad luck to give away all the newborn clothes. Said it was a surefire way to wind up pregnant again—"

Sasha rolled her eyes. "That would be about par, wouldn't it?" She imagined holding a baby in each arm while Cam pushed them out onto the deck like before. "Maybe I'd better keep them all. I don't want to start all over from scratch."

Linzy laid the back of one hand across her forehead dramatically. "Oh, no, what have I done? You'll have to build another room on the house to keep everything."

"Nah," Sash grinned. "Just kidding. I only pulled out a couple of favorites. Just in case." She took the clean, sleepy baby, cradled her against her shoulder, and turned around so Linzy could see Skye's face. "Say nighty night to your Aunt Linzy, Skye."

Linzy leaned forward and kissed the baby's chubby cheek. "Sweet dreams, little one." She patted both the baby and her mom.

"You're not mad, are you?" Sasha asked her sister.

Linzy kissed her cheek, too. "Of course not. I'm never mad at you, Sis. No matter what. But I do worry." She pushed at her bangs again. "I sound like Mom don't I—"

Suddenly there was a knock on the front door. Linzy dropped the dishtowel on the counter and turned toward the kitchen doorway. "I forgot I told Blue he could stop by and see you two." She started toward the living room, then stopped and looked back at Sasha. "Is that okay, just for a second?"

Sasha nodded and went back into the living room to their grandmother's old straight back rocker next to the fireplace. It had been stored in the attic for years. "It'll be good to see him."

"C'mon in," Linzy called, waving at him through the door glass.

Blue opened the door and ducked inside. He wasn't as tall as Cameron, not quite, but he'd knocked his head on so many things over the years, ducking came naturally. "Hey," his brown eyes lit up when he saw the three of them in the living room. "Is it too late for trick or treat?"

Linzy met him just inside the door and took his hand. "Nope. Glad you came by. We saved you a treat bag full of candy, pretzels, and roasted pumpkin seeds."

Sasha raised her free hand and stood. She turned like she'd done with Linzy, so he could see the baby's face. "She's growing fast."

"Yes, she is. And she gets cuter every time I see her." He took out his phone. "Okay if I get a pic of the two of you for Mom and Dad?"

"Of course." She moved the baby down into the crook of her arm and the little face immediately began to root around for the breast. Skye knew the bedtime routine. Bath, breast, sleep. And they'd stopped after bath, so the rest was inevitable.

"Oops," Sasha repositioned the infant back into the hollow of her shoulder so he could get a quick picture.

Blue's face reddened. He hastily clicked the picture. "Sorry for the interruption." He leaned forward and caressed the tiny head. "Now, feed that starving baby."

"For a single guy, you sure know your way around nursing mothers," Linzy joked.

"YouTube," he said, voice serious.

She laughed and eased down on the couch. Blue sprawled beside her.

"I should have left her pumpkin costume on her," Sasha said after she got the baby re-situated.

"It's okay," Blue replied. "Mom and Linz both sent me pictures." He held up his phone. "She's adorable."

Sash adjusted the lightweight blanket over her shoulder—and the nursing baby—for her own modesty. "You're always so sweet," she glanced at him. "I've never heard you raise your voice ..." She looked away for a moment, memories of Cam yelling and swearing surfacing in her mind. "Cam got drunk and pushed us out of our house." She swiped at a tear. "You probably already know all about it."

Linzy clenched her teeth. "But she's going back home tomorrow anyway." She seemed to be trying to keep her voice even. "I've told her she should stay here and rest, let me help with the baby for a while, regroup, think about everything."

Blue nodded, his gaze as level and even as Linzy's voice. "That sounds like a good idea." He hesitated, seemingly unsure of his role. "I don't know how things went down, but if you ever need me, I'm a phone call away, Sash. Anytime. Day or night."

The tone of his voice made her look at him. "I know. My sister says the same thing, and believe me, I do appreciate it." She gazed down at the baby, twitched aside the blanket a bit, to make sure she wasn't getting too warm. "It'll be okay. Cam and I have talked. He's extremely sorry, he lost a lot of money playing poker right before we met. He says he's going to start going to AA meetings—and I'm going to suggest something called GA, too. If he can find one." She laughed darkly. "I googled what would make someone do that…"

"I still say it's too soon," her sister stated bluntly. "If he's having some sort of crisis, I think we should give him time to work it out."

Sasha pasted a smile of patience on her face. "It's okay, Sis. Like Blue said, you are both just a phone call away. I'll follow all your advice about making an emergency go bag, and I will call you if I need you." She stood, pushing herself up with her free hand, baby still nursing at her breast.

Blue jumped up, assisted her with a palm beneath her elbow, and Skye continued to nurse as Sash made her way toward the bedroom.

She patted Blue's arm. "Thank you for being our rock. I think I'll go read to this little one, give her a good burp, and then tuck us both in for the night."

Blue slipped a modified hug around her shoulders. "Seriously, though. Call me. Anytime." The concern in his eyes was enough to give her a few more second thoughts. She seemed to be the only one who considered this episode a one-time thing.

"I will," she said. "I promise." At the doorway to the kitchen, she paused and looked back. "And if anything like this ever happens again, I will be out of there *permanently.* I won't even think twice." She smiled. "Goodnight, you two. Don't stay up too late."

"Love you," Linzy called after her. "Sleep tight."

Linzy and Blue settled back into the couch and turned on the TV. They kept the sound on low, but it was a good mask for conversation. "How bad was it?" he asked. He knew the gist of the story, but not the details.

"I don't know what would have happened to them if he hadn't

called me before he passed out." She gripped Blue's fingers tightly. "She couldn't even get in the car because her keys and phone were locked up inside the house." She lowered her voice even more. "And there was no way to get back into the house because he had turned off the electronic keypad." She looked away. "Sash says he told her it was accidental ..."

Blue held her hand. "He didn't hit her or—"

"No. But he took her by the arm and pushed her and the baby outside in the cold."

"Does she know you called me as soon as he drove up yesterday?"

"No, I didn't mention it." She released his fingers. "I don't care if she gets mad at me, but I want to keep you out of the argument. That way she will have someone she can trust to be neutral. I guess. Heck, I don't know. I'm just playing this by ear."

She sighed. "Tonight, she told him to come and pick her up tomorrow. I think I should pack her a 'go bag' myself. I've heard that's the thing to do. I won't leave it up to her. I'll put in baby clothes and diapers, maybe some bottles and instant formula, and then I'll get her a spare car key, house key, and telephone, one of those prepaid things you get at Walmart or Target." She paused. "That way, if it ever happens again, she can just get in her car and leave. Call me on the way home."

"Can she hide the bag outside somewhere?"

"Yes. Maybe in the little storage building where her kiln is located."

"But even if she gets to the go bag, her car will still be in the garage."

"Right ..." Linzy said. "And if he turns off the security again, then she can't drive away. She will have to just get the phone and call me." Linzy tapped her index finger against her chin, thinking. "Or simply call the Sheriff's Office again. They got there pretty quickly this time."

Blue nodded. "Good idea. Put the bag in the store house.

Make certain the keys and phone are in waterproof containers." He ran a hand over his head. "What else?"

Linzy pictured the beach house in her head. "You're right. The bag with the phone definitely has to be waterproof." In the back of her mind, she imagined a drunken Cam taking Sasha's iPhone and smashing it as he pushed her out the door again. "Hang on." She tapped an icon on her screen. "I'll check websites for those cheap phones."

Blue beat her to the punch. He held up his own phone with the closest Walmart website pulled up. "Check this out. They have prepaid phones *and* waterproof containers." He stood. "I'm going to run into town and get them. Is there anything else I should pick up while I'm there?"

Linzy stood and embraced him. "Lean down here, you lanky angel." He did as she requested, and she kissed him on the corner of the mouth.

That turned into a more passionate kiss before he allowed her to push him away. "Hurry back," she said. "I *want* to give you a whole list of things to buy, but I can't send the go bag home with her tomorrow. He'd see it."

"I don't mind—"

Linzy shrugged. "I know you don't, but I can buy it all tomorrow, then drive it down the next day while he's at work."

Blue grinned. "You need to go down there and make sure everything's on the up and up, don't you?"

"You know me too well, Little Boy Blue."

He embraced her and pulled her up to his level before kissing her again. Then he set her back on her feet. "Okay. If you insist. But I seriously don't mind picking it all up right now."

"Nah, it's all right. You picked me up. That's enough for one night. Let's get a glass of tea before you go."

"Or maybe we could have hot chocolate by the fireplace?"

Linzy laughed. "Of course, why didn't I think of that? Halloween calls for hot chocolate, not iced tea."

They went to the kitchen to make it. Lately, they'd been talking about setting their wedding date, but nothing was carved in stone. They were both on the same page when it came to Sasha. Linzy didn't want to start planning until she was certain Sash and the baby were okay. Taking care of her little sister had always been their agreement, even before this nonsense. One thing Linzy couldn't quite wrap her head around was how isolated Sash's new home felt now. She told Linzy the house directly next door to theirs was dark except for the usual twinkle lights. No one would come to the door, and the wind was so chilly.

She said if she hadn't had the baby, or if the wind hadn't been so gusty, she would have kept going on down the beach to the next house, and the next, and the next, but then she remembered the beach towels and that's when she thought it would be better to get out of the cold wind and wrap the baby.

Linzy related all that to Blue as they whipped up the hot chocolate and sat in front of the fireplace. They avoided talking about Sasha anymore, discussing work instead. She told Blue about her newest students, and he regaled her with tales from his new career as well.

When their mugs were empty, Blue practically leapt to his feet. Once he had an objective, he couldn't rest until it was done. "Going to get the stuff," he said. "We've got a little safety net, for Sash. Now we just need to put it in place."

Linzy walked him to the door, kissed him soundly, and stood by as he climbed into the pickup. Pushing a strand of wavy auburn hair back into its clip, she let her gaze follow the pickup as Blue drove out the gate. When she pulled her hand away from her hair, sparkly glitter from her witch's mask floated to the floor.

She smiled. Their jack-o-lanterns still glowed beside the gate, but it felt as if the trick-or-treaters had been days ago instead of only a couple of hours. She thought about Sash and Cam. Sasha was convinced everything would be okay, but Linzy knew she, herself, would have trouble trusting him now.

After cleaning up the cocoa makings, Linzy banked the fire and waited. Before long, Blue was back with the prepaid phone and waterproof zipper bag. "Oh, it's like the bags they give you for your phone at water parks like Great Wolf Lodge, isn't it?"

Blue nodded. "A lot sturdier than a plain old sandwich bag. Here, I got a couple extra for her keys and cash."

Linzy hugged him and asked him to help her go over how to set up the phone so she could teach Sash. That way she wouldn't have to stop and try to figure it out if she actually had to use it.

When they were finished, Blue reluctantly went home and Linzy started to bed. She almost called him to come back. Surely Cam wouldn't show up in the middle of the night, would he? She peeked in on Sash and the baby, surprised to see her sister had fallen asleep with her phone in her hand. Linzy wondered if she had been talking to Cam, or whether she was expecting a call from him.

She shook her head, then went through the house checking doors, windows, and the security system. Afterward, she checked on Sasha and the baby one last time before turning in. Sleep was elusive, but Blue called and wished her goodnight. He told her everything would be all right. She tried to believe him.

Cam arrived the next morning and Sash and the baby went home before the first pot of coffee was even empty.

Linzy told herself not to lecture, but found she couldn't stop her mouth from saying, once more, that she thought it was just too soon. "At least remember what I told you," she whispered in her sister's ear. "We're always here, no matter what."

Sasha hugged her and walked with her to Cam's Lincoln. "It's going to be okay, Sis. Cam and I have talked it through. Try not to worry." She put the baby in the back seat carrier that was already there, then Linzy took the one from her Buick and allowed Cam to put it in his trunk. "Be sure to put that back in your car when you get home," she told Sasha.

"I will," she said, hugging Linzy again. "I'll call you tomorrow and you can come down and see for yourself, okay?

Linzy nodded, but said, "Call me today and tonight and tomorrow ..."

Sasha smiled indulgently. "Yes, ma'am. I will."

Cameron surprised Linzy when he came around the car and stood beside the passenger door. "I don't blame you for worrying. But please know that nothing like this will ever happen again. Sash is telling the truth. We've talked it out and I promised her I will never take another drink. Not even a beer."

Linzy had heard that earlier. Repeating it wouldn't make it true. Besides, actions speak louder than words. Everyone knows that.

24

LINZY & BLUE

Linzy Skye Gaines. A round little three-month-old chub of grins and giggles and gas. She continued to bring a light into all their lives.

"I had my doubts," Linzy told Blue as they were leaving the beach house during the Thanksgiving break. "But Cam seems to have settled down. I've never seen Sasha so happy. I guess the Halloween episode was a fluke. Could it possibly have been a one-time thing? Do people fall off the wagon and then jump back on, just like that?"

Blue shrugged. He wouldn't say one way or the other, but Linzy got the impression he had his doubts, too. "According to him," Blue said. "He'd never been on the wagon or even needed to."

At Thanksgiving, Cam did his best to be the perfect host. "I feel like I have to tell you guys that everything really is back to normal. I mean, I never had a problem with alcohol before the Halloween thing." His voice wasn't pleading, just matter of fact. "I'm not saying I didn't drink, but I was just your regular, happy-go-lucky social drinker. Never a sloppy drunk a day in my life. Saw way too much of that growing up."

He rubbed his hand over the back of his neck as if those memories tracked across his spine. "Seriously," he said. "I can't explain what happened that night, but I can reassure you all that it won't happen again, because I will never put myself in that position again." His gaze sought Sasha's with a look that was so genuine, even Linzy couldn't find fault.

As they were driving away, Linzy told Blue, "I was afraid this whole place would be tainted now, but it's not. It's still so beautiful and serene." She scuffed her flip flops back and forth across the fine grains of sand coating the pickup's rubber floor mat. "I've really enjoyed walking the beach with Sash and Skye these past few weeks. It must be so nice to do it every day—"

"Or just to drink coffee on that huge deck, watching the sunrise over the Gulf, or sipping a tea in the evening while flipping burgers on that fancy grill." Blue grinned comically. "Maybe we should sell everything and buy us a place like that."

Linzy began to shake her head before he'd even finished his thought. "Maybe we'd better give that some more thought. Although, to be honest, I've often wondered if we should have sold the house after Mom and Dad … you know."

Blue laid one hand on her knee and squeezed gently. "I'm not sure where that thought came from. I mean, we would never sell your place. I think you would miss it, and to be honest, I can't imagine driving past the house and seeing someone else's car in the carport." He waited until she looked at him. "Besides, if you want a beach house for a wedding present, I'll get it for you. And we will use it only on weekends like the uber rich. We won't have to sell a thing." Under his breath he muttered, "Except my soul."

Linzy slugged him playfully. "I don't need a beach house for a wedding gift. We'll leave that to Cam-the-realtor and just be happy for their little family." She gazed out at the shore as they drove the length of the island. "Besides, even now, after all that stuff—and how thoroughly disgusted I was with him—Cam still says I am welcome to come down and spend the night, walk the beach, anytime I want with Sash and my little namesake. Maybe I was wrong about him."

"If you were," Blue joked. "It's gotta be the first time you were ever wron—"

She slugged him again before he could finish his snarky comment. "Oh, *you*."

Blue drew an X on his shoulder with his fingertip. "Right here," he said, rolling up his t-shirt sleeve. "This is where you slugged me."

Linzy rolled her eyes. "I can't hurt you, Superman."

He laughed and drew a bigger X. "And right here." He smiled innocently. "You slugged me twice, you know."

She tipped her head back, laughing.

"You gave me a boo-boo," he said. "And you know what you have to do with boo-boos." He tapped his shoulder. "Come on. Don't be shy." He drew the X again. Even larger.

"You have no shame," she said. Then she leaned over to kiss the boo-boos. First one, and then the other, and then another he pointed to on his jaw. And then one more on the corner of his mouth, that sexy, turned-up corner that always caught her attention when he was speaking.

She had to lean way over for that one, her elbow digging into the padded console of the pickup. "I don't remember slugging you here," she joked, kissing him again. "Or here." She planted one on his cheekbone for good measure.

"I think you did, right here, though. A few days ago." He tapped his index finger on his ear lobe.

Linzy giggled, kissed it, then nipped it, too. Just a bit.

"Ow," he yelped. "Now you've got to start all over."

And so it went, all the way back through Galveston, across the causeway, down the long, deserted highway, through tiny Brookville, and out the other side. All the way back to the house on Wisteria Way.

Just before they arrived home, Blue said, "Promise me we will always settle our disputes with kisses."

"That's a promise," she said. "But aren't we the ones who always agree on everything? I mean, we are so incredibly blessed. We've never even argued."

Blue reached for her hand. "We are blessed. We've got everything anyone could ever want—"

"Yes, we do. A lovely farmhouse, the mountain cabin at Stutter Creek ... did you know Sash signed her half over to me right before she married Cam? She didn't even tell me, just called Carla Brushow and had it drawn up. Said she did it so there would never be another chance for someone to take it out of the Everly family name."

She stopped talking and stared out at the familiar road. "It kind of worried me that she did that knowing she was about to marry Cameron. But—"

"But that business with Ancho and the other creep was probably what she had on her mind."

Linzy nodded vigorously. "Yeah, and she said when she told Cam what she'd done, he thought it was great. Maybe she was testing him. Anyway, I thought that was a good sign at that time." She scuffed her flip flops again, thinking. "By the way, if we don't want to stay with Sash and Cam when we feel the need to dip our toes in the surf, we can always rent a beachfront condo or something." She raised an eyebrow. "I think Cam's office has a rental branch, too."

They laced their fingers together. It was good to talk about something other than problems. The two of them were relieved to see how well Sasha and Cam were getting along. And how they both doted on Baby Skye. So what if Cam didn't do much feeding or diaper changing? Some men just weren't made that way. Sash was still mostly breastfeeding anyway. She only gave Skye a bottle now and then, to get her used to them before weaning.

Surprisingly, Skye wasn't even opposed. Such an easy baby. Such a blessing.

It was all brand new to Linzy. She had zero experience with babies. But eager-to-learn might be her new middle name. Everything the little one did fascinated and delighted her almost as much as it did Sash.

Life was grand again. It took on a sweet, even keel that floated them right through the end of November and into the middle weeks of December.

They were all excited for the baby's first Christmas. Even Mr. and Mrs. Ash were planning on being there. In fact, there was talk of finally going to Stutter Creek for a white Christmas. It always snowed in the mountains in December. "Looks just like a Christmas card," their mom used to say. Of course, that was before the forest fires and flash floods.

I'll call Beth again, Linzy told herself. Just as soon as Blue gets his work schedule lined out. Being the newbie, he had zero control of his time off. Veteran employees always got first dibs on holidays.

"We could take turns hitting the slopes," she'd told her sister on the phone, remembering how the two of them had loved skiing with their mom and dad. "But we would have to open the gifts here at home. I don't think they will all fit in Blue's pickup to be transported to the cabin."

"Did you go overboard on the baby, Sis?" Sasha asked.

Linzy held her hand up, thumb and forefinger about an inch apart. "Maybe, just a little." Skye was everyone's first. First baby, first niece, first "almost grandchild" (according to Mr. and Mrs. Ash) first *everything*. The kid was going to be incredibly spoiled.

"I have an idea," Sash said. "Since we've both got our trees up and decorated already, why don't we go ahead and do Christmas here, at Sunset Drift, then plan on a trip to the cabin afterward? Maybe for New Years or whenever Blue will be assured a few days off."

Linzy didn't even have to think twice. "That sounds like an excellent idea," she said. "Let's plan on it."

And so, it was set. Midnight services at the church in Brookville, then Christmas breakfast at the beach house—where the baby would get her first taste of Christmas morning and presents—and then Christmas dinner on Wisteria Way with Blue and his folks.

It will be the beginning of some new holiday traditions, Linzy thought. Of course, they would invite Mr. and Mrs. Ash to Stutter Creek for New Years, too. It was going to be one major holiday blowout. We deserve it, she told herself. Every one of us.

The sisters continued planning and talking things over with the rest of the family. But it didn't take much to convince everyone of their plan. Now, all they had to do was shop.

A few days later, Sasha pulled her Cadillac into the garage beneath the beach house. She didn't notice that the overhead door was already open, she just assumed it went up when she pushed the remote button on her sun visor. She and the baby had been to Galveston to a wellness check-up at the doctor's office, and then she had stopped to deliver some of her seashell Christmas ornaments to the consignment gift shop on The Strand.

Sash couldn't believe she was selling her tiny works of art on The Strand. She still went into the real estate office part time, taking the baby with her, but getting her agent's license had lost its urgency since Skye's birth. She still planned to get it, later, but right now Sash didn't see the point since she couldn't bear the thought of having to leave the baby to show houses. Maybe she'd take it up again when Skye was in school.

Fortunately, it hadn't taken Cam long to pull in a few more clients. He'd been working hard, all hours of the day and evening, showing homes in Galveston and moving into the larger Houston-area market too. He also talked to Sash more, keeping her abreast of their finances, teaching her how to take care of their bank accounts and investments. Sometimes they both forgot how young and inexperienced she was with money.

Since then, things had been wonderful. Just like the first days of their marriage when everything had been shiny and new. She'd especially enjoyed Linzy coming to walk the beach with her and the baby every few days, and she had been delighted to have everyone gather at her house for Thanksgiving. It was almost as if the Halloween incident had been nothing but the glitch of a new husband and father overcoming his own insecurities.

On the other hand, she thought that just maybe she'd had so much counseling that she somehow felt comfortable analyzing others' intentions. Shut up, overthinking brain, she thought. Just shut up.

Congratulating herself for making it into Galveston for her quick new-mommy wellness checkup, and for delivering the latest consignment ornaments to the gift shop, Sasha turned off the car and took the baby out of the back seat. She then tugged the diaper bag onto her shoulder and went through the garage to mount the half dozen steps leading up to the interior kitchen door.

The doorknob wouldn't turn. We never lock this door, she thought. The overhead garage door always closes so no need to lock this one, too.

Shuffling Skye to the other arm, she dug her phone from her pocket to tap in the four-digit security code that would unlock the security system, but the code blanks wouldn't come up.

Tapping at the phone, she tried to understand what was wrong. I know the security service was paid, she murmured, because Cam showed me how to find it in the monthly online bank statement. She tried to access the internet to recheck the statement to make absolutely certain she didn't miss anything.

This time she noticed the tiny internet wheel spinning around and around. The Searching for Connection message appeared. Well, no wonder it doesn't work. We have no internet.

She adjusted the baby to her other arm. Door locked, no internet, and no physical key. Funny, I never even thought about not having a key for this door. I do have a key for the shore-side door, though. But of course, it's in the diaper bag with my car key fob.

I guess I'll have to carry Skye and the diaper bag back down the steps, around the house, and up the other steps to the back deck. That's when she realized the overhead door had not automatically closed after she'd pushed the button.

Oh, well. Just a little inconvenience. When he gets home from work, I'll have to make sure Cam gives me a key for this door. It's probably tucked away somewhere because we've never needed it.

Sash exited the garage with the baby in her left arm and the diaper bag hanging on her opposite shoulder. She wove her way around the base of the house through the stout pilings holding their luxurious home above the sand. On Galveston Island, hurricanes and floods were simple facts of life and pieces of history. All beachfront homes were raised above the sand on stilts.

But that didn't matter just now. What matters is that we have become too dependent on technology, in my opinion at least.

Sasha continued grousing and muttering as she made her way through the last few pilings toward the shore side deck stairs. This is awfully similar to the night we were locked out by Cam, she thought. But I know it isn't that. He isn't even here. Besides, it's broad daylight, not dead-of-night. Still gave her the shivers, though, being locked out. Shouldn't be happening. Oh, well, if I can't get in this time, I'll just call Cam or get back in the car and drive to Linzy's.

She shook the thoughts from her head as she stepped up on the bottom step and started to climb. Halfway up, she had to stop and readjust the diaper bag on her shoulder. It kept slipping down the nylon fabric of her old blue windbreaker. The weather had been chilly and damp all day.

After a couple of mild curse words, she made it to the top of the wide deck. For a moment, she simply stood, catching her breath beneath the overcast sky. The Gulf was as noisy as ever behind her. Sasha loved that sound. It was only one of the many things she adored about her new home.

She'd left the Christmas tree lights on when she went to town, and now they shone out into the overcast day wonderfully blurred and muted behind the tinted floor-to-ceiling windows.

Look at all this, Sash. Look at all you've got … amazing beach house, beautiful Christmas tree shining out over the deck rails down to the beach, and your most perfect treasure, sweet baby Skye, cooing away, right here in the crook of your arm. Be thankful, right? Just be thankful.

She turned her face into the cool winter breeze to literally say a quick prayer of thanks, and that's when she caught a glimpse of movement from the corner of her eye. A distant silhouette in a funny looking hat and coat. Someone else out and about on their private, community only, beach.

Sash still didn't know all of the Sunset Drift owners. At least two homes belonged to snowbirds who came and went at various times. Another, owned by a couple who were the fur-parents of two adorable Yorkies, was occupied almost all the time. It was the third house down. She'd met them later, days after the Halloween incident, because she and Linzy had been walking the beach more often.

Glancing down the length of the sand now, Sash had to admit that the two empty houses between the Yorkie house and hers gave her a bit of a creepy feeling now. Those two owners must be snowbirds, Linzy had commented after never seeing anyone on their frequent strolls. She'd been determined to meet as many of the neighbors as she could.

Since that awful night, Cam had followed through on his promise to join AA. He didn't talk to Sash about it much, except to tell her when he went to the meetings, but as far as she knew, he hadn't taken another drink, not even a beer. But he'd also been working a lot more hours, so she and Skye were often home alone. She assumed that's why Linzy came down so frequently.

Sash wasn't frightened here by herself, not when she could lock and unlock the doors with the click of an icon. But since that wasn't happening, she would have to dig the keys out of the diaper bag—too much trouble to carry a purse and a diaper bag—and that made her feel a lot more vulnerable. Especially since glimpsing the odd silhouette down the beach.

She gritted her teeth and tried to get the bag off her shoulder so she could dig through it while holding the baby in one arm. Should have got the keys out while I was in the garage, she thought. She did not want to lay the baby on the cold deck. I'll put her in the stroller, she murmured, remembering how they'd shoved it under the edge of the patio table after their walk yesterday.

Plopping Skye into the familiar seat, Sash strapped her in and pushed her up to the locked door. Linzy had been here to pull the empty stroller up the steps after their most recent walk while she'd carried the baby up. And thank goodness Linzy *had* been there. They'd had the bottom of it full of shells they'd found. Now the shells were in the house, washed and drying in the bathtub on a towel.

Sasha faced the baby away from the constant breeze and opened the diaper bag. She had to dump out the bigger items so she could get to the things in the bottom. Sure enough, in the pale sunlight, her house keys winked up at her.

Ahh, she sighed. My new normal, a diaper bag instead of a purse. She looked at the baby. Skye was absolutely the best 'normal' anyone could ask for. Grabbing the keys, she quickly found the correct one and stuck it in the lock. The skin on the back of her neck crinkled as if the breeze had grown fingers. She whirled around, but no one was there.

Shading her eyes with one hand, Sasha glanced back toward the community's private pier. Cartoon-gray clouds graced the sky. They cast a slight shadow over that part of the beach. But the shadows didn't reach her deck.

She craned her neck, trying to see further, toward the outcropping of black rocks that marked the end of the private beach.

Nothing.

Giving up, glad for the windbreaker, she turned back to the lock, opened the door, pushed the baby inside, then leaned down to grab the diaper bag. That's when she became aware of a new light flickering outward through the floor-to-ceiling windows. It wasn't there before she unlocked the door.

Christmas tree lights? No. Those lights don't flicker. They're steady. They've been on all along. Looks like the TV. But I didn't have it on before I left, she thought.

Sweeping everything she'd dumped out back into the diaper bag, Sasha yanked it up and hurried inside. "Cam? You home?" Stupid question, her mind said. His Lincoln wasn't in the garage. Besides, it's early afternoon. She blinked, her eyes taking a moment to adjust from the bright shoreline to the dim interior. The flickering lights were unnerving.

She closed the door behind her, peered over at the big screen TV.

What the hell?

On the screen, a flickering image of Linzy straddling the lap of a swarthy faced man seen only in profile.

That can't be Linzy.

Sasha peered closer.

The woman on the screen looked like an exotic dancer

version of her sister. Short silvery skirt, sparkling sequined tube top, six-inch stiletto heels, and hair as straight and shiny-black as a shard of obsidian.

The strength left Sasha's legs. She dropped onto the sofa in shock. Aside from the hooker-type clothing and straight black hair, it was Linzy. It was her face looking over the shoulder of a swarthy man in a purple satin shirt. Her Linz, the one she could call anytime of the day or night. It wasn't her hair, that had to be a wig, but it was her, and there she was, grinding away on the lap of a ... *gangster?*

Sash examined the scene in disbelief. Her sister's long-fingered hands gripped the man's shoulders. Her tiny, shiny skirt was hiked up, pelvis pressing into his lap as she—*That's a lap dance. Oh my God, that's Linzy giving that creep a lap dance.*

Sasha glanced at the Christmas tree half expecting the beautiful lights to wink out under the onslaught of the horrible image playing across the TV.

She glanced toward the baby, gray wool filling her head. *Glad I faced Skye away from the TV.* Sasha closed her eyes, willing the gray wool to abate. *I will not pass out, I will not.* She made herself look again.

The swarthy-faced guy stared out at her from the TV screen, a grinning, gold-toothed Cheshire cat in black sunglasses and a purple satin shirt. A pimp. A gangster. So proud of himself and what he was doing. Sasha looked away, stomach roiling with disgust and disbelief.

25

SHERLOCK HOLMES

Bile burned in Sasha's throat. The image of Linzy's face, her stare vacant, her beautiful wavy hair covered by a straight black wig, chopped so the ends barely scraped her bare shoulders as she moved ... that image filled the screen.

Sash forced herself not to look away. The scenario appeared to be a dark, cavernous room, some kind of underground club with a disco-ball light scattering sparks about the walls and ceiling. That's the flickering, she thought.

She gaped at the mind-numbing scene.

Linzy and the man were in the foreground, a multitude of gyrating dancers in the background. Sparks of light bounced merrily off Linzy's tiny silver skirt and rhinestone covered top and heels.

Sasha blinked when Linzy looked directly at the camera. Her eyes were rimmed with black kohl eyeliner, brows shaped into dark wings, pupils huge, unfocused, her sister, but not her sister at all.

Struggling to make sense of things, Sasha mumbled, "Linz?" But the girl had already looked away. Sash closed her eyes, focused her mind, opened them again.

The screen blinked, then started up, replaying the exact same scene.

This time, Sasha sat up, making herself pay close attention to the entire video. She shook her shoulders like a wet dog shaking off water, trying to make her brain focus not on the swarthy faced man with the gold teeth and sunglasses, but instead on the young woman grinding on his lap.

Not Linzy's hair, nor her clothes. Maybe *not* Linz? Impossible to say. It looks like her face, her lips, her eyes beneath the heavy black liner. But could it be fake?

Sasha leaned forward, eyes squinted, memorizing every detail, knowing the young woman would glance her way again at any moment. And ... *bam!* There it was. Another quick glimpse directly into the camera.

Linzy. Yes. It was her face. Sasha knew it as well as she knew her own.

Mind in overdrive, adrenaline pumping, Sasha clenched her fists and watched as a silent message began to crawl across the bottom of the screen in bright white print. *If you want your sister back, come to pier. She in training now. Come alone or you never see her again.*

Sasha leapt up, clutching the back of the sofa with one hand, ready to go. But the words began scrolling again.

If you want your sister back, come to pier. She in training now. Come alone or you never see her again.

How could this be happening? Did it go along with what happened before, with Ancho? With the deaths of their folks? How could it? The money? Their inheritance? They weren't rich. This can't be—

The screen scroll began a third time. It cast a flickering pall over the entire room. The lights on the Christmas tree stood out like jewels.

Who would know about Ancho and Dom other than Blue, his folks, and the sheriff? And how could it possibly be related? How would a pimp, or a kidnapper, get my sister? More importantly, how can I get her back?

Sasha dug her phone out of her pocket to call Cam, but there was no signal of any kind. No internet or cellular service at all. So how is this video playing, she wondered.

The words scrolled across the TV screen again. Sash glanced at the baby. What do I do? Which pier? The private community pier, or Pleasure Pier, the amusement park on the seawall? Or is it just the name of some club, maybe the one with that glittery disco-ball? How do I find out? They didn't even mention money. Don't kidnappers always demand money? They just said come to the pier—oh, my God—do they want me, too? Should I call the cops? No. No cell service, remember?

She peered out the floor to ceiling windows. The surf appeared calm, the faint afternoon sunlight winking off the small waves breaking against the sand. It might be a disco ball under water. No. No. That's stupid. I'm not asleep. This isn't a dream. There's no disco ball under the water. She pressed her fingernails into the palms of her hands. I'm awake. I am. She looked at the tiny crescents in her skin.

The image of Linzy straddling the swarthy gangster's lap kept reappearing on the screen. Maybe it is a dream, she thought. A nightmare. I've stepped into another horrid nightmare. Her brain wanted to play the poor-poor-pitiful-me song—the why-do-these-things-always-happen-to-me song—but her logical mind wouldn't go there. Not this time.

Someone is sending me that trash over the internet … they must've hacked our system. That's why nothing else is working. Someone hacked us and is controlling everything, including my phone. Is that possible?

Or maybe it's all fake. Not Linzy at all. Just that AI junk, deep fake, or whatever it's called. And maybe, just maybe, I can send a text to Cam instead of calling.

Her fingers tapped Linzy's number first, just in case. "Linzy, where are you? Are you ok?" Nothing happened. The text did not send. A red error memo appeared.

Msg failed. Retry?

Oh, my God, Sasha prayed, willing her mind to focus. Please don't let this be real.

As if in answer, a text came in from her husband, Cam. "On my way home," it read. "Need anything from the store?"

Her thumbs flew over the tiny keyboard. "No!" She replied. "Don't stop. I need you here. Hurry!" She clicked send, her hand straying to her forehead, feeling for lumps or injuries. Did I fall? Hurt myself? Am I hallucinating?

She felt no injury, no wound.

Her phone blipped. Her first message to Cam appeared to send.

She hit Retry on her text to Linzy.

The error message appeared again. When she clicked over, the red error message had popped up beside her text to Cam, as well.

This can't be happening she thought as her hands began to gather fresh things into the diaper bag. Lord, help me, which pier? They didn't even say which pier. Oh, Lord, help me, I can't screw this up like I screwed up saving Mom and Dad. What if I never see my Linz again? She looked horrible, a hooker, all made up with that black junk, obviously drugged. Stolen. Trafficked. That's it. That must be it, sex trafficking, but how?

As tangled thoughts spiraled through her head, Sasha dashed around, gathering bottles from the kitchen, diapers from the nursery. One part of her mind said wait for Cam, the other part said go, go, go. She pressed 9-1-1 on her phone. Nothing happened. The phone screen was blank.

She heard a small noise from the TV screen, as if the video was about to start again. But nothing happened. Walking toward it, fresh diapers in hand, Sasha steeled herself for something terrible, an electronic explosion or some sort of firework. She held the thick disposable diapers in front of her eyes with one hand, in case of flying glass.

Still nothing.

Inhaling deeply, to settle her nerves, Sasha picked up the remote and pushed the power button. The TV appeared completely dead.

She glanced out the window, looking for something that might have interrupted the satellite signal. The skies were light gray, the wind blustery, as always. She checked the plugs to the wall and to the control box. Everything appeared normal, just dead. No little red light anywhere.

No one is this powerful, she thought. To have this kind of control. Yes, they are, and they can. If they have money, they can do anything. She turned, almost afraid to have her back to the traitorous TV. Now, it will explode, now shards of flying black glass will slice through my flesh and into my liver, my spleen, my lungs, my heart … the baby.

Oh, Lord, her mind scolded. If Linzy were here she would shake some sense into me.

Sasha stopped, glanced back out at the beach. Was that the shadow-figure, way off down the shore, long hair whipping sideways like seaweed?

She stared hard, but the harder she tried to make it out, the fuzzier the movement became until it seemed she was looking at nothing but foamy water caressing the sand, crawling up and over the black rocks at the community's boundary.

Fear creeping across her scalp, Sasha spoke to her sister aloud. "I'm coming, Sis. I'm scared, but I'm coming." She hurried back to the stroller. Skye had dozed off again. Such a good baby. Eat, sleep, play, repeat.

She heard another funny click. The message and images were on the screen again. *If you want your sister back, come to pier. She in training now. Come alone or you never see her again.* And there was Linzy, grinding away, flipping her hair over her shoulder, glancing at the camera, glancing away …

The screen went dark once more.

Obviously, a video. Actors. AI maybe. Not even real. Please, Lord, let it not be real.

It didn't matter. She couldn't take a chance.

She zipped up the diaper bag. Wait for Cam, her panic whispered. But she couldn't wait. Linzy was in trouble. My messages won't send. What if Cam stops by the store? What if he's been drinking? My God, what if this has to do with Cam, with the money he lost? Or worse yet, with revenge for the way Linzy tried to get me to leave him?

Something turned over inside her. Nausea rose in a sickening swell.

The words said come alone. But I can't leave the baby.

She ran for an unopened can of formula to go in the diaper bag. Just in case.

Skye dozed in the stroller. Such a perfect baby. Why can't everything stay perfect? Why does something bad always happen?

Sasha fought back the urge to grab the baby and run the other way. Leave her sister to her fate. *No. I would never desert her. We're sisters. We save each other. That's what sisters do. I'll leave Cam a note. He'll see the video, send the cops. If he can't make a call out, he can go get the cops and the gangster can't blame me. With luck, I'll have Linzy back by then.*

She rummaged through the corner desk for a note pad but came up with her journal and the checkbook they seldom used. If it's money they want, they can have it. They can have it all. She tore a blank page out of her journal, dashed off a note to Cam, and stuck it on the fridge. *But what if it is Cam? No. It isn't. It can't be.*

Skye woke and began to fuss. Sash realized it had been a while since her last diaper change. She popped a bottle from the fridge into the warmer on the kitchen counter. While it heated, she stuffed the checkbook into the diaper bag and then took Skye out, executed a two-minute diaper change, then tucked the baby back into the stroller and placed the lukewarm bottle in the seat beside her.

"I'd do anything to keep you out of this, baby girl," she whispered. "But we have to go find Aunt Linzy." We'll start with the private pier down the beach. If she isn't there, I'll come back and get the car, we'll drive down the seawall to Pleasure Pier.

Stowing the diaper bag in the compartment beneath the stroller, Sash rushed across the living room to the back door snagging her jacket sleeve on the Christmas tree in her haste.

She stopped, pulled her sleeve free, and rescued the tiny shell ornament that came off with it. Dashing outside to the deck, the image of her sister fresh in her mind, Sash hesitated. A dark silhouette beckoned to her from down the shore. Okay, she thought. It must be the private pier.

The wind kicked up and swooshed her blonde hair into her eyes, partially obscuring her view. When she swiped the locks aside, the image was gone.

She thumped down the stairs, backwards, tugging the stroller down one step at a time. The shore breeze flipped the baby's blanket and Sasha reached down and arranged it back around the baby's face. When she straightened, the silhouette was there again, waving her to hurry.

Sasha's heart galloped. She hesitated, now that she was outside, away from the sickening video. Her mind wanted to convince her it wasn't Linzy on the screen at all. That it was all some kind of ploy to get her out of the house.

She scrabbled her phone from her pocket, but the screen was still blank. Can't even get a picture, she thought. Is it possible for someone to drain my phone battery remotely? Surely not.

Of course, it is, her common sense whispered. Hackers can do anything. Her mind went on and on until it finally came back around to what her brain had hit on earlier.

Could Cam be doing this? Could anyone be that two-faced, that cruel, that evil?

Images of Ancho popped into her head, answering her question. Think about it, Sash. True kidnappers would've asked for some kind of ransom.

Her feet hit the sand. The figure continued to beckon. The front tires of the big stroller plopped off the last step. The wind whipped her hair across her vision. Something about that beckoning shape …

"I'm coming, Linz. I'm coming." She thought of the keys still in the door lock, but the dim silhouette waved frantically and suddenly she was reminded of a slender Sherlock Holmes, knee-length beige coat and an old-fashioned deerstalker cap pulled down low.

Linzy had dressed up exactly like that for Halloween one year. *She was Sherlock Holmes, and I was Watson. What a strange coincidence. Is that you, Sissy?* She recalled Cam copying that very photo from her Instagram page shortly after they married. He said he wanted a collage of his favorite photos for his office.

Suddenly, arms of iron grabbed Sash from behind. A ragged voice rasped, "Don't struggle."

Instinctively, Sasha struggled and slithered free. The nylon fabric of her old windbreaker slid like Teflon through the creep's grasp.

Sash shoved the stroller deep beneath the deck and lurched toward the black rocks down the beach. She wanted to lure whatever monster had grabbed her as far away from Skye as possible. If she ran fast enough, maybe he would forget about the baby stroller and simply come after her.

As she ran, an idea bubbled to life. I'll scramble through the rocks and circle around to Tim and Kev's house, the neighbors with the Yorkies.

Idea set, Sash ran a crazed pattern, praying the couple would be there, her nylon windbreaker flapping in the breeze. She was determined to lead the guy completely away from her house. Cam was on his way home. He would find the baby under the deck. *The same place we spent hours when he shoved us out the door on Halloween night. It should be the first place he looks.*

Something sharp poked her palm and she remembered the tiny shell ornament. She zigged toward a rare tide pool and tossed it in. It looked like a turquoise treasure left there by the sea.

"Yer makin' it too hard," a harsh voice shouted, hot on her heels.

A second form dashed out, intercepting her, huge hands grasping her arms.

Sasha slithered again, this time shedding the windbreaker completely.

A bit farther down the beach, the silhouette stepped out from under the empty house's deck. Sasha shot toward it like an arrow as another gust of wind grabbed the silhouette's odd cap and tossed it away. Messy dark hair whipped across the profile face. *Female, but not Linzy. Who?*

"Call the cops," Sasha shouted at the strange figure. "Please! Call the cops!"

Out of desperation, Sash yelled at the woman one more time, and then she zagged toward the water and dove into a wave, her high school swimmer's body remembering the strokes, the breaths.

The iron-armed creep came fast behind her, much too fast for such a large man. He yelled for her to stop, or he would shoot.

In the distance, the sound of an outboard motor cut through the chop.

Sasha's head crested between waves. She dragged in air and

saw a large, sleek yacht anchored in the distance. A small narrow boat seemed headed straight for her. Sash ducked back under the water.

Something grazed the side of her head.

Her last coherent thought was an image of the baby in the stroller. *Would Cam find her? Or would Sherlock Holmes get there first?*

26

TEENA

Teena stuffed her hair back under the Sherlock Holmes hat Chalk had rented from the costume shop. He'd trolled Facebook, Instagram, and TikTok until he found pictures of Cam's wife. The realtor had all sorts of things on his personal and business pages. It was clear he was stone cold in love with the woman he'd married.

She readjusted the cap. The thing itched. Probably has lice, she thought. But she couldn't stop to worry. The job had to be done before the shakes set in.

Chalk promised to keep her flush from now on if she would help him with this one little thing. He wanted Cam's wife and baby. Cam had humiliated him, and he wanted revenge.

Teena watched Chalk chase the young mother into the ocean. The woman kept yelling at her to call the cops, call the cops. Poor dumb thing seemed to think Teena was there to help. She felt a little twinge of guilt eating into her psyche, but the need for a hit overcame it and she hung around just long enough to see a splotchy-complected guy lean over the side of the narrow dinghy to pull the woman into the boat. Chalk was in the water, his fish-belly face straining as he pushed Cam's wife up from below.

Revolted, Teena turned away when she saw Chalk draw back his fist and begin punching the woman in the head to make her stop struggling.

The woman went limp, her face falling sideways into the waves.

The men manhandled her limp body up and over the side of the boat.

Teena pulled her rented coat tighter and hurried on toward the beach house. But the image of Sasha's battered head falling over into the water would not leave her mind. *Chalk. Hateful Chalk.* He had knocked out all the surveillance cameras to Cam's ritzy beach house when he hacked the security system. She remembered how impressed she'd been that he could do that. Especially since he appeared to be a brainless brute.

"You learn all kinds of good shit in lock up," he'd said.

The words had chilled Teena. But not enough to make her want out of their deal. She'd do anything for another hit. Besides, Cam was the one who'd broken off their relationship after only one hook up last year. That doesn't matter, her better sense cried. That girl in the water didn't do anything.

Teena hurried on, out of breath, sweating under the coat and hat. In moments she was there, at the house, grabbing the handrail and pulling herself up the seventeen steps to the broad deck looking out over the ocean.

All she had to do was get the kid and deliver her to a woman waiting at a hotel downtown. Room 461. Chalk said the baby would go to a nice, rich family who had offered him more dough than she could even imagine.

As she made the top step, shaking and gasping, Teena heard the baby's cries.

But not from the deck. Not even from the house.

She stopped to listen.

The cries were coming from down below. Teena stumbled

back down the steps to the underneath. *Stupid. You saw her with the stroller, what'd you think she was doing, driving it empty?*

An idea began to form in Teena's tortured brain. It was fueled by the fact that she'd had her own child once. His name was Arden. He'd been taken away by Child Protective Services when the neighbors found him wandering near the apartment complex pool. Teena didn't know how long she'd been passed out on the couch before CPS came banging on the door, telling her they had her son.

She barely remembered the boy now. Just his saggy little diaper and slurpy wet kisses. He's better off, she thought. Just like this kid will be. Growing up rich beats hell out of having a druggie hooker for a mom.

Teena caught her breath, looked around. *Idiot.* This kid's mom isn't a druggie or a hooker. You know Cam is well off. And he doesn't do drugs. Besides, you really think Chalk knows any nice, rich people? He's been in prison most of his life. If he is selling a kid, it isn't to a good family. More likely it's child porn. Human trafficking of the worst kind.

After Teena realized where the cries were coming from, it was easy to find the stroller and the fussing baby girl. The pastel quilt had fallen away, showing beautiful pink cheeks.

Teena didn't hesitate. Her adrenaline was high. She latched onto the stroller and pulled it back to the steps. *The beach house door is not locked. The keys are still hanging there.* She tugged the stroller up, one impossible step at a time.

At the top, chest heaving, she had to stop and breathe. To her right, Christmas tree lights shone like precious gems through the tall, tall windows.

Christmas. What would that be like in a home like this? She imagined shiny silver paper and beautiful red ribbons, some old Christmas movie on the big screen TV, a cozy little fire in the fireplace.

The baby squawked, wanting to be picked up.

Teena leaned down, smoothed the fine baby hair blowing in the breeze. I can't send Cam's baby into Hell, no matter what happens to me. Even after he found out I was a user, Cam never made me feel less than. I did that all on my own. Then I tried to use him to look big in front of Chalk. This whole thing is my fault. If I hadn't bragged about him being rich, Chalk never would have known.

Before she could chicken out, Teena pushed the stroller through the unlocked door into the house.

In the living room, sweating like a fiend, Teena stuffed her hair back up under the deerstalker cap, but shrugged out of the hot coat. She looked around. The Christmas tree was especially gorgeous up close. Even in her tortured state of mind, Teena could see Sasha's artistic hand all over the room, especially the seashell ornaments. *It's too late to save her, but maybe I can save this kid.*

Shaking worse than ever, the still-young and once-beautiful Teena made the most amazing decision to follow through and do the right thing.

Kissing the baby on her delicate head, Teena unsnapped the stroller bindings and pulled the baby out. A bottle fell out with her. Teena picked it up and plopped Skye into the playpen in the corner giving her a few drinks from the bottle to soothe her. Without allowing herself to rethink it, she snatched the empty stroller by the handles, and rushed back outside and down the deck steps.

She felt certain her heart would explode every time the stroller tilted precariously as she bumped it down each of the seventeen steps. Somehow, she made it back to the sand and hit the ground running, dashing down the beach to the place where Chalk's rental car waited in the carport of the empty home two houses away.

As she rushed the empty stroller along the sand, Teena glanced toward the yacht and the smaller boat. In her agitated state of mind, she imagined Chalk or one of his minions looking up, somehow realizing there was no baby in the stroller, then heading for her like demons from Hell.

She continued on anyway, scooping up the discarded blue windbreaker along the way. Teena was determined to get the car and get out of the security gate before Cam got home. It amazed her that he still used the same password he'd had at his condo—and that she'd been able to remember it. She really wished she hadn't, but she told herself Chalk probably could have bypassed it anyway.

Too late to worry about it now. She shoved the stroller behind a stout pier and tossed the windbreaker into the front seat of the car as she slid beneath the steering wheel.

She could see Cam's Lincoln approaching the gate. That was good, it meant the baby wouldn't be alone, but if he saw her, all would be lost, and she wouldn't get the junk Chalk had promised to leave in their apartment.

Stuffing her loose hair back up under the itchy hat, Teena yanked it down hard. Then she had a better idea and simply fell over in the seat, sideways, completely invisible through the dark car windows.

Chalk's words played through her head as she counted the seconds. "I'll take care of you, Tee. You just gotta get the kid and deliver it to the nice lady."

When she'd counted sixty, Teena raised her head. Cam's car was pulling into his own driveway at the end of the development. Rich guy, she thought, wanting to be angry. *Nice guy,* her mind replied. *Doesn't yet know his wife is missing.*

Shaking worse than ever, Teena started the engine, backed out of the carport, and headed toward the gate. For once, her luck held. The gate hadn't closed.

Teena stepped on the gas and zoomed through, taking the corner at the intersection much faster than she normally would. Get to the apartment, get the stuff, go somewhere else. Not the

Holiday Inn, not without the baby. *When Chalk finds out I didn't take the kid, I need to be far, far away.*

She spared one last look at the yacht anchored offshore. Was he still on there? Teena wasn't sure. She wished she'd listened closer to that part of the plan. Get the baby, take it to Holiday Inn, I'll deal with the wife, then I'll meet you there. That's all Chalk had told her.

On the way through town, Teena prayed to get home, get her drugs, and get gone. Her own car had been repossessed shortly after she'd lost her job at The Joker's Wild. Chalk had a friend rent this one so she could deliver the baby to the hotel. She would just have to drive it as far as she could until she was able to make enough dough to buy a bus ticket to another state.

Her cousin, Mara, lived in Colorado. She was the only one who still answered Teena's calls. *Maybe a couple tricks will get me enough for a bus ticket before dawn. Mara will let me stay with her. I'll just leave the car in a downtown parking lot. Use a fake name for a bus ticket. Start a new life. Maybe even get off the junk.*

But when she arrived at their apartment, Chalk met her at the door. Somehow, he'd gotten there ahead of her, probably brought the little boat back to shore while she was busy yanking the stroller up and down the seventeen steps.

"What are you doing here?" he asked, voice like death. "You haven't had time to deliver that kid yet." He had a towel in one hand. Fresh t-shirt in the other.

Teena's knees almost buckled. "I've got her out in the car. Just came for the stuff." She tried on a smile. "I'll go ahead and take her now." She tentatively held out one hand, palm up, hoping for her dope.

Chalk rubbed the towel across his hair, dropped it into her palm. "I'm coming, too. Now, I gotta be there when you hand it over." He pulled on the t-shirt, picked up a handgun from the bedside table and cupped Teena's elbow with his other hand. "I hope the nice couple is still waiting."

27

THE PHONE CALL

Linzy wiped her hands on her apron and grabbed her phone before it could jangle again. Her latest ringtone was soothing, a carol of bells. It invaded her thoughts gently. She'd been daydreaming about the Stutter Creek cabin as her hands diced onions and shredded chicken for Blue's favorite enchilada casserole. He was not at the fire station today. He was helping his dad harvest winter vegetables.

She put the phone to her ear and was immediately struck with such a profound sense of déjà vu it made her stagger. Yanking out a kitchen chair, she plopped down, wondering at the sudden shift in the atmosphere.

"Hello?" She wasn't certain the word made it past her lips. But it must have.

The other person began to speak.

Linzy's world slowed and tipped. "No, Sash isn't with me. Isn't she at home?"

She listened intently for a moment. "Missing? What do you mean, missing? She's probably just walking the beach—"

"She's gone," Cam interrupted. "She left the baby and took off. Left behind *everything*." He drew in a shaky breath and continued.

"She wrote a note saying you were at some pier, and she was going to get you. I guess if you aren't with her, then that was just an excuse. Maybe I deserve it." He stopped speaking and waited for her reply.

Linzy tried to focus on what he was saying, but her mind wouldn't go there. *Not again, not more tragedy, no. It can't be ...*

In her lap, the fingers of her left hand twisted the fabric of her mom's old apron tighter and tighter until it was wadded up in her fist like a soft handful of fear.

A tinge of exasperation in his tone, Cam said, "Linz, did you hear me?"

With the forefinger of her right hand, Linzy tapped the speaker volume, turning it to max. "She's not here, Cam. And she's not *gone*," she paused. "She can't be *gone*." She tried to make her voice pleasant, to catch him off guard. "Are you drinking again? I mean, Sash wouldn't go off and leave Skye. You *know* that. Besides, I haven't seen her, and I sure don't know anything about a pier."

Linzy kept the phone connection open even while, in her head, she had the sudden realization she needed to get there. To the beach house. Her sister would not go anywhere without the baby. Not outside, not to take a shower, not to run an errand. Not to walk the beach, and especially not to some random pier. *He must be drunk again. That's all there is to it.*

She stood to remove her apron. "Did you try to call her?" she asked Cam. "When did you last see her?" Her voice sounded authoritative, even to her own ears.

"Yes, I tried calling and texting. She doesn't even read them. Her phone seems to be turned off." He let out a noisy breath. "I saw her this morning, when I left for work."

A million horrific scenarios skated through Linzy's head, the baby alone, screaming in her crib, hungry, filthy diaper, mommy nowhere around. Then she realized Cam was still talking.

"—got home from meeting a client a couple hours ago and she wasn't here—just the note. And the baby."

Linzy closed the dumbfounded panic-hole whistling through her head and forced herself to pay attention. "Wait, are you saying she's been gone for hours, and you're just now calling me? What the hell, Cam? You know she wouldn't leave Skye alone. And she wouldn't go anywhere without letting you and me know. Is there something else you're not telling me?"

She made herself inhale and the oxygen to her brain helped to clear her mind. "Did you speak with her on the phone at all after you left?" She pulled up her sister's contact and sent a quick text without letting on. *"Where are you, Sash? Cam says you've gone to some pier to pick me up. Call me. Now."*

"No, Sis," Cam said, "I had showings all day."

Linzy bit her tongue. *Sis?* He never called her that. Sis was reserved for her and Sasha. Not him. She was not his sis. Since the Halloween episode, she was barely back to claiming him as an in-law. Although, to be truthful, she'd thought everything had smoothed out since then. Now, this.

Through a rising haze of worry and anger, Linzy heard Cam saying, "I got home from work, and when I didn't find her in the house, I went outside, checked the kiln house, checked everywhere. She wasn't there, so of course I came back inside. That's when I found the note saying she had gone to get you at some pier."

Linzy's suspicions were growing by leaps and bounds. "She can't be gone. We speak on the phone all the time." *But did we speak today?* They called each other so frequently the days sometimes ran together. Nevertheless, her sister would never take off without telling her. Never. At least not voluntarily.

Cam continued speaking, "She stuck the little note under the heart magnet on the fridge. The same one we always leave notes under. That's why I hurried down to the beach, to see if she was at the private community pier."

His voice cracked a little, but Linzy's suspicious nature had been triggered. She felt no sympathy whatsoever.

"Sis," he said again, "if she isn't with you, then she must've run off with someone." He hesitated again. "A boyfriend, maybe."

Linzy closed her eyes, took a deep breath, and willed away the creeping fear and anger. This reeked of deception. Her sister would not run off and leave that baby.

She took another deep breath, *inhale through the nose, exhale through pursed lips.* A technique one of the therapists had taught her and Sash to help them calm their minds when they felt like screaming. Or was it Pastor Sue who taught them that technique? *Who cares, focus, dammit, focus.* Panic gripped her in its claws.

Through clenched teeth, Linzy whispered, "Cameron. You know my sister does not have a boyfriend. Her baby—your daughter—is barely four months old. She has me, you, and the baby. That's it. Except for Blue and his family, and she certainly isn't with them. They would have called me if she suddenly appeared at their house without the baby."

Her breath felt like fire when she inhaled this time. *Think, Linz! We've been planning a big Christmas dinner. We've been talking about our menu since Thanksgiving.* She tried to force her mind to cut through the chaos, but none of this made sense. As she questioned him, another thought popped into her head. Their recent conversation about Stutter Creek. New Years and skiing and how good it would be to light a fire in the cabin's big fireplace.

"Do you think the baby will be ready for a trip to the mountains?" Linzy had asked.

"I think she might be," Sash had replied. "I know I will be ready. I don't think we've ever been away this long."

That's right, Linzy thought. We've been through too much already. Haven't made it back yet. She chided herself again, tried to pull her mind back to the present, but the thought of Stutter Creek wouldn't leave her alone. "I'll call you back," she told Cam, realizing he hadn't answered her question, *and* that her sister hadn't answered her text. "I'm going to call her."

It was easy to tap her sister's contact again. The little phone icon this time. But Sasha did not pick up. It went straight into the void. Nothing happened.

"Oh, Sash," she said tersely. "Where are you?" Maybe she is hurt somewhere, or had a mental breakdown ... maybe her phone died, and no. She would never leave the baby, no matter what. That's all there is to it.

Linzy clicked over to tracking to find her sister's phone. *Should have thought of this immediately.* But that didn't work, either. She pulled up the contact she'd made for the prepaid phone they'd put in the emergency go bag. It was off, too.

She called Cam back.

Her brother-in-law said, "She didn't answer, did she?"

"No, it's like the phone doesn't exist." She paused. "I can't even track her, can you?"

"I can't. I mean. It's obviously dead or turned off," he said. "That's why I think—"

"No, dammit. Do not say she ran off. Do not say that again. You know it isn't true. What do the cops say?"

He went on as if she hadn't spoken. "The reason I say Sash is missing or has a boyfriend is because in addition to her phone being turned off, her Cadillac is still in the garage, and she left everything, Sis. Even the—"

Linzy exploded. "What the *fuck* do you mean, she didn't even take the car?" Linzy never used the F word. Never. But now she flung it out like a pro. Like a rock star or some high-on-fame celebrity. "You let me sit here and call her and jack around while you sit there knowing she didn't even take her car? You *fuck*. How is she supposed to be gone somewhere to pick me up if she didn't even take the car?"

"You didn't give me a chance—"

"She did *not* leave home without a car. She did not leave home without her baby. No. No way." Her voice seethed with anger. "I'm asking you again. What did the hell did the police say?"

"Calm down," Cam said. "They said she was an adult and would come home when she was ready. I didn't call you sooner because I was embarrassed and pissed off and I was doing my best to keep the baby happy, because let me tell you, Skye was mad as hell. She did not want me, or her Stuffy Dog, or even a bottle. She wanted her mommy." And then Cam, the snazzy, card-playing, real estate magnate, lost it. He began to bawl, blubbering worse than baby Skye ever had.

"Okay," Linzy said, realizing she might have pushed him too hard. "Okay, never mind. As long as the baby is all right. Let's try and think, okay?"

But Cam was too deep in his head. He couldn't seem to stop. Finally, he said, "When I finally got Skye settled, I called the cops, but they didn't seem concerned because she left that note saying she went to get you at the pier. They seemed to think that meant she'd gone with a friend, that she'd probably be right back. I thought so, too. It seems stupid now, but the baby was beginning to fuss again, and I was trying to change her diaper, and you know, all of a sudden, I realized she was crying because Sash still wasn't home."

He tried to get better control of himself. "The note said she had to go to the pier. To get *you*. Do you understand what I'm saying? Do you know how that feels? It was like, like … I don't know. It wasn't like Sash. It was cold …"

Linzy tried not to blow up again. He's worried about how he feels? "Tell me the truth, Cam. Did you lock her out again? Is that why she left? Did you lock her out but keep the baby this time? Is she walking up and down the beach right now, trying other houses, looking for a phone to call me?"

She stopped talking, waiting on him to respond, remembering how she and Sash had packed the emergency go bag together.

They'd put in the prepaid phone Blue had bought, and Linzy

had even sprung for the extra key fob for the Cadillac so Cam wouldn't know. Together, they'd hidden the bag in the store house with the new kiln and equipment.

But if she didn't take the car.

Or the baby.

Then she probably didn't take the go bag, either. So, where's her regular phone? Where is *she*?

Panic dug its claws in deeper. Even if she had to walk all the way down the beach to town, Sash would've had time to call by now. If she could.

Cam's voice wriggled into her ear. "We didn't fight. I wasn't even home. I was at work, showing a house." He cleared his throat. "I know she would never endanger the baby by leaving that way."

Linzy agreed. The go bag had diapers and formula, and the prepaid phone. There was no logical reason to leave Skye alone. That's why she asked Cam if he forced her out but kept the baby.

But he didn't respond to that. He was still talking.

"She must've waited until I was nearly home before she took off. I messaged her to let her know I was on my way. But I didn't hear back from her. I assumed it was because she was busy or walking the beach. Now, I think that must be when she left. I still can't believe it. I was on my way home." He swallowed, hard enough that Linzy heard it over the phone. "It has to be another man. Maybe she's punishing me. For the other thing."

Linzy bit the inside of her lip to keep from blurting out all the hateful words that came to her mind about the *other thing*.

"Sasha is an excellent mother," she said. "She would not endanger Skye by leaving her alone." *Not unless she was forced.*

28

THE SEARCH BEGINS

Linzy glanced down at her screen to make certain there'd been no reply to her first text while she and Cameron were talking.

Nothing.

Something awful has happened. Regardless of what Cam said about a note, Linzy knew something was very wrong. In the back of her mind, she wondered if there was a note at all. *I have to get there. Check on Skye, see if Sasha took the go bag, find her. Not sure what's going on. Not even sure Cam is telling the truth.*

She grabbed her purse, keys, and phone charger. *Think I have one in the car, but better to be certain. What about the food on the counter? Leave it.*

Cam began speaking again. "The note says she went to get you at the pier. And that's all it says. Nothing about leaving Skye." His voice cracked.

Linzy listened with one ear. *I just have to get there. I'll call the police on the way.* Her walking shoes were by the front door. "I'll be there soon," she said bluntly. "I want to see that note. Don't throw it away."

She hung up the phone without waiting for a reply. She'd lost all confidence in him, once more. Even though she *had* begun to trust him again, this was different. Not calling her immediately? Worse than different.

Where are you, Sissy. Send me a message. Show me a sign. Something. Anything. For the first time in her life, Linzy didn't notice driving through the wisteria gate, or through the tiny town of Brookville, nor even over the long stretch of the Gulf Freeway to the causeway. Her mind was miles away, searching past conversations for clues to her sister's sudden disappearance. *Maybe she'll be there when I arrive. No, she would call me. Or Cam would, knowing I'm on my way. Wouldn't he?*

She crossed onto the island leaving the causeway behind, flowing with the rest of the twilight traffic headed to The Strand, or to the seawall beaches, or even just going home from work on the mainland. The sun edged toward the horizon, painting a yellow landing strip on the calm water.

Following the freeway curve that would take her to Broadway and 61st Street, Linzy tried to dispel the horrible sense of dread enveloping her. She couldn't feel Sasha. Anywhere. She could only taste salt, and it was bitter.

Turning west on Seawall Boulevard, Linzy soon approached Sunset Drive which would take her to the Sunset Drift community. Cam had made certain the gate was open. *Score one for him.*

The house was well lit, every window shining, the understory lights twinkling. Linzy immediately took note of the fact that her sister's Caddy was parked right there in the open garage.

Cam must've been watching for her. He headed down the steps before she even had her gearshift in park. "So glad you're here," he said, leaning into her space as she opened the car door. "Skye is going to be so glad to see you."

Linzy imagined the baby fussing in her crib while he was

down here, greeting her. "Is she in her room?" she demanded. "In her crib?"

Cam pushed the tips of his fingers into his sandy colored hair and stepped back so she could get out. "No, no. She's in her playpen, in the living room. Fussing a little. Probably getting hungry. Thank God Sash was introducing her to the bot—"

Linzy grabbed her purse and cell phone, an awful thought creeping into her head. *Did you wait until the baby was being weaned before you got rid of your wife?* She'd seen so many true crime shows in which the husband got rid of the wife when he tired of her or wanted someone else. *No! Don't go there. Not yet. Not her Sash.*

She pushed past him, headed for the stairs. "Tell me everything you know," she said. "What else did the cops say?"

"They said they're sending someone out to get the information."

"That's what they told me, too," she said. "I called them from the car." They didn't seem too worried, though. Like Cam said earlier, a grown woman who leaves a note didn't seem to be very high on their radar.

Even after Linzy had told the dispatcher about Ancho and how he'd murdered their parents, the dispatcher had simply said she'd pass it along and Linzy could fill in the details when the officers arrived. She started to tell the woman about the Halloween episode, but the woman just said to save it for the deputies when they arrived.

Linzy slammed the car door and hurried around to the back of the house and up the seventeen steps without waiting on Cam. The entire southwest wall of glass looked in upon the Christmas tree like a work of art. Linzy could've gone through the garage and into the kitchen, but something had beckoned her toward the beach.

The wide deck was painted from the side by the dissolving sunset, waves lapped, foamy and gentle, upon the darkening sand.

Linzy didn't stop to admire the view, just pushed open the door and walked straight inside. The house was immaculate. She passed the Christmas tree bedecked with Sash's sparkly shell art along with some of the familiar ornaments from their childhood. They'd split them up when the decorating began.

She went straight to the baby lying in her playpen. "Where is your Mama?" she whispered to the fussy child. "I know she didn't go off and leave you. She wouldn't."

Skye held up her plump little arms and Linzy plucked her up and carried her to the kitchen in search of a bottle of formula. To her surprise, Cam had one ready.

Without a word, Linzy tested the formula's warmth on the inside of her elbow, then gave it to the baby. Skye closed her eyes and began to drink. *If only you could talk, sweet baby.*

Linzy carried her to the bedroom, checked her diaper, it was dry. So far, Cam seemed to be on the ball. She found the baby's jacket and put it on her while she was still concentrating on the bottle.

"Umm, Linz, what are you doing?" It was clear from the tone of his voice that Cam thought Linzy was about to take Skye and leave.

"I know where Sash keeps the stroller, so I am taking that, and the baby, and we are going to search the beach for her mother."

Cam nodded and pulled on his jacket.

Together, they exited the house and went back down the steps to the underneath. Linzy didn't see the stroller out in the open, so she looked in the store house. She was somewhat dismayed to see the emergency go bag right where they'd hidden it in the corner.

But the stroller wasn't there.

Images of Sasha lying hurt or unconscious swept across Linzy's brain.

She took a calming breath and huffed it out, causing her bangs to flutter. Then she pushed her phone into her pants pocket determined to search every inch of the property before tackling the beach. *That stroller must be here somewhere. It's supposed to be here or under the deck. I can't get very far carrying the baby this way, but once the deputies arrive to keep an eye on her, I can go. I just don't feel right leaving Skye alone with Cam.*

She carried the baby back into the house, to wait. Cam was right behind them. Glancing toward the wall of windows, Linzy realized it would be dark soon. Giving each room a thorough search—looking into the closets and even under beds, feeling foolish for not doing so at first—she realized halfway through that she was also paying strict attention to any cleaning items, unusual smears, or errant stains splattered on the walls or ceilings.

Too many TV shows and novels, her mind insisted again. But she went through the rest of the house, anyway. She inspected the bathrooms and the laundry area, even peeked into the washer and dryer—to see if any towels had been laundered recently—but nothing seemed amiss.

Her sister had always been a conscientious housekeeper. She'd said it was one of the few things over which she had complete control.

"I've got to go to the beach," Linzy told Cam, an idea striking her out of the blue. "I just can't wait. Maybe I can use the baby sling, the one Sash wraps around her back and chest to hold the baby when she's out of the stroller?"

Cam appeared perplexed, then it dawned on him. "You mean that fabric thing Sash wraps around herself? I don't really know where she keeps it." His face showed the truth of his words. "I suppose it's in the baby's room. Probably in the closet." He started to walk, then turned back, snapped his fingers.

"You just looked in there, didn't you? Maybe she keeps it in the car. For when she's shopping." He led the way through the kitchen toward the connecting garage door.

She might've kept it in the car, Linzy thought. It wasn't much, kind of a long wrap that held the baby to her chest. But if it wasn't there, then she had no idea where it would be.

Cam went to the Cadillac and popped the trunk. "Here it is."

Linzy had a sudden need to see in that cavernous trunk for herself. *Can't believe I didn't look in there already.* She hurried down the steps. Sure enough, there it was. Folded up in a tidy pile, just where it would be most useful if Sash found herself in town without a stroller. There was nothing else.

In a calm voice Cam said, "Why don't you just let me search the beach again, while you stay here with Skye?"

"You can go, if you want," Linzy said. "But I also need to search for her. I know the places she loves. We've walked it together so many times ..." She attempted to wrap the sling around herself and the baby.

Cam took it from her, then took Skye. "I think I'd better just take the baby back inside. It's getting colder with the sun setting. I'll keep looking for the stroller. We'll catch up with you." He looked toward the gate. "Deputies should be here, soon."

Linzy let her gaze follow his. She hated to leave before law enforcement arrived, but she was itching to search. Holding up her phone, she said, "Please call me when they arrive."

He agreed, moving back toward the steps to the kitchen entryway.

"Oh," she called after him. "The note?"

Cam reached into his pocket, pulled out a small page of folded paper. He handed it to her without comment.

The page appeared to have come from a diary of some kind. The edges were ragged, as if ripped hurriedly. Linzy thought it very odd that her sis would write on that. She hated untidiness and these edges were the epitome of untidy. Not to mention the fact that the girl adored note pads and pens and all kinds of artsy paper and stationery. Why on earth would she write it on a page from her diary or journal? *Unless she was under duress and it was the closest thing to hand.*

She made a mental note to look in the kitchen later. One of the gifts she'd given Sasha for a housewarming had been a magnetic notepad that stuck to the fridge. It had a beach scene for a background. She'd assumed the note was written on that—after all, he'd said it was stuck on the fridge.

Then she remembered how he said it had been stuck under a magnet where they always leave notes for each other. *I seem to be trying to make everything a clue.*

"Wow." She scratched at the ragged edge of the paper lightly. "She must've been in a big hurry when she wrote this." She snapped a photo of the note with her phone camera.

Cam opened his mouth to say something but then closed it again. Apparently, her photo taking surprised him.

She didn't care what Cam thought. She just wanted to make certain the exact same note was handed over to the deputies when they arrived.

"I'll be back shortly," she said, delaying a bit longer. "Please don't forget to call me when they get here." She hated to leave Skye with him again.

"Of course," he replied, his tone stiff. "I'm sure you'll see them from the beach anyway."

Linzy knew she was being bitchy and bossy, but she had a pervasive fear that both he and the baby would disappear as soon as she was out of sight. That's just stupid, she told herself. Just paranoia. She thought of turning, grabbing Skye, running down the drive toward the gate to meet the officers who should be arriving. But that would be ridiculous. Not good for anyone. *I've got to get a grip. He isn't going to do anything with law enforcement almost here; besides, he seems almost as distraught as I am.*

Linzy stopped trying to figure it out. Somehow her feet were carrying her back around the base of the house toward the beach.

29

SEARCHING

The soft sand stretched away into the waning sunset. The foamy water fringed the shore like the ragged edges of the note. Linzy felt her panic rising again. She cupped her hands around her mouth to call out for her sister, knowing even as she did how fruitless her voice was against the Gulf. But she had to do something. This was quickly sliding from mystifying straight into terrifying.

"Sasha!" Linzy called, unable to help herself. "Where are you?"

No one was on this end of the beach. From this distance, every house appeared empty except for twinkle deck lights just coming on. For some reason, the house windows all appeared dark as well. Even though some were strictly weekend homes, where were the occupants of the others?

Linzy supposed some residents might be dining in town or at the community club. Maybe even out on their private yachts. She could see one out past the breakers, way out in smooth water. Or was that a cruise ship? From here, she couldn't tell. It seemed to be moving away.

Her feet took her a little farther from the house. Not too far, though. For all her smart words to Cam, she really had no idea where Sash might go without a car. Besides, she couldn't make herself leave the baby completely.

At last, her phone vibrated in her pocket. It was a text from Blue asking if she'd made it. She'd finally had sense enough to send him a text from the highway, telling him she was headed to Galveston because Cam couldn't find Sash.

"I made it, but still no Sash. Sorry I didn't let you know when I arrived. Cam was watching for me, and I forgot everything when I saw him without her. We haven't found anything yet. I'm on the beach, but there's no sign of her. She didn't take her car, or the go bag we packed."

"The baby okay?" he asked.

Linzy continued a bit farther down the beach, eyes scanning from water to shore to dunes and back again. "Yes," she texted back. "Skye is good. She's with Cam at the house. Deputies are on the way."

"That's a relief," he replied. "I'm almost there. I won't let you do this alone."

Linzy smiled, but it was a sad smile. Sad because she knew he wouldn't be coming if he wasn't worried. Also, because she realized her own house was vacant. If Sash found her way there, no one would be home. She could get in, though. All the codes were the same.

"Thank you," Linzy typed. "I should have just brought you with me. I'm not thinking right. I even left all the casserole makings on the counter." Her breath caught in her throat as she tapped. "This makes no sense, Blue. I'm really scared."

"I'll be there soon," he sent back. "Hang on."

"Okay," she replied. "Thank you."

The pulsing text ellipses started and stopped, indicating Blue was typing some more. At last, another message came through. "I know Sash wouldn't leave the baby. I'm afraid she fell or fainted somewhere. Don't worry. We'll find her."

Knowing Blue was coming eased Linzy's mind a little. She

started to put her phone back in her hip pocket. Instead, she dialed 9-1-1.

When the dispatcher answered, "9-1-1, what is the nature of your emergency?"

Linzy stammered, "I, um, I'm sorry. I called earlier, about my missing sister—"

"Let me transfer you. What is the address you're calling about?"

Linzy told her, then said, "I called once already. And my brother-in-law called, too. But I've come all the way from Brookville, and no one is here yet."

The dispatcher told her she was transferring her to the Sheriff's Department. "Please hold."

Another voice answered and asked her what the problem was. So Linzy went through it all again.

"Is your sister an adult, ma'am?"

Linzy turned her collar up against the breeze but kept her eye on the sandy shoreline. "Well, yes, but she's a young mother with a new baby, and she wouldn't go off and leave her alone like this. My brother-in-law says he also called in, but no one has ever come so I thought—"

"What is your brother-in-law's name and address?"

Linzy told her.

"Hold while I connect you with the correct department, please."

Taking a deep breath, Linzy leaned over to push aside a large clump of sea oats not too far from the house. The oats were not tall enough that she could be hiding there, but they were just tall enough that she could be lying there, unconscious or hurt, like Blue had said.

Linzy waited. She'd wanted to tell this new dispatcher about the kind deputies who had responded at Halloween. *Send them back, please.* But the woman didn't give her a chance. She put her on hold, instead.

Every few seconds Linzy checked her volume to make certain she hadn't muted it or disconnected the call altogether. But nope, still on hold.

She continued down the beach, slowly.

At the first dark house, she checked her phone again, then marched up to the lower area of the sprawling home. Like all the beach houses, this one was built on stilts, or pilings.

Underneath the first floor the area was dark except for the twinkle lights and motion-detector lamps. Linzy didn't know the people who owned the place, but she had greeted them a couple of times when she and Sasha had been walking the beach. The woman was older, the man a bit younger, or so it appeared, and they were both friendly. She recalled how the man chucked baby Skye under the chin making her giggle. Sash said it was the first time she'd ever seen them.

Linzy strode into the bright white of the first motion detector and climbed straight upstairs to the massive double doors. The interior of the house appeared dark. The drapes and blinds drawn. Linzy rang the bell and waited.

The view from their vast west-facing deck took her breath away. The last bit of sun dripped into the ocean as if the entire horizon were melting. Muted sparks of light played hide-n-seek in the waves, one last hurrah before the darkness replaced them with stars.

Linzy swiped a loose hank of hair off her face, her eyes watering from the stinging breeze. The wind off the Gulf blew constantly, seemingly much stronger around dusk. She held her hair in a ponytail grip on one side of her neck and held her phone in her other hand.

"Hello," she called out. "Anyone home?" She'd seen a Beach Bum 4-wheeler stored beneath the house, but no other vehicles. Speaking directly into the doorbell camera, she said, "I hope you don't mind if I look around. I'm searching for my sister, Sasha. She lives next door. You've met us both, walking the beach …"

She began to feel silly standing there talking to a camera, but she wanted to cover herself in case anyone wondered what she was doing. She assumed all these security systems were remotely connected to the owner's phone app. "Anyhow, I'm just going to look around down below. In case she fell and hurt herself or something."

Linz snapped her lips shut, then blurted, "Sash is missing. We can't find her or get ahold of her. Please, if you can hear this message, please tell me if you've seen her."

Turning away, she stopped, then glanced all around the deck. It wrapped the house on three sides; deck furniture scattered about in cozy groupings. There was nothing to indicate Sash had been there. Nothing was amiss.

She trod lightly back down the wooden steps, still holding her phone, but allowing her hair to blow free so she could hold on to the railing for safety.

Underneath the house, same story. No sign of her sister at all.

Linzy looked at Cam and Sash's house next door, not too far away, but at least a few hundred feet. Two more houses could fit in the space between them if this was a middle-class neighborhood. But this was high dollar, as their dad might have said. From here, she could make out Cam's silhouette, standing in the window of the baby's room. He had little Skye in the crook of his arm, his other hand holding the bottle to her lips.

The baby appeared to be drinking contentedly.

Linzy couldn't tell if Cam watched her, or the coming night. There were no law enforcement vehicles there, yet. She glanced down at the phone in her hand, and it squawked as if she'd conjured someone.

"Hello, Miss? This is Detective Banks. Sorry to keep you waiting. Are you there?"

Linzy glanced down at the screen, but of course it wasn't on Facetime. Just a simple call. "Yes, I'm still here. Can you help me?" She heard a chair squeak, maybe one of the old rollie types.

"I'll certainly try," he said. "Why don't you tell me the problem."

Refusing to let herself get exasperated, since she'd already told two dispatchers the problem, Linzy said, "I'm at my sister and brother-in-law's home," she gave the address, "and my sister is missing."

The squeak of the chair, thump of feet on the floor. "That's a pretty elite address, Miss ... what did you say your name was?"

"My name is Linzy Everly, but my sister's name is Sasha Gaines. I think my brother-in-law already made a report. He said that he did. And I called from my car, on my way here, to say I was coming. But no one has arrived yet, and I've come all the way from Brookville."

"What's his name, your brother-in-law?"

"Cam. Cameron Gaines. He's in real estate. Signs all over town—"

"Yes," Detective Banks interrupted. "I've seen those signs. Man. I'm in the wrong business if it nets a home in that area."

"He's well off, that's true. But my sis has her own money, and they've got a new baby, only three no, four months old. Sasha is thrilled to be a first-time mommy. She would never take off and leave her baby. *Never.*" By this time, frustration and fear were at war inside her. Tears clogged her throat.

"All right, then," the detective said. "Just stay put. I'm on my way. I have to apologize for not coming immediately. We had what appears to be a suicide at the downtown Holiday Inn. Lots of folks to interview, plus waiting on the Medical Examiner and Crime Scene folks. This time of year, depression can be worse. Unusual for us, here, but don't worry. I'm on the way now. We'll look things over. Do you know if she took her phone with her?"

Linzy tried to remember what Cam had said. "Not certain. All I know is that she isn't answering it, and we can't track her on it. I've tried and tried to call and text."

She continued looking around the beach while they spoke.

With Cam and the baby visible in the window, she felt free to keep going, check a bit further up where the native grasses and decorative sand fencing met the dunes. Sash could be lying back there, behind it. In her head, Linzy saw images of bare feet, blue lips, blood spattered grass in the wan light…

Her heart sped up as she pushed aside clump after clump, peered behind every strip of picket fencing, checked and rechecked the earth for any sign of footprints, or disturbance. But there was nothing. The surf had washed the sand as clean as if she'd tossed it in her mom's old Maytag back in Brookville.

The detective told her, once more, to stay put. "We're on our way," he said. Then he clicked off.

Linzy came to the second dark house. I'll do the same thing, she thought. Go up, introduce myself to the camera, look around. Maybe soon, Detective Banks will be arriving.

This home also had the required pilings with steps leading up to the deck. It was easily the largest house on this end of the development. Three stories, multiple decks, and she could no longer see Cam and the baby in the lighted window because of the other house in between. I'll make it quick she thought. Way too dark and spooky here. I wonder if it's normal for both houses to be empty at this time of year.

She remembered her phone flashlight and thumbed it on. As with the other house, the steps were lit by rail-draped twinkle lights, otherwise it would've been difficult to navigate. As before, Linzy walked right up to the doorbell cam and spoke directly into it after pressing the bell. She tried to recall if she'd ever met these folks but didn't think so. The Yorkies and their folks lived next door, the third house down from Sash and Cam.

After stating her reason for being there, she waited for a response. But there was none.

Holding her hair again, Linzy made her way around the three decks. From here, she could see all the way to the community entrance gate. Two vehicles were entering.

Linzy hurried back to the ground. The sun was completely down. Underneath the raised house it was dark as pitch except for the lights on the stairs.

Suddenly, a strong motion light flooded the area and there, in the bright glow, a familiar shape stood out. It appeared to be a balloon-tire beach stroller just like the one Sash pushed Skye in every single day.

Linzy gasped and her fingers flew over her phone screen. She activated the camera. First, she took a straight-on picture, and then another from the side. Carefully, she checked the area for footprints—there were many—lit up by the flood light. She peered all around, expecting to find her sister lying incapacitated in some way.

But she was not there. Nothing else seemed out of the ordinary, only some vehicle tracks leading in and out of the carport.

Oh, my God. Did someone grab Sash on the beach and stuff her in a car? Even if they had, it wouldn't explain why the baby was at the house while the stroller was here.

Linzy's sisterly senses began to blink her brother-in-law's name like faulty neon. *Cam. Cam. Cam.* He had to be involved. How else would he have the baby but not his wife?

"Sasha," she called softly, afraid of alerting anyone who might be holding her. "Are you here, Sissy?" Was she being held captive inside this very house?

Linzy didn't know what to do. She left the stroller untouched and sent a message to Blue telling him where she was. "Please bring the detective down to the big house if he is already here when you arrive." She thought about adding another text to tell him what she'd found, but her fingers hesitated in case Cam was standing near him.

30

SASH TRIES TO ESCAPE

The boat grazed Sasha's head, a glancing blow just hard enough to knock her under the water. Rough hands latched onto her. She fought them like a wild wet cat, biting and scratching, until someone began to punch her in the head—knuckles like ridges of rock—and then her face went under the water.

At the last second, she felt herself being shoved and pulled up and out of the water. More rough hands grasped her under the arms and dragged her violently into the boat. Salt water streamed from her sinuses and mouth, and she coughed and sputtered when she tried to scream.

The yacht waited out past the shallows and the small boat raced toward it at top speed. Sash felt semi-aware when they hauled her aboard, but a deep-as-night blackness overcame her when a hypodermic pricked her skin. The feeling was indescribably worse than any wave crashing over her head. It was a feeling of death beyond death.

Her last coherent thought was *Our Father Who art in Heaven ...*

~

Linzy stood to the side of the empty house, watching as Blue pulled into Cam's drive directly behind an unmarked car. She'd had to walk out onto the beach—past the sightline of the house in between—to be able to see all the way back to Cam's.

The night air had cooled quickly in the twilight. She pulled her sweater closer as she headed back. In moments, Blue emerged from beneath Cam's carport. His familiar blue-jeaned shape was easy to recognize. The moon was beginning to rise, lighting the beach just enough to see. Beside Blue walked a tall, slender man in a gray sport coat lighter than the twilight.

A Galveston County Sheriff's K-9 SUV pulled into the drive behind the unmarked car. Linzy had been so focused on Blue, and the man she assumed was the detective, she hadn't even seen the SUV come through the gate, just the earlier cruiser and the unmarked car. *Suddenly, everyone is taking it seriously.*

Her heart clutched like an old engine as the deputy driving the SUV stepped out, opened the rear door, and tugged a leash.

A large dog exited the vehicle in one smooth motion. Linzy recognized the long, floppy ears and jowls of a bloodhound. She inhaled sharply as Cam appeared at the bottom of the steps and handed something to the detective who gave it over to the K-9 Officer. He offered it to the dog's nose and said something she couldn't hear. The bloodhound immediately began to track.

This just got real, Linzy thought. She pressed one hand to her chest, feeling for her heartbeat as she looked at Blue standing beside the man in the suit.

As always, the Gulf wind swished her hair across her face. When she clawed it aside, the bloodhound was busy nosing around the posts of Cam and Sash's house. Linzy found herself running toward them.

In the seconds it took Linzy to get back to the house, the hound had followed its nose right up the seventeen steps to the beach-facing door. Everyone followed it up.

Cam opened the door. The dog and handler went inside, tracking straight to Skye's playpen. Through the door-glass, the rest of them observed the handler offer the garment to the hound's nose again, encouraging the dog to go through the rest of the house.

It went back out the door instead.

"Strange," the gray suited man said. "Why wouldn't it find her scent in every room?"

Linzy looked at the tan garment the handler held in one hand. The big, bald officer was bent over, offering it to the dog again. Tan. A tan something Linzy didn't recognize because she had never seen it before. *Tan?* Sasha didn't wear tan. She said neutrals were for people who lacked imagination.

She stepped forward, meaning to follow the pair as they went back down the steps.

The officer held up a hand in warning. "Stay back, please. Orson is working."

Linzy ignored him and said, "That coat, or whatever it is, doesn't belong to my sister. Who gave you that? Did Cam give you that?" She wanted to rush over and yank the thing out of his hands.

The officer appeared confused. He held the coat up, looked at it as if seeing it for the first time. "The husband gave us this for scent. Said it was his wife's most recently worn garment."

Shaking her head, thunder clouds building inside her skull, Linzy looked toward Blue and the gentleman she assumed was the detective. Cam was inside the house with Skye.

The detective in the gray suit looked at her as if for the first time. "You must be Linzy, the sister I spoke with on the phone." He didn't wait for a reply. "Why do you say this isn't your sister's garment? Couldn't she have a coat you don't know about?" His voice was smooth, no nonsense.

"She could," Linzy said. "But she's never worn a thing like this in her life, except at Halloween when we were kids. In day-to-day life, she would never wear tan. And certainly not wool." She nodded toward it. "Sash is allergic to wool. Gives her hives."

The detective took the coat from the officer, looked at the tag inside. "I believe you. But someone belongs to this coat. And they've worn it recently in your sister's home. Near the baby's playpen. Let's see where the dog leads."

Linzy's mind exploded, thunder booming. So many possible scenarios crashed into her brain, she felt faint. Then the obvious hit her. "Oh, my God. Let it go. Let the dog follow. If it goes to the stroller ..." She'd almost forgotten it in all the excitement.

And then the second thing hit her. "Why did Cam give us this? It isn't Sash's, I know it isn't."

The detective pulled out his phone, pressed a key, spoke into it. "I need to speak with the husband. Do not let him leave."

Linzy glanced back at the house. The deputy who drove the marked cruiser mounted the steps to the deck.

Orson, the hound, was halfway down the beach now. Apparently, he still had a good lock on the scent. Linzy knew where he was headed. The stroller. She hurried to keep up. Blue stayed beside her, touched her hand. She'd almost forgotten about him.

The closer they got to the second house, the faster the dog tracked. His nose never left the wet sand. The large officer struggled to keep up.

And then they were there.

Orson went straight to the balloon tire stroller and sat, waiting. The twinkly deck lights seemed incongruous in this tense setting. The motion light flooded the area.

Linzy felt a tearing at her senses, as if some major turning point had been achieved. "I don't know who that coat belongs to, or why Cam gave it to you, but apparently the owner of it pushed the baby's stroller here, without the baby in it." Her mind whirled. "Did they do that to lure Sash down here?" She pointed to the car tracks she'd seen earlier.

"But the baby is at home," Blue said.

Linzy shook her head. "I don't understand. But I know this. That dog will never find Sash with that tan coat to go on."

"Take him all around this house," the detective instructed the officer. "Find out if he alerts any place else."

The big dog went up and down the steps and the decks without alerting. Then it came right back to the area around the stroller and stopped where the tire tracks began.

Linzy hugged herself to keep from exploding. Panic, followed by rage, drove her blood pressure to the top of her head. "Obviously something horrible has happened to my sister. If you wait right here, I will get a shirt from my car. One of *Sasha's* shirts. She stayed at my house a while back, after her husband threw her and the baby outside in the middle of the night. I still have a couple of their things in a bag in my trunk."

She hurried back down the beach toward the car, hoping the man would take her seriously, thanking God she hadn't thrown the clothes in the washer the way she had intended.

The detective appeared to be sharing her information with someone else. His head was turned to the side, but she could see his lips moving as he spoke into his phone again. They all followed her back to Cam's house.

Linzy hurried around to her car, popped the trunk, grabbed a tie-dyed t-shirt her sis had made—and still wore frequently—and rushed it out to the officer.

The detective cleared the ground between them with an economical stride.

Linzy sniffed the t-shirt, not wanting to give it up, then held it toward the detective. "This is Sasha's. She wore it all the time until the Halloween episode. When the deputies got us back inside the house, she grabbed it out of her dirty clothes hamper to bring to my house so she would have something to wear. She didn't want to hang around there any longer than she had to. It was in the middle of the night when I had to rescue her and the baby. But after we got to my house, she found some of her old clothes, so she never brought this bag in the house. I forgot about it. Until now."

The man took the shirt. His hands were strong, long fingered, not young, they were his most prominent feature besides the thick eyebrows and piercing black eyes.

"Yes, I'm Linzy," she said, realizing she hadn't responded earlier.

His eyes met hers for a split second. "Detective Banks," he said. He looked at the shirt. "I want to hear more about the Halloween episode. Was it violent?"

Linzy gave him a shortened version of that night. "He's been perfect ever since, to my knowledge. I mean, I've visited many times since then and they both seemed very happy. The baby, too."

She took a breath to calm her fast-forward speech. "But when he called me this evening," she said. "He told me Sash was missing. I couldn't believe it. I talk to her every day. Nothing about this makes sense." She couldn't help herself. Her eyes sought the window where she could feel Cam watching.

"Describe your sister for me, I've only seen photos."

"Sash was thin, I mean rail thin. Beautiful blonde hair. After Skye was born, the breastfeeding made the pregnancy weight fall off her." She looked at the tag in the seam of the tan coat. "This is large. Even nine months pregnant, my sis never wore large. Besides, like I said, it's tan, and it's made of wool."

She pulled out her phone, tapped on a recent video she'd made of Sash and the baby. "See," she held it out to the detective. "Here she is. This is Sasha."

Motioning toward the coat, she plunged ahead. "The question is, why would Cam give you something that doesn't even belong to her?"

Now the sharp black eyes met hers and stayed. "You're certain about this?" The wind ruffled his feathered black hair. Threads of white peeked through.

Linzy nodded. Panic assaulted the backs of her eyeballs. Her head pounded. *Could I have a stroke, at my age?* She held her palms to the sides of her head, clearly in pain. "Take the t-shirt. Sasha's scent is on it. Come to think of it, her scent should be on every one of these pilings. We walked this beach every time I came down—at least once a week—that dog should be running around like mad, following her tr—"

The detective handed the officer the t-shirt who, in turn, offered the soft cotton to the wet, black nose. "Find," he said. The dog smashed his snout into the fabric, then immediately headed to the thick piling nearest the stairs. He stopped.

The bald officer gave him a pat, offered the shirt again, gave him another instruction, and together they moved to another piling, and another, and another, and so on right back out to the beach. That's where the big copper and black coated hound put his head down and really went to work.

Linzy and Detective Banks glanced at each other and at Blue. They all rushed to keep up.

Orson and his handler appeared to be a running a zig-zag pattern down the beach. First to the rocks, then back toward the water, then to the rocks and so on and so on.

Then as if on cue, the loose-jowled snout stopped, scented the air, shook his head, put his nose back to the sand, and followed it into the surf.

"Oh my God." Linzy's thought was half exclamation, half prayer. In the back of her mind, a dark fear surfaced. *Sissy in the water in the middle of winter? Why would she—*

And then an even darker thought breached. She must've been forced. Or she took her own life. She glanced at the detective to see if she had spoken that thought aloud. Suicide by drowning, a horrific way to go. Especially for a strong swimmer like Sash.

How would one even go about it? Take something, a drug, some kind of sedative or antidepressant? Had the doc prescribed anything for post-partum depression? No. Not for a nursing mother. Surely not. Besides, Sasha wasn't depressed. I would know.

"Try him further up the beach," the detective called to the handler. The wind whipped his suit jacket open and Linzy caught sight of the gun holster around his shoulder and the badge clipped to his belt.

She stayed at the place the dog had alerted near the surf. In the rising moonlight, her shadow appeared and disappeared with the tide. Orson kept going down the beach, nose to the sand, not stopping. He looked to be on autopilot, doing what his handler said, but not really excited since he'd been pulled back from the waves.

Detective Banks stood behind her. Near the spot where the dog had dashed into the water. He dug a giant X in the sand with a piece of driftwood, then he dragged the driftwood across the beach to the shallow rocks and sea grass, took a video of his handiwork, possibly marking the spot for future reference, no doubt knowing the tide would soon wash it away.

Linzy photographed it with her phone, too. She felt it was necessary. She *hoped* the detective knew how to tell if Sash had gone into the water.

Blue slid his arm around her shoulders. "Look," she said, indicating the detective's actions. "He's marking the spot. Just like me. In case they don't find anything further on." She stared at the detective standing a little way off, snapping pics and videos with his phone. She was forced if she went in there, Linzy wanted to scream. She wouldn't leave the baby. Not unless it was at gun point.

She looked back the way they had come. The dog's tracks, and their own, were slowly disappearing beneath the lacy foam.

Linzy watched the K-9 officer, and then she glanced back at

the rocks. Without thinking, she began to follow the zigzagging dog tracks. They reminded her of the way she and her sister meandered around when they went walking, looking for shells and interesting bits of driftwood, checking the tidepools, seeing what needed to be seen, what might be caught in the sea oats.

Blue went with her, slowly, from place to place, following the big paw prints in the wet sand. The prints would be gone before the moon was high, but not yet.

Linzy wasn't certain what they were searching for, she just knew she had to keep looking. Her own footprints, from when she found the stroller, were not near the water, they were closer to the houses. *Had Sash been running in a zig zag pattern for a reason? What reason?*

She crawled over a tiny tidepool, nearly dry. They had found sea glass there once, and a beautiful sea urchin, but there wouldn't be anything—

The glint from her phone flashlight reflected off something at the outside edge of the rocks. She leaned over, grasped handholds of sharp basalt, pulled herself carefully across a ridge, and there it was. "Detective, detective!" She plucked a glittering turquoise seashell from a narrow crevice and showed it to Blue.

Detective Banks jogged up—Linzy noticed he'd taken a second to drag another X in the sand, snapped another picture as well. "What've you got?" he asked, carrying a short chunk of driftwood.

She turned so he could see the small shell balanced on the palm of her hand. "Look," she picked it up by the silver hook attached to the top. "It's a Christmas ornament, see?" She pointed to the silver hook and the tiny rhinestone glued to the shallow center like a treasure.

"Not just a shell?" the detective asked.

Linzy looked at his face. "Oh, no. Sash has been painting and selling these in a local gift shop for a couple of weeks now."

"Definitely one of hers?"

Linzy turned it over in her palm. A tiny SG was painted on the other side. Painted white waves followed the minute ridges in the shell. "Looks like it came right off the tree in the living room." She nodded toward the floor to ceiling windows fronting the beach house. The Christmas tree was barely visible, blurred by the heavy glass.

"She put the tree up early to have a place to hold all the ornaments she was making. I went with her when she dropped off the first batch of them at the gift shop. They're a bit fragile. She packed them in flat boxes lined with tissue paper. The owner sells them in fancy little boxes as if they are precious jewels." She looked at the one in her hand. "Sash is so happy with her art. And with her baby. Being a mom suits her so well."

Turning the turquoise shell over again, Linzy went on, "I think she dropped this one here on purpose." She looked up at the detective's face. "She knew I'd look for her where we always walk. Maybe someone brought her out of the house by force, but she grabbed this little ornament off the tree on her way out."

She stopped talking, picturing everything in her head. "I don't understand the stroller, though."

"Maybe she put it there a long time ag—" he started to say.

"No," Linzy interrupted. "We used it yesterday."

"That explains the dog alerting on the stroller so strongly. Maybe it holds the scent of the person who wore the tan coat along with the scent of your sister." He held up his phone to video the K-9 handler as he and his dog did a second search of the area around the stroller.

"Yes," Linzy agreed. "And look. This ornament was put here very recently. If it was old, the paint would be washed away, chipped away." She abruptly stopped talking as if the next words hurt her to say.

"Someone must have taken her from her house, brought her here." She looked down at the jagged rocks. "Then they somehow forced her into the water where the dog stopped. Did they force her into the waves? Into the rip? *Drown* her? Did they drown her?" She glanced at the red warning flags flapping in the wind down the shore where the public beaches began. The flags were barely visible. But she knew they were there. Sash would have certainly seen them in the daytime. Those flags meant rip currents, no swimming.

Images of her sister struggling in the surf overwhelmed her. She fell to her knees, cold fear washing over her like icy water. "Sash would never go in the ocean when the flags are red. And she would never risk leaving the baby alone in the house to come down here. Never." Her voice took on a singsong quality. She glanced at Blue who had knelt beside her. "She had the baby in the stroller, and someone took the baby from it and carried her home, but they left Sash in the water." Her eyes welled with fear. With unshed tears of fear.

To her surprise, the detective knelt beside her and Blue in the sand. "This could be evidence," he said. "This could help." He pulled her to her feet. "Let's go back to the house—"

Linzy shook her head. "No. No. I have to search the rest of the beach, what if she left me other things?"

"Okay," he said. "We'll search every inch. Together." He glanced up at the house again. "But then I've got to get up there and find out why Cameron Gaines gave us that bogus jacket."

So, he did believe her. "Maybe he wants to throw us off," Linzy said. "He showed me a note. Said she left it on the fridge." She clenched her fists in anger. "I wasn't nice when he called me to come and get them the day before Halloween. When he locked them out that night."

The detective's face hardened. He tapped a few keys on his phone and told someone on the other end that he wanted two more officers out to the beach to help search.

Linzy wanted to throw her arms around him in gratitude. Her emotions threatened to unwind like kite string in the wind. "Thank you," she whispered. "We've got to find her. Baby Skye needs her mommy. I can't imagine what my sister must be going through." She swiped at her nose, turned toward the officer with the dog.

"Don't," the detective said. "Don't try to imagine." He clicked something else on his phone and started back down the beach.

31

THE INTERVIEWS

Following Detective Banks back up the long steps to the deck, Linzy took Blue's hand, and whispered, "Thank you for coming."

He squeezed her hand in reply. No words were necessary.

As they climbed the steps, they saw one of the deputies headed to the house where they'd found the stroller. He had a large roll of yellow crime scene tape in his hands. Linzy felt her heart threaten to seize up in her chest. She pressed her free hand there in alarm. Would the CSI van pull up next? Or would one of the deputies photograph and fingerprint the stroller?

Cam had all the lights on now. The windows shone like multi-paned beacons.

The K-9 officer led Orson back to the SUV and gave him fresh water and some kind of treat. "Ya done good, boy," Linzy heard him say as he ruffled the dog's loose skin around his neck. "Ya done good." And then his words were whipped away by the gusts of wind chasing each other beneath the raised house. The K-9 unit was parked on the street side of the property, along with the other cruisers and the detective's car.

At the top of the steps, Cam stood in the doorway. "I knew you wouldn't find anything," he said. "Even if the big dog alerted,

Sash walked that beach every day. It was her exercise and her happy place. Linz will tell you."

Linzy was surprised at his nonchalance.

"Actually," the detective said, "we did find a few things. The dog alerted more than once." He didn't pull the shell ornament from his pocket—and for that, Linzy was glad, though she couldn't say why—but he did stop and examine the other ornaments on the Christmas tree.

"Interesting ornaments," Banks said, lightly touching one of the other rhinestone shells. That one had a tiny crab painted on it. With a rhinestone, of course.

Cam's head bobbed. "The shells are organic, but she made the starfish ones in the electric kiln I bought her." He smiled slightly. "Even had a small cement slab poured so it would be level."

Detective Banks didn't smile. "I noticed the storehouse near the carport. Good place for the kiln. Dangerous things, sometimes. Well ventilated, I suppose?"

"Had a professional install it," Cam said. "Not taking any chances." He let his gaze drift to Linzy, then he caressed Skye's cheek, offered her the pacifier clipped to her blankie, though she wasn't fussing.

Linzy wanted to comment, but she didn't trust herself at all. In truth, she had to stuff her fingers deep into her pockets so they wouldn't fly at Cam's face, claws out. Why isn't he more worried? Why isn't he falling apart?

She expected the detective to tell Cam they'd found the baby's stroller, but it seemed he wanted to keep that to himself as well.

Detective Banks glanced around the open concept living and dining area. "All this color. Did your wife do the paintings, too? It seems she is quite an artist." He turned a half-circle, taking in the different pieces of beachy art adorning the walls. "Turquoise seems a favorite hue." He stopped turning so that he faced the floor-to-ceiling windows.

Linzy could almost hear the wheels turning in his head.

"Sash loved turquoise, the color of the water on a good day, she always said." Cam shook his head. "I never see that, though. To me, Gulf water always looks brown and muddy, but not to Sash, she saw things differently."

Linzy watched his throat move as if he wanted to say more but couldn't. It alarmed and infuriated her to hear him talk about Sasha in the past tense. She hoped the detective noticed.

The detective indicated the dining table across the way. "Mind if I sit?"

Cam strode over and pulled out a chair. "Of course." He gently placed the baby back in the playpen, glanced at Linzy.

Detective Banks sat, took out a small notebook. "I'd like to ask you a few questions," he said. "So that I can better facilitate these missing person reports, get the correct info out there to the public as soon as possible."

Linzy froze, wondering if she should stay or make herself scarce. She needed to hear what he would say. "Okay if we sit, too?" she asked.

"Of course," Banks said.

She and Blue sat beside each other on the opposite side of the table, while Cam chose to sit at the head. Baby Skye gurgled a bit, watching her bright paper starfish mobile in the playpen.

The detective poised pen above paper in the small spiral. "Let's go back to the beginning. Make sure I haven't missed anything. In fact, do you mind if I just record the conversation, to make certain I get it right?"

Linzy saw her brother-in-law's Adam's apple go up, then down. But he nodded okay.

The detective pulled a tiny tape recorder from his pocket and placed it on the table nearest Cameron. Linzy thought it was completely old-school but maybe he had a reason. She had to admit; it made her heart quicken when he pushed the record button.

"First things first," he said. "You have the right to remain silent—"

Cam's eyes nearly bugged out of his head. "Are you arresting me?"

"Oh, no, no," the detective soothed. "Standard procedure when we record someone. Sorry. Did I not say that?"

Linzy watched both men. Shrewd move on the detective's part. If he did that rights thing to get a response from Cam, it worked.

"Okay," Cameron said, voice shaky. "I have nothing to hide. I just need my wife to be found."

Detective Banks finished reading Cam his rights, all on the recording, then proceeded. "When did you first learn your wife was missing?" His voice sounded almost nonchalant.

Cam cleared his throat. "Today, when I came home—"

"About what time was that?"

"Around two o'clock," he said. "She'd been to the doctor for her checkup—"

"Was she sick?"

"What? No. Just a regular checkup. New mother stuff, I guess. Plus, she was going to take some more of the little painted shells to the shop." He appeared perplexed for a moment. "Anyhow," he continued. "I texted her that I was on my way home in case she wanted me to pick up anything for dinner. But she didn't respond." He cleared his throat. "I figured she was walking the beach and didn't hear the message alert."

Detective Banks made a note in his little notebook. It looked like shorthand. Linzy felt her heart rate pick up, just a bit, wondering what he found worth noting even though the recorder was running.

Cameron continued. "It didn't take long for me to get home. But she wasn't here. When I glanced back at my phone, there was a 'not delivered' message there. And I couldn't find her anywhere."

He fiddled with the edge of the placemat before him. Sash had painted them with Skye's handprints before Thanksgiving. Had them laminated at the office store in town. Very colorful. Handprints like little turkeys with primary color feathers.

"Did your wife take anything with her?" Detective Banks asked, as if it wasn't unusual for a new mom to go running off without her baby that way.

Linzy was amazed to see how red Cam's face had become. She recalled how her own heart sped up at the reading of the rights.

"What do you mean? I haven't seen her. She wasn't here. How would I know what she took with her?"

"Her cell phone?"

"Maybe. I mean, I haven't found it. I've called and texted over and over. No response."

Banks made another notation in his notebook. "Tell me how it went, exactly. When you arrived home. It was what time?"

"I got home around two p.m. The baby was in the playpen, and the lights were on, and those of the Christmas tree, but since she wasn't answering the phone, I thought she must've walked down to the beach—"

"Have you ever known her to do that? Leave the baby alone to go to the beach?"

"Well, no. But I'm not here in the daytime, usually, so if the baby was asleep," Cam swiped at a bead of sweat visible in his hair line. "Maybe she just needed another shell or something."

"Was the baby asleep when you arrived?"

Cam shook his head. "No, in fact, she was starting to cry. I picked her up and gave her the bottle in the playpen with her."

"Is that how your wife usually feeds the child?"

"No," Cam said. "Not at all. I found it very strange, but since Skye was fussing, I gave what was left to her."

"Where is that bottle now?"

Cam looked toward the kitchen. "I put it in the sink, rinsed out the milk—then I made another one, in case she didn't get enough that time. It wasn't full, you know."

Banks followed his gaze, made a note in his notebook, then typed a quick text and sent it to someone.

"Did you see any of your wife's work laid out, as if she'd suddenly felt the need to run down to the beach for another shell?" He glanced around. "Because I don't notice anything. Perhaps she worked on them in another room?"

Cam cut his eyes at his sister-in-law. "No. She usually did it here, at the table. That was just a thought. I *hoped* that's where she was. After all, she was here when I left for work this morning. Everything was fine."

"But you didn't find her on the beach?"

Linzy could see the knuckles on Cam's fists standing out beneath the dining room lights.

"No. I didn't," he said.

"Did you see the baby's stroller anywhere?"

"What? No. I don't know where it is." His fists clenched even tighter. "I had to carry the baby around outside to look."

"Do you often have anger issues, Mr. Gaines?"

Cam's face paled. It left two red spots on his cheeks. "I don't. Why do you ask?" He looked at Linzy. "You told him about Halloween?"

"Of course she did," the detective said. "Why wouldn't she? It was traumatic for Sasha and the baby. Her sister, too, I imagine. If she had disappeared *that* night, you clearly wouldn't have known."

Now Cam dropped his head. "You're right. I deserve that. I made a horrible mistake, and it never happened again. Will never happen again. I'm going to AA." He looked at the detective. "I've absolutely nothing to hide." He started to stand, then turned to the detective. "Okay if I get a glass of water?"

Banks nodded but rose to follow. "Just allow me to move this bottle so the lab can get prints off of it when they arrive." He stuck his ink pen in the end of the just rinsed bottle and moved it over to a dry dish towel on the counter. "I wouldn't mind a drink of water myself," he told Cam. "How about you, Ms. Everly? Mr. Ash?"

"Yes, please," Linzy said. Blue shook his head.

Cam almost kept his hands from shaking as he took three glasses and added ice and water from the dispenser on the front of the fridge. He handed one glass to Banks, then drank his own right down. But before taking the other glass of water back to Linzy, Cam reached into the refrigerator for a can of Coke. The bright red can with curly white lettering seemed cheerful. Too cheerful. He seemed to be drawing things out, delaying the interview, perhaps.

Linzy scolded herself in her mind, feeling like an idiot, focusing on the red can as if it echoed his cold nature.

At the table, he avoided eye contact as he handed Linzy her glass.

"Thank you," she said, thinking to herself how their stiff manners felt like old taffy, so brittle they were on the verge of crumbling.

Things were moving too slowly. She couldn't believe they were sitting here, drinking ice water and Coke, not knowing where Sash might be or what she might be going through.

Linzy felt certain Cam knew more than he was telling. The muscles in her jaw began to ache as she talked to herself in her head, the way their favorite therapist had taught them. Biofeedback, the woman had whispered to them as her assistant placed the electrodes on their skin.

It had been one of their first sessions after their parents died. "Once you learn these techniques, along with your deep breathing, you will be able to talk your anxiety down when you're on your own." She'd smiled and whispered, "Without all the gadgetry." And she was right. Linzy and Sasha had both used the techniques more than once. They'd helped each other incorporate it into their prayers and meditations.

"I'll need a photo for our media department," Detective Banks was saying. "They will send it out, post it, give it to the news reporters, all the things that need to be done to get the public looking for your wife."

"Of course." Cam pushed his chair out, as if to physically go somewhere in search of the photo.

"Oh, you can just text me one," the detective said. "Everyone has pics on their phone, right?"

Cam nodded, took out his phone, began scrolling through his photos.

"I've got a ton if you don't," Linzy said. She wasn't sure the detective wanted her input, but it was the truth. In addition to the video clip she'd already shown him, she had dozens of candid photos of Sash and Skye. With and without Cam.

"I've got tons, too," Cam said. "Just trying to choose the one that's the clearest—"

Detective Banks held out his hand. "If you don't mind, I'll just pick one and send it to myself. Then forward it to the office so they can get it posted."

Hesitating only a moment, Cam handed him the phone.

In her head, Linzy gave up counting backward and began to recite The Lord's Prayer. It was part of her nighttime ritual. Not biofeedback this time, just prayers. It almost always relaxed her enough to sleep. Maybe it would help now.

Her fingertips crept to her jaw muscles and began to massage by pushing up and back toward her ears, then pulling gently down again, toward her chin. She hoped it would release some of the tension in her face. Maybe stave off a debilitating headache later. Stop messing around, her mind cried. Let's get busy searching.

Detective Banks appeared to watch her from the corner of his eye. She didn't care. Not one whit. Every now and then, her fingertips moved around to the muscles in her neck too.

In her head, Linzy imagined herself rubbing away the image of Cam up here in the house, doing nothing while she and the detective were trailing Orson Welles and his handler all over the beach. How is it possible Cam hadn't even been able to find the baby stroller two houses down? And why didn't Banks call him on it?

"I see what you mean," Banks said to Cam. "You do have plenty of pictures to choose from. Beautiful family, Mr. Gaines. Absolutely stunning." He clicked on something. "This will be the one." He handed the phone back. "I put my number in so you can send it directly to me."

Cam nodded, looked at the picture the detective had chosen.

Linzy was surprised to finally see tears leaking from the corners of his eyes. A response to the photos, perhaps. Her own emotions were screwed down tight. Just like her jaw muscles. She pressed into them with her fingertips again.

Cam clicked a couple of keys and sent the picture.

Detective Banks did the same. Apparently, he'd already prepared a text message to go with it. "Your wife drives the gold Cadillac, right?"

"Yes," Cam said. "I bought it to match my Lincoln." He swiped a knuckle under his eyes discreetly. "The plate number is—" He rattled off the numbers from memory.

Detective Banks punched the numbers into his phone. Linzy had no idea why he would need them. "Since she didn't drive away from the house," Detective Banks said, "we will continue to concentrate our search in his area. I need to see the note, please."

Linzy noticed the change. Is he trying to anger Cam, to throw him off balance?

Cam retrieved the ragged edged paper, handed it to the detective.

Banks examined the paper front and back. "Definitely her handwriting?" He showed the note to both Cam and Linzy for affirmation. They nodded. Both reached out again, as if it was a touchstone. He examined Linzy's face. "You say it makes no sense? You did not call or send her a text about a pier?"

Linzy shook her head. "Not at all. I was at home, making dinner when Cam called and said she was missing."

His head swiveled toward Cam. "That's what he said, missing?"

Cam looked at the tabletop. Fingered his Coke can, waited.

"Yes," Linzy said. "I didn't understand how he could say she was missing. I mean, he'd just got home. Did he even have time to search the house and the whole beach?"

Banks looked at Cam fidgeting. He began to examine the note again. Waiting.

Linzy felt her jaw tighten back up. Her fingers crept toward the offending muscles.

At last Cam said, "I knew she was missing. The baby was here. Sash was not. Her car was here, but she didn't answer phone or text. Then I found the note that said she'd gone to pick up her sister at the pier."

Linzy noticed he didn't call her sis in front of the detective. What did that mean? It seemed important, but then everything seemed important, now.

"Did you think it odd that she said she went to pick up her sister but didn't take her car?"

"Yes, of cour—"

Banks continued, voice growing sterner as he spoke. "How did you think she went to pick up her sister, exactly?"

"Well, I thought she walked down to our pier—"

"What was she going to do, carry her home, piggyback style?"

"No, I guess I thought she would just meet her, you kno—"

"And why wouldn't she take the baby? Was she in the habit of going out without her child? She had the nice stroller, after all." The detective wasn't peppering him, but he wasn't letting up, either.

Cam closed his eyes, rubbed his forehead with his stiffened fingers. When he opened his eyes again, he said, "No, Detective, she never went anywhere without the baby. I thought she either walked down the beach to meet Linzy, or that someone came and picked her up."

"But without Skye, right? I mean this time. She did go without Skye." He seemed to be using the baby's name on purpose. It had a jarring effect, coming from his lips. As if he knew them, personally. "Do you see why I'm having trouble with this scenario, Mr. Gaines?"

"I—I don't know what could have happened," Cam began. "I told myself the baby was probably napping when she left, and she knew I was on my way so …" He closed his mouth, looked directly at the detective. "Please, just help me find my wife. She is my whole world. Her and Skye. Without them, I'm nothing. *Nothing*."

Linzy noticed he didn't say "I have nothing," he said, "I *am* nothing." Again, that seemed important. Every little thing, important.

Detective Banks ignored the emotion, stared at Cam's hands. "You must sell a lot of property, Mr. Gaines. Luxury vehicles *and* this amazing place." He glanced pointedly toward the windows at the stunning view. Then he looked back at Cam. "Especially with a nonworking spouse and a new baby." He let that sink in, then said, "Were you having financial difficulties, Mr. Gaines?"

The question hung there between them, thinly veiled, the real meaning seeming to imply if you're having financial difficulties, maybe you want your wife gone so you can claim her assets. Or a fat insurance policy. Or both.

Linzy's gut rolled. Did he take her down to the beach and drown her when he got home? Is that why she left the turquoise shell? She had no doubt Sasha was worth a lot both dead and alive. Her sis had mentioned life insurance once. "Can you believe he took out a million-dollar policy on me?" Sash had said. "And on himself, too?"

"Of course," Linzy remembered answering. Then she'd made a mental note to discuss it with Blue, but he'd been out on a major structure fire—the high school in a neighboring town had caught fire, something about excess tar on the roof—and she hadn't wanted to bother him with it. *I felt like a mother hen, worrying over everything.*

Eventually she'd convinced herself that Cam was a wealthy businessman, of course he'd have big insurance policies. Besides, the beach house was worth more than that, and on top of everything, Sash had her own bank account. Surely Detective Banks knew all this.

She pulled herself back to the present in time to hear the detective say, "Mr. Gaines, I want your authorization to allow us to go over your finances." The detective's face was deadpan, voice dry as toast. It wasn't a demand, but it wasn't a polite request, either. It fell somewhere in between.

Cam sat back in his chair, and Linzy thought she heard the crackle of aluminum as his grip on the Coke can intensified.

"That seems invasive. My wife has just gon—"

"Do I need to get a warrant?"

Linzy barely heard the question, the detective's voice was so low.

Cam stopped the pressure from his fingers. "No. Of course not." He pushed the phone across the table. "It's open, look all you want."

"I'll need to take it downtown to our IT department," the detective said. "We'll want to look through your business records, too."

Linzy was glad they would look at both.

Cam nodded. "Do what you need. Anything that will help you

find my Sash." The tears that had been building now leaked out. He calmly wiped them away with his thumb. "I just hate to be without my phone in case she calls. Or texts. What if she needs me?"

To her surprise and relief, Linzy finally felt sympathy for him.

32

SASHA WAKES

The room glittered; the reflected light stabbed at her eyes like a million tiny knives. Sash tried to raise a hand to shield them, but her arms didn't work. *Do I have arms, or did I drown? Is this what it's like to be a spirit?*

Her vision took in the limited scene. Every surface dazzled. Can't be diamonds. Must be rhinestones. Or sunlight on a billion drops of water. Is it the disco ball? She couldn't force her thoughts to make sense.

The light faded to black.

~

Detective Banks stood, gazing at his phone as if reading his messages. "If you will follow me in your vehicle," he said to Linzy. "I will follow Mr. Gaines in his vehicle. I want to interview both of you at the station."

Linzy looked up. "Shouldn't someone stay here in case Sash comes back?"

The detective looked around the house. "Your friend, Blue, can stay. And my men will be here, continuing the search. I'll make certain one is always near the house." He glanced at Cam. "Do I have your permission to search the house and garage and outbuildings?"

Cam nodded, face strained. "Of course. Whatever it takes. Just please find my wife. Please."

The detective nodded and picked up the recorder. "There will be officers searching the entire area."

"And the beach again?" Linzy asked. "All those other houses? Maybe someone is home now."

Detective Banks nodded and touched her shoulder reassuringly. "We're just getting started. Let's go downtown. Sometimes a change of scenery is necessary to jog one's memory."

Blue took her hand. "Will you be okay?"

Linzy nodded, bit her lip against the words she wanted to say. "I'll be fine. Thank you for staying. I can't imagine leaving no family here."

"I'll stay as long as needed." He squeezed her hands. "And I'll call Mom and Dad, too."

For some reason, that made tears spring to Linzy's eyes. She swiped at them almost angrily. "Thank you," she whispered again.

"I'll get the baby," Cam said. "You can't imagine the shock I felt at finding her here alone." He stabbed his fingers into the front of his thick hair. "I just assumed Linz and Sash would show up at any moment." He shook his head. "The note …"

He seemed to need some sort of reassurance from one of them. Or both of them. Something to tell them he'd done the right thing or at least wasn't to blame for waiting.

But no assurance was forthcoming. They both just looked at him. Then Detective Banks said, "Don't be alarmed at the crime scene tape two houses down as we drive out, it's just the place where Linzy located the stroller."

"Wait," Cam said. "You found the stroller?" He stopped, midstride, eyes wide.

"We'll discuss it at the station," Banks said, turning on his heel to lead them out. Once again, Linzy got the feeling he was baiting Cam with the info that she had found the stroller when he hadn't found it himself.

No one spoke as they each went to their own vehicle. The detective waited patiently as Cam put the baby in his Lincoln.

Linzy glanced around at all the first responder vehicles. It looked like an unlit circus. None of the vehicles had emergency lights going, but the street was certainly crowded. I guess rich people don't wander out to watch someone else's misfortune the way we do down in the lower classes. She chided herself for thinking that way, but she still wondered why no one came to check out all the law enforcement activity.

After a moment, she stopped trying to make things make sense and simply got into her car, ready to follow Detective Banks to the Sheriff's Office. He'd already instructed Cameron to lead the way.

Why did he do that, Linzy wondered. Why did Banks ask both of them to drive their cars instead of riding with him, was it so he could search Cam's car at the station? Or had they already done that? Surely, they have. We looked in Sash's trunk, but not Cam's. It didn't even occur to me.

Now, she watched the road carefully, scrutinizing the highway for signs of blood leaking from Cam's car.

A fleeting image of an officer opening the trunk of the Lincoln flickered in her head. Nah, the bloodhound would have alerted if there'd been anything suspicious. Wait, is that the reason Cam gave them the beige coat, so the dog would be thrown completely off track? Where'd that coat come from anyway?

Something to bring up in the interview.

Her mind entertained a million questions and scenarios all at once.

As she pulled away from the beach house, she saw Blue

watching from the deck. He stood tall against the backdrop of the waves, but the beauty of the luxury home site had been completely tainted. All she could think of was the possibility of Sash out there in the Gulf, struggling to keep her head above water.

It felt so wrong to drive away. *We need to get this interview over with. Get on with the search. Cam should at least give me the baby.* He isn't trustworthy now. He gave them the wrong coat. Couldn't even find the stroller. And where is the diaper bag? Linzy felt certain it was stuffed in the bottom of the beach stroller, behind the crime scene tape. Where else could it be?

Inside her chest, the vise began to squeeze. Soon, the beating, vital organ known as her heart would be flattened, useless. *Where are you, Sissy?*

She followed the detective's car right past the yellow tape. It glowed eerily in the early darkness.

At the Yorkie house, two officers stood on the deck. Apparently, the owners were now home. One of them—she couldn't tell if it was Tim or Kev—stood there with the officers. He had one hand on his mouth as if in shock.

Linzy wondered what Cam thought of all that as they drove by in their separate vehicles. As far as she knew, he still hadn't been told anything other than the location of the stroller. The detective had Cam's phone. He couldn't even call anyone.

Their three-car caravan drove on through town and into the Sheriff's Office parking area designated Staff Parking Only. Linzy chose a spot near the detective and opened her door cautiously, half-expecting him to say, "You can't park here, go back to the public parking out front."

But he didn't do that. He simply slid out, pulled the flap of his jacket over the butt of his gun, then directed her toward the well-lit double glass doors set flush into the wall beneath a small canopy.

Cam joined them, carrying Skye in her car seat carrier. He still looked slightly pale.

"Detective," Cam said. "I need to know everything about that yellow tape back there—"

The detective scanned an ID card, and the doors opened soundlessly. "All in good time, Mr. Gaines. All in good time."

Cam grabbed the detective's arm, "Just tell me if they found my wife with the stroller. *Please*." His voice grew more strident with each word. The baby began to fuss, no doubt alarmed by her father's panicky tone.

Detective Banks looked down at Cam's hand on his arm. "Of course not. I would have told you." He glanced at the hand again. "The deputies are continuing their investigation."

Cam released him. "Just please ..." he began.

"Soon," Banks said. Then he motioned for Linzy to enter the double doors, and she found herself in a brightly lit hallway with floor tile so shiny she could've touched up her lipstick. If she'd been wearing any.

Banks motioned her to continue down the hall. "Make yourself comfortable." He indicated a small waiting area with orange Naugahyde chairs and two vending machines, one for drinks, one for snacks, and told her he'd be back to get her soon. Then he motioned for Cam to keep walking.

Linzy peeked around the doorjamb to watch where they went. She kept expecting Cam to turn back, ask her to take the baby. But he didn't.

They stopped at a door with a small sign hanging above it: Interview One.

She'd had a bit of experience with law enforcement stations after Ancho was arrested, but this was different. This time she was on her own. And it was Galveston County, not Wister County. There was no Attorney Brushow to show her the ropes. No Mr. and Mrs. Ash to hold her hand. No Blue to keep her sane.

She ran her fingertips over the smooth Naugahyde chair seats.

Proudly made in Stoughton, Wisconsin, she thought, recalling a paper she'd done on Made in America businesses when she was in high school.

Why is my mind playing with trivia right now? She toyed with the bracelet Blue had given her that awful year. The year of Ancho. The bracelet was inscribed *In case of emergency, call Blue.* She wanted to, oh how she wanted to.

Detective Banks stuck his head around the corner. "How about a soft drink?"

"Water?" Linzy asked. "The other makes me burp."

He smiled.

She felt like an idiot. What a thing to say. As if she were sixteen again.

"Sorry," she said, when he returned with the bottle of water. "I'm nervous and very, very worried about my sister." She plunged ahead. "Also, worried about baby Skye." Tears threatened to burst through her words. She twisted the cap off the bottle and took a quick sip.

"Come with me," Banks said, starting back down the hall to a different interview room.

Interview Two, the dangling sign read. Linzy wondered how many there were.

The detective bypassed Interview Two and continued down the hall to an office with his name on the desk. "This won't take long. I just need to get some background from you before I talk to Cam." He indicated a comfy chair snugged up to his desk. "It won't hurt him to cool his jets a minute while you and I chat."

Linzy was glad he hadn't made *her* cool her jets. "I just hope he knows how to take care of Skye. Sasha is the main caregiver. Nursing her, changing her, everything . . ."

He nodded, set the small recorder in the center of the broad desk the same way he'd done back at the house. "Mind if I record?"

Linzy shook her head and placed her water bottle on the glass desk protector and her hands in her lap. "He's trying to send me a message by keeping Skye with him at all times." Her thoughts popped out unbidden. Just put a microphone in front of me, she thought.

Banks pushed the record button. "What makes you say that?"

She screwed around in the chair, took a solid breath. "He seems a good guy, but that night he locked them out, he was like someone else."

He made a small hand gesture that said she should continue. "How so?"

Another tiny sip of water, then Linzy said, "Incredibly drunk and nasty. Locked them out in the middle of the night, then called me and bragged about it. As if he wanted to punish all three of us, me, Sash, and even the baby." She gulped, then continued. "Only psychopaths do that sort of thing, right?"

She went on without waiting for him to answer. "And that beige wool coat? Who does that belong to? And why would he give it to the K-9 officer? To throw them off Sash's trail, I'll bet. But most of all, why would that note say she was going to pick *me* up at some pier? Is that to implicate me in some way? I mean, we had no plans of any kind. She would *never* leave the baby."

Detective Banks didn't stop her rambling, but he didn't offer any answers or opinions, either.

Finally, Linzy ran out of steam. "Nothing makes sense," she murmured.

"Would your sister have run off? Maybe to get away from him?"

Linzy started shaking her head before he even finished the question. "No. No. Not without Skye. Besides, if she needed to get away, we've got property in Stutter Creek, New Mexico. A cabin. She could have easily gone there—her and Skye—if she didn't want to stay with me. And she knows I would've helped. But she couldn't have gone there because she didn't take her car."

She barely noticed how the detective's eyebrows when they

went up at the mention of Stutter Creek. She was too busy replaying an image of their beloved cabin in her head. The memories were always accompanied by the burbling of the creek, the clear, fast-flowing water, the swimming hole near the cabin.

"No," she repeated. "She wouldn't have taken off without Skye. Or without telling me." She glanced up at the detective's piercing gaze. "Sash and I have been through a lot together. Starting with the murder of our parents by our so-called uncle when we were teens. He intended to kill all of us, and when that didn't work, he had the nerve to move in with us and try to bilk us out of everything we'd inherited because of him—including the Brookville farm and the Stutter Creek property." She unknowingly hugged herself as she spoke. "It was a horrific couple of years."

Closing her eyes, Linzy murmured, "Please, find my sister. Someone has her, or knows where she is, I feel it, Detective. I feel it in my bones."

Detective Banks sat back for a moment. "Tell me what happened with your parents, if you can. Why do you say your *so-called* uncle?"

Linzy consciously released herself. She'd had such a grip on her upper arms, it felt like letting go in more ways than one. Taking a deep breath, she let the image of Ancho's horrid face enter her thoughts. Since before the trial, she'd made it a priority to completely erase him from her mind. Now, she reversed that idea and opened her mouth to tell him the rest of the story.

Banks glanced at his watch and stood. "Can you hold on for one second? I'm going to check on Mr. Gaines. I don't want the baby to be too much of a distraction, and I'm afraid she will be getting even fussier by now."

Linzy wanted to hug him for that. All she could think about was what might be happening to her sister, and what would become of Baby Skye if they couldn't find Sasha. "I'll be right here," she said. "Please let me help with the baby if possible."

He nodded. "That's exactly what I'm hoping."

From where she sat, Linzy could hear the detective out in the hallway. She overheard him tell a uniformed deputy to make certain Linzy didn't leave and that no one was allowed to go into his office where she was waiting. "And run a financial on her and her properties," she heard him say.

"Looking at motive?" the deputy asked. "Think the hubby and sis-in-law could be in on it together?"

She thought she heard Banks chuckle, then he said, "Don't think so. Just need to tie some threads together. The sisters had been through a lot before this guy even entered the picture. We need to make certain Mr. Gaines wasn't part of the earlier scheme. The one that ended in the death of their parents."

"Then you definitely want to read this file."

There was a pause in the conversation.

Linzy held her breath, leaned toward the door, listening intently.

Papers rustled, then the detective said, "Maybe the husband is not what he seems," he hesitated and Linzy could imagine him turning pages in a file folder. Then he went on, "Father a convicted felon, Cameron Gaines not his original name … has a brother here as well. We will want to interview the brother, too."

More page turning, then his tone of voice went back to authoritative. "So, what have they found at the house?"

"Everything clean so far. Don't know if it's in the file, but apparently, his dad is still in prison."

Detective Banks said something she didn't catch, then said, "Thanks for the file and for the heads up. Looks like Mr. Gaines and I will have plenty to talk about."

Linzy peeked out the office door just in time to see him enter the door marked Interview One. “Sorry for keeping you waiting,” she heard him say before he closed the door and cut off her access.

She wondered what he meant when he said Cameron Gaines wasn’t Cam’s original name. And why would his father be in prison, furthermore, did Sash know all that when she married him?

33

COAT

When Detective Banks reappeared a while later, Linzy could hardly contain herself. Her brain had been working overtime. "Sash was going to donate some outgrown baby clothes to Goodwill next week. Maybe the beige coat was a gift someone had given her, that she couldn't wear. She would never tell a gift giver she was allergic. Sash would never hurt anyone's feelings. Maybe she decided to donate it and that's why she had it out." Coming back to herself, Linzy glanced at the detective. His expression seemed dubious.

He cleared his throat. "I asked your brother-in-law about it, again."

Linzy sat forward.

His eyebrows formed unreadable arches over his sharp black eyes. "He admitted it might belong to another woman. That could explain a lot of things."

Linzy collapsed back into her chair, shoulders slumped. "If Sash came across a coat belonging to another woman, it's easy to imagine her questioning him, maybe running out of the house in a fit of anger or despair." She gripped her bottle of water tighter. "She would feel so betrayed."

Banks nodded. His look seemed to say now we're getting somewhere.

Linzy clenched her teeth. "But if that were true, then everything Cam said about her being gone when he got home is a lie." She thought of the breakdown in his story. "It would mean he was there when she disappeared—" Her eyes flew to the detective's calm gaze. "Oh, my God." She inhaled, one hand on her chest. "That would mean he really did give you the coat knowing it isn't hers. That he knows where she went—that even the note is fake."

Banks's gaze was steady. "Is that possible?"

Linzy nodded, but it was uncertain. "I don't trust people easily, Detective. Not since Ancho. But this …" She exhaled, took another tiny sip of water, worried she would choke if she took a normal sized drink. *Should I just spew out all my suspicions and be done with it? No. Better roll 'em out, slowly. See how they sound in the open air.*

She forced herself to blink even though it meant the tears threatening to fall would spill out. Her voice trembled. "It was the day after Halloween when he came out to Brookville and took them back home. The next day I went to check on them—at her request—and wound up helping with laundry and cooking. He was very late coming home, although he was in contact with Sash by phone off and on all day."

Her glance rose to the detective's face. "Sash said he was only working late because he knew I was there to look after her and the baby." She hesitated, then said, "I was afraid he was avoiding coming home, you know, not really working at all. Just avoiding seeing me." She patted her chest as if to still her stammering heart.

The detective leaned forward, paused the tape. "I want to hear all about this, but if you need a minute, that's okay." His eyebrows rose as his blunt forefinger hovered just above the pause button.

When she shook her head, he pressed it again, and the taping resumed.

Linzy said, "I couldn't get past the change from the night he called me, so haughty, telling me to come and get them, he had kicked them out. Does that make sense? I mean, two different people completely." She paused. "I know I'm slow to trust, like I said, but now she's missing. *Missing*."

She closed her mouth, tried to frame her next thought into the most coherent sentence possible. "How can he be two such different people," she said. "How could he have shoved them outside in the middle of the night if he truly loved them? Is that a mental disorder? Split personality or something? I just can't—"

The detective pursed his lips. "That's the big question, isn't it?"

Linzy nodded. The tears rolled. "When I got there, that night, driving eighty and ninety miles an hour the whole way, I pulled up to the house and found my sister sitting in a deputy's car, cradling the baby. The deputy said she'd found Sash in a deck chair, covered with a beach towel, baby Skye wrapped in another towel, nursing at her mother's breast."

She squeezed her eyes shut to block out the memory. "I'm the one who called the sheriff's office to come and check on them. I kinda hoped they would send the same deputy out this time, too. Since she knows the history already."

"Do you recall her name?"

"Yes, it was O. Pollard. She told me when she moved the towels to help Sash out of the deck chair, she could see that her breast was covered with chill bumps." Linzy swallowed. "Imagine how cold the two of them must've been, sitting there, in the dark."

This time the detective *punched* the stop button on the recorder.

He sat back in his chair, none too delicately, causing the old swivel to squeal. His lips were no longer pursed as if to speak, now they were pressed into a thin, hard line.

If only Blue could see me now, Linzy thought, dabbing at her eyes and nose. He'd often teased her about her poker face, said she had it down so good, he often had to ask what she was thinking. It made her proud, somewhat. She'd worked hard at hiding her emotions, in those years after losing her parents. It had seemed safer that way. But this was different. She didn't think she could keep everything under control another time. Not again.

She made herself focus.

Detective Banks was speaking. "Pretty cold, locking them outside in the middle of the night that way."

Linzy nodded. "I couldn't believe it. Still can't, when I really think about it."

Banks ignored that. "Strange that he called and told you what he'd done, though. Or did your sister call you on her mobile? I want to make certain I have this straight."

"Cameron called me. About two o'clock in the morning, woke me up, told me in a slurry, haughty, voice that he'd put Sash and the baby outside and I should come and pick them up." She said it all in one long breath, knowing if she hesitated her voice would break.

He looked at something on his phone. "So, you jumped in the car and headed that way?"

Linzy nodded. "It didn't take long. I was just thankful there were few other cars on the road." She shuddered. "How could he lock a newborn outside? His own baby?"

"Didn't she have anyone closer she could go to, could call?"

"No. She said her phone was in the house, so she tried the first neighbors within walking distance, but no one was home. She said it was so windy on the beach and the baby was wailing ..." Linzy gnawed at the cuticle around her thumb. "Sash said she hurried back to get under the towels. I mean, he *literally* pushed them outside onto the deck with her in her nightgown and the baby in her little onesie. Then he slammed the door and locked it." Anger had rejoined the angst in her tone.

"Then he called you before he passed out?"

Linzy cleared her throat and reached for a tissue. Banks had placed a box on the desk near her. "Apparently that's exactly what he did. He was still completely dressed when the deputies saw him passed out on the bed. Outside, Sasha thought nursing Skye would keep her warmer. Said it was all she could think to do." Linzy barked, a short, hard laugh. "She said she kept expecting him to realize what he'd done and unlock the door, bring them back inside."

Banks nodded but didn't speak.

Linzy dabbed at her cheeks. "She pounded on the doors and windows, but he didn't respond. She couldn't even get in the car. The key fob was in the diaper bag in the house."

His expression didn't change, but Linzy thought he was as appalled as she had been, as she still was. "She said she was about to drag a deck chair down the steps to the store house, where the new kiln was located, because it would at least be out of the wind. But then she spied the headlights coming down the street." Linzy swallowed. "I just wonder how the deputies got through the security gate ..."

"We have override codes for security gates," Banks said. "Go on with what happened next."

"She said he apologized the next day. Told her he would never take another drink." Linzy pinched and rubbed at the areas on either side of the bridge of her nose. She hated crying. Her sinuses always stuffed up.

"I'm not surprised you called 9-1-1 that night. In light of all you and your sister have endured."

"Thank God I did. The two deputies went right out. Cam never even knew when I got there and brought them home." She clenched her teeth. "He appeared to be unconscious. I've never seen anyone that drunk." She closed her eyes, briefly. "But we've never been exposed to drinking at that level. Maybe that's how a real drunk looks when he passes out. Until our parents died, Sash and I had led a very sheltered existence. Or so it seems now."

She sat quietly for a moment, thinking something was off. Then it dawned on her. "Isn't there a record of all that in your files somewhere?" Linzy felt like she'd been duped into retelling everything she was certain he already knew. Why would he make her do that? To double check *her* story?

The detective seemed unconcerned. "I have the desk clerk looking at backgrounds for all of you but hearing it firsthand is always better and quicker." He tilted his head sideways, toward the direction of Interview One. "I have to know everything before I go back in there."

Linzy clenched her fists and deliberately placed them on the edge of the desk even though she really wanted to pound them, to make a scene.

As calmly as possible, she said, "Well, here's some more background for you." She went on to retell him all about Ancho and the way he'd flown to Texas after her grandfather passed away. How he'd disabled their old furnace vent while pretending to be just stopping by for a visit.

"He wanted to kill us all so he could inherit everything that once belonged to my dad. Sheriff Peach of Wister County is the one you want to speak with about that. He and the insurance investigator—I've forgotten his name—are the ones who put all the facts together when they discovered that the furnace vent pipe was damaged."

She sat up straighter, relaxed her clenched fists. "They traced Ancho to Brookville through airport footage and a receipt from a hardware store in town." Linzy didn't know how much information he wanted. This couldn't be related to Ancho, could it? She recalled the way Domino leered at her. He hadn't gone to jail. Could he be behind this?

Poker face, she told herself. Poker face, Linz. No, she thought. Poker face be damned. She rushed ahead, regaling the detective with all the background on Domino, too.

Banks halted his questions, obviously deep in thought. For the first time, Linzy noticed how stooped he was. As if he shouldered these burdens with her.

After a moment, he said, "I appreciate your candor, Ms. Everly. I'm going to do some more research before I speak with Mr. Gaines again." He gave her a sudden, hard look. "Was Gaines in the picture when your folks were murdered?"

That idea took Linz by surprise. "No. We didn't meet him until later, when Sasha got into the work-study program in high school." She paused. "He knew about it though." Her glance met his again. "His brother's niece is one of Sasha's best friends. Her name is Rose. She's the one who recommended Sash for the receptionist's job in Cam's office."

Detective Banks seemed momentarily speechless. "Tangled web," he said at last. "Probably nothing more than coincidence. Small town, everyone knows everyone."

Linzy nodded. "What happened to us was such a big deal. My folks knew everyone through the pecan business, so everyone in Brookville knew what happened. They knew about Ancho, too. The trial, you know."

He sat back in his chair, more carefully this time, only a slight squeak as he swiveled his knees back into the kneehole. "I see I've got quite a bit of research to do. Wonder if Ancho is serving his time at the same place Cam's father is serving time?"

An awful chill gripped Linzy. "Until now, I didn't even know Cam's father was in prison. Sash never mentioned it."

"Maybe she doesn't know." Banks said. "You girls have been through the wringer. First your parents' deaths, then finding out it was murder by a so-called uncle, now this character. Cameron Gaines. I don't trust a man who drinks to excess or puts his hands on a woman in anger. Never did. Never will."

He tented his fingers in front of himself on the desk. Before he spoke, he seemed to realize the prayerful position he'd presented. He lowered his hands and smoothed them across the near pristine surface of the glass. In the upper corner, a sticky note had been written. The letters were small, blocky cursive.

She couldn't read it from her angle, but Linzy knew at once the writing belonged to the detective. She'd seen him writing in his notebook. He was old school. Methodical. Concise.

She felt safe with him.

She trusted him.

He would find Sash. If anyone could.

"I'll need your help on this," he said. "Time is of the essence —" He hesitated as if not sure how much to tell her. "I'm going to see if I can break through Mr. Gaines's façade, and I don't have time to finesse him. What else can you tell me about his past? I noticed quite an age difference between him and your sister."

Linzy attempted to still her nerves. She wanted to jump out of her seat. Enough with the questions, she wanted to scream. Get the search going again. Instead, she sucked up her feelings one more time so she could play along. "I didn't like the age difference at first, but having lost our parents when Sash was only fourteen, it kind of made sense she'd fall for someone older. Someone more settled. Especially after the mess with Ancho and Domino."

The detective waited, giving her room.

"Cam hired her right away. Sasha trusted Rose's opinion. She thought the world of him both as an 'uncle' and as a boss. Rose said she wanted someone she trusted to fill her shoes before she got married and moved away. Looking back, I wonder if she recommended Sash as a way to help my sister out of the fishbowl our highschool had become. I mean, she and Rose have been best friends forever." She nibbled at her thumbnail as she thought about what she'd said. "I called Rose to see if she'd heard from

Sash. She hadn't." Linzy looked up at the detective. "Sitting here is killing me."

"Trust me," he said. "This is necessary. And time is not being wasted. I have people scouring their home, their computers, his phone, and his finances. It nearly took an act of Congress to get the digital warrants so quickly. I made Mr. Gaines think it was routine, but I'll tell you, it was not routine. I called in favors. A number of them." He cleared his throat. "I want her found, too. Something about this thing stinks to high heaven and I'm going to find out what it is."

"Okay, you're right. Cam was always on the phone or computer. If he's involved, there's probably something on his laptop or tablet. Maybe even the phone." She stuffed her hands under the sides of her legs to keep from chewing.

"Do you feel he is involved?" Banks asked bluntly.

Linzy pulled her thoughts up short. That was the second time he'd asked her outright. If I say yes, will that narrow his search?

She fidgeted, stuffed her fingers deeper under her thighs, then said, "I don't want to believe it, but he was a different person that one time, like I said." She looked down, obviously wrestling with her words. "And I wasn't nice." She glanced up at the window behind his head. "I was very vocal when he came back to get her after he locked them out. I didn't want her to go back with him."

"And you told him so, huh?"

Linzy nodded. "That was only a few weeks ago. I convinced her to stay with me one extra day, just to rest, but I hoped she would stay for good. Her and Skye. Sasha vetoed it, though. Wanted her marriage to work." She pulled her hands out, placed them back on the desk, unfisted this time. "Please, Detective Banks, we've got to find her. She may be hurting, or being hurt —" Her voice dissolved into tears.

He pushed the tissue box closer.

Linzy cleared her throat, pushed through the pain. "Right from the beginning, I mean the very next day after he threw them out, he started texting her, apologizing." She rolled her eyes. "The day after that, he came and got them." Crumpling the tissue into her palm, Linzy touched the edge of the desk with the tips of her fingers. *The stories this desk could tell. I can almost feel them. Will this be just one more?* "I can't imagine Christmas without them, Detective." She looked at him, eyes swimming with tears. "Can you just ... *hurry?*"

"We're doing everything in our power." He didn't lose patience, just continued, "You said he acts different lately?"

Linzy quashed a sigh. "Yes, aside from that episode, Sash said he had been staying gone, working late, but not at the office, at places where she couldn't or wouldn't go. Meeting clients at odd times, going to bars, stuff like that." She thought hard, sifting through the things her sister had said after it happened.

The detective's pen magically appeared between his long, knob-knuckled fingers. He tapped it on the desk. "Doesn't sound like he is exactly settled."

Linzy recalled their walk down the shore, the detective's suit coat flapping open in the breeze while they searched. She wondered if the wet sand had ruined his shoes. "I think his problems started after the baby was born. He seemed excited when Sasha found out she was pregnant—they got married right away—but maybe it came as a shock to him. How much time and energy a baby requires. He said he'd never been married before." *Shut up, Linz. Don't make the entire thing about him ... what if it's Domino? Let the detective look into everything. Don't make them lean toward Cam just because you don't like him.*

"Not even divorced?" Banks asked. "That's unusual. Something to look into." He stopped the pen and looked directly across the desk. "You've given me a lot to go on. All these things are what we call flags. And they are a good place to dig in." He pulled his phone from inside his jacket pocket. A silent text must have come in.

Linzy's nerves sizzled beneath her skin. Maybe this is why people drink, she thought. To still the buzzing nerves.

"Okay," he said, after reading the text message. "His computers are clean. Nothing illegal. Bank accounts are low. But that's the worst of it—"

"What about his phone?" Linzy interrupted. "He told Sash he'd been playing cards somewhere. That's how he lost the money. Said he was trying to recoup some cash the night he went home drunk."

"Still looking at the phone," Banks said. "He has a ton of contacts."

She wanted to say please, keep me in the loop, but what came out was, "This could make him very angry."

"He has a problem controlling his anger?"

She looked into Detective Banks' dark eyes, then added, "Only that one time as far as I know. And he was drinking. He didn't seem this way at first, although, to be honest, I always thought there was something odd about him." *Oh, why did I mention that again? Let him get on with it, Linz. Stop talking, just stop talking.*

"Odd? How do you mean?"

"He bought her that beach house. Knowing he couldn't afford it." She closed her eyes. *Should have stopped talking. Now, here we are, going over everything. Again.* "He gave her that and told her it was so she could see the moon over the waves every night. Said he'd promised her the moon and that was as close as he could get. He has a romantic side, but I guess he went overboard. Financially, I mean."

"Is that the odd part?"

She took another tissue and dabbed at her leaking eyes. *How can I formulate a way to tell him I just don't trust Cam anymore? I can't. He might stop looking at other people. Can't have that. Tunnel vision is never good.*

After a couple of seconds, she wadded the tissue into her other palm. "I felt he had some kind of secret. Maybe it's just his dad being in prison. But you know, he's very successful. Face on billboards, nice real estate office, fancy cars, and yet … sometimes he wouldn't look me in the eye. Like I said, I have trouble trusting people. Maybe it's just me."

"Was he jealous? Of you always being around?"

"I'm beginning to wonder," she murmured. "Ever since he called me that night and said if I cared anything about them, I'd better come and get them." This time she really did have to blow her nose. "I mean … who does that?"

The detective stopped the recorder again, said something under his breath.

Linzy wasn't certain, but it sounded like he said *who indeed?*

34

ESCAPE

Detective Banks stood. "I'm going to interview Mr. Gaines again," he said. "A bit more earnestly now that I have a little more background." He laid a hand on her shoulder in passing. "And I'm going to bring in his brother and sister-in-law. Whatever is in his past, they will know about it."

Linzy nodded. He would help her. Some people were good. She had to keep that in mind. Stupid, she chided herself. Just think about Blue and his folks if you need reassurance about good people in the world.

As if on cue, her phone chimed.

The detective stopped in the doorway.

It was a message from Blue. "Just checking on you," the message read.

She knew the detective waited at the door. "It's my fiancée, Blue."

"Of course," Banks said. "I'll be back soon. And then I'll let you go." He went out the door, heading back toward Interview One.

"Thank you," she murmured to the detective, then she told Blue everything that had transpired so far, and he relayed the information from the house, which was nothing.

Another text came in. From Detective Banks this time. "Cam is bringing you the baby."

Before she could reply, Cam walked in with Skye and the carrier. He also handed Linzy a plastic grocery bag with a couple of disposable diapers and a can of instant formula. There were two clean bottles in the bag as well.

Linzy couldn't believe she hadn't seen him pack all of that before they left. But it was another plus for him. Blue asked what was happening and Linzy told him she was getting Skye from Cam. "I'll keep you updated," she said before signing off.

Cam waited patiently. Then said, "They're giving me a lie detector test in a few minutes. They're getting it set up now. Detective says it's just to corroborate everything I've told them." He kissed the baby on the head as he handed her over. "I don't mind," he said. "I just want to get this all out of the way and go back to looking for Sash." He paused until Linzy got the baby positioned in the crook of her arm.

"I know," she said. "Feels like we aren't doing anything to help." She clasped Skye gently, her own body softening to conform to the sweet little shape. "But we are doing something by giving them all this information, right?"

Cam nodded. "That's what I keep telling myself."

Linzy could see Detective Banks waiting in the hallway. "Go ahead with the detective, we'll be fine. Maybe we can all leave soon. Get back to the search."

Cam started to turn around, stopped, said, "She's coming home, Linz. I know she is. I *know* it."

The statement surprised Linzy so much it rendered her speechless.

Detective Banks motioned him to come, and together he and Cam walked down the hall past the interview rooms, then turned the corner to go down another hallway.

Once again, Linzy peeked out the door to see where they went. She lost sight of them when they made the turn past the interview rooms, but something else caught her eye. At the end of the hall, the glass doors framed the dark night. Inside the brightly lit building, time seemed to stand still. Out there, Sash was deep into nighttime, all alone.

~

Cam stopped outside a door marked restroom. "Okay?" he asked, jerking his thumb at the door. "The thought of a lie detector makes me a little nervous."

Banks nodded. "Tech's still setting up. Go ahead." He looked down at his phone. It seemed to have calls and texts coming in constantly. "Banks here," he said, turning his back to Cam as he spoke into the device.

Cam pushed the restroom door, pretending to go inside. Instead, he bypassed the doorway and kept going. The side door loomed. He hoped no alarm would go off when he went out, but he had to chance it. I'm not under arrest, he thought. They can't force me to take that test. Not yet anyway.

Adrenaline coursed through him. He'd told Linzy the truth. He didn't mind taking a lie detector test, but more than that, he needed to get out and look for her himself.

He had an idea of what had happened now.

It all circled back to the creep with Teena in the parking lot that night. The brute had obviously felt humiliated when his robbery plan went awry. Maybe this was him getting his revenge.

Sitting in the interview room, alone except for Skye, his thoughts had begun to clear. His wife was in terrible trouble. He had to find her. At first, Cam was convinced she really had gone to meet Linzy for some reason. Like the note said. Or even to meet up with some guy using Linzy's name as a ruse … but after all this, it became apparent that simply couldn't be true. In his heart, he knew she would never leave Skye alone. What a fool I've been, he thought.

Sasha was a brand-new mother, the most perfect example of love and kindness he'd ever known. While he sat there in the interview room with their precious child, he finally decided his own moral failings had been coloring his entire outlook. *Because I had no trouble lying to her, I half-expected her to do the same to me. I'm an idiot. I'm a guilt-ridden, dyed-in-the-wool idiot. I wouldn't blame her if she had run into the arms of another man.*

But even after chastising himself for one thing and then another, there was something that still didn't make sense. The fact that he'd gotten falling down drunk on two beers the night Chalk and Teena attempted to rob him. The night he'd shoved Sash and the baby out into the cold.

They put something in my beer. They must have. Teena had her hands on my glass. That wasn't a coincidence. It made me crazy. I've never manhandled a woman in my life before this. I wouldn't. Especially not the two loves of my life. Not in my right mind, that is.

He'd wanted to share his thoughts with Detective Banks, but he knew it sounded like he was making excuses for his past behavior. Besides, the man came through the door insisting on a lie detector. Cam had heard those tests could take a couple of hours. Now that he had an idea about who might've taken Sash, a couple of hours seemed too long to wait.

He wanted to tell Linzy his plan, the one he'd been formulating while she was talking with Banks, but he couldn't take the chance. He needed her to stay safe to take care of Skye.

The side door did not sound an alarm, which he found very odd. Don't look a gift horse in the mouth, he told himself. In seconds, he was outside in the cold December air. His Lincoln sat right where he'd parked it. He'd given them permission to search it, but he was pretty sure they wouldn't find anything. Unless they found his hidden compartment. Doubtful, though. He had installed it underneath the center console himself.

He climbed into the Lincoln as if he didn't have a care, moved the seat back to its original position, flipped the sun visors back up into place, readjusted the mirror, started it up, and drove it right out of the parking lot.

Once on the highway, he opened the secret compartment and took out the burner phone that had lived there since he first bought the car. He usually had his 9mm in there, too, but he'd taken it out and left it in the door pocket that night at The Joker's Wild. But after that fiasco, when he pushed Sash and the baby out in the night, he'd taken to leaving it locked up in his office. That's how badly the episode had scared him. Made him question his own sanity.

He ran his hand across his chin, feeling the stubble there, but not really noticing. He was determined to think his way through this mess. He'd begun to figure it out after Linzy clued them in to the impossibility of the wool coat belonging to Sash. Then, when Banks had finally told him where they'd found the stroller, and the tire marks, all the little jigsaw pieces had started falling into place. That's when he'd truly started thinking about Teena and Chalk and the night they tried to rob him.

Burner phone in hand, he sent his brother, Brandon, a quick text. "Legend, I'm about to call you." He sent him the text using Brandon's childhood name so he would know to answer the call from an unknown number.

Brandon picked up after the fourth ring. "Bro, what's going on?"

"Listen carefully," Cam said. He quickly told his brother about Sasha and what he thought happened to her.

Brandon listened.

"I'm sending you another text with some instructions," Cam said. "Counting on you to do this for me. And for Sasha. Make sure no one follows you. I'll drop this car and head there on foot."

It had occurred to Cam that he'd been allowed to leave the Sheriff's Office way too easily. They probably had a tracker on the Lincoln. Detective Banks had sent his regular cell phone to their IT people so they obviously couldn't ping him with that. But of course, they could put a tracker in or on his car. No problem.

He turned into a convenience store with a back door that was never locked. He intended to go through the store, leaving his car in the parking lot. From there, he'd hotfoot it over to an old warehouse scheduled for demolition. He'd had his realtor's eye on it for a while. It would be an excellent property for a new apartment complex.

Best of all, it was secluded.

Cam went in the front door of the all-night store in full view of the security cameras. Fortunately, he knew this particular store did a little trade out the back door, so there were definitely no cameras there. In moments, he was through the door and sprinting toward the warehouse.

After hearing about how Sasha had tossed the seashell ornament where it would be found, and how the stroller had been left at the neighbor's house like a decoy, also recalling how the tan coat had been draped over the playpen like a tiny miracle ... it had begun to make sense. All except for the part about the note and the pier. Cam still couldn't figure that out. But he would, eventually. He couldn't believe how late it was already. The moon was high now; it coated the quiet asphalt streets with silver.

Thinking as he walked, he realized Teena was the only woman he'd been with who could've known his security code. The one he'd been too stupid to change.

Plus, he'd seen firsthand what shape she was in now, and how Chalk seemed to have her under his control. Now, he needed Brandon to find out who this character really was and what kind of stuff he was into.

Which is exactly why Cam had instructed Brandon to get a message to their dad in prison. Before he went in, he had told Brandon if he ever needed help, all he had to do was call. Cam had cut all ties with the old man even before he got caught and convicted. Now, he could only hope his dad's offer applied to him, too. Neither of them had ever called on him before this. But as someone once said, desperate times call for desperate measures.

Cam didn't want to take everything into his own hands this way, but even if Banks had listened to him, the detective would have spent precious time going through legal channels, warrants and all that, before he could act on his hunch—providing he believed it at all—and Cam was afraid they didn't have that kind of time. Not if the kidnappers took Sash by boat the way he suspected.

He waited impatiently for Brandon to call and tell him everything he'd learned. Finally, his cheap phone buzzed.

"Dad told me to call his old partner. I did and he called me back right away," Brandon said. "Apparently, he told Dad he'd be here for us, so he's living up to his promise."

"That's wonderful," Cam replied, trying to rein in his sarcasm—he'd never had any respect for his dad or his partner—but that was then, as they say. Now, he'd lean on anyone to help find his wife. "What can he *do*?"

"He said he knows a guy in Galveston. Gave me some numbers to call and some instructions on what to do when, and if, we can actually get to them. He said we would have one chance with these guys, so we can't screw it up. We have to be convincing. Make the buy. You're right, he says it sounds like human trafficking. But if they don't believe we are buyers, we're screwed. There won't be any backup. All we have to work with is the cash Dad left us, and an offshore bank account number if needed."

"I knew I could count on you, Bro," Cam said. "We'll do whatever he says. Whatever it takes." Then he explained how he'd simply walked out of the Sheriff's Office through the side door. "I didn't *want* to appear suspicious, but they probably think I'm on the run." He paused to make sure Brandon understood what he was saying.

"I get it," Brandon said. "They will think I'm helping you escape. I don't think they will shoot to kill, though." He laughed darkly. "Not yet. But I guess that means I'd better put the pedal down. See you in a few." And that was the end of the discussion until he slid into the vacant warehouse parking lot a few minutes later.

As soon as he saw the unfamiliar SUV, with his brother behind the wheel, Cam rushed out of hiding and leaned into the window. He clapped a hand on Brandon's shoulder. No words of gratitude were necessary.

"Get in and put on this suit I brought you," Brandon said. He held up one arm so Cam could see he was already wearing a business suit himself. "You can change while I drive." He handed his brother a new burner phone from his house. They'd learned to keep several on hand growing up with their criminal father. "I told Maura just to say I got a call and had to leave. I don't want her mixed up in this if we can help it. I assume the deputies will show up at my house looking for you at some point."

"I don't want to get your wife involved either," Cam said. "If you talk to her, tell her the whole blame lies with me. I just had to get out of there to look for Sash."

Brandon nodded, glanced at his watch. "It's been about twenty minutes. So far, so good."

Cam stripped out of his clothes. He didn't ask any questions, he trusted his brother completely. But he did wonder where Brandon had come up with this unfamiliar SUV in the middle of the night. "So, what else did the old man's partner tell you?"

Brandon pulled out of the deserted parking area. As he drove, he relayed what he'd learned and then handed Cam a note he'd jotted on computer paper. "He said this guy is an acquaintance of Pug's at The Joker's Wild. His name's Reggie. He works the docks in Houston, but supposedly, if trafficking is going on anywhere in this area—with Chalk or without him—Reggie will know about it."

Fastening the buttons on the clean shirt Brandon had brought, then sliding his arms into the sleek sport coat, Cam said, "I don't think the old man would steer us wrong. I hope not." He changed his pants and stepped into the rich looking shoes a high-level criminal might wear. "I hate to say this, but I'm afraid Chalk may have kidnapped Sasha to get revenge on me."

"Why would he want revenge?"

"I humiliated him in Joker's parking lot when he was with Teena. It's a miracle he didn't get Skye, too. I believe I have Teena to thank for that." He remembered the feel of her hand on his arm as Chalk pulled her out of the car that night. How she'd said, "I'm sorry. I didn't mean for this to happen."

His brother glanced at him. "Maybe God was working through Teena."

Cam looked at him. "Seriously?"

Brandon shrugged. "My wife makes me go to church. Taught me to pray. You know this is the best life I've ever had. Never thought it was possible, did you?"

"No, I know what you're saying. It was my best life, too, until now—"

Brandon cut that off by grabbing his brother's hand. "God, please, steer us to Sasha. Help us get her back, safely. Amen." He ignored Cameron's shocked expression by saying, "You'll find a 9mm in the console." Then he slipped on a pair of dark sunglasses and grinned. "I study the Bible, but I also own a reprint of Poor Richard's Almanac in which Ben Franklin famously said, 'God helps those who help themselves'."

Cam rolled his eyes. "Bro, I read too, or have you forgotten? That pearl of wisdom came straight out of one of Aesop's fables."

Brandon shrugged. "Whatever, try these on." He handed him a pair of black glasses.

Cameron put on the sunglasses, looked in the visor mirror,

and said, "You don't think they'll be suspicious of sunglasses at night?"

"Nah – and don't worry. I'm not taking it lightly. We don't have a choice. These and this hair gel, it's at least a little bit of disguise. You'd do the same for me. And you're right, we can't wait on the law, Sash will be long gone. Time is of the—"

"Essence," Cam finished. "Just like the old man always said. Time is of the essence." He slathered his hair with the styling gel. It did look much darker afterward. He glanced in the mirror again. *This could go so wrong.*

They drove on toward the Galveston Wharves, while Cam entered the phone number from the piece of paper into his cheap phone.

Brandon said, "We'll do whatever he says to get this show on the road."

"Yeah," Cam replied. "I sure hope we're on the right track."

"Dad's old partner said he knew Pug from way back. Said he's not into the trafficking. Just the gambling. He said we can trust him."

Cam nodded. "We have to, don't we?" The phone number he'd entered finally began to ring. An automated voice answered and instructed him to leave a message. Cam left a voice mail for Reggie and mentioned the name of his dad's old partner.

The phone jangled in his hand almost before he'd clicked off. A voice told him exactly where to go and with whom to speak. The voice also said to take plenty of cash.

Brandon nodded toward the floorboard where a medium-sized, hardshell case rested. "Hundred thousand, unmarked."

"Dad's stash. Can't believe you never dipped into it." Cam shook his head. "What if they want more?"

"That other number on the page I gave you. That's the offshore account."

Cam opened his mouth, then closed it again. After a moment,

he said, "Dirty money. I don't even care where it came from. Whatever it takes to get my Sasha back."

Brandon's phone buzzed. "Guess they contacted Reggie." He listened to another set of instructions, then relayed the information to Cam, telling him they would be met by a driver at a certain wharf. "Reggie said he knew exactly what's going on. Says once we meet the driver and are taken to the ship, you'll pretend you're shopping for yourself and your backers. You are not Cameron Gaines. You are Royal River Rhodes, brother of Legend, and son of Kingston Rhodes." Brandon's voice changed. "I never thought I'd be using our old names again. Or be glad our old man is incarcerated for one of the most imaginative money-making con games of the last decade."

Cam agreed. "Guess this means the criminals still respect him."

"Yeah, and they know he's due to be released in a couple of years. They'll want to please him by pleasing you. There won't be any problem as long as you've got the cash. And the insurance of the other account as a last resort."

Cam nodded, appreciating the verbatim message.

"There's just one more thing," Brandon said. "I've been thinking about it. You're right. These sunglasses and hair gel may not be enough. Someone might recognize you.

"But they're expecting both of us," he said. "A pair of brothers. But you're right, I probably do need to hang back. We can't let this stop us ... there has to be a way." All at once, an idea struck him like a thunderbolt. "Linzy's fiancée," he said. "Blue Ash. He loves Sash like a sister. Took care of both of them after their folks were murdered."

Cam looked at his brother. "I'm going to call him to go with us. I'll be there, but I won't speak, I'll be the backup, or the driver, or whatever. I'll keep my cap pulled way down, like an underling."

Brandon was shaking his head. "Bro, I know Blue. He's

straight as an arrow. He'll call the cops, turn us in. He probably thinks you did something to Sash. I mean, you left the cop shop without telling any of them."

Cam smoothed his hand over his greasy hair. "I think he will help us. Besides, we need someone else we can trust. I would call Linzy, she'd help us in a heartbeat. But she has to take care of Skye." He pulled out his phone, pressed some digits. "I'm afraid we don't have a choice."

35

THE PLAN

Cam could hear the doubt in Blue's voice when he answered the unfamiliar number. "Hello?"

"It's me, Cameron. Don't hang up. Just listen." He spat out the entire, horrific story in a nutshell, ending with, "I need you to pretend to be me, the old me. My brother will be there, and I'll also be along. But I can't be the one doing the deal. They might recognize my billboard face."

"I'll be there," he said without hesitation "But I have to tell Linzy. She'll never forgive me if I don't."

Cam didn't try to prevent it, he simply said, "Is that wise? Won't she insist on coming along?"

Blue didn't speak for a moment, then he said, "You're right. She's still with Detective Banks anyway. If she calls and I don't answer, she'll most likely assume I got called out." He spoke again, "I'll send her a quick text telling her that. So, she won't worry."

"Good," Cam replied. "It's not exactly a lie. And it would be too dangerous if she knew the truth. Skye needs someone here in case things go south." He paused. "Dress like a businessman," he told Blue. "They're expecting big money. In fact, forget changing.

You can just wear my suit. I was planning on going in myself, until my brother pointed out that my face is everywhere in Galveston."

He told Blue where to meet them so they could drive together to a certain wharf where a small boat would take them to a private yacht.

"Did you have any trouble getting away from the house?" Cam asked when Blue pulled into the meeting place.

"Nah," Blue said. "Just told the nearest deputy I was called in to work.

Cam handed him a sport coat and pants. "I think they'll fit." He rebuttoned his own shirt as he spoke.

"They'll be fine," Blue replied, climbing into the roomy back seat of Brandon's borrowed SUV. "Let's go get our girl," he said. He began to strip without waiting for more instruction. "Y'all can fill me in as we drive."

Brandon nodded and put the vehicle in gear.

"Okay, here's our plan," Cam began, telling him exactly what they intended.

Blue mumbled agreement through the shirt halfway over his head.

Cam continued. "Did you turn your phone off so the law can't ping it?"

Blue grunted yes as he unbuttoned his jeans and changed into the slacks Brandon had brought. So far, everything fit near perfectly.

Cam continued to fill him and Brandon in on what had happened with the police so far. "I made everyone suspicious when I gave that damn tan coat to the K-9 officer to track." He glanced away. "Especially, Linzy." A look of regret crossed his face. "It was an honest mistake, though. I assumed if it was in my house, it belonged to my wife. Now, I believe that coat belonged to Teena."

He rubbed the back of his neck as if to kill the tension

accumulated there. "That stupid coat was draped over a chair near Skye's playpen—"

"Yeah," Blue interrupted. "That really made Linzy think you're involved. Funny thing is, she said that coat reminded her of ones she and Sash used for Halloween dress up one year, back before their folks were murdered. They went as Sherlock Holmes and Watson."

Cam said, "That's why I felt like I recognized it. I've seen that Halloween pic. It's on Sash's Instagram account."

"Don't beat yourself up, Bro. Now, here's where we are going. Reggie told me he would arrange some guys to take us to an 'invisible' yacht operating in the near Gulf—that's what he called it, 'the near Gulf'—he says they pay people big bucks to keep them off the radar. Said this is the only one of their 'invisible' ships in our area at the moment, so if Sasha was taken, that's the one they put her on."

Cam gritted his teeth. "This must be a well-financed operation. We have to be on our toes. Blue, your name is Royal Rhodes. Brandon is your brother, Legend." He paused. "It's a long story, but those are our real names. Brandon's and mine." He glanced at his brother. "We'll answer any questions when we have more time."

Blue nodded. "Go on …"

"You work for a billionaire—never named—who sent us to buy some girls and boys for one of his private party clubs. Think Jeffrey Epstein and his sex island. Reggie said this particular ship we're boarding started out as a floating hospital, but when it got old, the dude with all the dough bought it and repurposed it.

Now, they operate on the victims they kidnap, sell some organs to the highest bidders on the *red* market—that's the black market for organ trade—and that way they can make millions off each person by parceling them out. But for someone willing to pay an even higher price, they can buy the whole person instead.

Use 'em in whatever way they desire. Reggie told Brandon they refer to the victims as specimens."

"That's a horror movie," Blue said. "Worse than a horror movie." He covered his mouth with his hand. "That makes me feel ... I don't know. I just can't believe it. I mean—"

"Mind blown? Or as if you've taken a hard blow to the head?"

"Yeah," Blue said. "Something like that."

Cam nodded. "I'm trying not to actually think about it. We just have to go get her back." He nudged his brother and he and Brandon switched places. "Now, remember. I'm just the driver. My name is Bill if you have to use a name for me. Let's all get in character."

Blue sat back in the seat and straightened his new suit. "I'm good," he said. "I've got an idea about how to act. You know, Brookville is a small town. Most of us have heard rumors about your dad ... seems his sketchy past may be helping us now. So don't worry about me questioning anything. I'm here for Sasha. Whatever it takes."

"Glad to hear it," Brandon began.

"Heads up," Cam interrupted. "Our turnoff is coming up." He slowed the SUV, then said, "What's this?" A white pickup was approaching. The driver motioned for them to follow. "I think we are about to find out what's what," Cam said.

The truck turned and then immediately took a hard right into an anonymous parking lot.

Cam pulled in behind the double cab truck. Only in Texas would the bad guys be driving a big white pickup, he thought. Then he realized that almost every work truck on the road was a white pickup. Almost like hiding in plain sight.

He stayed in the SUV while Brandon and Blue stepped out and stood beside the vehicle, case full of cash in hand.

Cam heard Brandon introduce Blue as the buyer, and himself as his brother. He inclined his head toward Cam, dismissively. "Our driver will wait here."

The burly passenger of the white pickup shook his head and motioned toward the truck. "You all come." His voice was flat, hard to read.

So far, Blue hadn't said a word. Just stood with his sunglasses on and his chin in the air. If the circumstances had been different, the scene would have been comical, especially when Blue checked his watch as if to show they were wasting time. But the reality was that this entire thing depended on whether these punks believed their act or not.

Cam got out of the SUV and all three approached the truck. He kept his head down and sunglasses firmly in place. Each man was given a ski mask with the eyes sewn shut. Cam breathed a sigh of relief after he removed his sunglasses and pulled the disguise over his face. He assumed Brandon and Blue also donned theirs. It made him wonder what the three of them must look like in their business suits and ski masks with no eyeholes.

All three men were told to step up into the back seat of the double cab pickup.

Suddenly, Blue bellowed, "Watch it, fool!" It sounded as if someone attempted to force him into the truck. Cam hoped that's all that happened. Just before they had come to a stop, Blue said he intended to turn his phone back on and shove it under the floor mat. "Don't worry, it's on silent," he'd assured them.

Cam almost vetoed the idea, but Blue insisted they needed some kind of backup plan. They both agreed Linzy would know to alert Banks and the sheriff if she tried to track Blue and saw his phone there. It was not a very good backup plan, but better than nothing.

Suddenly, Cam heard another scrabble at the pickup. He figured Burly must've grabbed Blue when he stumbled. It sounded as if the barrel-chested thug yanked him back and slammed the door shut. Cam heard a thump that might've been Blue's face up against the closed window. "Spread 'em," the guy growled.

Cam's heart sank. He must have seen the phone.

The guy grumbled something unintelligible.

Maybe he's just searching him, Cam thought, fighting the urge to rip the ski mask off and see for himself. He heard the truck door open again, and a loud grunt issued from Blue as he said, "Hey, idiot, watch it. Kinda hard to find the step with this thing on my head, you know." This time, it sounded as if Blue fell into the truck with a hard "oof."

Cam and Brandon were then treated to what Cam assumed was the same rude search before being forced into the backseat alongside Blue. Maybe he hadn't seen the phone, Cam hoped. If he had, this whole thing would be over and we'd probably be dead.

He found himself saying a prayer the same way his brother had done earlier. Only he did it silently, in his head. So far, he'd kept the horrific fear of what his Sash might be going through at bay. But now, sitting here under someone else's control, unable to see where they were going, those fears were about to explode.

Without another word, the truck started driving. They made turn after turn, probably so the three of them couldn't retrace the number of stops and turns before they arrived at the final, correct wharf.

After the fifth or sixth U-turn, Cam began to feel it in his gut. Their hands were not cuffed nor were they restrained in any way. *If I have to puke, should I yank off the mask? Or will that get us all shot?* He kept waiting to taste the salt air of the Gulf as they neared the docks, but it didn't happen. Maybe because of the mask.

Finally, to Cam's immense relief, the truck slid to a stop. Without removing their masks, the three of them were taken out and ushered across a small landing pad. Cam recognized the sound of a helicopter in the process of starting up. "Hey," he said. "Where we—"

"Don't worry," said a man said with a heavy rolling accent. "Tis a brief jor'ney."

Cam couldn't place the accent, nor did he care to try. All he wanted was to find his wife and get her home ... *but a helicopter?* How would they get her back to land if a helicopter was necessary to get there? Brandon had been told a small boat would take them.

As things grew more and more complicated, Cam's self-confidence began to lag. What have we gotten ourselves into? Is Brandon's cash going to be enough to pull this off, or will we have to turn over everything and then find ourselves prisoners, too?

His thoughts were cut off as they were once again forced to step up, this time into the helicopter. The roar of the rotor—when it amped up—drowned out any possibility of conversation. The ski masks caused extreme disorientation.

Cam's stomach lurched as they lifted into the air. *Oh, God. Please don't let me be sick.* Thankfully, God heard his prayer. It was a very quick jor'ney just as the man had promised. In minutes, they set down on the deck of a ship.

They were allowed to remove their masks. It turned out to be a yacht the size of a small cruise liner. Now, everyone else was masked. Not with ski masks, though, the people who stood there to meet them wore regular old health care masks. The ones that covered everything but the eyes.

Everyone exited the helicopter. The rotor was so loud, speech was still impossible.

They were led across the deck to an actual strip of carpeting that was probably red but looked dark brown in the moonlight.

Brandon stepped forward first. His footsteps went silent when his feet hit the carpet.

Cam's sense of the ridiculous went into overdrive. Red carpet for a supposed crime outfit? No, for the minions of a supposed billionaire. Us. He prevented himself from gawking, but he was well aware of the dark water surrounding the ship.

At the end of the carpet, a fastidious man waited. He didn't offer to shake hands, just nodded and smiled. All the other figures were large, like the burly guy. Their faces appeared ruddy in the ship's hanging lights.

These were the types of boys their dad had played with that had caused his fall from grace. No one had to see whole faces to know they were in the presence of evil. It permeated the finally salty air.

The head honcho bowed slightly, then told them he was on a tight schedule. "I'm simply pausing here as a favor to your father." He touched the blazing white shirt cuffs peeking from the edges of his navy jacket sleeves. His white deck shoes were so immaculate they glowed. He appeared to be the world's tidiest ship captain.

Brandon inclined his head toward Blue. "We appreciate it. My brother is beginning a new venture with our father's backing."

Cam stood behind them. No one acknowledged him. He was just the driver. Brandon was the spokesperson, and he carried the cash. It was evident Blue was the buyer, but also evident he was simply there to make the selections, as if the cash exchange was somehow beneath him.

The captain stood aside and waved his hand toward the double doors that would open into the centrum of the ship. Brandon went first, then Blue, and then Cam, following along like an afterthought.

"Ready for tour?" the fastidious man asked.

Brandon nodded.

Cam thought it an odd question. A tour? What were they doing, sightseeing? He didn't have time to ponder. A sudden worry added to the churning pit in his gut. What if Sash isn't even here?

36

THE PRESS CONFERENCE

Shortly after sunrise smudged the sky with color, Linzy found herself on the private beach at Sunset Drift again. She slowly walked every inch of it as the sun rose. Before she arrived at the black rocks marking the far boundary, her text alert dinged and a message from Detective Banks popped up. "Press conference in front of the Sheriff's Office at nine a.m."

Linzy replied, "I'll be there." Then she trudged back toward the house, past the yellow crime scene—the stroller was no longer there, it had been taken to the lab for fingerprinting—and up the seventeen steps to the deck. There were no more deputies on duty. They had completed their search last night while she and Cam were at the Sheriff's Office. Detective Banks said they had even gained entry—by permission from the out-of-town owners—to search inside the home where the stroller was found. He said they expressed deep concern for Sasha and the baby, but nothing was found.

That didn't alleviate Linzy's fears. She'd seen the tire tracks going in and out of the carport area. She knew in her heart it had something to do with Sasha. She just couldn't figure out what.

Locking the beach house up tight—wondering again where

on earth Cam had gone and if he was now the chief suspect in her sister's disappearance—Linzy hurriedly poured a thermos of coffee, toasted a slice of whole grain bread, and grabbed a framed photo of Sash and Skye before heading out to the car. It wasn't nearly time for the press conference yet, but she couldn't stay in the house. Did a press conference mean they had new information?

Galveston County Sheriff Alan Crevier, Detective Arthur Banks, and Diek Evans, Chief of Beach Patrol, made their way to the wide front entrance outside the Sheriff's Office. Reporters were already gathering. A local TV channel had sent a cameraman with their reporter.

Detective Banks had sent Linzy one more text message shortly after the first one. "In addition to this press conference," he wrote, "I've also notified the Stutter Creek Sheriff's Department to put your cabin on their door-check service just in case she shows up there." Banks had added, "Trust me when I say we are covering all bases."

Linzy wrote back, "Thank you, I do trust you, and I also called our friends in Stutter Creek. The ones who take care of the cabin for us." She stopped typing, then added. "I'm headed your way now. I assume there is no new information, or you would have told me already, right?"

He sent back a check mark.

That single symbol sliced through Linzy like a razor. She couldn't even respond. Didn't mention to him how she had driven herself half-crazy walking the beaches this morning while watching her Wisteria Way home on her phone-camera link. She thanked God they had put up those security cameras after Ancho. Otherwise, her mind would've been torturing her, wondering if Sasha had found her way home.

Finally, the detective messaged again. "Let me know when

you arrive. We're going to get this out to the public. See if anyone knows anything."

Linzy wanted to ask him why he had allowed Cam to walk out of the station after his interview. They'd been there for a couple hours, and then, poof. They simply let him leave, but she didn't feel comfortable questioning his tactics. She assumed they knew what they were doing. Surely Banks had something up his sleeve.

Her thoughts continued round and round as she sat in her car and dozed, waiting for the press conference to start. She cracked the window open so the cool Gulf breeze could fill the interior.

For a second, Linzy felt an inexplicable ray of hope. God would not take her sister the way he'd taken her parents. He wouldn't be that cruel. The voice of Pastor Sue whispered in her head, "God didn't take anyone, Linz. Evil took them. An evil, greedy, lazy, entitled, man."

Linzy jerked fully awake. Evil, lazy, entitled … could Ancho be behind this? Even from prison? It was like the unanswerable question. One she kept returning to. Especially since Dom hadn't gone to prison. He could be anywhere. There'd been nothing tying him to the murder of her parents. But would he do Ancho's bidding now?

She turned on the radio to drown out her thoughts, and to listen for a report about any major fires or accidents. Blue had been called out, Sash had been gone nearly nineteen hours and apparently, Cam was somewhere in the wind.

It was almost nine o'clock.

Pushing her bangs off her forehead, straightening her spine to work out the kinks, Linzy pulled out her phone to see if she had missed any texts while she had dozed.

Still nothing.

Not like Blue to be out so long. It must be a very large fire or some sort of terrible accident if they had to call in off duty firefighters. If it was a real catastrophe, there should be a news report. Something didn't feel right.

After she left the Sheriff's Office last night, Linzy had taken Skye and gone straight back to Sasha's house. Blue wasn't there, so after bathing the little one and giving her another bottle, Linzy rocked her in front of the huge windows looking out onto the beach. It felt strange, sitting in Sash's big rocking chair, looking out upon the place where she might have been taken, but Linzy hadn't been able to make herself go home in case Sasha somehow reappeared. She felt unmoored. Adrift.

She was glad when Janine Ash drove down from Wisteria Way to check on them but completely surprised to learn Mrs. Ash didn't know about Blue's off duty run. She said he had not texted her nor even called. Linzy felt both relieved and somewhat dismayed when she agreed to let the sweet lady take Skye home with her for the night. She only did so in order to get up early and walk the beaches again.

It had been several hours since Blue texted to say he'd been called out. Linzy expected him to return by daybreak, or at least to call or send a message, but there had been nothing. This morning, he seemed to have stepped into the void just like Cam. Linzy couldn't remember ever losing track of Blue this way.

She wanted to text Detective Banks to ask about Cam again, about why he'd allowed him to leave so casually. He'd already told her they had done it on purpose. "We hope he can lead us to your sister," he'd said. "We aren't certain he had anything to do with her disappearance. Just covering as many bases as possible."

Linzy hadn't had the foresight to ask anymore at that point. She was still, truthfully, quite stunned that they'd let him walk out that way. *Maybe I'll learn more at the press conference. If not, I'll try to pin him down after.*

Something about the idea of a pin, of pinning him down, made her think of a way to find Blue. *A pin. I can track Blue's location on the map. Can't believe I didn't think of it until now.*

She tapped his name in her messages. A tiny map popped up on her screen and a miniscule icon appeared to show his location. Goodness. The Port of Galveston. What's he doing there? Could be a dock fire, or some sort of industrial spill.

Sensing movement outside the car, she realized the press conference was about to begin. She'd messaged Banks and told him she was waiting in the car. But her thoughts were muddy and jumbled. She wished Blue was here to help her survive this press conference.

A few reporters had formed a half-circle around the sheriff and Detective Banks. Behind their heads, variegated bands of clouds hugged the horizon like streaky artist's wishes. The sky could have illustrated a wall calendar labeled *December Morn, Galveston, Texas.* It reminded Linzy of Sasha's current fascination with all things art.

Her phone dinged.

It was a text from Detective Banks asking her to join them at the makeshift podium. She scrambled from her car and hurried to the group. She recognized the sheriff from her trip to the station earlier, but until now, she hadn't actually met him.

He patted her on the shoulder and began the session by telling everyone the reason he'd called the press conference. He then introduced Linzy, and she held up the photo of Sasha and Skye.

The Sheriff of Galveston County was a trim man about Linzy's height. He wore an impressively perfect dark gray suit topped by a pale gray cowboy hat. It reminded Linzy of Cam's billboard photo. He'd always had that gray Stetson on his head, accompanied by an engaging grin. She gripped her framed photo tightly. Made herself pay attention.

The sheriff seemed to gaze above the reporters' heads as he spoke. His no-nonsense voice was as neat and tidy as his suit. If Linzy hadn't seen him earlier, she would never have suspected he was the sheriff of the entire county. His suit seemed no different than that of a Texas banker or businessman.

His voice carried well. "Sasha Everly Gaines was last seen at the doctor's office yesterday afternoon for her regularly scheduled new-mom checkup. Doc said she appeared to be in excellent health." He paused as if to think over his next statement. "Her husband, local businessman, Cameron Gaines, arrived home at Sunset Drift between two and three p.m. where he discovered their four-month-old baby had been left in her playpen, alone. We are quite concerned for the whereabouts of Mrs. Gaines."

He shifted his shoulders forward, then back, inside his suit coat. "This is Detective Arthur Banks." He turned toward the tall man beside and slightly in back of him. "Detective Banks is in charge of investigating this case. Please direct all questions to him."

Banks stepped forward, touched the microphone. Adjusted the angle slightly upward.

Linzy half-expected him to tap it. *Is this thing on?* But he did not. Apparently, it wasn't his first press-conference-rodeo.

A blonde reporter in jeans and a plaid lavender blazer started the questions. "When was she reported missing?" She was the only reporter with a cameraman, and she zeroed in on the missing husband immediately. "And where is Mr. Gaines?"

Everything happened quickly after that. By the time Linzy was asked to show the photo again, her head was spinning.

She held the picture high and told everyone she knew her sister was in danger because she would never leave her baby alone. "Little Skye needs her," Linzy murmured. "We all do." She glanced into the TV camera. "Please, check your security cameras and call the Sheriff's Office if you see anything out of the ordinary. Especially in the beach areas."

All the other reporters held their smart phones a little higher for a better vantage point with their phone cameras and microphones. The lavender-jacketed woman wanted to ask another question, but the sheriff pointed at a different reporter in a green dress.

"To be blunt, Sheriff," the reporter began, "why such a big push for a woman who hasn't even been missing for twenty-four hours yet?" She tilted her head expertly to one side to make the hair slide off her cheek while still holding her cell phone steady. "And exactly where is Mr. Gaines?"

Sheriff Crevier gave her a look that could wilt a new rose. "Nursing mother. Extenuating circumstances. Conference over."

After that, things wound down and everyone dispersed. Linzy felt deflated. Why *isn't* Cam here? she asked herself. Where has he gone? Why did he take off? She stopped her swirling thoughts and looked the detective square in the eye. "Is Cam the extenuating circumstance?"

The good detective shook his head. "Sheriff only meant that since you and your sister have already been through one attempted murder plot, we aren't wasting any time in throwing our full resources into searching for her now." He continued walking with her back to her car. "Don't freak out, okay?"

Linzy's heart galloped. She laid a hand flat on her chest. "Don't freak out? Why? What? Oh my God, have you found her?"

He clasped her shoulder. "No, no. Not at all. I just wanted to let you know that while we *were* tracking Mr. Gaines at first, he has now gone off the grid."

She looked up at him. It felt like looking at a scarecrow in a cornfield, it was that surreal. "What does that mean? Gone off the grid. I don't understand why y'all let him walk out of the station. And why you didn't tell that in the confer—"

"We knew when he left the office last night. We were tracking his car, but he is no longer with it. We've lost track of him. We have his car, but not him. He isn't at his brother's house, and neither is his brother. Officers are scouring their places of work, going over everything. Brandon's wife says he received a call and left the house abruptly. We assume the call was from his brother."

He stood facing the breeze, the rising sun creating planes of light and shadow across his bony face. "Now, Brandon is in the wind, too."

Linzy felt sick. Brandon helping Cam escape? An idea occurred to her. "What about Rose, his niece?" Linzy said. "She and Sash have always been so close. Maybe she knows something."

"We've interviewed Rose already. She and her husband drove in as soon as they heard your sister was missing. She is devastated. Doesn't know anything."

"Thank God she's here though," Linzy breathed. Knowing Rose had arrived made her feel somewhat better. But worse, too. It took away the tiny shred of hope that Sash had sought out her old friend.

Banks relaxed a bit. Relieved, perhaps, that Linzy wasn't going to fly apart.

She chewed at her thumbnail. "I can't believe Cam is gone. Now, Brandon's gone, too. I've got to go and call Mrs. Ash, check on Skye." She didn't tell him she planned to call Maura, Brandon's wife, as well.

The detective nodded. "I understand, but remember, if you hear anything, from anyone, call me first."

Linzy said she would, but her insides were still thrumming. Before the detective could get away, she said, "Please be honest with me. Is Cam the main suspect? Is that why he took off?"

"He has not been named a suspect. We didn't have anything to hold him on. No evidence of *any* wrongdoing. At all." He pulled a length of vertically folded flyers from inside his jacket. His black eyes were steady. He handed her the flyers. "Now, this is not much, but I thought you might want to start putting them up."

Sasha's face stared up at her from the first flyer. It was a photo of her holding newborn Skye. The baby's little face wasn't visible, but the caption said she needed her mommy to come home. "I thought folks might be more inclined to pay attention to a new mom and baby," Banks explained. He had apparently had his office print the flyers from a photo on Cam's phone.

Linzy hugged him. She didn't care if it was proper or not. "Thank you, I will start putting them up immediately." She took the papers, then realized she would need a way to attach them to posts and windows.

Detective Banks handed her a roll of clear packaging tape in a plastic dispenser. "Take this, it sticks to everything." He smiled a wan smile. "I'll be in touch. Let me know if you hear from anyone; Cam, your sister, anyone."

Linzy took the tape and said, "Of course." But before they separated, a wiry bow-legged cowboy in an ancient, sweat-stained hat approached her with his hand out. "Ellis Barton," he said, shaking her hand gently. His fingers were gnarled, his pine-knot joints making Banks' knobby fingers appear smooth as silk. "I saw you speak just now."

He glanced down at the flyers. "Ms. Gaines is your sister. She's a beautiful young woman." He paused, and Linzy saw his Adam's apple go up and down as he swallowed. "I lost my daughter over twenty years ago. Had to do something to keep my sanity. Now I help others search for their loved ones as a volunteer with EquuSearch. If you don't know about us, we are an equine search organization founded by a wonderful man who also lost someone dear to him."

He swept his hat off his head, shifted his stance, and continued, "We are horseback volunteers dedicated to finding missing people. I'll fill you in if you want. I'm just a spokesperson today, here to let you know what we are doing out at Sunset Drift and further inland." He turned to Detective Banks. "How are you, Arthur?"

The detective held out his hand. "Good to see you, El. Thank you for getting here so quickly." He patted Linzy's shoulder. "I'll leave you with Ellis. Trust him. He knows what he is doing. EquuSearch has carte blanche when it comes to people searches."

He nodded at them both, then started toward his unmarked car. "I'll be in touch," he said.

Linzy knew about the organization. She'd seen them on the news helping out during disasters like the horrible flooding in Central Texas earlier in the year. She was so glad to see them, and she was already thinking about how she would make certain to tell her new friend, Ellis, about the tide pool where she'd found the turquoise ornament.

37

SASHA

Sash went into the water headfirst, a shallow dive. She was attempting to outrun the bad guy chasing her. He grabbed her arm and the other man, in the boat, nearly wrenched it from its socket trying to yank her up. *The big one hit me, over and over. Shoved me up and out of the water. Blood on my tongue. Are you the one in that awful video? Where's my baby?*

Reality came and went. In her head, she kicked and kicked, reliving everything again and again. The brute slapped and punched her. Stars appeared but she couldn't tell if they were overhead or just peppering the edges of her blurry vision.

Something pricked her arm and her body went limp. She lost sight of even the confusing stars as hands clutched her arms, her legs, her whole body. She felt herself lifted and handed across a rough surface. There followed much guttural cursing.

"Damn!" Someone grunted. "She *dead weight*." More grunting and groaning as she was yanked and flopped into the bottom of a tiny boat.

"Hope you didn't kill her, you fool," a different voice growled. "If she is dead, you answer to boss. *You*. Not *me*." More cursing, groaning, yanking. Sash remembered her head flopping this way and that. Out of her control. Her vision had gone from star-peppered gray, to black. Then to nothing. Blank.

She'd awakened in the sparkles, then another prick from a needle sent her back to black. Later, she awoke to the sparkles again. This occurred over and over. Sasha couldn't tell if she was dead or alive, underwater or above. The sparkles were like drops of sunlight on waves. Each time she came to, she prayed to know about Skye. But there were never any answers.

Blackness always swallowed her again.

Cam and Blue followed Brandon through the doors. Blue's posture said he could own the place if he so desired. What an actor, Cam thought. The cash valise was placed on a center table and opened. The contents were inspected, and the men were frisked again.

"Level three," the tidy captain said, turning to the burly guy from the white pickup.

Burly nodded, then pointed them to an elevator across the lobby. Everything shone, polished to perfection. Here and there, rhinestones were embedded in the expensive wood like so much cheap bling. Up close, the pattern appeared random, but at a distance, artsy waves were visible. The rhinestones picked up the electric lighting, scattering it randomly across the interior of the yacht.

To Cam, the whole thing felt like the inside of an old dance club or disco, something from a movie, way before his time. He was tempted to pry one of the rhinestones loose, make certain it wasn't a diamond, but of course he wouldn't do that. They had their roles to play. Perhaps the most important roles of their lives.

Burly stopped in front of the elevator and pressed a button to open the doors. He then stepped aside so they could enter the small, wood-paneled car. After the big man got in, there was no more room. Thankfully, it was a short, downward trip. When the smooth doors slid open, they found themselves in a triangular hallway intersection. A larger set of elevator doors stood immediately to the right. Those doors appeared to be burnished steel.

Freight elevator, Cam thought.

Across the odd hallway, another set of double doors—wide, similar to the ones on the upper deck—but not fancy. These were utilitarian, like in a hospital. They were inset with narrow vertical windows surrounded by black rubber just like the doors.

No nonsense, Cam thought. All business. He recalled the comment about black-market organs. He pictured his Sash on an operating table, sliced open, flesh splayed, internal organs gleaming, heart still beating…

Every muscle in his body tightened up. He peered through the vertical door windows. Plain hospital beds were visible. They angled the walls on both sides. A human form lay perfectly still upon each mattress. Pristine white sheets were pulled halfway up each person, tucked in around the edges. It was difficult to gauge the size of the room. More rhinestone art glittered across the walls in swirling waves. Cam's belly roiled as his eye followed those rolling waves. They seemed to give the ship even more motion than he actually felt.

Burly was speaking to Brandon. Cam made himself listen.

"—is the display deck." He cleared his throat. "Do not touch. Tell me the bed numbers of the ones you choose. You may procure the entire specimen, or parts thereof." He glanced down at his cellphone. "I will input the numbers here and the specimens will be readied for shipping to your agreed upon location." He opened the door and motioned them through.

Wait. What? Cam sought Brandon's eyes. He hadn't mentioned anything about shipping or *parts thereof*. Cam assumed—stupidly, of course—that they would pay the money and carry her home in a smaller boat. Of course, that was before the helicopter. Not thinking, he told himself. Not thinking at all.

As the doors closed behind them, the four men stood just inside the large stateroom. A center aisle ran the length of it. Stainless steel IV poles stood sentinel at the head of each slanted bed. Walls must have been removed to get so many beds in one place, Cam thought.

In the far corner of the room, a male nurse in blue scrubs, wearing a stethoscope around his neck, tapped at a computer cart on wheels, charting data. The bottom of the cart held medical supplies. Everything about the room sparkled.

Cam began to hate rhinestones. Still hanging back behind them all, he slipped his sunglasses out and put them on. *I don't know who the old dude reached out to in order to gain us entry, but it must've been high level.*

Somehow able to hide his shock at the high-tech glitz, Brandon started forward.

"Ah ah ah," the guide scolded, wagging a finger like a schoolmarm. "Must wear these." From somewhere he produced paper masks, gloves, and shoe covers.

Brandon appeared annoyed, but did as requested.

The guide nodded. He already sported a mask, now he pulled on the rest of the coverings. "Some specimens already bought—waiting on shipping. Must not infect." His eyes—the only part of his face visible—crinkled at the corners. "Damaged merch go in tube." He indicated the corner of the room. "Boss lose big dollar."

Something about the man's voice and eye crinkle, as if he were grinning beneath his medical mask, made Cam recoil inwardly. Outwardly, they all complied without protest. Blue never flinched. His character seemed made of ice. Cam wanted to ask which ones were already paid for, but then he saw small red tags hanging from three of the IV poles. I'll bet those tags say sold, he thought.

He wondered if Brandon could feel him itching to do

something. *Anything*. This was too weird. He found it odd that the Burly man sometimes spoke formally, while other times he sounded like a gangbanger off the street. *Some info must be memorized. Or he's reading off that phone.*

"You don't need to go any further," Blue told Cam and Brandon brusquely, as one would a pair of employees. "I'll decide if these are worth anything." He glanced around, daring anyone to contradict him.

Brandon nodded and stepped aside, allowing Blue to go ahead for the first time since they'd boarded the ship.

After donning the appropriate mask and other items, Blue ignored the guide and proceeded directly up the center aisle. Cam was amazed at his transformation from good-old-boy firefighter to ruthless black-market businessman.

The guide looked momentarily bewildered, then recovered himself and caught up. "All you see are for sale unless marked. Whole specimens, here. Partial ones on lower deck. They go to tube after operations." His voice remained gruff, but softer, lilting. He clearly enjoyed this part of his job. "You look for whole specimen?" He waved his large, uncalloused hand toward the beds. "These are fresh. New."

Cam tensed. He could hear every word. *If that bastard hurt my Sash, he will pay.* He felt his fists clench and realized that might be dangerous in here. He didn't even know if she was here, yet.

He forced himself to relax and breathe behind his paper mask.

Blue slowed beside every bed, pretending to assess each *specimen*. Of course he was looking for Sasha. Cam knew he would recognize her. She told him Blue had been in her life since she was a kid. Forever, maybe. He forced his fists open further.

Cam hoped Burly couldn't see through Blue's act. The temperature was set to frigid in here. At least there's that. And the masks helped. *Thank God.*

In the car, he had combed his sandy hair into a sleek, off-the-forehead arrangement using the tube of hair gel Brandon had brought. Now, the stuff felt greasy. He wanted to scratch his neck where he was certain a single drop had melted and was inching its way into his collar, but he resisted the urge. *Sash is here; I feel her.*

It took a supreme act of willpower to keep himself from scratching, and worse yet, from rushing one bed to another while Blue stalked the aisle, viewing the "specimens."

When Blue stopped suddenly beside the third bed on the left, Cam could tell it was Sasha. Blue's body language changed dramatically.

Cam moved forward, unable to prevent himself any longer.

Her beautiful sun-streaked hair splayed out around her head like a silky fan. It appeared to be styled, as if someone had arranged it across the blue vinyl mattress so it would be even more eye-catching. A needle sprouted from her left inner elbow. The head of her bed was slightly raised. She looked like a modern-day Sleeping Beauty.

Cam's heart crashed into his ribcage. He looked away before the guide could see his eyes. *Was she alive?* He peered closer. The rhythmic rise and fall of her chest told him the answer was yes.

"This one," Blue murmured. "She's the one I want."

Burly frowned. Even beneath the mask, it was obvious. A deep line had appeared between his eyebrows.

Cam caught it, realized Blue may have spoken too quickly.

Blue seemed to realize it, too. "Now, let me see the rest." He glanced down the aisle. "I want several."

The guide's forehead smoothed out and they left Sasha, unconscious, unaware. Cam moved as close as possible before stopping near his wife. He cleared his throat and brushed her hand with his knuckles.

A tear slipped from the corner of Sasha's eye.

Cam watched Blue, willing him to play this right. *I'm not leaving without her. No matter what happens.*

Blue moved on as if this was just another business trip. He

pointed at a specimen toward the end of the row. Cam saw the young girl he indicated. The girl looked so young; he knew that's what drew Blue to want to help her, too. He probably wanted to buy them all. Save them all. Cam felt the same way.

Instead, Blue changed the topic. "That the tube?" He indicated the fat white ceramic cylinder rising through the floor near the far wall.

"That's it," the guide said, turning them around to have a look at the other half dozen beds. "You see more specimen you want?"

"That one." Blue pointed in the general direction of another still form—a boy, twelve, maybe fourteen, so slight it was impossible to judge his age—strapped to a bed opposite Sash. But he couldn't seem to help glancing back at the thick white tube. Cam's gaze followed his.

The tube stood waist high, rising up through the floor. The opening looked to be at least sixteen inches in diameter, the size of an extra-large pizza. A round porthole covered the top of the mammoth cylinder. The horizontal porthole window was made of thick glass, hinged so it could be opened. It appeared to be the same kind of safety glass used in the narrow door windows.

Cam followed Blue's gaze. Blue appeared to have an intense desire to open that window-cover and look down inside the tube. Cam understood why. He'd never seen anything like it. He'd heard Burly say damaged specimens go in the tube. He imagined an odor clinging to it, but the hospital disinfectant smell and the paper mask made it impossible to be certain.

"That's what gets rid of the … leftovers?" Blue asked.

Burly's eyes crinkled. Probably grinning again. "Garbage, that's all." He seemed to backtrack on his earlier braggadocio. He motioned for Blue to progress back toward the front.

As he turned around, Cameron's eye examined the tube. He spied a trickle of pink on one side. *Flesh pink, just like one of Sasha's acrylic paints. That color is flesh pink.* His skin crawled with disgust. *Garbage? Medical waste. Human beings. These people are for sale, for any purpose. Including his wife. What happens to them is of no concern to these monsters. It's like an immaculate abattoir.*

A veil of guilt descended on Cam. It nearly sunk him to his knees. *I did this. I put her here. Birds of a feather. I brought the birds to her and Skye, to our nest. The hawks, no, the vultures. I brought the vultures to our little nest and now ...*

His vision filled with red. Adrenaline charged through his veins. He wanted to rush to Sasha, unhook the IV, run out of there with her no matter the consequences. *I came in here unarmed with a ghost of a plan—*

"Señor?" the guide was speaking to Blue. "You are ready to complete your transaction?" The man's rehearsed speech brought Cam back to reality.

"Yes," Blue said. "I've seen all I need to see. My associate gave the cash to your boss." He raised his chin. "But now that I've viewed all the stock," he glanced around the room. "I like what I see." He paused a half beat. "I want them *all*."

Cam almost fell over. That statement changed everything. There couldn't possibly be enough money to buy them all, some were already sold, and those that weren't surely wouldn't fit in the helicopter. He stared at Blue. *Do you know what you're doing, buddy?*

Burly's eyes showed momentary disbelief. He quickly recovered his composure and pulled out his phone, sent a quick text. "I take you to boss," he said, glancing down at the incoming reply. "He say you mus' have a more luc-ra-tive arrangement in mind." The word lucrative almost tripped him up. It was obvious he was reading now.

Blue nodded and Brandon pulled the folded sheet of notepaper from his pocket. "Tell your boss I have a bank account number that will allow you boys to wrap this up so you can all retire early." His voice sounded nonchalant. Cam was both impressed and dismayed.

Burly walked them back toward the black rubber doorway. "Let's get starte—"

Helicopter blades chopped the air above the ship. That was our ride, Cam thought. *They're leaving us.* He looked to Brandon and Blue to see if they were as panicked as he felt. *What have we done?* A loud thump sounded on the floor above them. From the hallway, they heard the elevator open with a ding.

Excited voices assailed them as two thugs rushed through the rubber-lined doors.

Gunfire tattooed the air.

Cam flung himself across Sasha's inert body as Burly spun around, yanking his sidearm out of a hidden holster quicker than anyone would've thought possible.

Blue rushed forward, set his feet, and smashed the heel of his hand upward into the burly man's nose taking him down with one hit. On the way to the floor, the guy struggled with his weapon, fumbling it as he did.

The gun slid across the floor toward Brandon.

From the corner of the room, the nurse who had been entering data rushed into the scene and kicked the gun away.

Brandon scrambled after it.

Soccer dad still got game, Cam thought. *But why would they come in shooting unless they know we're imposters?*

38

PANIC AT THE DISCO

The first shot spun Cam around and knocked him away from Sasha. The second shot hit Blue. Cam fell to the floor beside Burly. *Through and through,* he thought, *please let the shot be through and through.*

Brandon made it to the sliding pistol but found himself under attack before he could pull the trigger. One of the new guards smacked him upside the head with the butt of the very gun he'd chased across the floor. They also hit Blue as he struggled to gain his feet. When Blue went back down, he grabbed for the rolling cart and spun it wildly.

The larger of the thugs said, "We'll give 'em to the Big Guy, let *him* find out who sent them here." Grasping Brandon under his arms, they dropped the now unconscious man beside his brother.

The fewer bullets fired on a ship, the better, thought Cam.

From her bed, Sasha moaned. Even hooked up to the paralyzing drugs, she seemed aware that something terrible was happening.

Brandon began to come around as the toe of someone's boot nudged him in the temple. "What do we do with them until the boss arrives?"

Brandon moaned and tried to rise but the guard popped him on top of the head with the butt of his gun. "Stay down," the guard muttered.

"Take them to surgery," the male nurse said. "We'll make some money off them before the tube. That'll make the boss happy—"

"This one took a hit," the smallest of the guards indicated Cam with a jerk of his head. "Might as well go ahead and—"

"Nah." The nurse pulled a rubber tourniquet from the pocket of his scrubs. "Tie the arm off with this. Stop the bleeding. Doc can sew it up. Their hearts and lungs may be viable. Probably kidneys and spleen, too." He turned away and busied himself cleaning up blood and checking IVs and vitals on each specimen.

The guards laughed. "Take him apart, then we feed him to the tube." The biggest one said something in a language Cam couldn't understand. It made his blood run cold.

He kept his eyes slitted, looking for a chance to get loose before they could bring on the drugs and restraints. Right now, they thought he was unconscious. He would try to use that to his advantage.

Without moving his head, he shifted his point of view. Sasha made another sound, and he wanted to leap up and charge toward her. *This rescue is not working—*

The smaller guard noticed his eyes move. Cam barely caught a flash of something before the gun butt smacked him just as it had done his brother.

The men bundled Cam and Brandon onto gurneys and swept them out the door and into the freight elevator. They ignored Blue, inert under the bed in the corner.

Both Cam and Brandon were knocked out, strapped down, and taken out. But Sash seemed to be coming around. From his hiding place, Blue could see Sasha. Hearing Cam's voice, and then the gunshots, plus all the noise of the struggle, seemed to have brought her close to consciousness.

Strangely, she wasn't flailing about or saying anything, but Blue could clearly see her eyes move. Then he noticed how in all the commotion, the IV in the crook of her arm had become partially dislodged. Apparently, the medicine no longer flowed directly into her vein.

Across the room, a doctor arrived. "I've got this," he told the nurse. "You go help with those men. That was too close for comfort. We need to get all these specimens offloaded and get ourselves home." He looked around. "I don't know what their deal was, but it probably isn't going through now. See what you can find out."

The nurse nodded. "I'll be back when they are secured below, Dr. Sita."

The doc dismissed him with a wave of his hand, then he moved on. Blue watched carefully. The man's motions were not as smooth as they could be. It seemed the gunshots had rattled them all, but Blue didn't recall seeing this guy in the stateroom when they entered so where did he come from? Maybe he heard the gunshots, or one of the guards sent him in as they removed Cam and Brandon.

Whatever, the guy hadn't been overly friendly with the nurse, he had a true doctor's air about him. Then Blue realized the doc appeared to be whispering to the "specimens" as he checked on them.

"I'm sorry," Blue heard him murmur. "My uncle paid for my medical school, I didn't know he worked for the cartel. Now, I work for them, too. Not by choice. Not at all. I was ignorant."

He adjusted the IV flow and moved on to the next bed. Blue heard him continue his rhetoric. It felt like he was talking to himself more than to the patients in the beds. "What was I supposed to do?" the doc said. "When my uncle tried to make them cut me loose, they beheaded him, dumped him at our family's gate. It was not safe there anymore. I had to hire the coyote to bring them here. Fifteen thousand dollars each for Mamá, Papá, mi abuela, and Celina—my little sister.

Now I'm the one who is stuck. My uncle paid with his life, now I'm paying with mine and yours. Catch-22." He adjusted his round glasses and glanced at Sasha's bed. "You do it for family, right?"

Sasha followed him with her eyes. Blue could barely see them from beneath the bed, behind the sheet hanging down.

"But you know what?" the doc went on. "Today, I'm done … I can't do this. They said red-market surgeries, taking care of patients who sold their organs to save themselves or family members." He shook his head. "Then I saw you, little mama." He seemed to speak directly to Sash now. "I see your milk, leaking. You have a little one somewhere. I won't do this … not anymore." He detached her IV but left the tubing taped to her arm.

Blue held his breath.

"No more …" the doc muttered. "Dr. Carlos Sita, new kid on the block." He pushed his glasses up again as he moved on to the next specimen. "Sent my soul straight to hell with this trip. Gotta make it right." He made the sign of the cross on his chest.

Blue began to hope.

Stunned from the bullet, Blue had crashed into the rolling cart then fell behind the bed nearest the far door. He could feel blood trickling down his face from where he'd grazed the metal corner of the cart on his way down.

He wondered why Dr. Sita didn't rush toward him. Surely, he wasn't completely hidden. But no, the doc appeared to be more focused on the patients. Probably thinks I'm dead or unconscious, Blue thought. But as he watched the man through slitted eyes, he began to get a different vibe. The doc continued to adjust IVs and talk to himself and the patients. He made the sign of the cross each time he stopped at one of the beds. In fact, he seemed genuinely concerned about their well-being.

Blue felt he had to take a chance. "That's my sister," he rasped, pushing aside the corner of the sheet that had fallen over the side of the bed. He pointed at Sasha.

The doctor glanced at her, then looked straight at Blue and placed his index finger against his lips. He glanced over his shoulder at the double doors, as if expecting someone to burst through at any moment.

He casually stepped over to the cart, took two rolls of gauze from a shelf beneath it, and pushed them under the bed at Blue. He indicated Blue's leaking head and chest wounds, then he grabbed a wheelchair and turned away without a word.

Sasha began to moan. Every now and then Blue thought he could make out a word, something about an angel in glasses and bad men drowning her. She chilled his senses when she shrieked, "Where's my *Skye*?"

Blue longed to go to her, soothe her, let her know Skye was okay, but before he could do or say anything, he saw the doctor lean over Sasha's bed and whisper something in her ear. Sasha settled back into silence.

Knowing he needed to move, to figure out how to help not only Sash, but now Cam and Brandon too, Blue carefully slid aside the sheet so that he could watch the quiet doctor tending to the other people. I seem to be the only one still mobile, he thought.

Sasha began to moan again, but this time, the doctor did not shush her. Instead, he continued on to the next bed and the next and as he left each one, the subjects all began to make small noises.

He's taking out the IVs, Blue thought. Unhooking them from the drugs.

That's all it took. He slithered out from under the bed just in time to hear the elevator ding. The sound was muted by the rubber-sealed doors.

But Blue didn't have time to worry about that, even as he tried to stand, using the head of the bed for support, the doors opened, and two uniforms appeared. "Coast Guard," one of them barked. "Stay exactly where you are."

The other elevator dinged and two more Coast Guardsmen stepped out.

Blue tried to stand straighter as the doctor pushed a wheelchair past him toward Sasha's bed. Sash was muttering about spider legs and blue in the floor. *I think she meant me, Blue, on the floor. But I don't know why she keeps going on about spider legs.*

"Here," Dr. Sita called to the first guardsman. "Help me get this woman in this chair. Her brother is there," he nodded toward Blue. "He appears to have a gunshot wound to the upper chest. Inflicted by the cartel."

The guardsman helped the doc slide Sasha off the bed and into the chair. The doctor showed him how to strap her in so she wouldn't slide back out. Her head lolled on one shoulder and her eyes rolled, unfocussed.

Dr. Sita turned over control of her wheelchair to the men. "Get her to safety and take him as well."

The guard in the lead turned to the other two who had arrived. Between them, they lifted and half-dragged Blue to another wheelchair.

Blue caught the doctor's eye and nodded toward Sasha. "Thank you," he said.

Dr. Sita acknowledged him but turned back to the other specimens.

"Stay here with him," the lead guardsman said to his partner, indicating Dr. Sita. "He is part of this whole thing ... at least until the law says otherwise." He turned to Blue. "Are you Blue Ash?"

When Blue nodded, the guardsman said, "Detective Banks called us, gave us your last known location." He stepped back and pronounced, "We've got a medic on deck. Thank you for alerting us to this travesty."

Blue wasn't sure what to say, it had been nothing more than desperation that led them to put together their haphazard plan. "Thank you for coming to our rescue. Her husband and his brother were with me. They were taken down to the surgical suite. We need to get to them right away."

"Don't worry, we have the ship under control. All is well."

His partner pushed Sasha, still moaning, to the elevator, while he took control of Blue's chair. The other two stood at the ready, one near the doctor, the other near the door.

As the guardsman helped him into the chair, Blue realized he and his friends had probably heard the cartel helicopter leaving because they found out the Coast Guard was on the way. That must be when the two thugs had rushed in, determined to kill or corral them.

His plan about turning his phone back on seemed to have

worked. Linzy must have tracked it, realized he was nowhere near his department's jurisdiction, and shared the information with Detective Banks.

He imagined the detective following his phone signal to the Burly man's white pickup. That must be when they got the Coast Guard involved. Had to be how they located the ship so quickly.

As the elevator doors opened, Blue heard a series of shouts from below decks. Apparently, someone had tried to escape.

In the elevator, Sasha appeared to waver in and out of consciousness. She still mumbled about spider legs falling through the air, and that she was headed to the top of the world. A heavy weight seemed to keep her from moving her arms. Her head lay over on one shoulder as if her neck no longer worked.

Blue wasn't certain she knew who he was, even though he spoke to her and kept one hand on her arm the entire time. At one point, just before the on-deck elevator doors opened, she said, "Thank you, sparkly angel." It didn't make sense to Blue, but he didn't have time to worry about it. Getting off the ship and making certain Cam and Brandon were found, that's what concerned him. "By the way," he said, before the doors closed behind them. "That doc in there really was trying to help … maybe that will count for something in the long run."

The guardsman just nodded.

39

BACK ON LAND

"There were demons," Sasha said, gazing up at her sister. "Purple and black demons." She closed her eyes as if the dim light through the tilted hospital blinds caused her pain. "I know how it sounds," she murmured. "But it's real. And don't let them put that 5G stuff in your house either. It makes spider legs." She opened her eyes for a split second. "See them floating?"

Linzy didn't know which of those things to respond to first.

While she was trying to decide, Sasha whispered. "Look, in the corner." She pointed her chin toward the upper corner of her room. "Is that a nest?" The bedside monitor beeped as her heart rate soared.

Linzy reached toward the button to call the nurse.

"Don't do that," Sasha hissed. "If anyone opens the door, the breeze will make them multiply. See them floating?" She tried to raise her hand but only her fingers came up off the bedsheet. She rolled her head to the side as if to avoid something floating down.

Leaning closer, stroking her sister's arm from shoulder to wrist, gently, oh so gently, Linzy said, "It's okay, Sissy. I promise. They aren't real. I know you see them, but it won't always be that way. It's just from the drugs they gave you on the ship." *Oh, God, I hope it won't always be this way. What if those drugs damaged her brain permanently?*

Sasha's eyes closed and her heart rate finally began to slow.

Linzy collapsed in the heavy duty orange chair beside the bed. The nurse had already shown her how to make it recline so she could sleep there tonight. It wasn't easy to manipulate, but of course this type of furniture had to be made extra sturdy to withstand so many distraught bedside companions.

Drifting away, Linz dozed fitfully. She wanted to walk down the hall to the elevator and take it to the surgical waiting room to check on Blue. He was still in recovery. But she couldn't leave her sister. Wouldn't leave her. Detective Banks said he would let her know as soon as there was any news on Blue.

After boarding the yacht, the Coast Guard evacuated all the 'specimens' and their rescuers. Ambulances waited to take them to hospitals in Galveston and Houston while the bad guys were rounded up and held on the ship for processing by the appropriate law enforcement agencies.

"I woke up on a ship," Sasha whispered when she came around again. "It wasn't like waking at all, it was more like becoming." Her eyes sought Linzy's. "Like just now. I hope you know what I mean ..." Her voice faded out. "Somehow, I became aware of movement, and ridiculous, dazzling lights. Every surface glittered. And then there was that spider."

Linzy didn't know what to say, but she was trying to understand. "What do you mean every surface glittered?" She had heard very little about the interior of the ship.

"My throat," Sasha rasped. "It's so dry."

Linzy jumped up to grab the cup of ice chips a nurse had brought in earlier. She held a plastic spoonful to her sister's lips. "Take your time," she said. "Let them melt on your tongue."

Sasha nodded, let the ice melt in her mouth, then her words tumbled out, one on top of the other, breaking painfully on every other syllable. "I have to tell," she murmured. "I feel things fading." She swallowed a piece of not-melted ice and choked, coughing harshly, the coughs weakening to gasps for air.

Her bruised face broke Linzy's heart. The huge swelling on the side of her head looked like half an egg under the skin. Linzy raised the head of the hospital bed more and more until her sister was sitting nearly upright.

Sasha finally stopped choking and breathed again. "I didn't know where I was or how I got there but I remembered running, then diving into the ocean only to have big hard arms pull me up, out of the water, and into a small boat."

She opened her mouth for another bit of melting ice before continuing. "Someone hit me. And hit me. After that, I couldn't move because of all the bright sparkles. I thought it was the disco ball from the TV. I couldn't speak, or call out, or move any part of my body."

Purple demons, spider legs. Now a disco ball? Linzy didn't know what to think about any of that. Had to be the drugs.

"Are you in pain, Sis?"

Sasha shook her head once, then twice, frowning as if trying to recall. She opened her mouth for another bit of ice.

"Don't forget to melt it on your tongue," Linzy reminded her.

Sasha nodded. "Am I sick? My throat is stuck together on the inside. My neck hurts."

Linzy didn't know how much she was allowed to say. She'd been told not to direct her memories except to tell her she'd been drugged. "It's the drugs they gave you, Sissy." She paused. "But you're going to be okay. I promise." Linzy was trying to follow protocol. As much as she knew how, at least.

The detective said he wanted her to remember the men that took her all on her own. In case she had to testify against them later. The paralytic drugs will wear off the doctors told them. It just takes a little time.

Eyes closing again, Sasha croaked, "So tired."

Linzy set the cup of ice chips on the bedside table and glanced at the two-way mirror on the wall, hoping she was doing things by the book. She picked up her sister's inert hand. "Do you know who I am?" she asked, voice soft.

"My Linzy," Sash said, then she cut her eyes to the side, "More ice?"

Linzy carefully placed her sister's hand back on the pristine sheet where it lay, immobile. It alarmed her that there seemed to be no function there at all.

"Here," she dipped the spoon, retrieved a few ice chips, put it to Sasha's lips, but the girl could no longer bend her head forward to take it. The short conversation seemed to have sapped all her strength.

Linzy slipped a couple of tiny chips between Sash's lips. "Let it melt slowly," she reminded her. She held her hand behind her sister's head, bending it slightly forward.

Sash let her head fall to the side, but as Linzy was removing her supporting hand from behind her sister's head, Sash murmured, "Where baby?"

Linzy glanced toward the mirror, uncertain if she should answer.

"Baby dead?" Sash also glanced at the mirror, eyelids fluttering, sleep imminent. "The purple demon there? The one that made you dance on his lap?"

Linzy tried not to look at the mirror again, she couldn't believe Sash had noticed. This was such uncharted territory. She didn't know what to do.

"Sissy," she placed her hand on top of Sasha's still one again. "I heard you say everything in the ship glittered."

Sasha said, "Ship?" Her eyes opened, then closed again, slowly. "Glittery except the spider legs and the tube." Her voice trailed away.

Linzy cringed. She hadn't heard anything about a tube, but it was too late to ask. Sash was already back asleep. Or so she thought, until Sasha whispered, "It was white. Like a sink or a tub. And it smelled." She wrinkled her nose as if sniffing the air.

"Smelled bad?"

"Nurse man told angel doc he could never get the smell of feces off his fingertips from stuffing the tube."

Linzy rocked back in her chair. *Was that part of her hallucinations?* "Did you see them stuffing things in the tube?"

Sasha's eyelids fluttered again, then stilled. "Sparkly angel doc. Cam's voice. I was alive. Cam and Blue. I don't know."

Linzy couldn't speak.

"Where baby?" Sash croaked again. Her voice had fallen so low, almost too faint to hear. Her eyes did not open. *"Baby Skye, dead?"*

Tears welled in Linzy's eyes. She placed her free hand over her mouth. After a deep breath and a prayer, she said, "The baby's fine, I promise." Her sister didn't respond. "Sasha?" She touched Sasha's cheek. "Sissy …"

Sash didn't answer. She was used up, back in LaLa Land where she'd been—off and on—since being rescued.

Linzy resumed her prayer, holding her sister's motionless hand between both of her own. "Dear Lord, please let my poor sister rest without hallucinations. Please help her heal. Amen."

Detective Banks opened the door, motioned for Linzy to step out into the hall.

She didn't want to leave Sash in case the purple demon came while she was wandering around in sleep, alone, but Banks opened the door wider.

Finally, Linzy let go and crossed the room, glancing back at Sasha lying perfectly still. Her skin was as bluish-pale as her own still-leaking mother's milk.

Banks held open the door and whispered, "Is she out?"

Linzy swiped her fingers beneath her eyes. "Asleep, or unconscious, I can't tell which." She glanced at her fingertips, surprised at the amount of moisture there.

Detective Banks touched her back lightly, as if to direct her down the hallway.

"Can we go in that room?" Linzy pointed at the observation room attached to Sasha's. "So, I can keep an eye on her?" She glanced back at the door.

Keeping a slight pressure on her upper back, he propelled her past the security guard posted outside Sash's door. "Of course. C'mon." They entered the closet-like room next door. It was blessedly empty.

"I didn't even know there were hospital rooms like this," Linzy said, standing in front of the mirror that looked in on her sister. "She looks so frail."

Banks nodded, bade her sit in one of the three chairs in front of the mirror window. "There are a couple of these rooms, strictly for observation of injured or ill offenders. Especially those who might be contagious or violent. Cops hate to wear hazmat bunny suits unless absolutely necessary." He smiled. Linzy wasn't sure if he was serious or joking.

"But Sash is not contagious or violent, is she? Oh my God, I hope she isn't contagious. I never thought of that. She was on some kind of hospital ship. Were there diseases? Will we give the baby some horrible disease?"

Shaking his head, Detective Banks sat in a chair beside her. "No. Nothing like that. Your sister is a special case." He loosened his suit coat a little, adjusting his tie. "You see, we're pretty sure what Sash has been through is just the tip of the iceberg. Those things she was telling you, about doctors and nurses stuffing human flesh down tubes into the ocean ... that seems to be true."

Linzy felt her mind tilt sideways. "Not hallucinations?"

He swung his head back and forth, slowly. "Afraid not. The tube was a way of disposing of human remains. The crime scene techs are going over it now."

Letting his gaze rest on Sasha's inert form through the mirrored glass, he continued, "As for the demon and all the sparkles, we discovered that the bad guys lured her out of her house by sending a fake AI film of *you,* kidnapped and dressed like a hooker, being forced to give a lap dance to a purple-shirted pimp in an underground dance club. Of course it had a huge, sparkling, disco ball."

He pressed his lips together, as if in disgust. "The ship itself had rhinestones set into every surface. They seemed to think it made the horrific display suite more attractive to buyers." He shrugged. "Maybe it did. Anyway, thank you for allowing us to tape your conversations this way. I believe it will turn out to be very helpful."

Linzy couldn't speak. She felt the tears rolling down her face, but there was nothing she could do to make them stop. "Sash was going to be sold, wasn't she? I hope it was okay to tell her that Skye is safe." She took the handkerchief he offered. "I didn't know what to say when she asked. But she remembers some things. Did you hear her? She kept asking if the baby is dead." Her voice broke, her shoulders heaved, and she collapsed into sobs as the detective patted her awkwardly.

"I heard, yes. But you did fine. Later you can tell her that it was a woman named Teena who saved Skye. It was Teena's coat, by the way. The tan one. She must've shed it when she came into the house and grabbed the stroller. Probably she was in withdrawal by then. Not thinking straight."

"But straight enough to leave Skye, at least."

Detective Banks nodded, stood. "And then she either jumped, or was pushed, from the fourth-floor balcony of a hotel downtown."

"Horrible," Linzy said. "Poor Teena. So much death and destruction associated with these criminals." She swiped away tears again. "I hope you catch them all."

Banks rocked back and forth on his heels and changed the subject. "You can bring the baby in as soon as the doctors give their okay." He slipped his hands in his pockets. "Your sister is strong. She's going to be all right."

Linzy stared at Sasha, thought of the long road ahead. *She will heal physically, but what about mentally?* She thought of Blue and Cam and Brandon, downstairs, being treated for their own wounds.

She couldn't believe the things Blue and Cam—and Brandon—had done to track Sash and rescue her. The Three Musketeers, she thought, amazed.

Linzy longed to see Blue. Longed for the feel of his arms around her, comforting her, holding her together. But mostly, she needed to see him to make certain he was okay. The detective said Blue and Cam had been shot, but they were going to be okay. Linzy needed to see that for herself. She grasped the edges of her chair to keep from jumping up and running down the hall.

Detective Banks patted her again. "It's going to be fine," he said. "We may not get all the bad guys, but we're getting a ton of evidence from that floating crime scene, and we've got your sister and her three heroes to thank for it."

Eyes glued to Sasha's still, white, form, Linzy said, "I don't really understand what was happening on that ship, or yacht, whatever it is."

Banks looked at his watch. "Technically, it was a medium sized hospital ship—the size of a large luxury yacht—that had been re-outfitted for human trafficking. They also did a little red market organ sales on the side."

"Oh, my, God. Trafficking and red market as in selling them off in pieces? I mean … all that and no one knew?"

"Brand new operation," he said. "The current bad boy go-between, the one they called Chalk, was just out of prison and literally waiting on that ship to come in. Seems he'd made some good buddies in prison. They were the ones who hooked him up with this wonderful trafficking opportunity. Big money. Grabbed a lot of their victims off certain streets in Houston, but this time he decided to get revenge on Cameron by grabbing your sister and the baby. Although Teena foiled at least part of his plan. Thankfully."

Linzy thought it over. "Why did he want revenge on Cam?"

Detective Banks said, "Well, don't get me wrong, it was both revenge and money. Always money. But yeah, apparently, Cam humiliated Chalk in the parking lot with Teena, around Halloween."

Before Linzy could open her mouth to ask, Detective Banks went on. "Yes, the Halloween episode. Looks like one of them spiked Cameron's drink and that's why he didn't know what he was doing that night."

"And this creep was going to sell Sash and Skye, but Teena intervened."

"Looks that way. There are no morals whatsoever in that cadre of evil. But Teena didn't appear to be part of that bunch. Not even a wannabe. She was just a drug user looking for her next high." He looked down at the floor. "I'm surprised they didn't take her as well. Guess she was too damaged to sell."

Linzy clutched her belly, trying to absorb it all without getting sick. "I guess those evil people are everywhere, even right here in Galveston."

"I'm afraid so," Banks said. "Sometimes feels as if we're fighting a losing battle. There just isn't enough money for some people. They will do anything for more."

Focusing her gaze on Sasha's form, Linzy said, "I can't believe my little sister was about to be one of their sales."

He nodded. "But think of it this way. *Because* of your sister and her heroes, we were able to shut down a brand-new avenue for trafficking. And we rescued almost a dozen other victims, too."

Linzy held up one hand in a stop gesture. "Wait." She closed her eyes, then opened them again, feeling a bit more in control. "This is almost too much. But I do have one more question … do you know what sort of things were done to Sasha? Had she already been used in some way? Was she operated on, was she going to be stuffed down that horrible tube?" She felt her stomach begin to churn again and slapped a hand to her mouth.

Banks pulled a peppermint candy from his pocket, handed it to her.

Linzy tried to undo the cellophane wrapping, but her shaking fingers could not get a grip.

He took it back, split one end of the clear sheath, presented it to her half in and half out of the wrapper.

She popped it into her mouth hopeful it would allow her to hear the rest of the truths without having to dash across the hall to the bathroom.

"Better?" Banks asked.

"I don't know how you do this day after day—"

He glanced in at her sister. "We get some wins, like your sister. That's what I live for." He inclined his head toward the one-way glass. "Besides, if I don't do it, who will?"

Linz took a peppermint breath in through the nose, out through the mouth, slowly, quietly, the way she and Sash had been taught. "I thought losing our parents was the worst," she said. "And then Ancho came, and we learned he was behind their deaths." She pulled the end of her ponytail around her neck and tucked it into her fist, holding it like a lifeline. "Now, this."

Banks made the crinkly wrapper disappear and Linzy imagined him at the end of the day, emptying his pockets at home, candies and bits of cellophane tossed onto the bureau with his keys and mobile phone.

"Don't think of what has happened," he said. "Think of how you both survived."

Linzy let loose of the end of her hair, met his gaze. "This is mind bending. I don't see how she will ever be the same."

The force of his gaze held hers. "We don't believe she was

used in any way. She hasn't been missing that long, and the drugs she was given will wear off. She *will* recover."

"If it was revenge, it seems this Chalk person could have just drowned her out there in the surf—"

"She's so young and beautiful, selling her would make a lot of money. Just like all the others that were on the ship with her. And don't forget, he thought he was getting the child, too. He probably thought of it as a two-birds-with one-stone sort of deal."

Linzy let that sink in. "She keeps talking about spider legs and 5G internet and the purple demon—"

Banks frowned. "Pieces of conversations, struggles to wake up, and that graphic video of you on the lap of the purple-shirted pimp. Did you ever see that old *Star Wars* movie, *Return of the Jedi?*"

"*Star Wars*, sure."

"Remember Jabba the Hutt? Big old nasty blob—"

Linzy nodded. "Umm, yeah, had Carrie Fisher on a chain—"

"That's the one." He glanced in at Sasha again. "Picture Jabba the Hutt in a purple shirt, just as gross, just as nasty, even more evil, and you'll have a fairly accurate picture of the guy we think runs the ships part of this crime outfit."

"Did you say ships. Plural?" Linzy shivered, hugged herself.

"Yes. Cartels and crime families have been having their pick of 'humanity for human consumption.' That's our code for this lane of crime. HFHC. These days we have too many people on the fringe of society. Too many go missing every day with no one to report them." He clenched his jaw muscles, smoothed his fingers down the deep lines on either side of his mouth.

"You don't mean *actual* human consumption, do you?"

He remained silent.

"Oh, my God. You do. They can buy people for anything, can't they?" She closed her eyes, let her mind form a prayer of thanks. *Thank you, God, and thank you, Teena, for saving our baby Skye.*

Thanks to Cam and Brandon and Blue, the Three Musketeers, for finding Sasha so the Coast Guard could rescue her. She finished the impromptu prayer of thanks and looked at Detective Banks. "Thank you for your part in saving my sister."

"Don't forget to include yourself in there," Banks said. "And that quick thinking boyfriend of yours, too. If not for his phone, we wouldn't have known about that private helipad. Since we found it, we figured it had to be so they could board a ship."

Linzy dug her own phone out of her pocket and glanced at her texts. Nothing. She tapped a quick message to Blue to tell him she would see him soon. He was doubtless still in recovery, but the text would be there for him when he could read it. Maybe his mom would see it and read it to him. She hadn't left his side since the ambulance brought him in.

40

HOSPITAL - BABY

Detective Banks's phone dinged. He pulled it out and glanced at the screen. "Your brother-in-law is awake. They're bringing him up to see his wife. Someone is bringing the baby, too. Seems Mr. Gaines won't take no for an answer."

Linzy felt her scalp tighten. Even though it appeared Cam was completely innocent in the abduction, Linzy hadn't found a way to forgive him yet. If he had been the kind of husband her sister deserved, the bad guys never would have known where they lived.

She sat up straighter, the gray walls disappeared; the mirrored glass disappeared, and the entire room narrowed to that one spot, the doorway to the hall. "What are we waiting for?"

Banks stepped around her, blocked the door with his body. "One second." He waited until she looked into his face. "What is the current plan for the child? For my report?"

Every part of Linzy's body vibrated like the detective's phone. "She can come home with me until Sash is well enough to take care of her again." She knew Brandon's wife, Maura, had Rose to help with Skye, since Janine Ash was staying with Blue, and Brandon's wife was sitting in the room with him.

Banks said, "Don't forget, Cameron Gaines has been cleared of any wrongdoing. He is the father. The rightful guardian."

"You're right," she sighed. "He will want to take her." She'd simply assumed she would take Skye home and Sash would follow when she was released. *Why did I think I needed to take care of them again?* "You must think I'm such a control freak," she said.

Banks smiled. "I think you and your sister have been in survival mode for so long it's become second nature to take care of each other." He let that sink in, then went on. "But it does need to be discussed. I would rather CPS *not* get involved. I can see the baby will be in good hands with you and Mrs. Ash, or with his family, if necessary. But he is her father, and he has now been cleared—"

"Of course," Linzy said. "Cam has legal custody. That's how it should be except I may need to care for mom, baby, and dad if he is injured." She laughed self-consciously. "I hope you know I mean that in the best way."

"I believe you," he said gently. "Your little sister, and your niece were in grave danger. You don't get over that feeling just because we tell you to." His expression softened to match his voice.

She took a step back, glanced through the glass at Sasha who had begun to moan. "Okay. I'll stay right here. Just don't ... don't let me down."

Sasha's moaning grew louder. Her fingers began to clutch at the sheet, her legs scissoring ever-so-slightly.

"Hey, Detective?"

He looked over his shoulder, one hand on the door.

"I changed my mind. Okay if I go in with Sash instead?" Linzy tilted her head toward the glass.

Banks nodded. "Go ahead. I trust you won't make a scene." Then he was gone, coat tail flapping behind him.

Linzy walked out of the small room into the hall, immediately pushing into Sasha's room next door. She moved to the bed and took Sasha's hand between both of hers. "Hey, Sis," Linzy said.

Sasha's legs stilled. Her moaning stopped.

"You're okay," Linzy whispered, wondering if someone at the nurse's station was watching on the camera. She leaned a little closer. "Baby Skye is here. They're bringing her up."

As if on cue, Janine Ash came through the door with the baby in her arms.

Linzy was surprised, she'd thought it might be Rose, but Mrs. Ash said, "Blue is doing fine so I had to come up. I couldn't go a moment longer without seeing Sash for myself." Tears dotted her cheeks, but she wiped them away and passed Skye to Linzy.

Linzy hugged the baby to her chest. Skye appeared to have been crying, too. Her little face was streaked, big blue eyes swimming with tears. "Oh, sweetie," she whispered, pressing the baby's cheek to her own. The baby's pudgy little hand reached for her face.

Turning toward the bed, Linzy called her sister's name. "Sasha?"

The young mother's legs were scissoring again, fingers grasping at smooth white cotton. Linzy noticed the wetness staining her hospital gown. Milk stains. Need breast pads, she thought. I'll ask the nurse.

Mrs. Ash pulled the smaller chair up to the bedside and began to caress Sash's legs as if she were a baby like Skye.

Linzy brought Skye to the bedside, holding her angled slightly down toward the bed. "Here, Sash, here's your baby." She positioned Skye just close enough to allow the baby's grasping fingers to touch her mama's face.

"Baby," Sasha croaked. "Skye." A slight smile graced her lips even though she had yet to re-open her eyes.

Skye wriggled toward the sound of her mother's voice, reaching, bending, holding her arms out, doing her best to get to her.

Linzy bent closer.

Sasha visibly relaxed, finally able to open one arm out to the side. The way she would if she were about to breast feed.

A nurse burst into the room. "Don't let the baby nurse! Drugs are still in your sister's system."

Linzy backed up a few steps, pulling the baby away.

Detective Banks followed the nurse into the room. He pulled the folded blanket from the foot of the bed, motioned for Linzy to sit in the reclining chair, and covered the pair of them with the blanket. "A bottle, please," he told the nurse. He seemed to take offense at the way the nurse had yelled.

Linzy felt a debt of gratitude toward the kindly man. He'd been with them through this whole thing.

He winked when he saw the look on her face. "Four kids of my own," he whispered. "Everything will get back to normal. This is just a temporary pause." He turned to the nurse as if to ask why she was still standing there.

Janine Ash said, "Here, in the diaper bag. We're like scouts, always prepared."

The nurse looked at her. "I can warm it under the hot water tap. Won't take but a few seconds."

"Oh, thank you," Mrs. Ash said. "A little warmth would go a long way." She handed over the bottle.

"Thank you," Linzy mouthed, unable to speak aloud. She smiled and patted the baby on the back. I'll never let you and your mommy out of my sight again, she thought. The nurse handed her the warm bottle and Linzy offered it to the baby. Skye took it eagerly.

The room quieted as everyone watched the baby latch on to the bottle.

They were all surprised when Cam burst through the door a second later, hair disheveled, eyes wild, hands shaking. He wore a hospital gown thrown over a pair of dress pants. The pants and untied gown were both dotted with spots of blood.

Detective Banks steadied him as he entered. "I meant to bring you in myself," he said. "But I heard a note of alarm in a nurse's raised voice, so I followed her instead."

Cam's face was raw and pale, voice tremulous. "Linzy, Sasha, oh, my God, Skye." He wiped at his stubbly face with his bandaged arm.

Linzy looked at Banks. "Is he all right?"

The detective examined the tall man gripping the silver bedrail, misery twisting his features. "A through and through bullet wound treated in the Emergency Department. He will be fine." He glanced toward Mrs. Ash as he spoke, perhaps wanting to let her know Cam was no longer under any kind of suspicion —since she was the one who had been caring for the baby.

"He told us everything. Simply caught in the middle, really, but he felt so guilty that he might have caused this entire mess with his gambling, he could barely function. He called his brother and with their father's contacts from prison, and help from Blue, they came up with this crazy plan to get his wife back."

Sasha began to moan again, and Cam swayed on his feet.

"Perhaps it's a tale for another time," the detective said.

Linzy realized the baby had turned loose of the bottle at the sound of her father's voice. He walked wobble-legged to her side, knelt beside their chair.

The baby reached for her daddy like a life saver.

Cam's hands went to the sweet little girl and drew her into his arms, nestling her into the hollow of his shoulder as if he'd never let her go.

"Daddy's girl," he murmured. "Daddy's two girls." His eyes focused on Sash while adjusting his daughter against his chest.

Linzy stood, pulled the orange recliner as close to the bed as possible, and offered it to Cam.

He acknowledged her with a half-hug, then sat gingerly. Linzy gave him the baby's bottle, and he adjusted Skye in his good arm and offered the bottle to her, again. She took it and went back to drinking eagerly. Cam's other hand crept onto Sasha's bed and found her fingers. He held on lightly, connecting the three of them by touch. Finally, he lay his head back, seemingly at ease at last.

As the baby drank her formula, Detective Banks said, "The young woman who jumped or was pushed from the hotel balcony yesterday has been positively identified as Teena Reynolds. We've just notified her cousin in Colorado."

Linzy thought he must be repeating the information for Cam's benefit.

"She used to work at The Joker's Wild club," Cam said. "I met her there back in the day, when I was single."

Detective Banks nodded. "That was likely the connection. The FBI interviewed everyone on the ship and one of them quickly gave up the name of Chalk."

"He was Teena's new boyfriend. Or dealer. Both, I guess." Cam shifted in the chair, careful to keep the baby comfortable. "The two of them tried to rob me in the parking lot of the club shortly before Halloween." He glanced at Linzy. "I think she may have put something in my beer that night. I saw her touch it on the bar."

He seemed ashamed of what he was telling them. "I shouldn't have even been there. I thought I'd get in a quick card game, win back some of my losses so I wouldn't have to admit them to Sash, but apparently Teena told that creep I had money. Guess he thought I was an easy mark." He pressed his lips together for a moment, obviously thinking back.

"After I foiled their plan that evening," Cam continued, "Teena whispered that she was sorry she'd ever mentioned my name to him. I could see bruises on her face and arms where he'd abused her."

Linzy exhaled. She hadn't known all the particulars, but in her mind, she could imagine Teena taking the baby stroller and running down the beach to the empty house to spare little Skye the same fate as Sash.

"We think the kidnappers were counting on Teena to bring them the baby. She was definitely the one who drove the car found at the empty house," Detective Banks said. "But we think she left the baby in the playpen knowing Cam would come home and find her. Apparently, she left her coat there, too."

"And I was too stupid to realize it didn't even belong to Sash."

"Not stupid," Janine Ash spoke up. "Distraught."

Linzy's phone buzzed, and she pulled it from her pocket. It was a text from Blue. "Are you here?"

She responded immediately. "I'm upstairs with Sash, but Cam and your mom just came in so I'm coming to your room right now." She squeezed her eyes closed and said another tiny prayer of thanks.

At last, her jangled nerves began to settle back into their normal places.

41

TYING UP LOOSE ENDS

Detective Banks instructed the officer outside Sasha's hospital room not to allow anyone else in to visit, and then he and Linzy left the room.

"Can you tell me more about these people," she asked, as they headed for the stairwell. They both avoided the elevator without discussion. "Is my sister still in danger?"

"We don't have all the players. Probably never will, but there were so many victims—eleven more unconscious, just like your sister, and several others in the operating suite on a lower deck—that we will be tracking information for a long time. With help from the Feds, that is. In fact, the personnel on the ship came from all over the world. The criminals went right into clinics and medical schools and recruited both doctors and nurses as if they really were running mercy ships. Bold. Very bold. Don't worry, we're rounding them up."

He stopped, realizing her biggest fear perhaps. "But don't worry about Chalk. We got him first, thanks to a friend of your husband's named Pug." He shook his head. "Big coward Chalk turned out to be as soft as chalk. Caved almost immediately. Turned over all the names he knew and some he only suspected."

He opened the stairwell door, then turned back. "Oh, and when you hear about Dr. Carlos Sita, he was the one Sasha calls 'the angel doctor'. He was instrumental in helping your sister and all the others on that deck. That will go a long way toward assisting him with his legal problems down the road." He gave Linzy a thumbs up and told her he'd be in touch.

She continued down to the surgical waiting room. The bullet that lodged in Blue's chest had to be removed.

The hospital aide sitting at the desk in the surgical waiting area directed Linzy to Blue's room. He was just out of recovery. Taking a deep breath, Linzy swept her bangs off her forehead, straightened her shoulders, and opened the door.

Blue lay in the bed, a large bandage on one side of his chest, a smaller one on the side of his head. Linzy's heart nearly stopped. "Oh, my God," she breathed. She meant it as the beginning of a prayer, but Blue heard.

He opened his eyes. "Linz?"

She rushed to his bedside. "It's me." She leaned over and pressed her lips to his forehead.

"Hey, there," his voice was hoarse.

Linzy melted into the chair beside his bed.

"You okay?" he murmured.

She laughed, both her hands gripping his near one lightly. "You're asking me if *I'm* okay?" She leaned in and kissed his cheek.

"Right here," he said, lifting one corner of his mouth.

Linzy kissed it.

"Here." He touched the tip of his tongue to the other corner.

Linzy complied, leaning over. She couldn't help laughing at him putting her at ease with their old game.

"Right here," he said, puckering his lips like a duck.

She kissed him soundly, sweetly, her hair grazing his face, making him smile. "I was so worried about you," she whispered.

"Same, baby, same," he replied. "How are Sash and Skye?"

"Skye is great. Cam is there, giving her a bottle. He and Detective Banks agree the waitress from the bar where Cam played poker must have slipped something into his drink the night he locked Sash and Skye out on the patio. You know, back at Halloween when this whole nightmare began."

Blue lay so still Linzy wondered if she had overloaded him with too much information. She didn't know nearly enough about gunshots and head wounds. Banks had said after Blue was shot, he fell and gashed open his head on the corner of a cart. If the good doc hadn't helped him, he might have laid there and bled out.

Linzy eased back into her chair.

His grip tightened on her hands.

"Are you in pain?" Linzy asked.

He grinned, closed his eyes. "Just a touch of double vision."

"How about a cool cloth?"

"Yes, please."

Linzy found a pristine white washcloth, ran it under the cool tap, folded it lengthwise, and laid it across his eyes.

"Better," he murmured.

"Reminds me of the night you and Sash sat with me in the bathroom. After the news about Ancho coming to live with us." She perched on the edge of the chair and took his hand again. This arm was clear, but the one on the opposite side of the bed had an IV. Linzy was careful not to jostle anything.

"That was a bad time."

"We're on the good side now," she said. "I know we are. Everything will be hunky-dory from here on out. We're all together, that's the main thing."

"Cool," Blue murmured. "Like this wonderful thing you put on my eyes."

Linzy looked at his beloved face. She couldn't tell if he was teasing or not. "Head hurts?"

"Nah," he said. "Well, maybe a little. But I still want to hear more about how Sash is doing. That ship, Linz. You wouldn't believe."

"The detective told me a little. It must've been horrible. Thankfully, Sash is recovering," she said. "Along with you and Cam and Brandon. When you're all better, I want to hear about everything you saw and exactly how you three amigos found her."

His grin didn't falter. "That's a deal," he said. "Go ahead and talk, please. I love hearing the sound of your voice. Was afraid I might not. Hear it again."

Linzy's heart melted. "Well, first off, Sash is still having some hallucinations from the drugs they gave her. They must've been so strong. She sees strange things, spider legs floating through the air—"

Blue squeezed her hand. "One guard had a spider tattoo on the side of his neck. It appeared to be crawling out from under his collar. Creepy, and I wasn't even on drugs."

"Gross," Linzy said. "Sash must've seen it—"

"Probably," Blue said. "Will they stop? These hallucinations?"

"The nurse said yes. But if they don't go away soon, they will do an MRI to check for brain damage from other trauma." The threat of tears gripped her, and she had to swallow. Saying it out loud that way made her realize she wasn't quite as steady as she'd thought.

Blue brought her hand to his chest. "Other trauma?"

"She told me someone hit her and hit her … I could see lumps and bruising on the side of her head."

"Yes," Blue said. "I saw the bruises. Pretty severe."

Linzy was dumbfounded. "I never thought about how they actually took her. She didn't go down without a fight, did she?"

"Not our Sash," Blue said, adding, "Is Cam the only one still in there with them?"

In light of the topic, this question did not surprise her, even though she'd already mentioned it. She squeezed his fingers. "Your mom is there, too."

Blue smiled. "She told me she was going to the cafeteria for a cup of coffee after she took Skye up."

Linzy laughed. "I'll see that she does."

"We've got to take care of her," he said. "And my dad, too."

"Yes," Linzy agreed. "They've certainly taken care of us all these years."

"That's right," Blue said. "And we will do the same, for as long as we can—until we're just a couple of old fogies."

"You mean we aren't already?"

"Nah," Blue interrupted, his old jolly nature shining through. "Not too old. Gotta lotta livin' yet to do."

"That's right," Linzy murmured. "A lotta living. Thanks to you and your new buds."

"And God," Blue murmured, pointing toward the ceiling with his index finger.

She glanced at his eyes. They had closed again. In moments, his chin dipped to his chest and his breathing deepened. Linzy stood and whispered in his ear. "You rest while I go up and check on everyone. I'll be back soon."

He squeezed her fingers, and one corner of his mouth went up.

She kissed it, then pressed the pad of her thumb there, to seal it. She called Janine Ash and asked if she was ready for a break, but she replied not yet, so Linz made her way down to the cafeteria for a cup of coffee and a turkey and cheese sandwich. It was surprisingly delicious, and it occurred to her she had no idea the last time she'd eaten.

But she couldn't sit still. As soon as she finished the quick meal, Linzy grabbed a bottle of water and hurried back to the stairs. If Cam wasn't occupying the orange reclining chair in Sasha's room, she intended to make it hers for the night. Sash should be coming around again, soon. Linzy wanted to be there when she did.

~

Mr. and Mrs. Ash took Blue home after a couple of days and Sash went home the day after that. Cam was released the same day as Blue, and Brandon had been released after just one night. He had a concussion from the beating he took but he convinced the doctors he would be more comfortable at home.

Sash was so thrilled to be able to sit up and walk around, with assistance, that Linzy doubted they could have kept her any longer if they'd tried.

Brandon's wife, Maura, and dear sweet Rose, came to the beach house, often. They also took turns looking after the baby so Linzy could rest.

By the time Sasha was considered drug free, Skye had lost interest in breast feeding and simply continued with the bottle.

Things progressed and the sisters began to talk about what they wanted to do for their shared Christmas. "I want normality," Sasha said. "But I also want your help. At least for this first one." She'd glanced away, then back. "If it won't be too stressful, that is." Her eyebrows went up as if she'd asked a question.

Linzy hugged her. "After this, I can't imagine ever being stressed out over a holiday gathering."

Blue vowed to help. Since becoming a full-time firefighter-paramedic, he'd learned to make a few dishes on his own. The guys at the station all had to take turns cooking for their shift at least a couple times a month.

That's how it came to be that Linzy and Blue took over Sasha's kitchen to make the Christmas feast. Sash helped out and observed, afraid if she didn't pitch in now, she might never do it. The nightmares and hallucinations still plagued her from time to time, but mostly as memories and bad dreams. The doctor said that would fade in time.

As a result, they all humored her when she talked about spider legs, purple demons, and 5G conspiracies. For that, Sash was grateful. She told them so. Often. They still didn't know why 5G seemed so frightening to her, unless she equated it with the video hack that lured her out of the house that day, but they humored her without question.

The entire ordeal brought all three families closer together. Trust was restored, and Linzy was certain transparency had a lot to do with that. No question or topic was off limits. Not even when it came to Cam's family history. He surprised them all when he made a delicious, boiled-milk caramel pie with graham cracker crust. "It's the one thing Dad taught us that didn't involve evading arrest," he joked.

"I finally began talking to him again after all these years," he said, as they devoured the pie after Christmas dinner. "It's only through letters," he said. "But it tells me a lot." He laughed. "It tells me the old guy hasn't changed much. I don't think he's the least bit sorry about cheating all those people out of their money." An expression of shame darkened his face. "But if not for him and his contacts, I don't know how we would have found you."

Sash patted him and hugged him. "If I ever meet him," she said. "I will thank him personally for saving me."

Everyone in the family agreed no person was one dimensional. The fact that they had avoided tragedy with the help of criminals wasn't lost on any of them. Since their parents' deaths, the black and white world they'd grown up in had gone completely, unequivocally, gray. The only thing that hadn't changed was Linzy and Blue's relationship and their new habit of praying together. The bunch of them even attended Pastor Sue's church for midnight services on Christmas Eve.

God works in mysterious ways, Blue said later, in private. Linzy had to agree.

And just like that, Christmas was in the books. It had gone off without a hitch. Little Skye seemed astonished by the beautiful lights and gaily wrapped gifts under the tree. Between her doting parents, her aunt, and the Ash family, not to mention Brandon and Maura's family, the baby received so many toys she could probably open her own toy shop one day.

For New Years, they all agreed to celebrate with Sash and Cam on the beach. It would be Skye's first glimpse of community pier fireworks. Cam said they would watch from the deck so it wouldn't be too loud or scary.

Sasha had trouble leaving the house after her ordeal. She didn't like for Cam to leave her and the baby alone, either. As a result, he had taken to working from home every morning, setting up viewings and conferencing with clients, and then around noon, he would begin his showings in person after Linzy arrived with her laptop. She would teach her students from the beach house until Cam came back home around six.

During the day, Sash would clean house, read to Skye, take her for walks on the beach if Cam or Linzy could accompany them, and practice cooking.

Baking and trying new recipes had become her strength. Skye loved it, too. She would happily swing in her new little wind up swing, cooing like a dove, while her mommy whisked and stirred and sometimes hummed along with the kitchen radio.

Linzy was certain Sash would pick up her art again at some point. Right now, everything from before seemed a reminder just waiting to trigger another flashback memory.

Life was good, as long as no one expected Sash to be alone.

Linzy talked to Blue and Cam, and even to their old therapist. All agreed it would simply take time. So, they went on this way, everyone pitching in to make things easier for Sash, but Linzy knew her sister better than anyone. She remembered how Sash sometimes had to be prodded to make a change.

"Maybe the reason she can't get past her fear," Mrs. Ash

offered. "Is because there was no one to actually prosecute for her abduction."

Linzy had looked at her visiting soon-to-be mother-in-law with newfound respect. "I'll bet you're right," she agreed. "She never really knew who took her. No wonder it all seems like a nightmare from which she can't escape."

"That's exactly how it seems, Sissy," Sash had said, walking in on them from the hallway.

Linzy smiled sheepishly, embarrassed at being caught discussing her problems with Janine Ash. "I thought you were napping with the baby," she said.

"Obviously," Sash smiled. "But it's okay. I know you just worry. And I'm glad that Chalk person turned on the others and got so many rounded up, but geez. It does seem like I'm just supposed to simply forget about it and get back to the way things were before." She rolled her eyes. "Kind of like when Ancho accepted that plea deal. I was glad we didn't have to testify, but at least we knew *he* went to prison. This feels like it's ongoing. I think Mrs. Ash is right, we need some sort of ending. I worry about myself, too."

Glancing around her spacious living room and at the wide, floor-to-ceiling windows looking over the beach, she said, "At least I don't see the spider legs anymore. But I sure remember them. How real they seemed. How light, and floaty."

She shivered, rubbed her palms up and down her arms. "And even though I know they were just hallucinations from the drugs and that creep's tattoos, I just can't shake the way they appeared out of nowhere, over and over. Like all these bad things did. Every. Single Time. They just appeared out of nowhere and disrupted our lives. Tried to kill us."

Her eyes were huge. It was obvious she'd given the topic a lot of thought. "Besides all that, I can't stand the idea of being alone anymore. How will I ever go back to work at the office, never knowing who might come through the door when I'm there alone, just the baby and me?"

Linzy leaned forward and clasped her sister's hands. "It's only been a few weeks. The lawyers and detectives will get it all straightened out and put the bad guys away. That will give us some closure. But until they do, we will pray for strength and emotional closure. Remember, we are all here for you, forever. You will never be alone, okay?"

Sasha nodded. Her long blonde hair covered one side of her face, and her voice was low. "When I couldn't move, I could still hear people around me, but everything was white and sparkly and my mind decided I was in Antarctica, some place I could never truly be. It was pristine, but it seemed as if my leg was broken. It had to be because I was lying down while everyone interacted with each other around me. They would come in and go out, and I could sometimes see their shapes, but I couldn't speak to them. The drugs had me paralyzed. Everyone acted as if I didn't exist. It was terrifying."

She took a breath, then continued. "And when I consciously tried to close my eyes, the spider legs would float down onto my face." She laughed self-consciously. "Cam says it was just my eyelashes fluttering."

Janine Ash reached toward her, to comfort her. From the bedroom, where they had put the crib, Skye made a little murmur. It was picked up on the baby monitor.

"Once, I was struck with the idea that we were waiting on the end of the world. There was a timer ticking down. We only had fifteen minutes. Everyone thought we were nuts, going there—to Antarctica, the land of sparkling everything—to await the end. But we all seemed to want to be there, so that if we were going to die, at least we would see it coming."

She pushed a tear off her cheek, one eye barely visible within the curtain of hair. "We had only minutes to call our loved ones—those of you who didn't believe the world was about to end—in order to say goodbye, but I couldn't call. I didn't have a phone, and no one would talk to me even though I seemed to be literally sitting right on the crisp cusp of the Earth, a point of light the only thing showing my location."

Linzy opened her mouth to speak, but Sasha held up one hand. "I know what you're going to say, it makes no sense, but it did at the time. It was awful and beautiful and terrible. And I go back there nearly every night, as if my mind is still trying to understand."

The last part of her sentence was spoken so softly both women found themselves leaning forward to hear it. As one, they enveloped her in their arms. "Oh, Sissy," Linzy said.

Mrs. Ash said, "Oh, honey."

And then they were quiet as Sash finished her tale. "Somehow, the world didn't end. Instead, I wound up in Georgia, hot and swampy and slow." She laughed self-consciously again. "I was glad the white sparkles were gone. Soon, I became friends with an elderly man who took pity on me and invited me home to meet his family. They lived in a wonderful old southern craftsman home with a wraparound porch and a yellow kitchen. A tiny ancient woman kept constantly sweeping and cleaning, but she wouldn't acknowledge me at all." Cam says that sweeping sound was probably the rhythm of my own blood pressure inside my head."

Sasha gazed into the corner of the room, remembering. "He has answers for everything. But in my opinion, I think the woman was Sipsy from the *Fried Green Tomatoes* movie. I believe my mind conjured up a nice person to rescue me the way Sipsy rescued Ruth's baby from Frank Bennett in the movie."

She paused. "Then came the lady of the house. I don't know who she was, but she seemed elegant in her linen capris and floral blouse. She was tall and willowy, with soft, silver-white hair piled loosely on top of her head like an afterthought. I kept trying to see the clips or pins holding it in place, but I never did." Sash smiled softly. "It was such a beautiful home."

"That sounds like our grandmother," Linzy said. "You were only a baby when she died. Did they welcome you with open arms?"

Sasha shrugged. "I sat at the honey-colored dining table under the soft white lights and watched the tiny woman sweep and tidy the yellow kitchen, and no one ever spoke. Not even the gentleman who'd brought me there."

Linzy could feel the oppressive tension her sister must've felt at being completely unable to communicate with anyone, but in the back of her mind she was thinking the white sparkles were probably the rhinestones embedded in the walls that Blue had told her about. They must have sparkled so brightly under the overhead fluorescents. The others moving through her dreams had to have been the nurses and doctors. Doubtless one of them might've been a janitor of some sort. Cleaning and scrubbing around the beds. Around the horrible tube, perhaps.

Maybe I'll bring it up with her later, Linzy thought. But not yet. No way.

"The elegant lady was also an author," Sash continued. "The one in Georgia. After a little while, we all traipsed into town, down a soft, red dirt road. We walked very slowly, either because of her age or my bum leg, straight to the old-fashioned library, where she was scheduled to speak. There was a copy of her book on a fancy display stand. The cover of the book was light green and gold with a perfect ripe peach in the center like a cameo."

"What was the title?" Janine Ash queried, seemingly right there in the library with Sash.

"*My Georgia Home,*" Sasha said. "But the author's name was in such an ornate script I couldn't quite make it out."

"Granny's family was from Georgia," Linzy said. She wondered if her sister had experienced a near-death experience. Or something else supernatural. But she couldn't make herself bring it up, yet. Instead, she kept Sasha talking. "Where'd you go next?" She found herself seriously intrigued. None of this had been shared before. Was it just surfacing in Sasha's memory, or had she simply been afraid to tell them about it?

"I went to Louisiana. New Orleans, I think. Or it may have been Baton Rouge. I wanted to catch a bus, but by this time, neither of my legs would work. It felt as if I were dying, little by little, limb by limb.

In Louisiana, I couldn't get around at all. Someone had propped me up on a bench in a park. I believe the Georgia folks dumped me there, like an unwanted pet. People hurried past. They glanced in my direction, but no one spoke. And then Denzel Washington appeared."

Janine Ash covered her mouth with her hand.

Sash sat up straighter, allowing their arms to fall away. "It's okay to laugh. I know how it sounds. It's all crazy and mixed up. And why Denzel Washington? I mean I like him as an actor, but of all the people to dream up—"

"A famous character who rescues people," Linzy said. "*The Equalizer*, remember? He rescued random people. We always loved that movie—"

"Blue loves it, too," Mrs. Ash interjected.

"So did our dad," Sasha said. "So, I guess that makes sense. Just like Sipsy rescued Ruth's baby. But I'm a little upset with myself for not conjuring Cam or Blue or even you, Sis. I mean, y'all are the ones who came for me so why did my mind insist on showing me all these famous strangers?"

Linzy chewed at her thumbnail. "Maybe your mind was triggered by things around you on the ship. To be honest, I wondered why you didn't conjure up Superman or someone like that to rescue you."

"Hmm, things on the ship. Yeah, that makes sense," Sasha said. "Maybe the doctor, Carlos Sita, reminded me of Denzel in some way, rescuing strangers, I mean—"

"The one you called your angel doc?"

Sasha shrugged. "He did at least try to rescue us that day. Blue said he made the sign of the cross over each and every patient. As if saying prayers." She looked at Linzy. "And he stayed there when the Coast Guard came, so he could make sure we were all okay. And you know, I saw him once, when I first came to consciousness. He put his fingers to his lips and motioned that I should be quiet. I think that's the first time I actually became aware of reality." She looked at her sister as if to make sure she was still speaking rationally.

Linzy nodded. "And then?"

Silence for a moment while Sash gathered her thoughts. "That's right after I thought I heard Cam's voice. And Blue's. That doctor's coffee brown eyes … they did remind me of Denzel's, kind and intelligent." She fell silent. Seemingly back in the past.

"And then—" Linzy prompted again.

Sash looked up, as if from a distance. "Loud noises, gunshots." She paused again. "No. I may have it mixed up. The loud noises and gunshots occurred before the doc shushed me. And I never saw Cam, only heard his voice. Didn't know anything about Brandon. I just remember someone sliding me off the bed into a wheelchair and then the feel of Blue's hand on my shoulder in an elevator."

Her eyes closed, perhaps against the onslaught of memories. "I felt liquid. No bones, no muscles, just … liquid. I was so glad when that elevator stopped, and Blue's hand was still on my shoulder." Her voice trailed away.

"Thank God, Sissy," Linzy said. "Thank God for Blue and that doctor and the other two Musketeers."

"Amen," Janine Ash chimed. "Thankful for them, and thankful that all three musketeers recovered from their wounds."

"Yes, ma'am," Sasha agreed. "All three had gunshot wounds or head trauma, yet I'm the one everyone seems concerned about."

"Well," Linzy said, "you have been through a lot—"

"I guess so," Sasha interjected. "My whole life seems to be getting over one trauma after another. Learning how to 'get sane' again." She paused as if to make certain her next words were okay to speak. "Don't jump to any conclusions, but this ordeal has made me think I might be good at helping trauma victims recover. Mentally, I mean."

Linzy started to reply, but Sasha held up her hand. "Hang on, Sis, I want your input later, after we've all given it some thought."

Her sister nodded, so Sasha continued, "This mental stuff has made me think I may want to pursue a degree in psychology. Counseling, perhaps. Those hallucinations were so vivid, so unrelenting—"

Linzy couldn't help herself, "Yes!" she said. "And you could use your artistic talents as well. We've all heard of art therapy—"

Her interruption was then interrupted when Skye let out a fussy wail. They all laughed and looked at the baby monitor. Linzy stood, patted Sash's shoulder, and said, "I'll get her. Be right back." On her way to the baby's room, she glanced out at the waves, the winter sun was weak but still warm. She gave another silent prayer of thanks for the end of the nightmare. Hearing Sasha's recollections—and her ideas about the future—made her believe they'd turned a corner in her healing process. Just like the day they had burned the prayers and letters in the chiminea, sharing was like lancing the wound.

When she stepped back into the living room with the sleepy baby in her arms, she saw Janine Ash touch Sasha's hand with her fingertips. "Trust me, sweetheart, whatever you decide to do, there is no hurry. You're going to be fine, just fine."

"We all are," Linzy said, walking in with Skye. "We are all going to be just fine, now."

EPILOGUE

"We didn't quite make it for New Years," Linzy said. "Or any other year since we lost mom and dad. But we're here now, and we're together. Better late than never, right?"

Sasha sucked in a breath as they stepped out of their vehicles at the observation point looking down into the valley. The compact village of Stutter Creek twinkled with light. It nestled into a near-perfect bowl at the foot of Sierra Blanca Peak. The view was every bit as breathtaking as they remembered.

Linzy pointed at a sprawling shopping center just off the new four lane highway. "It has changed some. I mean, resort towns are not supposed to have big box stores and massive highways, are they?"

Blue massaged her shoulders. "It has become such a popular destination, I guess it was inevitable. Let's hope downtown hasn't changed."

"I just want everything to be the same. Vintage. Retro."

He slid an arm around her waist. "The playground of our youth."

She blinked, holding back the tears. "It doesn't matter, right? The main thing is we're all here, survivors." She glanced at Cam and her sister standing near the rail, showing Skye the twinkling twilight view.

"I can't wait to see Beth and John—" Blue said. "Hard to believe your folks always invited my entire family to come up in the summer and again in winter for skiing. We could never stay long with all the farm work to be done, but we sure had fun when we could. We had idyllic childhoods, didn't we?"

"Yes, we did," Sasha agreed, overhearing his comment. "I can't wait to see little Danny, and Turk, the wonder dog."

Blue laughed. "I doubt if Danny is little anymore. And old Turk. Such a good dog. I hope he's even still around. It's been a while since any of us have been back." He cut his words short when he realized what he'd said. The reason none of them had been to Stutter Creek was because of the tragedy on Wisteria Way.

Linzy laid a hand on his arm, to ease his discomfort. But the melancholy mood seemed to have its grip on them. She led the way back to their vehicles and they climbed inside and headed on into town.

Only about ten blocks in length, there wasn't a whole lot of downtown to see. But as they came to the first of the three traffic lights, Linzy touched Sasha's photo on her phone to call her.

"It's still there," she said, when Sash answered. "The Drugstore is still there."

Linzy knew Sash didn't really think it might be gone, she was probably just so glad to see that some things hadn't changed.

Sash and her little family were directly behind Linzy and Blue, Skye's car seat was tucked neatly into the backseat of the Lincoln the way it was supposed to be.

"I'm so glad to see that downtown hasn't changed much. Looks like they've had some snow." Pushed up drifts of the white stuff lined the sides of streets and parking lots.

"Guess it was recent," Blue said. "Not even gray yet."

Sasha piped up, still connected by phone. "Some of the store names are different, but I guess that's to be expected. The main things are The Drugstore and next, the creek. We'll find out about that one after just one more stoplight."

Linzy laughed, the pall of melancholy pushed back by happy, little-kid memories. "We'll see it soon, right where the old bridge crosses over Stutter Creek. I can't *wait.*" She hugged Blue's arm to her side.

He grinned.

"Look!" She gave Blue a shake. "There it is!"

Sasha sighed audibly though the phone. "So glad it looks the same. Remember to roll down your windows when you go over."

They drove slowly, rolling down the windows as they drove across the picturesque wooden bridge, gazing out the car windows, listening carefully for the burbling sounds of the rocky creek. "Now, it feels like we're home," Blue whispered.

"Yes," Linzy replied. "And here's our turnoff to the cabin."

Within minutes they were all standing in the recently cleared driveway, looking at the well-kept log cabin. Sasha lifted Skye from the backseat. When she turned to Linzy, there were tears in her eyes. "Here we are," she said. "Here we finally are."

Linzy understood what she meant, and how she felt. They'd been through so much since the last time they'd seen the little cabin in its dusty green pocket of pines. "The last time we were here was with Mom and Dad," she said.

"I remember," Blue said. "I came up later, with my mom and dad. But somehow, we were able to stay for two whole weeks. I think we had the best duck fights that summer."

"Yep," Sash said. "All of us summer kids at the swimming hole by the big boulder. Even Danny and Turk were there."

"Turk, the Wonder Dog," Linzy laughed.

They trooped up the steps and entered the cabin.

Linzy gazed out the picture window at the thin covering of

snow. The cabin was immaculate, windows clean, surfaces free of dust, and the fireplace was stacked with a well laid fire for later. "John's been here," she said. He'd been their caretaker for as long as she could remember.

"Beth, too," Sash added, indicating the loaf of fresh cinnamon bread on the counter.

Linzy smiled. "That's why it smells so wonderful in here. We'll have to make The Drugstore our first stop tomorrow."

"Oh, look," Sasha said. "It's beginning to snow."

They all crowded onto the long front window to enjoy the view of the fresh flakes. From experience, Linzy knew some version of the white stuff would fall daily for at least another month.

"We're fortunate they haven't had a really big storm recently," Sasha said.

Blue glanced toward the top of the mountain. "Yeah … makes me wonder how the skiing is this year?"

"You always loved those slopes."

He nodded. "Didn't we all?"

"It was wonderful," Linzy said. "Summer trips, winter trips, swimming, hiking, or skiing. But no matter what, we always had to stop at The Drugstore Café for Beth to feed us." She smiled.

"Skye will grow up loving our Stutter Creek as much as we do," Sasha said. "And if you and Blue will get busy and start your own family, she might even have some little cousins to share it with."

Blue raised his eyebrows. "I'm down with that plan."

Linzy elbowed him. "I'd like to plan our wedding first. Nothing big, or fancy, just family and a few friends."

"I know an Elvis impersonator in Vegas," Cam said. "Does a bang-up job." He hugged his wife.

Sasha beamed up at him. "I wouldn't trade it for the world." She glanced at Linzy and Blue. "Although, I would have liked to have you two there."

Linzy said, "Maybe we'll skip Elvis, you know how I hate to be a copycat." She tickled Skye under the chin. "We'll get this little one some cousins, though. One of these days."

Cam leaned down and kissed Sasha gently. He was so different since everything that had happened. Now, he seemed laid back and happy. As if the horrific ordeal had been a real wake up call. "Reality struck me right between the eyes," he'd told them. "Almost lost the two most important people in my life."

Blue walked up behind the rest of them at the picture window. "You know, we are truly blessed everything worked out the way it did. I've said many thank you prayers for your father and your brother." He spoke directly to Cam. "And for the woman known as Teena, too."

"Yes," Linzy said. "The Lord saw fit to show all of you the way to find and save our Sasha and the other people on that ship." She turned and squeezed Blue in a hug. "And for that," she said, "we are eternally grateful."

"Amen," they all murmured. And then Blue whooped and rushed to the front door. He hopped down the three wooden steps just in time to meet a giant tan and black dog threatening to break out the window of a blue 4x4 pickup truck.

"Turk!" Sasha cried as the big dog was released from the back seat.

"And John," Linzy laughed as a tall bear of a man crossed the drive behind his furry pal.

"What kind of dog is that?" Cam asked. "He's *huge*."

Beth stepped out of the passenger side of the truck and waved. "Hello! You must be Cameron. Say hi to Turk, our Anatolian Shepherd."

A skinny, dark-haired teen also exited the truck and held up one hand shyly. "Hi - I'm Danny," he said. "Don't worry about old Turk's size. He is nothing but a giant furball with teeth."

Everyone laughed and hugged, and Skye began to cry from too much excitement.

Turk stopped, looked for the sound of the cry, then made a beeline for the baby—

still in her father's arms—and nosed her little foot with his wet black nose.

Her tears dried right up. She immediately began to coo and gurgle and wriggle to touch this amazing new creature.

"Look at that," Cam said as Skye held her hands out toward the giant dog. "My daughter's going to be a wild animal tamer."

Sasha laughed. "She can be anything she wants. We will see to that."

Beth held her arms out for the baby. "Wanna come to Aunt Bethie?"

To everyone's surprise, Skye went without hesitation.

"Now," Beth said, settling the baby on her hip, then looking directly at Linzy and Blue. "Let's talk about this wedding stuff I sense is on the horizon." She picked up Linzy's hand to admire her diamond ring. "You know The Drugstore caters weddings, right?"

Linzy and Sash looked at each other, eyes wide. "A Stutter Creek wedding? Now why didn't we think of that?"

Blue nodded, and Turk stood up on his hind legs, planting gigantic paws on his old pal's shoulders, licking his face and giving him a massive doggy hug.

John laughed. "I think he's telling you he will be glad to stand up with you at the wedding."

Blue hugged the big dog right back. "I believe you're correct. I just hope we can find a tux in his size."

"One more thing we will make happen," Danny chimed in, grinning. "We're just so glad to see you all again."

Once more, much hugging commenced.

This time, there were happy tears all around.

PLEASE REVIEW

We hope you enjoyed *Wisteria Winter* by Ann Swann. If you did, we would ask that you please rate and review this title. Every review helps our authors.

Rate and Review: Wistera Winter

MEET THE AUTHOR

Ann Swann was born in a small West Texas town with red-brick streets and roll-up sidewalks. Like Stevie in her *Stevie-girl and the Phantoms* series, Ann grew up riding her green Stingray bicycle all around that much-loved town. That's also where she began writing stories.

Ann still lives in Texas, although in a much larger town, with her indulgent husband, Dude, and a fat tuxedo cat named Mojo.

When she isn't writing, Ann is reading. Her to-be-read pile has taken on a life of its own. She calls it Herman.

OTHER TITLES FROM

5 PRINCE PUBLISHING

www.5PrinceBooks.com

Having the Werewolf's Baby *Courtney Davis*

Courting the Lion *S.E. Reichert*

Mistress and Mage *Blythe Brandenburg*

Having the Vampire's Baby *Courtney Davis*

Come to the Cape *Emi Hilton*

Time To Byrne *S.E. Reichert*

Bookish *Bernadette Marie*

Dare You to Choose Truth *Lauren Lipp*

Enlightenment *Nicole James Kelley*

All the Little Moments *Savannah Reed*

The Rocking of the Ocean *Barbara Matteson*

New to Newport *Emi Hilton*

Trusting the Alpha *Courtney Davis*

Sweet Summertide *Sarah Dressler*

No Words After I Love You *S.E. Reichert*

Demons and Tea Leaves *Courtney Davis*

Shadow of the Throne *Russell Archey*

Shadow Among the Stars *Courtney Davis*

The Pack *E.C. Saulness*

www.ingramcontent.com/pod-product-compliance
Lightning Source LLC
LaVergne TN
LVHW050915080826
845145LV00001B/88

* 9 7 8 1 6 3 1 1 2 4 4 5 7 *